NOWHERE
LIKE
HOME

ALSO BY SARA SHEPARD

YA
Pretty Little Liars Series
The Lying Game Series
The Perfectionists Series
The Amateurs Series
Wait for Me

ADULT
The Visibles
Everything We Ever Wanted
The Heiresses
The Elizas
Reputation
Safe in My Arms

NOWHERE LIKE HOME

A NOVEL

SARA SHEPARD

DUTTON

DUTTON

An imprint of Penguin Random House LLC
penguinrandomhouse.com

LIBRARY OF CONGRESS CATALOGING-IN-PUBLICATION DATA

Names: Shepard, Sara, 1977– author.

Title: Nowhere like home: a novel / Sara Shepard.

Description: New York: Dutton, 2024.

Identifiers: LCCN 2023035477 (print) | LCCN 2023035478 (ebook) |
ISBN 9780593186961 (paperback) | ISBN 9780593186978 (ebook)

Subjects: LCGFT: Thrillers (Fiction) | Novels.

Classification: LCC PS3619.H4543 N69 2024 (print) |
LCC PS3619.H4543 (ebook) | DDC 813/.6—dc23/eng/20230825

LC record available at https://lccn.loc.gov/2023035477

LC ebook record available at https://lccn.loc.gov/2023035478

Printed in the United States of America
1st Printing

BOOK DESIGN BY DANIEL BROUNT

To Maya

NOWHERE
LIKE
HOME

PROLOGUE

t's hard to sum up this place. Hard to craft a sales pitch. It took me a while to get it right, but I needed the perfect thing that would persuade someone to take the plunge. I'm nothing if not persistent.

This is what I came up with.

Maybe you're stuck. Maybe you're sick of yourself. Maybe you want answers about who you really *are.* Maybe you want to make lasting relationships, true friends, not like the acquaintances you think you're close to now. Maybe you think, *If only I could get away. If only I had time to really think, really breathe. Everything would be better. I'd know what I want. I could change.*

So come, then. Here, things are different. We have stunning sunrises every morning. Fresh food every day. Good company, always. Your children will grow up appreciating nature and community instead of burying their faces in screens. You'll grow your own food, really *feel* the soil between your fingers. You'll understand what life is supposed to be. You'll get the answers you're looking for. You'll find peace. You'll heal. I *promise*. Because here, you can start over. Here, you can be who you want to be. Here, we're all friends. At different points of the day, we pause after screwing the lid on a mason jar, or conjugating a French verb with our children, or while we're holding up the beam of the new shed, or while we're trying to find the center of ourselves at meditation. And we think, *We've really cracked the code.*

You want that. Of course you do. So come. We're living the dream. We're becoming better selves. Out in the desert, with the stars as our witnesses. Out in the desert, with its natural beauty as our model and guide. Out in the desert, you can escape.

Pretty good, right? Admit it—I've got you curious. Not that it's the real reason I want you here. It's only the means to the end. But once I've hooked you? Once you arrive? You're *out in the desert* . . . alone. And I'm waiting for you.

Because out in the desert, friend, no one can hear you scream.

PART
ONE

LENNA

The first troubling thing that happens when Lenna Schmidt arrives in Tucson is she nearly falls flat on her face on the Jetway. She catches herself and the baby using one of the ground transport guys' shoulders.

"Whoa," the man says, staggering backward. "You okay there, ma'am?"

"Fine, fine," Lenna mutters, her cheeks blazing. "Sorry."

"Think you frightened your little guy!" He gestures to Jacob, her five-month-old son, who has broken into a fresh round of sobs.

Lenna gives the guy a grimace-slash-smile. If only her baby were merely startled. There have been ten minutes of blissful silence since they began traveling. As Lenna walks down the ramp, her son's screams rise in volume. She can hear passengers deplaning behind her groaning. *There goes that baby again.*

The Tucson airport is small, with only one terminal and a few shops that are open. Lenna walks hurriedly, bouncing Jacob ineffectively and trying to convince herself that the fall and Jacob's renewed cries aren't some sort of omen that she's made the wrong choice. Just in case, she squeezes her fist five times, counting the squeezes in her head, making sure she's got it right. Then she searches the airport for something yellow. *There.* A bright yellow soccer jersey on that little kid. *Better.*

"It's okay, it's okay," she repeats to the baby as he moans. Blearily, she pokes her head into various women's bathrooms until she finds a changing table that seems somewhat sanitized. The diaper change helps his mood a little, and his screams trickle to whimpers. "All dry now," she says cheerfully as they exit the bathroom.

But he starts crying again as they get to baggage claim. She needs to get the baby's car seat, too, waiting next to at least twenty hard-case golf bags. Rhiannon told her to leave most of her possessions behind—*That's not what this place is about*—but Lenna would feel naked without them. As she hefts a suitcase off the carousel, she hears little jars of Stage 1 baby food clinking. A few travelers give her funny looks. She wonders if they think she stashed a bunch of beer bottles in there.

An airport attendant helps her load her things on a luggage cart and push through the Ground Transport doors—Rhiannon said she can't pick Lenna up personally, and that no buses come out to the community, and Lenna tries not to see this as an omen, either. The desert heat smacks her in the face as soon as she steps outside. It's so stiflingly hot that it's difficult to suck in a breath. Lenna's lungs feel like they're inside a pizza oven. There's a shiny sedan waiting at the cabstand; a man with leathery skin, wearing a barn jacket, leans against a wide-open passenger door. The A/C wafts from within. Lenna gravitates toward it, zombielike.

The man perks up when he sees her. "Need a ride?"

After he's helped her shove all of her things into the trunk and get the baby semisecure in the car seat, Lenna swings into the back seat next to Jacob. "Shh, shh," she says, trying to fit a pacifier into his mouth. He swats it away angrily.

The cabbie catches her eye in the rearview. "Set a' lungs on that one, huh?"

"Sorry." Lenna wants to burst into tears herself. "He isn't usually like this." A lie. Jacob is *always* like this.

She fishes a prepared bottle from the pocket of her backpack. She doesn't want to get him too attached to bottles or formula, but it's an emergency. Jacob accepts the nipple and falls silent. Lenna shuts her eyes. *Peace.*

The driver peers at her expectantly in the rearview mirror. "Oh. Sorry. The Texaco station just past Three Points on Ajo Way, please. There's a mile marker, too. . . ." It's the address Rhiannon gave her. She repeated it over and over to herself on the plane ride like a chant.

He looks puzzled. "That's almost an hour's drive. And not much out there. You sure?"

"Positive."

They start out the airport drive, heading due west—Lenna can tell because the sun is behind them. Her phone buzzes in her pocket. *Daniel,* reads the text ID. He has texted an image of the hastily scrawled note Lenna left for him this morning. And a question mark.

The time on the vehicle's dashboard clock is 8:30 A.M. Daniel is nothing if not predictable: Upon waking, he goes immediately to their home gym, which is next to the bedroom. He finishes, showers, gets dressed for work, and makes his way into the kitchen at 8:30, often on the dot. Her note, on the kitchen counter, was likely the first thing he saw when he came out to make coffee. She banked on this, being a whole state away before he even opened his eyes. Less chance that he'd convince her to change her mind.

She waits for another text. A reaction beyond just a question mark. *Bon voyage,* she expects he might say. Or an indifferent *See you later.* Maybe *Thank fucking God.* But nothing comes.

The A/C smells musty, so she breathes through her mouth. She looks at her baby, worried about the chemicals he might be inhaling. Five more fist clenches. And there: yellow words on a billboard for an injury lawyer. *It will be all right,* she tells herself. It has to be. Otherwise, what is she doing? Why is she subjecting her child to this upheaval if not for all the things Rhiannon promised? Serenity. Community. Help. *Answers.*

Well. That last one is a goal, not a promise. She just hopes that Rhiannon will comply.

The first part of the drive, there are cars whizzing east, turn-offs for housing developments with names like Sonoran Sun and Grande Iguana Casitas, and a casino on Tohono O'odham tribal land, jam-packed with cars. There are stoplights, then blinking stoplights, then stop *signs,* and then nothing, nothing, nothing but human-shaped cacti and dirt. They drive on a road called Valencia, then Ajo, small mountains rising before them.

With the hand that's not feeding the baby, Lenna opens the text chain from Rhiannon. Let me know if you find a flight, her old friend texted very late last night, when Lenna had bolted up in bed gripped with the notion that maybe she *should* come. (*Friend?* Can she call Rhiannon that again?) Now, Lenna replies. Landed, coming your way. Hope that's still okay!

"There's an observatory out there," the cabbie says, and Lenna jumps. He juts a thumb out the windshield at a purplish mountain rising in the distance. "Kitt's Peak. They use it to watch for UFOs."

"Pardon?"

"Kidding. But sky's real clear out here. On a good night, you can even see the International Space Station every ninety minutes." He chuckles. "You shoulda seen your face! UFOs!"

Lenna closes her eyes. She's too keyed up for jokes.

Rhiannon hasn't texted back. Neither has Daniel. To calm her nerves, Lenna focuses on her baby's relaxed features—miraculously, he has fallen asleep. His eyelashes look like little stars against his cheeks. His plump, pink lips are parted just so, blowing out soft breaths. When she eases her pinkie into his fat, open palm, his fingers gently close around it.

Her heart melts, twists, explodes. And with it comes that fierce, stomach-clenching love—a love that almost hurts.

Twenty minutes later, the driver's GPS announces that they are arriving at their destination. He pulls into a vacant lot. "*This* is where you want me to drop you?"

The lot might have been a gas station—in another decade. There is a bleached-white empty building that might have been a garage, and disruptions in the concrete from long-ago gas pumps. An empty plastic water bottle rolls across the lot, but it certainly didn't come from a mini-mart anywhere close. Not a single car passes going either direction. If a bug were to crawl past, Lenna might hear its scuttling legs.

She looks at her phone for what seems like the millionth time this hour. She's lost service.

"Um." Her voice cracks. She thinks of what Rhiannon said in the café last week: *The land where the community is? Marjorie always says it's special. It has a way of revealing the truth.* She thinks, too, of Rhiannon's kind eyes, the way she said, *I think you should come. You'll find what you're looking for. And I'd love to have you.* She even sang Lenna and Jacob a lullaby of sorts.

Hush, little baby,
No sound will you make
Mama, come to Tucson
'Cause you need a break.

But Lenna also thinks of how they left things off—before. The fight. The absence. The silence. And then what Lenna did.

A dusty cloud suddenly appears from inside the desert like a twister. Tires scrabble on the dirt. The cloud gives way to the shape of a dusty Chevy Suburban. A relieved laugh escapes from Lenna's lips.

"There she is," she tells the driver.

The cabbie shifts. "An off-the-gridder, huh? Watch out."

"Why?"

"They don't rely on the system. Most of them are criminals—or they have something to hide. My uncle was like that, slippery as hell. Excuse my language." He eyes her in the mirror. "You trust this person?"

Something to hide. Lenna shivers. Little does he know, the cabbie is describing *her.*

The Suburban comes to a stop, and Rhiannon Cook looks out. The light through the window hits Lenna's old friend in all the right ways. She looks the same as when she and Lenna were close, her auburn hair wild around her face, her chin sharp, her green eyes bright. But now, her frame carries a few extra healthy pounds. It suits her. And her skin, which used to be prone to breakouts, is clear and shining. When they'd reunited in LA a week ago, Lenna had prepared herself for Rhiannon to look either really wrecked or so transformed she was unrecognizable. But this version—it's inspiring.

"You came!" she bellows.

Lenna glances at the cabbie's ball cap, pulled low, and then back at her friend again. She lets her palms splay free. *Please, please, please,* she thinks, trying to push down a shudder of dread. *Make this worth it.* But also this: *Please let her have forgiven me if she already knows . . . or have mercy on me once I tell her the truth.*

She looks at Rhiannon. "I came."

2

LENNA

The lights in the dressing room line in the H&M store at the Beverly Center were an eerie shade of orange, even though it was nowhere near Halloween. Lenna stared down at her hands, which held a few questionable items she was pretty sure wouldn't look good on her tall, gangly, straight-up-and-down body—in this strange light, her skin looked positively ghoulish. Every indication was saying she should leave this store; she wasn't even sure she liked the clothes she was trying on. And yet, something was compelling her to stay. Just for a moment.

Lenna was a believer in signs. Her mother had been the same; the two of them even had a game where they opened up the newspaper in the morning, and whatever story they felt pulled to would set the tone for their day. These days, whenever Lenna felt that something might be an omen, good or bad, she saw it as maybe a message *from* her mother, from the other side. Lenna didn't always give in to the vibes, but today, the anniversary of her mother's death, she felt she should.

In the line in front of her, a mother stood with a little girl who looked to be about four—sporting pigtails, bright pink leggings, and a plastic backpack all her own, emblazoned with a pink girlish cartoon pig. The girl had been placid a moment before, but suddenly she pitched herself onto the floor and started screeching.

"Get up," the mother hissed, yanking the girl's arm.

But the girl made her body go slack. "Mommy just wants to try these on," the mother begged, holding up several dresses. "Can you please just help Mommy out and come into the dressing room with me?" And then, under her breath: *"Just this once?"*

"I don't want to!" The little girl kicked her legs. "I don't like this store!"

Other people waiting in line shot the mother a dirty look. Lenna shifted the clothes in her arms. She felt bad for the mother and wanted to help, but she felt uncomfortable initiating conversations. Especially with people she didn't know.

Then someone behind Lenna stepped from the line. "Hey there." She dropped to her knees to where the little girl lay. "Want to see something cool?"

The woman had bountiful auburn curls that spilled down her back and was wearing, Lenna was almost sure, the very skirt-and-blouse combination on a mannequin in the shop's front window. She held her phone out to the girl. "Wanna watch something with me while your mommy tries on clothes?"

The girl looked at her mother—who seemed at first startled, and then suspicious. "No, no," the mother said. "It's fine. She's fine. We're getting up right now, aren't we, Cassidy?"

"We'll sit right here on this rug," the auburn-haired woman cooed. She had the kind of raspy voice Lenna envied. There was a girl from high school who had a voice like that—like she'd been out all night singing at the top of her lungs, or smoking too many cigarettes, something else subversive and brave and way beyond Lenna's comfort level. "Take your time, Mommy. Seriously."

The mother waffled, but then turned back to an open dressing room. Someone had just left; it was her turn. "Mommy is right here," she told her daughter, pulling the curtain closed. "Right behind this curtain, Cass. Yell out if you need me."

"Uh-huh," the little girl said, smiling smugly. She stared at the screen. A mechanical *bloop* tinkled, and Cassidy gasped. "Ooh, a kitten!"

"Yep. There are kittens in this game," the auburn-haired woman said excitedly.

"Kittens?" the mom called from inside the dressing room. There were clicks as she took clothes from a hanger. "What are you looking at, baby?"

Lenna watched the two of them on the ground. All of a sudden, the same sort of universe-force that had pushed her into H&M compelled her to bend down and speak to them.

"Can I see the kitten, too?" she asked shyly.

The auburn-haired woman looked up and smiled. "Sure." She tilted the screen toward Lenna.

Pixelated kittens flew across the screen. "Wow," Lenna said. "That *is* really cool!"

"I *know*," the little girl said.

Lenna chuckled. The little girl reminded Lenna of Farrin, a spunky four-year-old she'd nannied for the summer between high school and college. Lenna used to come home with a plethora of Farrin-isms to share with her mom. Silly things the girl said and did, how she seemed old and wise beyond her years.

Her mom, who'd been so healthy back then, showing no sign of what was to come.

Lenna turned to the auburn-haired woman. "Nice of you to give the mom a break."

The woman shrugged. "No biggie." She swiped to a new level. Another kitten flew across the screen.

The dressing room door opened and the mother came out, holding the clothes she'd tried on draped over one arm—only a minute had passed; she must have really hurried. Her gaze fell on her daughter. "All done, monkey." She looked at the auburn-haired woman. "Thank you for dealing with her," she said gratefully.

The woman straightened up and smoothed down her skirt. "It was really no trouble. She's very sweet."

The mother took the little girl's hand and led her to the checkout line. Halfway there, the girl turned back to Lenna and the woman with the phone and waved, shyly, at both of them.

"What a cutie," Lenna murmured as she waggled her fingers. "Bye!"

Then she looked at the auburn-haired woman again. There were tears in her eyes. "Are you okay?" Lenna blurted out, startled.

The woman's mouth wobbled. She nodded but then seemed to change her mind and shook her head. It was all very subtle; no one else in the line even noticed. Then she dropped all the clothes she'd chosen onto the discard shelf next to the dressing room. "Are you busy right now?" she asked Lenna.

Lenna looked around. "Me? I guess not. . . ."

"Want to get coffee? I'm Rhiannon."

THE LINE AT THE STARBUCKS IN THE BEVERLY CENTER WAS TOO long, so they went across the street to the restaurant at the Sofitel hotel. Lenna didn't want to tell Rhiannon that this was the first drink she'd ever had with someone else in Los Angeles since she'd moved here six months before. She went out by herself sometimes— always at a nearly deserted bar, and always only for one drink, and usually when a baseball game was on, as these days the Dodgers were the number one topic of conversation with her dad.

But this was her first *social* drink. When she was alone, there was no one to judge her self-soothing quirks. Like the coasters on the bar right now: If she were alone, she'd straighten the stack nearest her, and then the stack a few stools down, and so on, until the whole room was neat as a pin. People would look at her strangely, but then she'd finish her drink and leave, so she didn't have to suffer the discomfort for long.

"They have a great ginger mule—if you'd rather get a cocktail," Rhiannon said as she looked at the menu. Her tears were gone, but the tip of her nose was still red. She was talking in a boisterous, forced way like she was maybe pretending it had never happened. Which was strange, because Lenna figured she wanted to get a drink in order to unburden something to a stranger. Perhaps she still would?

"They make their ginger beer in-house using a ginger bug," Rhiannon added.

A couple at the other end of the bar got up, leaving their coasters askew. Lenna's fingers twitched.

"I think I will have a cocktail," she decided, hoping it would settle the itch.

They went through normal pleasantries: which part of the city they lived in (they both lived in apartments to the east), where they'd come from (Lenna, farther up the coast; Rhiannon, Nevada), and how long they'd been here (Rhiannon for two years, Lenna for six months). Lenna was twenty-eight, Rhiannon twenty-nine.

Lenna was trying to figure out if she should ask Rhiannon again if she was okay—*she* teared up randomly in stores, often thinking about her mom, but she'd never come upon anyone else who did that. But then Rhiannon pointed at Lenna's tote. "You're a writer?"

"Oh." Lenna's tote was so threadbare and well-worn, she had kind of forgotten that it read *USC Journalism Program*. She sighed. "No. I mean, *yes,* I'd like to be, but this . . ." She touched the tote. "I went there for the first few weeks. But I couldn't make it work."

"I've heard conflicting things about journalism degrees."

"No—I *wanted* to do it. I loved the program." Lenna disliked the notion that someone would presume she'd quit because she couldn't hack it. "But there was this thing with my mom, so I had to withdraw. I never got around to going back."

Lenna reached out for the coaster stack in front of them. She could at least organize these without it seeming too strange. "Are *you* a writer?"

"Well, I work for this magazine, but I'm more of an editor." Rhiannon named the magazine she was working for, a publication called *City Gossip.* Lenna had heard of it. It was a weekly paper that documented scandals taking place in Hollywood, though celebrities' publicists paid for most of the stories.

Lenna must have unconsciously made a face, because Rhiannon added, "It's not a bad gig. They have awesome benefits. And you overhear some interesting gossip."

"I'm not judging," Lenna said quickly. "I'm just at a textbook publisher, so who am I to have an opinion? A gossip magazine sounds more interesting." *And,* she added to herself, *probably a step in a good direction toward loftier publishing dreams.*

"Totally true," Rhiannon said. "I'd love to run my own magazine someday. Either that or run away to an intentional community. No in-between for me!"

Lenna blinked. "You mean like a commune?"

"More like a work-live farm. It's hard to find a good one, though. I tried this one farm up north right out of college, but it was kind of weird."

"Aren't they *all* kind of weird?"

Rhiannon looked into the middle distance. "If you found the right fit, it would be so idyllic, I think. A built-in family. I've never been one for traditional marriage—or even relationships, really. Romantic ones, I mean. Don't get me wrong, I've had flings . . . it's just, I like my privacy, you know? I like my life solo." Lenna nodded, though mostly because she figured that was what Rhiannon expected. "But a community of some sort," Rhiannon continued, "that feels right."

Their drinks came. Lenna took a tentative sip, reflecting on what Rhiannon had just revealed. She wasn't sure she'd ever met anyone who flat out didn't want a romantic partner. She decided to change the topic. "That little girl in the store was so cute. I nannied for a little bit before college. Kids are a lot of fun."

"You were good with her."

"You were, too. That mom really appreciated it."

Rhiannon shrugged. "Frazzled moms are kind of a trigger." She looked at Lenna. "You want kids?"

"Yes," Lenna said emphatically. "But who knows when it will happen. Dating is so hard."

"*So* hard."

"You want kids, too?"

Rhiannon shook her head vehemently. "Absolutely not."

"You could still have them, even if you lived in a . . . community." She stumbled over the last word, hoping she'd remembered the right terminology.

"I don't think so."

Lenna waited for Rhiannon to explain herself—here it was, surely, the reason for her tears at the store. But she didn't. In fact, she looked like she was somewhere else entirely, maybe ready to leave.

Lenna worried she'd blown it. Maybe she'd asked a question that shouldn't have been asked. It was no wonder she had trouble making friends—she didn't have the natural knack for conversation.

"Sorry," she blurted.

"Huh?" Rhiannon's head shot up. Her face softened. She looked at the drink coasters in Lenna's hands. They were balanced between Lenna's palms, the edges perfectly lined up. Lenna needed to keep them that way. If she let the corners shift, Rhiannon would *certainly* leave. There would go her first chance at a friend.

Without another word, Rhiannon stood and walked to the end of the bar. She scooped up a few more stacks of coasters and brought them over. She said nothing, just leaving them in a pile in front of Lenna.

Lenna blinked. It was like Rhiannon had performed a magic trick. "How did you know . . . ?" She eagerly scooped all of them up and started forming a neat tower.

Rhiannon shrugged. "I had a roommate in college who liked to organize stuff, too. I got your back." She winked.

"I didn't used to be so . . . organize-y," Lenna explained, suddenly mortified. Were her behaviors that obvious? "It came on recently."

"Oh yeah?"

And then it spilled out of her: her mother's diagnosis, how quickly her illness progressed, how Lenna didn't even have time to catch her breath. But also how *preventable* it felt—and how desperately Lenna missed her. Surely there was something she could have done. Corners she could have straightened. Yellow she could have searched for. She vowed never to be caught off guard again. And so came the rituals.

Rhiannon listened, nodding as patiently as she did with the little girl outside the dressing room. Lenna couldn't remember—had anyone listened to her like this before? Well, besides her mom.

One drink led to another. The baseball game went into extra

innings. It was so magical, Lenna nearly forgot that it was supposed to be a dark anniversary, six years to the day since her
mother passed. There was brightness instead. But as they were
getting up to leave, Rhiannon paused. Her gaze was on something
across the room.

"What is it?" Lenna asked. She followed Rhiannon's line of
sight. All she saw was an ordinary-looking dark-haired woman,
staring at her phone.

"Do you . . . know her?" Lenna asked.

"She's just this woman from my office building, I think," Rhiannon said. "Josie? No—Gillian. I see her around a lot."

"Do you want to say hi?"

Rhiannon swung the strap of her purse over her shoulder. Her
movements were slow, maybe tipsy. Lenna felt tipsy, too. "Not
really," she said. *"But."* She turned to Lenna, placing her hand on
her arm. "You and I should totally do this again."

Instagram post from @GillianAnxietyBabe

May 2

> [Image description: A young woman with wavy brown hair sits cross-legged on the floor. She holds a white piece of paper up against her chest. The paper has the words "baby steps" written in all caps.]

♡ ▢ ◁   ⊓

Hiiiiii fellow Nervous Nellies of the world! Sorry I haven't been around! I've MISSED you!

I know I've harped on this before, but seriously: How do normal people DO it? I know "normal" is a useless word, because who's even normal, anyway? But you all get what I mean. How do normal people just go out in the world and . . . deal?

I'm preaching to the choir, amiright? #SocialAnxietyStrong! #IntrovertsForTheWin. For us, everything in that department is a struggle—even talking to a barista to order my morning coffee. (Thank God you pre-order on the app.) It still amazes me S wanted to be friends. (But RIP S and me these days. Sob!)

Still, I'm trying. Like my therapist says, I'm doing my homework. I'm trying to EXPOSE myself to uncomfortable situations. I'm trying to VISUALIZE the person I want to be—and sometimes, that means faking it until I make it.

Speaking of which, there's this person I want to know better. You know when you see someone and you're like, I bet we'd click? I see this woman, R, around a lot. I love her style: stacked boots, colorful skirts, a really good tattoo game. I really, REALLY want to be normal enough (there's that word again!) to speak to her, just a simple hello. But you know how it goes. When I get near her, it's like I've been hit with a freeze ray. I keep telling myself that if she actually got to know me, she'd like me. (Positive thinking!) All I have to do is take that first step.

But THEN (sorry! I'm rambling!), I was at this bar yesterday, and I saw her again. Completely by accident! Like a sign. I said to myself, G, this is your moment. You're going to talk to her. Only, she was with this other woman. They were sitting at the bar, talking. Laughing. I was so jealous. It reminded me of me and S, back in the day.

I moved a little closer to the two of them. I couldn't hear what they were saying, but I had a better view of them together. R was letting the other woman talk, which made me think she's a great listener. The other woman was tall, and kind of unsure. She also seemed to have no idea she was very pretty. I liked her laugh—she tipped her head back but then, after, she'd clap her hand over her mouth like she'd just done something embarrassing. I wanted to tell her that she looked great laughing. That big laughs are welcome in my world.

The more I watched, the more I realized they'd just
met . . . and they were forming a friendship, not building on
one that already existed. It felt like my chance. Why make
one friend if you could make two? But as usual, there were
heavy blocks in my feet, and my mouth felt sealed with hot
glue. I stayed where I was.

So I guess that's why I'm checking in. I'm hoping for some
support. Some wise words. Keep me accountable, will ya?
Love you guys. Don't know what I'd do without you.

TOP COMMENTS:

@anxiouskitten23: We'll keep each other accountable!   ♡
Rooting you on, babe!

@RTGz69: All my support, honey! How's the new job,   ♡
by the way?

@mimi_has_troubleZ: Do it, G. Seriously. They need   ♡
you as a friend. You're a GEM.

@lonely_girlRZ4540: Hi. Love this account sm.   ♡

3

LENNA

Rhiannon eyes Lenna's pile of luggage, stuffed into the cab's cargo area, and smiles. "I told you *not* to bring your whole house."

She helps Lenna to heft one of the monster-sized suitcases into the Suburban, which is cluttered with gardening tools and dirt. The stench of rotting vegetables hits Lenna hard. She tries not to gag while placing the car seat base in the back, which is also dirty. She gingerly snaps Jacob, who is still conked out, into the base, praying he doesn't wake. Next to him, a little boy with auburn hair and green eyes lounges in a front-facing car seat. He looks at Lenna solemnly, his familiarly shaped eyes inquisitive, his mouth clamped closed.

Lenna grins. "Is this your son?" she says in a near whisper.

"Yep," Rhiannon says softly back. "Say hi, Teddy! *Quietly.*" She gestures delicately to the sleeping baby.

Teddy blinks. Lenna looks from Teddy to Rhiannon, astonished. So it's true, then. Rhiannon really has a child. There was a small corner of her mind that had wondered if Rhiannon was play-ing a very strange trick on her.

"He's beautiful," she breathes.

"Aw, I like him, too." Rhiannon beams. "Ready to go?"

Rhiannon pulls out of the abandoned gas station and drives back into the desert, on something that's barely a road and more of a sandy path. She steers easily, with one hand. Only a quarter mile in, it's like the desert has swallowed them up—when Lenna turns back, she doesn't see the highway anymore. It makes her shudder, just a little.

"How far into the desert is this place?" she asks.

"Four, five miles?"

"Do people ever walk out to the main road?"

"Oh God, no." Rhiannon shakes her head. "That would be un-wise."

". . . Why?"

Rhiannon shrugs. "It's the desert." As if this is the only answer that matters.

They pass towering saguaros and twisted mesquites. Dirt and dust. Actual tumbleweeds. The desert is stark, but it's also beauti-ful with soothing, muted yellows and browns. The cacti and suc-culents flourish, despite the dryness. The sky stretches high, a pure, unblemished robin's-egg blue.

After about five minutes, the road forks. A dilapidated shack stands behind a rusted cattle gate. A giant satellite dish juts from a tin roof. Several rusted vehicles stand on blocks in the yard, along with other junk—building tools, a plastic swimming pool, shredded tires. Flies buzz angrily around overflowing garbage bags. Lenna doesn't realize she's squeezing the flesh on the back of her leg until it pinches.

"Oh, that's the Rivers' place," Rhiannon says, clocking Lenna's uneasiness. "We're not going there."

Then the car takes a left, where the road gets bumpier. A fence with coils of barbed wire at the top begins. When Lenna looks ahead, a jagged rock structure interrupts the horizon like a giant raised thumb. She gasps; it seems to have come out of nowhere.

Rhiannon smiles. "Isn't it cool? And that's not all you'll see. We've got all sorts of mountains, and ravines, and caves."

Lenna's heart slows. "It's gorgeous." Then she laughs nervously. "I still can't believe I came."

"I'm glad you did."

Rhiannon gives Lenna some history about the community—Halcyon Ranch, they call it. Lenna had tried to google the place, but it had no online presence. Rhiannon explains that's because the woman who founded Halcyon prefers it that way. To come here, you must be invited.

The community sits on sixty-two acres of prime Sonoran desert. Ten years ago, a land trust purchased the property. The woman who started the collective, Marjorie, built the house herself. "Marjorie poured the foundation, built the walls. Put in the floors, the tiling, the windows, the doors," Rhiannon says. "A lot of stuff's pretty basic, but a lot of it's really impressive."

Marjorie lived in a trailer until the house was ready. She worked hard to make the property completely independent of public utilities but still with the creature comforts of modern life. "Homesteading was the whole idea, but Marjorie didn't want residents to have to live like they were pioneers in covered wagons, so she installed a huge bank of solar panels and hooked up the electrical system," Rhiannon says. A geothermal cooling unit regulates the brutal Arizona heat; Marjorie drilled for a well and placed in a septic tank. Then, she handpicked others to live here with her. Intrepid women who needed a place like this. A respite. A reward.

"Seriously, *no one* else helped her build all this?" Lenna asks.

She feels a little of her old envy. Rhiannon seems to worship this Marjorie person, maybe for good reason.

Then they come around a bend. The fence running along the property is even higher, and the barbed wire is wider.

"What's with all that?" Lenna says, pointing at the sharp edges.

"To keep out animals, mostly."

"Mostly?"

Rhiannon pulls to a stop at an iron cattle gate. She hops out of the Suburban and types a code into a keypad. It lets out an angry beep. Rhiannon groans. "Marjorie's always changing this . . ." she mutters.

She punches in another code. And another. *Well,* Lenna thinks, *at least the Rivers family won't be breaking in.*

Finally, there's a metallic *clunk* as the bolt unlocks and the door swings open. Rhiannon climbs back into the driver's seat and steers the SUV through. Ahead are picnic tables, a fire pit, and a playground. A huge garden and animal pens full of goats and chickens. The house is one story, made of adobe, and sprawls like a shopping mall across the land. It's painted with a giant mural landscape in all the colors of the rainbow, consisting of so many disparate drawings that Lenna's eye doesn't know where to go first. Across the door is a shining golden sun with an eerie smiling face. Painted across the left wing are the twenty-six letters of the alphabet with corresponding pictures: *A for apple, B for banana.* Painted across the right part of the house . . . is that the Pythagorean theorem? It's like a psychedelic Sesame Street.

Not a single person is outdoors, maybe because it's so swelter-ing. Lenna feels self-conscious as they pull around to the back of the house, wondering if the other residents are watching her from behind windows. She swallows hard, then looks at Rhiannon. "Does anyone know I'm coming?"

"I told Marjorie. She's probably told the others by now." Rhiannon opens the door. "Come on."

As soon as the car stops moving and the engine shuts off, Jacob's eyes spring open. Sure enough, he starts to scream.

"It's okay, it's okay!" Lenna cries, unbuckling her seat belt and rushing to the back seat to tend to him. Her baby's face is bright red. He shakes his fists furiously.

"Shh, shh," she moans, lifting him out of the car seat and holding him in her arms.

Sweat pools in her armpits. It feels like she's standing on the surface of the sun. Her tote bag is slipping down her shoulder, and Jacob is now so distraught he's doing that choking sort of cry where he doesn't breathe. Part of her feels the tiniest bit disappointed, too. She'd thought the moment they'd pulled onto this property, a great weight would release from Jacob—and her. It was certainly how Rhiannon had described the place.

Was this a mistake?

Rhiannon stands on a little side porch, smiling and waiting for Lenna to catch up. She unlocks the door, holds it wide, and says, over the sounds of Jacob's screams, "After you."

Lenna eyes the house nervously, then her son even more nervously. "Are you *sure*?"

Rhiannon laughs when she catches Lenna's meaning. "Honey. No one here is afraid of a crying baby. I promise."

ONE THING IS GOOD, ANYWAY. THE INSIDE OF THE COMPOUND IS SO starkly cold and dark that Jacob stops crying purely from the shift in sensory input. It's *freezing*, actually, so much so that Lenna's arms break out in goose bumps. She must squint to make out the furniture so she doesn't bump into it.

Rhiannon gestures around. "So this is the main living area. Most comfortable part of the house, temperature-wise. Adobe walls. Superthick."

"Is it always this dark?" Lenna asks, knocking into a chair leg.

"Yeah, keeps it cool. But here, let me get a light."

She snaps on a lamp. Lenna's eyes start to adjust. The inside walls of the room are painted with doodles, snippets of poetry and song lyrics, and growth charts. There are a bunch of couches and a lot of bookcases. The place isn't messy, exactly—but it's certainly lived-in. An ordinary living room, albeit one that houses a whole bunch of people and children and animals. A large sign by the doorway reads: *Shake out your shoes.*

Lenna points at it. "Why?"

"Scorpions."

There is a tangle of various woven rugs on the floor, colorful and vibrant. One has a big chunk taken out of it. "Are there lots of pets?" The idea of animals cheers her. She'd always wanted pets when she was little, but her mother was allergic. Daniel thinks they're too messy.

"I would say so." Rhiannon waves her hand blithely. "Five, six dogs? Two cats. Well. We *had* two cats. One ran off."

"Is that dangerous, out in the desert?"

Rhiannon glances at her son. "The kitty went to another home," she says slowly, loudly. But to Lenna, secretly, she widens her eyes in a doomed sort of way. "That's why we keep the other kitty indoors from now on."

On one wall are pencil-marked half moons Lenna can't figure out. She moves closer to them, squinting. One fits inside the next. Each moon is dated.

"That's a pregnancy belly tracker." Rhiannon points at it. "From when Melissa had her baby, last year. Cute idea, right?"

"Someone else here has a baby that young?"

"Yep, she's the youngest one, and then Teddy. She was born last year. In the house!"

"Really?" Lenna thinks of the long drive from the road—and then the long drive *on* the road.

Rhiannon shrugs. "Marjorie took some midwifery courses. It all worked out."

"But *Teddy* wasn't born here, right?" Lenna asks.

Rhiannon looks away. "No. He wasn't." Then she smiles and touches Jacob's nose. "But like I said, all of us are used to babies! Even adorable crying ones with cute button noses!" Jacob hiccup cries.

"He's really out of sorts." Lenna's voice is suddenly shaky again. Her emotions are such a roller coaster. "On the plane . . . in the airport . . . you should have seen the looks . . . maybe I shouldn't have done this to him."

Rhiannon shakes her head. "Lenna. Seriously. You did everything right. And this is what we're *here for.* To give you some help. Remember?"

Lenna tries to nod, but it's like her emotional floodgates have opened. "I just feel like such a failure."

Rhiannon scoffs. "You're not." Then she turns away, pointing at the pictures on the walls. "Look at that pretty lady, huh?" Rhiannon narrates, pointing to a figure drawing, then a group photo. "And that's called calligraphy! And look! There's me and your new friend, Teddy!"

Lenna peers closer at the photo. It was taken at the front of the property—she recognizes the leering sun artwork on the door. Women and children stand shoulder to shoulder. Lenna spots Rhiannon in the back, holding an infant Teddy.

"How old was Teddy when you came here?" she asks her friend softly.

Rhiannon squints at the image a beat. "About three weeks?" Then she turns away. Lenna feels a lump in her throat. She pictures who Rhiannon used to be. Despite her moment with the little girl in H&M, she had a low tolerance for the messiness of children. One time, they were having brunch and the waiter seated a family with two cranky toddlers next to their table. Rhiannon stood up before they even got their mimosas. "Can we move?" she asked wearily, wincing when one of the kids let out a shriek.

How did someone change so much? Maybe it's different when it's your child.

Voices carry from down a hall. First there are lower syllables from an adult, and then higher responses from kids. *The pod people,* Lenna thinks as her stomach drops.

"So how many kids live here, total?" she asks.

"Nine. My Teddy, Amy's Matilda. Melissa has Casey, Marlo, and Susan—two of them were born here. Ann's got four kids—Riley, Bear, Nickel, and Hester. Some people count Coral as a kid, but she's over eighteen."

"Does anyone *not* have kids?"

"Naomi. Gia. Oh, and Marjorie has kids, but they're over eighteen. They aren't here anymore. Sarah doesn't have kids, either." She steps around a pile of clothes. "But she's working on it. She's not here right now."

"Where is she?"

Rhiannon smiles. "Monitoring. She's about eight weeks along, from IVF. The clinic we use is kind of far—it's easier just to stay overnight and get all the appointments out of the way. We have pooled collective funds to pay for the treatment for residents, if you want it."

"Really?" Rhiannon hadn't told her this at the café. It seemed . . . odd. But maybe Lenna just needed to get used to a communal way of thinking.

"A lot of people are desperate to be mothers when they come, but it hasn't worked out for them yet. Sarah's one of those, actually. It's taken her nearly two years of trying. Or they wanted to do the single-mom route, but, well, not everyone wants to go it alone."

"So lots of women want . . . help."

"Of course." Rhiannon says it like it's a no-brainer. "Takes a village, right? There's no reason for mothers to be so isolated. It's not how our species evolved." She nudges Lenna playfully. "We like to call it a *mommune,* actually."

"I get it," Lenna says quietly.

As they walk down the hall, Lenna catches mingling scents of coffee, essential oils, and dog hair. From somewhere down a back hallway, a woman sings a nursery rhyme. A child's shriek rings through the air.

"Melissa's in there with all the littles. She's their teacher. Already got some of them reading. She also makes medicine out of herbs and other plants. She's very holistic."

"Doesn't she have a one-year-old? Who's watching *her* baby?"

"Everyone else." Rhiannon laughs. "That's the point. We all watch everyone's kids." She looks down at Teddy. "Do you want to go in with Auntie Melissa, honeydew? Learn some shapes and colors?"

Teddy nods, and Rhiannon swishes him off. He pads down the hall, knowing where to go. Rhiannon smiles proudly, and Lenna feels a stab of envy. Rhiannon told her that Teddy cried as relentlessly as Jacob when he was a baby, too. But there's no sign of that child now. *Is* there magic here? Or is it because Rhiannon is simply a better mother?

Then Rhiannon pushes through another door. "This is the kitchen."

The floor may have been white at one point, but it's been colored over so heavily with permanent marker that it now resembles a Jackson Pollock painting. The countertops and table are covered in papers, pots and pans, magazines, and art supplies. But there are two refrigerators. The modern appliances are incongruous amid all the clutter. The stove is actually the same high-end stove Lenna heated soup and bottles on at home with Daniel. *Daniel.* She pushes guilty thoughts from her head.

Hanging on one wall is a large chalkboard outlining the meal plan for the next week. Lenna appraises the menu: *Tacos. Polenta. Corn soup.* It sounds homey but also somewhat gourmet. There is a line on each meal square delineating who will prepare the meal. *Coral,* it reads, after *Street tacos.* And *Chicken adobo.* And *Corn soup.*

To the right of the menu board is another chalkboard, this one even larger, marked *Chore Chart.* It's a chalky grid of various activities. The squares are divided into days of the week, Indoor and Outdoor jobs, and times of the day the jobs need to be completed. The leftmost side of the board bears a list of names—Lenna spots Rhiannon's. Next to each person's name is a number. Someone named Naomi, for example, has been awarded the number 20. Next to Rhiannon's name is the number 15.

"Are those rankings?" Lenna asks.

"Points. We're assigned jobs every day, and each of them carry a point value; if we accumulate enough during the week, we can trade them in for some time off or some other treat. Since it's Monday, no one's accumulated that many points yet. You have to get to one hundred for the perks."

"And what are the other luxuries besides time off?"

"Items from the outside world, like chocolate bars. A certain brand of soap. We have a stash. The pooled money buys it all, but then we dole it out." Rhiannon shrugs. "It gives us incentive. A goal. Most people don't really need it, but we all have days where we don't feel like getting out of bed, just like everyone else."

Lenna rolls her jaw. "And does it feel satisfying? Like, instead of being out there in the world, having a job . . ."

"I've tried both ways. I always thought I'd like this way, and I do." She smiles. "Maybe you will, too, Len. It's not as weird as it looks."

It's not weird, Lenna almost says, a knee-jerk politeness. But it kind of *is* weird. Her stomach starts to hurt again.

"I'll show you the patio, if you don't mind going into the heat again." Rhiannon holds up a hand preemptively. "Jacob will be fine out there. We have misters that will spray his head. And if he cries, all the better. It'll scare off the critters."

With that, she pushes a heavy door into the elements. The sun is still sweltering, but like Rhiannon said, the misters installed on the porch help. Lenna tries to stand under the spray with the baby, but he squirms and shuts his eyes and looks like he's winding up to wail again.

"Okay, okay, we'll go over here," Rhiannon says.

There are some kids gathered around a small outbuilding and playground, all barefoot with messy hair, in baggy pants rolled up at the ankles. A few of them don't wear shirts. Their skinny limbs tangle together as they play.

Rhiannon notices her looking. "They're growing up together. One big family."

The kids shriek and laugh. They *do* seem like friends. The noisiness soothes her. Lenna pictures what she'd be doing if she were home right now. On a normal day, Daniel would already be at work. Jacob's sobbing would be the only noise in the big, airy house. When Daniel would come home, she'd make desperate attempts to soothe the baby, because while she has learned to tune it out, sort of, Daniel has not. She might take Jacob on a walk, or bobble him on the patio—although she worries about bothering the neighbors. She might just plop him into the car and drive him around.

It's in those desperate, groggy, lonely hours that the thoughts creep into Lenna's mind. The visions. The *memories.* They grow

worse and worse, twisting from what really happened on that awful morning into something even more terrible, something involving her son. It's what happened last night, actually, what made her
bolt up in bed, text Rhiannon that she changed her mind, and look
up a flight online that left mere hours after she purchased it.

A scraping sound catches her attention. A woman drags Ad-
irondack chairs into a circle around a fire pit full of ash. She wears
rubber clogs, and her close-cropped hair is nearly all gray, her
torso is thick, and she has bulging blue veins in her calves. She
stands up, wincing and clutching at the small of her back. Her forehead is beaded with sweat.

"This is getting harder and harder every year." She turns to
Lenna. "You're Lenna, right? Rhiannon's friend? I'm Marjorie!"

The famous Marjorie, Lenna thinks.

"The famous Marjorie," Rhiannon says.

"Oh please." Marjorie waves a hand, humble but also proud.
"It's the rest of them who do all the work these days. I just found
an ugly heap of land and did something with it."

"Not so ugly," Lenna says, gesturing at the mountain, the sky,
the phalanx of saguaros. "Your place is beautiful."

"It's 'nowhere like home,' am I right? In the best of ways, of
course." Marjorie shrugs. "Then again, this place doesn't belong to
me *really*. We're all just guests here. In fact, we regularly acknowledge the people who came before us. Small offerings, a round of
songs, that sort of thing." Rhiannon nods solemnly.

Then Marjorie turns to Lenna again. "So you're thinking of
becoming a resident?"

"Uh . . ." Lenna feels caught off guard. "No. Sorry. I'm just visit-
ing for a few days."

"But clearly you've come for a reason," Marjorie says, her gaze
unwavering. "This land is very special. It has a way of revealing
the truth."

Lenna's mouth falls open. She isn't sure what to say.

"I told her that," Rhiannon says eagerly. "We're called here, you know?"

Jacob lets out another wail. Marjorie turns to him. "This one giving you trouble, Lenna?"

"I mean, he's not *trouble*," Lenna says quickly. "I adore him."

Marjorie snorts. "I wasn't questioning *that*. But babies under six months are impossible, they cry and you don't know why! Do you know that my boy cried for days, and eventually we found that he had a hair wound around one of his fingers? We didn't even see it! Wish he could have told us!"

"Oh my." Lenna glances at her baby's fingers, wondering if she's missed tiny tourniquet hairs. But they seem fine.

Marjorie's gaze fixes on something over Lenna's shoulder. The door to the house has opened, and a few more women stream out. Two are chatting boisterously, but as soon as they spy Lenna, they hurry over.

"Hello there!" the first calls, circling her. She is tall and has large, friendly features and strong, square teeth.

The other, a petite, birdlike woman with darker-colored skin, twisted braids, and small eyes with long lashes, approaches, too. "Who's this?"

Rhiannon acts as ambassador. "Lenna and Jacob, meet Melissa and Amy."

"Welcome," Melissa says. *Melissa*, Lenna thinks. The one who just had the baby. The teacher.

"Aren't you a cutie?" Amy, the one with the braids, pats Jacob's head affectionately. Jacob responds with a lazy smile, a rarity. He's getting drowsy. It's Lenna's favorite time with him, because he goes from angry and sobbing to sleepy and almost pliant. She smiles proudly, reveling in the moment of calm.

"Mel teaches the kids reading and science and does a bit of

apothecary work," Marjorie says. "Amy handles new construction, property upkeep, and teaches health and art. Her daughter is Matilda. You'll meet her later."

"And you do all that *and* chores?" Lenna asks, incredulous.

Marjorie laughs. "It's way less than most women do at home!"

A third woman approaches next. She is freckled and sunburned, and has a pixie cut. She wears her sweater sleeves over her hands despite the heat. She gives Lenna a closed-lips smile, unreadable behind her glasses . . . but not entirely unfriendly. "I'm Ann."

"Ann's in charge of our four-legged members," Marjorie explains. "And the planting."

"And this is Coral." Rhiannon points to a young woman with brown eyes, tanned skin, and a kerchief covering her hair—only a few frizzy pieces stick out the bottom. She wears a long hippie skirt, clogs, and rubber cleaning gloves. She's a slip of a thing, petite with slender limbs and arms. "Our chef extraordinaire."

"*You* cook those meals?" Lenna asks. *You're so young,* she wants to add.

Coral smiles shyly. Rhiannon jumps in. "She's incredible. A real talent."

Coral's about to speak for herself, but then her phone rings. The tone is a mourning dove's call.

"Sorry," Coral says, and turns away to answer. Lenna's surprised that women get calls in such a remote place. She wonders who they speak to from their old lives.

Then the women point out their children to Lenna. Many are playing under the misters. There are too many names for Lenna to keep track of. The women coo over Jacob, asking the usual questions—"How old?" "Is he a good sleeper?" "Is he good at nursing?" (They presume Lenna *is* nursing.) They ask to hold him, though Lenna shakes her head. "I should warn you in advance, he cries a *lot.* We'll just keep him sleeping for now."

"Crying doesn't scare us," they all say.

Then Lenna realizes that another woman is lingering on the porch. She has black hair cut at a sharp, bold angle at her chin. Her skin is ivory and flawless, and her eyebrows are groomed. She wears a wine-colored silk shirt that looks expensive, and flowing black pants. Her shoes are flats with crepe soles. It's only when the others move toward the circle of chairs that she offers her hand as though Lenna is fortunate to have her attention.

"Gia Civatelli," she says. Her voice is tempered. Snotty. Almost like she expects Lenna to know who she is.

"Hello." Lenna glances toward Rhiannon and Marjorie, expecting one of them to fill in how long Gia's been here, or what skill she's brought to the table. No one offers any explanation. In fact, Rhiannon brushes her hands together.

"I'm going to take Lenna to her room," Rhiannon announces.

"You've told her the rules, yes?" Marjorie asks.

"I will," Rhiannon promises.

"Rules?" Lenna asks.

Marjorie smiles. "Don't worry. Just some basics."

Back in the house, they turn to a long hallway. A stained-glass window at the far end glows. Lenna can still hear everyone talking outside. "They all seem . . . nice," she says, because it seems like the thing one *should* say. Though they do seem friendly—except for that woman in the silk, who Lenna is sure won't enjoy her child's constant cries. She hopes her bedroom is far away.

"Oh, they are," Rhiannon gushes. "It's a great community."

"What are these rules Marjorie was talking about?"

"Oh. Yes. I've got them memorized—one, respect everyone's property. No messing with people's things. Two, no littering, and no excessive or wasteful use of products. Especially no plastics."

"No plastics?" Lenna looks nervously at the plastic water bottle in the pocket of her backpack.

"Marjorie doesn't think it's respectful to the land. And plastics are basically toxic, you know?" Rhiannon keeps going. "Three, try and be your best self, and always strive for gratitude, peacefulness, and truth. Four, there are some rules about toilet flushing and the septic system, but you'll see those posted on the bathroom door. Five, we expect you to come to at least three community meals a week—for the others you can do whatever you want. It's a good group, though—I usually go to all of them. But not everyone does. Six, this is a women-only property, but you already knew that. Seven, there's the chore chart, which I'll go through in more detail later. You will be expected to do some chores while you're here, but it won't be much."

"I don't mind." Hopefully her chores will be with Rhiannon, so they can get time together.

"And finally, we're sensitive about people asking about our pasts," Rhiannon goes on, her voice dropping. "People see coming here as a rebirth. A fresh start. A lot of people don't want to talk about who they used to be. It's very important that we're respectful. Don't talk about someone's past unless they bring it up first. Marjorie's serious about this one. It can be grounds for expulsion."

"Wow. Okay. Got it."

Rhiannon avoids her gaze, but Lenna wonders if she's aware of the question that's burning on Lenna's lips. *Do you tell them who you used to be?*

They come to a door at the end of the hall. "Here's your room." Rhiannon opens it to show off a small room with a queen bed, a dresser, and a desk. A small crib is in the corner. There are even decent blankets inside. Lenna lifts one of them to her nostrils. It smells fresh. But the doubt creeps in, and the anxiety. *Squeeze, squeeze.*

They drag in all of Lenna's luggage and set it in the corner. Then Rhiannon shifts her weight. "So."

"So." Lenna feels like she should say something profound. About *them*. Their friendship. Who they used to be. What happened.

But then Rhiannon looks away, and the opportunity is gone. "Anyway, I thought you might want to rest."

Lenna makes a big deal of glancing at her watch. "Jacob's way off his schedule, but I guess that doesn't matter." She should just let him sleep.

"There's some iced tea." Rhiannon points to a pitcher on the dresser. "Melissa made it. She used cucumber. It's really good."

"Sounds delicious. Thanks."

"Take as long as you like. I'll be here. I'm glad you decided to come," Rhiannon says with a small smile.

After she's gone, Lenna carefully places Jacob in the new crib. Amazingly, he doesn't stir. Then she flops down on the bed with exhaustion. She needs to squeeze her fists again. It's unthinkable she actually did this. What would her mother think of her bizarre decision? Up and leaving her husband without explanation . . . and for what? A friend who walked out of her life? She thinks of what Gillian used to say: *Why does she have such a hold over you? It's like you're obsessed.*

Gillian.

The room grows quiet, then. *Too* quiet. The rushing sound starts in Lenna's ears. She presses her fingers to her temples. *It's okay,* she tells herself. She's gotten better at controlling it. But here it comes, regardless. The memories. *The two of them, standing on that ravine, the gray morning drizzle. Her twisted smile. Her sneering laugh. The pebbles, scuttling beneath Lenna's feet. And then, her scream.*

"No," Lenna whispers, holding the sides of her head. *"No."*

She rifles through her bag for headphones. Shakily jams them into her phone jack. She needs noise. White noise, brown noise, radio, *anything.* A different kind of whooshing fills her ears. Lenna jams the heels of her fists into her eye sockets until she sees stars. Eventually, the visions fade, turning gray, then translucent.

But they're still there. Always lurking, a constant reminder of what she did. This land reveals the truth, Marjorie said—what if it's true?

4

LENNA

Rhiannon's office was in Hollywood on a busy, touristy block. Inside the office building, a portable A/C rattled, and a female security guard with a name tag that read *Honey* sat behind a high desk, reading *Variety*. Lenna gave Honey her name, and Honey called Rhiannon's office to tell her that she'd arrived. When the guard hung up, Lenna moved to hit the button on the elevator, but Honey said, "Actually, darling, she said she's coming down."

Lenna stood in the corner to wait. This all felt like a dream. She and Rhiannon had talked constantly since their first serendipitous meeting. Rhiannon sent Lenna jokes and recipes, book recommendations, songs to listen to, and even a funny opinion piece. Articles for how to make ginger bugs. Fake news from *The Onion*. Screenshots from their favorite Twitter account, @BestOfNextdoor. They found the same things funny. They discovered they had the same taste in modern literary fiction. Neither of them had been to Will Rogers State Beach yet, or the Santa Monica Pier, or eaten at

Gracias Madre, and they both agreed that these were LA staples that they would tackle together.

They'd built up a rapport, so it seemed incredible that this was only the second time they were meeting. Rhiannon was bringing Lenna into her office, hoping that she could get her a job. "You could totally be a gossip writer," Rhiannon had said to her on the phone.

"I *could*?" Lenna was incredulous.

"Yep. You've got this. I can tell."

What can you tell about me? Lenna wanted to ask. No one had made these sorts of pronouncements about her before, not even her most encouraging teachers, not even her mother. Certainly not a friend.

Friendships were tricky for Lenna, always had been. She was more comfortable reading books than actually talking to people, probably because she had spent so many hours at the public library with her mom, where she had worked. Her mother would bring her stacks of fiction that she'd read and loved, and Lenna would devour the books, and after she was done, she and her mom would discuss them together. Characters felt like friends. She didn't need real people.

In high school, she was friendly with a few other bookish girls who also helped out at her mother's library. She was content enough, but she lost touch with those girls upon graduation, and when she saw them at her mother's funeral, they felt like strangers. In college, she made a concerted effort to socialize, joining the school paper, signing up for a running group, even rushing a sorority. But she quit the paper after the first staff meeting, which had been a harrowing experience where everyone was supposed to "pitch" ideas for stories—everyone else was so loud, so full of thoughts. She trained for a half marathon for exactly four days with a group of girls, trying her hardest to fit herself into their mold. She heard rumors about brutal sorority hazing so ditched that idea, too. There was a group of girls in her dorm that she ended up hanging around with, characters who weren't particularly memorable; by senior year, she did most things alone.

"You're just like me," her mother always sighed good-naturedly. "We're more suited to being by ourselves. I like to think we're just more independent than most people. But you need people, too, Len. You need *someone*."

Still, Lenna's independence—or loneliness—never truly mattered when her mom was alive; *she* was Lenna's someone. Without her, Lenna felt like an astronaut whose tether had been disconnected from the shuttle. She was just hurtling through blackness. She had no idea when she'd stop.

The elevator dinged, and Rhiannon walked out, her long peasant skirt swinging. She waved to Honey. Her face lit up when she saw Lenna waiting in the corner.

"Hey!" Rhiannon chirped, beaming. "Get here okay?"

"Easy," Lenna said, then gestured to the elevator. "Should we go up?" Someone named Rich was interviewing her at noon. It was five minutes till.

Rhiannon's face clouded. "Actually, Rich had to move some things around. Your interview isn't for another hour. Wanna grab lunch?"

Lenna had taken the afternoon off from her current job, so she had time to linger in the warm sunshine. Rhiannon led Lenna to a little taco place wedged in between a junk store that sold Los Angeles souvenirs and an ungainly CVS. They took their fish tacos to a bench across from the building. Lenna brought out a mini bottle of sunscreen and rubbed some into her part—and then the tops of her hands, for good measure. Rhiannon looked at her fondly. "You're always prepared, aren't you?"

"Pretty much," Lenna said. "I got it from my mom. She used to be so organized, too." Then she cocked her head. "What's your mom like? I'm sorry, I hardly know a thing about your family."

Rhiannon's mouth twisted. "Actually, I haven't seen my mom in years."

Lenna slowly chewed. It was hard to imagine someone having a living mother and not seeing her. She thought, again, of the tears in Rhiannon's eyes at H&M. Rhiannon had never explained what brought them on. Lenna kept waiting.

Then Rhiannon reached into her purse and pulled out a prescription bottle with an orange top. Lenna tried not to stare as she shook a pill into her palm. They were small, round, pale yellow. Lenna knew those pills. She'd taken them after her mom died, in order to sleep.

"Those don't knock you out?" she asked.

"Nah. And I don't always take them. Half the time I give them away. But sometimes, I just get kind of worked up. Panic, maybe." She swallowed the pill and then glanced at Lenna. "You asked about my mom. She was *way* different than yours was."

"How so?" Lenna asked tentatively, trying to be sensitive.

Rhiannon stared into her lap. There was a thin string stuck to her sleeve. Lenna resisted the urge to pull it off. "When I was little, my mom loaded me and my brother into the car and . . . well, she got into this accident and our car drove off a bridge."

The can of Sprite that Lenna was holding slipped a little in her grip. *"What?"*

"It was fine. Well. *I* was fine. Someone pulled me out. I remember waking up in the hospital, later, and a social worker—I guess that's who she was—telling me that my brother didn't make it. They'd taken my mom away. People were saying she'd done it on purpose."

Lenna's hand was clamped over her mouth. "Jesus. That's awful. I'm sorry."

"Thanks." Rhiannon sighed. "The news wrote their opinions about my mom's mental state. People couldn't understand how a mother could do that to her children. Everyone tried to keep me from hearing any of it, but when I was older, I went through this phase where I searched for *all* of it. You can find anything, if you go looking."

"I would have done that, too, if I were you."

"Anyway." Rhiannon tossed the wrapper into the trash. "You asked me about kids, too. It's why I don't want them. I just . . . I would worry, every day, *What if I'm just like her? What if it's inside me? What if I would do that, too?*"

"But you wouldn't. You'd know the warning signs."

Rhiannon shrugged. "What if I didn't?"

Lenna thought of the little girl in the store. The frazzled mother. How Rhiannon had stepped forward and given her a respite. "It must have been hard without a mom."

"My dad did his best, I guess." Rhiannon sighed again. "He was a drinker, and it certainly didn't get better afterward, but he always treated me okay. And he's sober now, so that's good."

"He must have been so broken. Having lost your brother . . ."

"Mm-hmm." Rhiannon touched a gold locket under her sweater. "I still wear this in honor of him. Got it for my birthday when he was still alive—apparently, he helped my mom pick it out."

"I'm so sorry." Lenna took a breath. "Do you still see your mom?" she asked.

Rhiannon scoffed. "No fucking way. Would you?"

A low-slung exotic car purred at the light. Lenna rubbed her eyes, trying to imagine the trauma of going through such an event. Of course it would shape you for life. Of course you'd cut your mother off. That kind of mother, anyway.

"You didn't have to explain the no-kids thing to me," Lenna said softly. "I shouldn't have asked in the first place."

"How would you know? And lots of people ask after they see how good I am with them," Rhiannon said. "Especially if they don't know. Most people don't, and I don't tell them." Her gaze cut to Lenna. "I hope you're okay that I shared this."

"Of course," Lenna said quickly. And she was okay about it. *Touched,* actually. "The work-life farm," she then remembered. "That's why you want to go? The . . . family thing?" *Because you didn't have one?*

Rhiannon looked thoughtful, as though this hadn't occurred to her. "Yeah. Maybe. You could be right." She turned so that she was facing Lenna head-on. Her eyes were full of remorse. "Listen, I have to tell you something. Rich filled the gossip writer position yesterday."

"Oh." Lenna's heart sank. "Then . . . why am I here?"

"Well, when I say I have someone's back, I mean it. And listen—there's another position available. It's not as glamorous—just a copy editor. It doesn't pay as well, but I think you could do it. Plus, we could work together." Rhiannon's eyes softened. "I'd really like that."

"A copy editor," Lenna repeated, thinking.

"For what it's worth, I'm sure you're qualified."

Actually, Lenna agreed. It was certainly less flashy, more suited to her introverted ways. It probably wouldn't be that much fun, but it was this—sitting in the sun on this touristy street, a friend telling her things, *making her feel needed*—that she really craved, anyway.

She said she'd interview. Rhiannon grinned. "Let's go up and talk to Rich, then."

As they turned to leave, someone shifted on a nearby bench. When Lenna glanced over, she realized with a double take that it was that woman from the Sofitel. The one Rhiannon had seen and turned away from. Now, she walked toward them, a bounce in her step. Rhiannon's smile dimmed.

"Hey!" There was an eagerness about the woman's expression—her eyes were a little bit too big, her smile a little bit too wide. "I'm Gillian, remember?"

"Oh. Uh, hi. Rhiannon." Rhiannon glanced at Lenna. "And this is my friend Lenna. She's interviewing for a job at *CG*."

Gillian looked Lenna up and down. "Fun! I'm in the building, too." She waved generally toward the lobby. "You guys eating lunch?"

Rhiannon shifted uncomfortably. "Yes," she said after a beat, like it was obvious. "We just finished."

Another ocean of silence passed. Gillian stood there like she expected something. An invitation, maybe.

"Anyway," Rhiannon added, turning away. "We need to get to Lenna's interview."

"Cool." When Gillian looked at Lenna, her smile was still as eager as ever. "Good luck! I know you're going to do great."

They walked back into the building and into a waiting elevator car. Rhiannon's shoulders were stiff. "That's the same woman from the bar, isn't it?" Lenna murmured.

"Yes."

"Do you see her around a lot?"

Rhiannon shrugged. "I catch her watching me, sometimes. You know those people who just don't get the hint that they aren't your type?"

This had rarely happened to Lenna, as she hadn't ever been forthcoming enough to make that many new friends. Though she nodded all the same.

And it felt good, admittedly. Because though Rhiannon was saying that Gillian wasn't her type, she was also—maybe—implying that Lenna *was*.

[Image description: A young woman with wavy brown hair lies on a bed with a white comforter, the covers pulled to her nose. Her eyes are wide.]

♡ ◯ ◁   ⊓

OMG, friends. You would not believe it. You simply would not believe it! Remember how I stated my intentions? How I was sure I'd spotted my SOULMATES but felt too emotionally paralyzed to talk to them? Thank you for all who commented that most friendships are made by being just a little bit pushy, exactly like I did with S. I took that to heart, I really did. But for a while, I was too afraid to really do anything.

But then something amazing happened!!! I already knew where R works. And there I was, outside the building, and I saw both of them on a bench. Together! And this time, I went up to them! And said hello!

TBH, I kind of grayed out. I came back to myself afterward, and they were walking back into the building and I was like, "Wha? Wha? What happened?" But I did it. And the taller one, L—who seems really friendly—turned back and smiled at me. Which feels like a total win.

Sadly, it's back home to S for me now. It's still frosty between us, brrr! The other day she threw a shoe at me. Can you imagine? It was probably my fault. It was my shoe, and she tripped over it coming into her house . . . clearly I don't belong there. But don't worry! One of these days I'm going to get off the damn struggle bus and just be a normal human. And it's going to be amazing.

TOP COMMENTS:

@RTGz69: We're all on the struggle bus together! You're doing great! ♡

@CortFF22: WTF re: S? You gotta get out of that situation, girl. ♡

@lonely_girlRZ4540: Rooting for you ♡

5

LENNA

While Jacob takes a nap in his crib, Lenna listens to the sound of waves crashing in her headphones. Finally, her heart starts to slow. Exhaustion setting in from barely sleeping the night before.

A half hour later, she opens her eyes. Her phone lies face up on the mattress next to her. Daniel has finally sent a follow-up text to the elusive question mark.

What the fuck are you thinking?

She sits up in bed, groggy and dry-mouthed. Daniel isn't some-one who uses *fuck* in daily speech, let alone his texts. She hadn't expected him to feel so vehement. Surprised, sure.

Though maybe that's unfair to think Daniel would be fine with the sudden disappearance of his wife and child. Sure, he has no concept of the baby's schedule, and sometimes she swears she catches him standing in the baby's doorway agog, almost afraid, but maybe she underestimated how much he cares.

After all, her husband was the one who suggested kids in the first place. Not that Lenna didn't long for one . . . but it all still felt so soon to think she deserved one, after that day at the canyon. She still felt shaky, undeserving of love. And their relationship felt so new, too. Like it was moving swiftly with her just going through the motions.

The day Daniel brought it up, they were out at a Thai restaurant; it was one of their first outings as a married couple. Lenna was still bowled over by this plot twist in her life. Daniel was so nice. Couldn't he see she was damaged? Surely she wasn't hiding it *that* well.

But after a waitress set down a plate of spring rolls, Daniel bit into one and said, like it was nothing, "Let's do the kid thing, Len. You want them, right?"

Lenna's chopsticks slipped between her fingers. "Excuse me?"

"You love them. And it's what you do when you're married. First comes love, second comes marriage, then comes Lenna with the . . ." He trailed off, his eyes dancing.

Lenna was getting used to Daniel's spontaneity. He sometimes just did things out of the blue. (It was one of the reasons she thought he'd be okay with her coming out to the desert on a whim.) He'd even proposed spontaneously, five months after they got together, before she felt she even truly knew him—and certainly before he knew nearly anything about her. He'd simply said, "I know something good when I see it, and I don't want you to get away."

It was startling, someone seeing her—as how Rhiannon had seen her, in fact. Daniel was so earnest, but she couldn't help but think it was an act. Could anyone blame her, after Rhiannon and then Gillian? The people she thought she trusted?

Daniel took her hands calmly, a big, gentle smile on his face. "I just think it would be cool, you know? *Pwease?*"

It was what he called his "sad dog voice." Lenna laughed. Daniel was so kooky, which gave her the space to be kooky, too. She was loose with him, her silliest self, not second-guessing her coolness like she used to with Rhiannon. She was more comfortable with her rituals around him, too. Daniel also had his particularities—all the tassels in the rug combed neatly, all the books on the shelves alphabetized, and he despised dust. But it was also because she'd been so certain the relationship wouldn't last—not because she wanted it to end, but because she still felt such self-loathing and uncertainty.

At the same time, there were so many things to love about Daniel. He truly listened to Lenna when she talked about her mother. He seemed to understand the breadth of her grief, and even though he'd never met her mother, he mourned her, too. He remembered her birthday and the anniversary of her death. He went with Lenna to visit her at the cemetery. He was more supportive than Rhiannon had been, actually. His kindness made Lenna feel guilty about all she wasn't telling him.

Despite everything, Lenna really did want a baby. In fact, maybe a baby would *save* her. Lift the fog that surrounded her. She fantasized about the distraction and purpose of loving something unconditionally, the way she loved her mother, the way her mother loved *her*. Maybe she should drop the worries about the relationship with Daniel being too new, or that she still had visions about the awful thing that happened, or that perhaps they should wait to start a family until Lenna was brave enough to share with Daniel what she'd gone through. The truth was, she'd probably never tell Daniel if she could help it.

And so, she looked at Daniel and smiled. "Okay, let's go for it." The very first month of trying, Lenna's period was late. Her hesitation over the whole endeavor turned to joy when she took in the positive pregnancy test. Two lines! The first shot! A miracle.

Daniel was happy, too. During her first and second trimesters, his enthusiasm remained high. Granted, she took over buying all the important things for the baby and setting up the nursery, but he was busy with work, and she was only freelancing. It was good to throw herself into a task.

She was so wrapped up in Jacob's arrival that she didn't quite realize Daniel was suddenly acting a little . . . distant. Unsteady. In the delivery room, she was vaguely aware of Daniel there, and it was only after she was holding the baby—the *crying* baby, because Jacob had started his crying right out of the gate—that she happened to look over at Daniel's face.

He seemed overjoyed. But he also stood very, very far away from the bed, his face white as a sheet. "You can come closer." She laughed. "I promise he won't bite."

Daniel just blinked. "I'm good," he said in nearly a whisper. It was something Lenna wondered if she should google: a condition, maybe? *Sudden Male Onset Baby Paralysis?*

In the weeks that followed, Lenna did all the work with the baby while Daniel doted from afar. He bought Jacob toys, stuffed animals, a board book of black-and-white pictures to stimulate his growing brain. He stocked the pantry with foods Lenna liked and baby formula in case Lenna needed to supplement. He made sure there were diapers and clean burp cloths. Occasionally he held Jacob's legs when Lenna was changing a diaper. But he hadn't really held Jacob for any length of time. He seemed terrified of dropping him and leery of his constant cries.

Lenna found herself in a quandary. She would sound ungrateful if she complained; Daniel was literally doing all the housework. But in so many other ways, he seemed so disconnected—from the baby, but also from her. None of their goofy couple banter existed anymore. She found herself not knowing how to make conversation with him—her whole life was the baby, and she wasn't sure if he wanted to hear how much Jacob had eaten, or that he'd had a good nap, or that he really seemed to like the song "Baa Baa Black Sheep."

It was why, when she decided to come to Halcyon last night, she figured Daniel would be okay with it. They needed a break—Rhiannon's lullaby was right *for both of them*. Maybe time and distance would set things right. And yet she knew that maybe she was trying to rationalize everything. Why else had she left as early as she did? Why had she left him that note instead of talking it through with him, even if she would have had to wake him up in the middle of the night? She knew this deserved a *what the fuck* kind of response. The thing was, she wouldn't have been able to explain Halcyon to him, not in a way that didn't sound like she was going off to a cult. *A commune for women deep in the desert with no GPS coordinates.* Not to mention the fact that she was going with a friend she'd never even told him about. If the roles were reversed, she'd be wild with panic, too.

The baby stirs. Lenna wrenches her gaze away from her phone and looks into the crib. "Hi, Noodle," she coos, feeling that familiar burst of joy she always gets when she sees Jacob. She picks him up, unlatches her bra, and pushes him to her nipple, where he latches.

She listens to the sounds outside. Dogs bark. Children shout. She needs to talk to Rhiannon. But first Daniel's text? He's her husband. He deserves to know she's okay.

After Jacob is finished eating, she feels a burst of hunger. She'll find lunch, then deal with Daniel. She wraps the baby in the sling at her chest and steps into the hall. Jacob starts fussing, but his whimpers are halfhearted. First, she turns right, but a few doors down, she hits a dead end—that stained-glass window she saw when Rhiannon led her here. Odd. She was *sure* she'd come here from the left.

She backtracks, passing her door again—she only knows it's her room because there's a chalkboard pinned to it bearing her and Jacob's names, with a heart—and heads the other direction. Finally, it opens into the familiar cryptlike common room with all the couches.

There are a few lights on. Someone is curled up in a chair in the corner, reading a book. Sprigs of gray jut from the crown of her head, but her face looks youngish. As Lenna gets closer, she realizes it's Melissa. The one who teaches the kids, the one who had the baby last year.

"Oh, hi," she says, stepping into the puddle of light from the lamp next to the chair. "Sorry about this guy. He's so noisy. Oh, and thanks for that tea."

Melissa looks up and squints at her. "What?"

"In my room? Rhiannon said you made it. It was really refreshing—and relaxing. She said you made it with cucumber you grow yourselves." Lenna blinks at Melissa's confused expression. "Sorry. Rhiannon said . . ."

Melissa lays the book facedown on her lap, her gaze flitting from Lenna to her baby. "I'm sorry, who *are* you?"

"Lenna." Lenna's vision tunnels. "I met you outside . . ."

"I don't *think* so . . ."

Melissa's voice sounds different—more of a fry, more California cool. Lenna looks around, trying to hold on to something in this room that's real. "Oh. I'm sorry. Maybe I . . . maybe we didn't . . ."

"Naomi," comes a sharp voice. And here is *another* Melissa, rushing forward. "Hey. You've met Lenna. She just got here. Rhiannon's friend."

The reading woman—Naomi?—is on her feet now. She places the book on the table. "Oh. That explains it. She thought I was you."

Melissa turns to Lenna. "Sorry. Naomi and I are sisters."

"Twins," Lenna says, feeling idiotic.

"Yes." Melissa tries to laugh. "It's been a while since we've had anyone new here. It's hard to tell us apart . . ."

Melissa's smile is twitchy, like she's trying to smooth something over. The tension is palpable. Even Jacob can feel it, his whimpers escalating. Lenna clears her throat. It feels like it's up to her to smooth this over. "So you're both residents? Is that fun to be here together?"

"It can be," Melissa says carefully.

"It's a real trip," Naomi says at the same time—sarcastically. Then she looks at Lenna. "So. What did you do to her?"

"Pardon?"

"What. Did. You. Do. To. Rhiannon?"

She holds Lenna's gaze a beat too long, a whisper of a smile on her face. Lenna's heart bangs. "Wh-what do you mean?"

"To deserve to come to this place, I mean. Must've been something *remarkable.*"

Lenna lets out a shaky breath. There are spots in front of her eyes. "Um, I don't . . ."

"Naomi, come on." Melissa grabs her sister's arm. "You know you're not supposed to ask those questions."

"Whatever, I have to do chores now anyway." Naomi stands. "Nice to meet you, Lenna. Hope you find what you're looking for here."

"Thanks." Lenna's head begins to hurt.

"Sorry about her," Melissa says after Naomi leaves, her jaw tensed. "I have to love her because she's my sister, but sometimes, I swear, I wish she was someone else." Then she winces. "Forget I said that. So. Do you need anything?"

"I'm fine." Lenna peeks once more over her shoulder. Naomi

has disappeared down the hall. She thinks of the hunger she felt in her room. It's been replaced with a ball of nerves.

"You see the rain?" Melissa asks as she guides Lenna into the kitchen. "Swept through half an hour ago."

She gestures to the open door to the outside. Lenna gasps. The front yard, which was dusty and dry, is now damp and shimmering. The temperature has also dropped at least thirty degrees. The mountain has turned a grayish pink. The sheds and outbuildings glimmer. And yes, there is a goat pen, off to the left. The animals are actually frolicking. It's amazing what a change in weather can do.

She feels lighter—and clearer, too. Suddenly, she has the words for Daniel, a way to explain.

Excusing herself, she turns with purpose back to her room and grabs her phone. Daniel's text is still on the locked screen. **What the fuck are you thinking?** She dials his number. *Think good thoughts,* she tells herself. *It'll be okay.*

He answers immediately, breathless. "Lenna! Holy shit!"

"Hey."

"Jesus Christ. What the *hell*?" His voice is choked, like he's been crying. "Where are you? I've been waiting here, thinking you're coming back!"

She's startled. "You didn't go to work?"

"Of course I didn't go to work! I thought you were *dead*! Where's the baby?"

"I left you that note," she says shakily. "Everything's fine. The baby is with me."

"'This is something I need to do? I think it'll be good for us'?" he reads with an incredulous inflection from the note she put on the counter early this morning, tiptoeing out before he woke. *"'Don't worry'? 'We'll be okay'? 'We'll be back soon'?"*

"It's all true."

"But . . . where are you? My God, I've been frantic!"

Lenna bites her lip. "I thought we might take this as a break. I thought you'd be relieved, actually." She laughs self-consciously. "No more crying!"

"Excuse me?"

But he heard her. He breathes out huffily. "I know I've been . . . it's been *hard*. But what, this is your idea of punishment?"

"This isn't about you. I just . . . I need to be here right now. I need some help."

"Help? I'm Jacob's father. When did you even think this up? What am I supposed to say when people ask where my wife and child have gone? *Actually, I have no idea. They ran away before I woke up.* You realize that's kidnapping, right? You've kidnapped our child?"

A streak of nerves goes through her. Her heart starts to thump. "Daniel, I'm safe. I'm with people I know and trust. And I'm coming back soon. Of course I'm coming back. I haven't kidnapped anyone."

"Who are you with?"

She hesitates. But then Daniel guesses. "It's that friend, isn't it? The one who showed up?" He lets out a baffled little whimper. "Who even *is* she?"

"A really good old friend." Her voice catches on *good*. She thinks, again, of Gillian: *Why does she have such a hold over you?* "Besides just having a little mental break, besides being around other mothers who might be able to shed light on how we can get Jacob to be happier, Rhiannon and I need to talk through some things. In our past. I want—"

"But you haven't seen her in years. You never told me a word about her. Why would you go somewhere with her at the drop of a hat? And don't use the baby as an excuse. That's bullshit."

For a moment, Lenna is speechless. "You don't know how hard it is," she whispers.

Then she hears a footstep in the hallway and stiffens. The last thing she wants is for someone to overhear her arguing. "I have to go. But we're fine. I promise."

"Lenna! No! I'm sorry. I know it's been hard. I agree. But I thought we were doing okay."

She shuts her eyes. "It's not just the baby. It's also me. I've been . . ." She searches for the word. *Haunted. Tormented. Visited by demons, pretty much since we got together.* But how can she tell him at this point? He'll want to know why she didn't say something sooner. And he won't be satisfied with half the story. He'll want the whole thing.

"What aren't you telling me?" Daniel begs when she doesn't say more.

She wishes she could tell him. But this thing she's suffering with? It's her very worst secret. Her *only* secret. If she told Daniel, he'd divorce her.

And take her baby.

6

LENNA

JUNE
TWO YEARS BEFORE

The *City Gossip* summer kickoff party was at a West Holly-wood establishment that seemed to tick various bingo squares of California cool: a wall of succulents, *check*. A vegan tasting menu, *check*. A neon sign proclaiming a swishy catchphrase—*You Do You*—*check*.

Lenna stared into her glass of red wine, trying not to peek into the back hallway to the bathroom for the tenth time. Rhiannon had gone nearly eleven minutes ago, and she hadn't yet come back. But Lenna could survive for a few minutes without her friend, couldn't she? She knew most of the people here—as a copy editor, she inter-acted with people daily because she corrected their stories. But it wasn't like she ever chitchatted with them. The magazine was about gossip, after all, but she was never good with infiltrating a clique. Plus all of her lunches and coffee breaks were with Rhiannon. She hadn't gotten a chance to really hang out with anyone else.

There was a strategic reason to get to know her other coworkers, though. In Lenna's interview for the copy editing position, Rich, the managing editor, said that if she wanted to eventually write, the best way to start off was by going out on assignment with the more established writers. If she built a rapport with them, they'd eventually let her report on some of the story, too, and share the byline. But Lenna was hoping Rhiannon could pave the way once she came back from the bathroom. Break the ice with her charm.

There was one guy, Frederick, who'd caught Lenna's eye for other reasons, too. He wrote a lot of gossip stories about TikTok stars. They'd chatted in the break room, and Lenna had gotten a nice, gentle vibe. Frederick wore blazers and belts while the other guys rolled in wearing sweats. He never drank coffee, only packets of hot chocolate, and the one time he noticed Lenna reorganizing the messy stacks of coffee cups, he thanked her. He carried around books of poetry, said he wrote some, too. He reminded her of someone her mother might choose for her. Someone literary and thoughtful. Someone who also might have spent hours on a library couch as a child, inhaling novels.

About a week before, Lenna had told Rhiannon about her crush in a roundabout way. Casually, like it didn't mean *too* much. "Huh," Rhiannon had said. "Yeah, I guess I can see that." It felt like she'd given her blessing.

"Hey, watch out," called a voice.

Lenna shot up. Staring at her from the bar was that woman they'd seen the day of Lenna's interview. Gillian.

Today, Gillian wore a short black dress and blocky silver heels. One hand cupped a lowball glass. The other pointed at Lenna's feet. "You're spilling your wine," Gillian said.

Lenna looked down. She'd been so lost in thought that her glass had tilted. Wine splashed on her red suede ballet flat. "Shit." The shoes had been a splurge.

"It's okay." Gillian snatched a bottle of club soda from behind the bar and a cocktail napkin. "This should help."

She leaned down and blotted the splotches on Lenna's shoe. Soon enough, the stains were gone. "Wow," Lenna said. "Thank you."

"Club soda is a miracle."

They stood back up. Gillian smiled sheepishly. She didn't actually seem that creepy up close. Certainly not the way Rhiannon portrayed her.

"You're Lenna, right?"

"Yeah," Lenna said. "And it's . . . Gillian?"

"That's right." Then Gillian saluted her. "Anyway. See ya later. Happy summer." She wended through the crowd.

Lenna felt a hand on her shoulder. "Hey." Here was Rhiannon, finally. "Sorry that took so long. And, ugh, sorry this party is so lame."

"No worries." Lenna took in Rhiannon's flushed cheeks and darting gaze. Her hands were still wet from the sink. "You all right?"

Rhiannon's mouth twitched. She eyed Lenna's wine. "Can I have a sip of that, actually?"

Lenna gave her the glass and watched as Rhiannon drained it. She laughed. "Do you want your own?"

Rhiannon placed it on the bar and shook her head. Her gaze was going in every direction. But then her eyes narrowed. "Why's *she* here?" She was looking at Gillian, who had moved to a vacated bistro table in the corner and was typing something on her phone.

"Oh," Lenna started. "Uh, I don't . . ."

"This is a party for *our* office. Not the whole building."

Lenna chewed on her pinkie nail. Did it matter? She pointed to the writers. "So hey. Mind if we talk to them? I want to network."

Rhiannon scanned the group. "I can't even be near Philip right now. That guy is dead to me."

"What did he do?"

Rhiannon just shook her head and muttered something under

her breath. She was like this, Lenna had noticed. Black or white. You were everything to her, or you were absolutely nothing.

Then Rhiannon turned to Lenna pleadingly. "Can we just go? Max is coming over. I think he has a thing for me. I swear he can't take a hint."

"Max has a thing for you?" Lenna looked at the guy in question. Max was tall and had wavy hair. He was definitely the most handsome person in the office. "And that's *bad*?"

"He's not my type. I swear, all I did was have a nice conversation with him, maybe laugh at a joke that was legitimately funny . . . little did I know it would turn into this." She rolled her eyes.

Lenna was always so puzzled about Rhiannon's aversion to romance. Her friend attracted people wherever she went. She always said friendship was more important to her. Less *messy*.

"Seriously, let's get the hell out of here before he gets down on one knee," Rhiannon pressed. "Otherwise, I'm going to make you plan the wedding."

"Um . . ." Lenna glanced longingly at the group of writers. She hadn't seen Frederick before, but now he had joined the group, presumably from the bar. Her stomach swooped at the sight of him.

"But writing. I really want to do it, and I feel like this is a good opportunity . . ."

Rhiannon waved her hand. "You can meet them in the office. I'll personally set you up with one of them. I mean, it's at your own risk, though. Everyone here sucks."

Lenna paused. "Everyone always seems so busy at work. And half of the writers are out on assignments."

"We'll figure out something. I promise. I've got you." Rhiannon's purse was already slung over her shoulder. "We'll go somewhere more fun." She pressed her palms together in prayer. "Please? I'll be your best friend."

You already are, Lenna thought. She glanced at Frederick again. His jackets had patches on the elbows. He nodded sagely at something another guy was saying. Her heart felt tugged in two different directions. But then she closed her eyes. "All right. But you owe me."

The double doors whooshed open to usher them out. When Lenna glanced over her shoulder, it didn't even seem like Max was paying attention. Guess he took the hint after all.

Instagram post from @GillianAnxietyBabe

June 2

[Image description: A young woman with wavy brown hair stands in front of a mirror, smiling. She wears a short black dress and silver heels and holds a cocktail in one hand and a sign in the other that reads "Milestone!"]

♡ ○ ▽   ⊓

Hi friends! Just a quick post. I think I'm making headway and had a REALLY good night—out in public! L seems like SUCH a sweetheart, but I'm not sure about R anymore. I'm getting chilly vibes from her, and it's not just my social anxiety speaking. I was at this party today, and I caught her doing something . . . surprising in the back hall. I almost wanted to tell L . . . but I don't like gossiping. It's burned me before, you know?

Anyway, heading off to bed! Love you, my Anxiety Babes. Let's have a better day tomorrow!

PS: I'm hiding in my room, btw, because S seems really unstable tonight. I swear one of these days she's going to SNAP.

TOP COMMENTS:

@anxiouskitten23: Amazing news about a good night   ♡
out! Such a win! Keep it up, babe!

@GGigiFfen-sick: Spill the tea on what you saw R   ♡
doing! So curious.

@lonely_girlRZ4540: I'm worried about you and S.   ♡

7

LENNA

Because of the break in the heat, Rhiannon suggests an after-noon walk up on Chiricahua Peak, the mountainous struc-ture in the middle of the property. It's named for the endangered Chiricahua leopard frog, though unfortunately there aren't any in the area anymore. Rhiannon promises it's an easy hike to the top, though the walk is a bit long. *Perfect,* Lenna thinks. They'll get time to talk.

"There's a quicker way up the rock face, but that wouldn't be easy with a baby in a carrier," Rhiannon says. "Unless you want someone down here to keep an eye on him . . ."

"Um . . ." Lenna feels uneasy leaving Jacob with a stranger. "It's okay. I don't mind the exercise. And who knows? Maybe it'll calm him down." She laughs self-deprecatingly.

Rhiannon looks at her for a long beat. "I'd never tell anyone how to parent, but I will say—babies sense tension."

Lenna bites her lip. Is it that obvious? She feels so jittery after the call with Daniel. She's clenched her fists so many times her finger joints ache.

"Look, by all means, feel all the feelings," Rhiannon adds. "I'm absolutely not telling you to relax. But babies do pick up on energy. How about I hold him on the walk so you can just be?"

Lenna looks down at Jacob. Could it really be that easy? "Well, okay," she says softly. "I guess we could try."

They strap the baby into the carrier over Rhiannon's shoulders. As soon as Rhiannon starts moving, Jacob's cries slow. Then they stop. Lenna gapes. "Wow. I *am* a failure."

"You're his mom. He loves you best. I just want to give you a break."

Teddy wants to come along, too. The boy toddles over to Rhiannon and lifts his arms for her to pick him up, but Rhiannon gestures to the baby on her chest. "I'm holding Auntie Lenna's baby for a little, okay?" Rhiannon tells him calmly. "You be a big boy and walk with us."

Teddy turns to Lenna and gives her the same suspicious look he gave her in the Suburban on the drive here.

Teddy points and grunts at Rhiannon's insulated lunch bag. "You want something?" Teddy nods. "You want some cheese?" Teddy nods again. Rhiannon unzips the lunch bag, and looks at him again. "Okay, what's the sign for cheese?"

Teddy thinks a moment, then flutters his hands. The sign for cheese, presumably, because Rhiannon grins. "Good!"

She hands Teddy a slice. Lenna lets out an impressed murmur.

"What?" Rhiannon asks.

"Sorry. It's just—I'm really glad for you."

Rhiannon squints. "What do you mean?"

"I'm glad you have Teddy. I know you . . . struggled. Because of your mom. Remember how you used to say that?"

Rhiannon's smile dims. She looks down. "Yeah. Well. I'm glad to have him, too."

She turns and starts up the path, Jacob bouncing. Lenna gnaws on the inside of her cheek. Surely Rhiannon must know that Lenna is wondering how Teddy came to be. How *any* of this came to be. Is she withholding the information because of the years they've spent apart . . . or to punish Lenna somehow? *Does* she know more than she's letting on? She thinks of what Naomi said, in the house: *What did you do to her?*

How odd it had been to receive a text from Rhiannon completely out of the blue last week. Lenna hadn't heard from her friend in years. Considering all that had happened, she figured she'd never hear from Rhiannon again.

Passing through LA, the text said. Wanna meet up?

Just that. Easy breezy. Lenna was baffled. Also, how did Rhiannon even know Lenna was still in California? Lenna was careful not to be findable online. She didn't have any social media accounts, and she'd asked Daniel never to tag her—she claimed it was for the baby's privacy. Even the freelance work she still did for magazines was all behind the scenes, just copy editing and proofreading, stuff that didn't lead to a byline.

Rhiannon had also used Lenna's new phone number. Lenna's old phone, the one she used to communicate with Rhiannon back when they were friends, was cracked and ruined at the bottom of the canyon. After what happened there, Lenna contacted Rhiannon with the new number, but Rhiannon never responded. Not that Lenna blamed her. She figured Rhiannon had worked out what Lenna did to her and never wanted to talk to her again. And yet, she must have received the message after all, carefully saving Lenna's information.

Lenna had waffled about meeting Rhiannon. The confrontation

scared her. Conflict was never her strong suit, and what if this was
an ambush? When she mentioned it to Daniel, she'd had to explain
who Rhiannon even was. She minimized Rhiannon's importance.
"I mean, it would be nice to catch up with her," she'd said casually.
"Relive old times."

"I didn't realize there were old times to relive," Daniel said.

Something inside Lenna felt spiky and hot. She had a lot of
love for Rhiannon, still. She knew she would regret it if she let the
opportunity pass. Gillian was right, after all. Something drew her
to her old friend. Something still made her feel like she couldn't
say no.

On her way to meet Rhiannon, Lenna gave herself a bunch of
boundaries: She would only go for twenty minutes. She wouldn't
eat anything. Every three and a half minutes, she would squeeze
her fist. She would not bring up the past and only discuss things
if Rhiannon asked. As she entered the café, she tried to breathe.
She searched for something yellow. The room smelled like espresso
beans, pungent cheese, and oiled wood. Someone called Lenna's
name from the corner, and when she looked over, it was Rhiannon,
the same Rhiannon, more or less, waving her arms back and forth
exuberantly.

"Hey!" Rhiannon stepped around the diners and came toward
Lenna with her arms outstretched. "How *are* you?" she breathed,
grabbing her hands and swinging them.

"Uh . . ." Lenna's stomach flipped. She'd expected Rhiannon to
be way more tentative. Testy. Something to indicate she was holding a grudge. She felt herself softening toward her.

Rhiannon peered at Jacob in the stroller. "Hi, pumpkin!" she
whispered. "He's beautiful. Congratulations!"

Lenna had no idea what to say. She must have been standing
still for a few beats too long, not speaking, because eventually
Rhiannon turned back to the table. "Let's sit!"

Lenna wheeled the stroller awkwardly next to the table and adjusted the pillow under Jacob's little head. Rhiannon watched the whole time, a vague smile on her lips. "How's motherhood?"

"It's . . . okay."

"You're married?" Rhiannon asked. Lenna nodded. "How'd you and your husband meet?"

"A crazy coincidence. There was this car accident right in front of us—we were witnesses. He drove me home, and, I don't know, we just started dating. Easy as that."

"That's strange . . . but romantic?" Rhiannon chuckled. "It's going well?" She looked at the baby. "Kids can throw a wrench into things."

Squeeze, squeeze. Yellow lemons in a bowl. "Daniel works a lot. But . . . it's fine. Really . . ." She trailed off. Why was she even getting into this? She owed Rhiannon nothing. "I'm just tired, is all. He cries a lot. A *lot.*"

"Tiredness is the worst," Rhiannon said, clucking her tongue. And then she leaned forward and took a breath. "I felt like it was too much to mention in a text, but I have a kid now, too."

Lenna's eyes boggled. *"What?"*

Rhiannon rummaged in her purse for her phone. She tapped the screen, and up came a few pictures of a chubby-cheeked toddler with Rhiannon's same auburn hair. "Teddy."

"But . . ." Lenna took a moment to collect herself. Their relationship was in the past, maybe she'd remembered incorrectly? But no. *No.*

". . . How old?" she finally asked.

"About two."

Two? Rhiannon mysteriously left town two years and four months ago. Why wouldn't she have told Lenna she was pregnant? Lenna would have been ecstatic for her.

"Teddy's the best," Rhiannon went on. "But, I mean, it hasn't been all rainbows and unicorns."

Lenna's mind was spinning. "Are *you* married?"

"Me? Hell, no." At least that was consistent, anyway. "I live at this compound, actually. Full of women. *Only* women." She crossed her arms. "Remember how I was always talking about that idea? I finally found a place!"

"Whoa." Rhiannon sounded so happy. "That's great. When did all this happen?"

"Been there for almost as long as Teddy's been alive. Exactly what I thought it would be. It's so weird—you always think actually living your dreams won't live up to your expectations. But in this case, it totally did."

"How did you find it?" Lenna asked—trying not to sound skeptical. As delighted as she felt that Rhiannon was living her dream, she doubted these types of communities advertised on reputable websites. She imagined flyers in shops that sold crystals and jade vaginal eggs.

"The universe called me there. It calls all of us. Well—people who need to go. People who are lucky enough."

"That's . . . wild," Lenna said diplomatically. It was exactly the answer she expected. "Did you go there after, um, leaving LA?" *After I got you fired.*

"Not exactly," Rhiannon said, averting her gaze. "There was some time in between here and there."

Was Rhiannon deliberately being cryptic? And surely this was the moment that Rhiannon would call Lenna out. Say she knew what Lenna had done and that she hated her guts.

Instead, Rhiannon lazily opened the menu. "So I'm thinking about the burrata salad. Sounds good, right?"

"Teddy!"

The child's name snaps Lenna back to the present. She's on a mountain now, and Rhiannon's kid has run up the beginning path. He's trying to negotiate up a steep, rocky divide.

"Wait for me." Rhiannon walks faster, Jacob's legs dangling at her waist. Jacob *still* isn't crying. "Mommy will help you." She takes Teddy's hand. "There we go!" she whoops, guiding him up the rock.

They start up the path. It's uneven, but maintained almost as well as a national park. "Taking care of the hiking trails is one of our duties at Halcyon," Rhiannon says. "We clear out weeds, dropped branches, that sort of thing." They pause to observe the reddish rock, then the vistas. The desert stretches out in front of them, endless. It's like looking into eternity. Lenna's heart slows. For a moment peace feels possible.

Then she turns and looks down at the property below. The women and children scurry. One of the mothers and her child walk into a greenhouse. Other kids are splashing in a makeshift pool formed out of aluminum. Lenna spies one of the women in the yard. She fills a trough with hay, the muscles in her arms working efficiently. Lenna has forgotten her name, but she was one of the boisterous, friendly ones. Not Melissa—or Naomi, certainly—but another. When she sees them, she waves. Rhiannon waves back.

"Which one is that?" Lenna asks.

"Amy. You met her."

"Right." Lenna skirts around a boulder. "Oh. After Jacob's nap, I met Melissa's twin sister."

A grimace passes across Rhiannon's face and then subsides. "How'd *that* go?"

"She got kind of mad I confused her for Melissa."

Rhiannon shrugs. "Those two are interesting together." She pauses, as if considering saying something. "I think Naomi hates that her sister had a baby while she's still trying. They both wanted kids. She doesn't want to be stuck in an aunt role."

"Maybe she'd be happier somewhere else, where she isn't constantly reminded? Do she and Melissa have to stick together?"

Rhiannon gives her a strange look but then turns away.

"What?" Lenna asks.

"It's not that easy."

"What do you mean?"

"I mean, this place, it's sort of . . . picky. It'll tell you when you're allowed to leave. When you've done what you need to do here."

"The *place* will?" Lenna stops and looks at her. "What if you want to leave before it thinks you're ready?"

"I don't know. No one's tried that. And I'm not talking about *you*," Rhiannon insists, as if reading Lenna's mind. "I just mean people who made the commitment to live here. It's hard to explain." She waves her hand.

They walk for a few paces in silence, their shoes crunching on the sand. Rhiannon seems a little rankled. Lenna feels the urge to apologize, like she always used to with Rhiannon. She was always like this, letting her mercurial moods show on her face.

But ten seconds later, she scoops Teddy up again, all smiles. "Now, if you *do* choose to stay, Len," she adds, raising her eyebrows tantalizingly, "then we'd have to talk about all of that for real."

"I can't stay," Lenna says quietly.

"What, because of your husband?" Rhiannon makes a face. "Too bad. You and I would have lots of fun."

Lenna looks away. Even after all this time, Rhiannon's approval gives her a special kind of euphoria. Not even Daniel's love and affection move her in quite the same way. She'd started feeling this pull in the café, when Rhiannon looked thoughtfully from Lenna to Jacob and said, "Maybe you want to come to Halcyon for a while?" When Lenna demurred, Rhiannon gave her this whole speech—a sales pitch, really—about feeling stuck and wanting answers and making meaningful friendships. "Maybe you think, *If only I could get away. If only I had time to really think, really breathe*," she said. And then something else about living the dream with the stars as their witnesses.

If someone else had said all this, she would have laughed, or thought they were trying to indoctrinate her. But coming from Rhiannon, it was tempting. And flattering; Rhiannon wanted to spend time with her again. They parted ways with Lenna saying she couldn't get away, but the invitation stuck with her, germinating, until it shot from the soil, seeking sunlight.

And yet. The same question she'd wondered at the café last week still lingers: *Aren't you the littlest bit mad at me? Are we ever going to talk about that?*

"Your other residents seem interesting," she says, deciding to change the subject. "Everyone is so different. I can see some of them choosing this life. Like who's the one who takes care of the animals?"

"Ann."

"Right. She makes sense. But others—like that one girl, the chef? She's just a teenager."

Rhiannon shrugs. "Coral came here when she was under eighteen. I don't know the story behind that, but she somehow convinced Marjorie to let her stay even though you're supposed to be an adult and pay into the group fund. She's totally sweet, but I feel like it was some sort of abusive household situation, maybe."

"What about Gia?" Lenna glances at Rhiannon out of the corner of her eye. "She's so . . . refined."

Rhiannon's shoulders rise and fall. "Gia's okay. But I'd leave that situation alone."

Lenna's whole body stills. It's a lot like what Rhiannon said before—about Frederick. Does Rhiannon realize?

She peeks at her friend. *Surely* she must. But Rhiannon keeps walking.

"Why should I *leave it alone*?" Lenna tries to emphasize the phrase, just a little, to jog her friend's memory.

"Just take my word for it." Rhiannon clears her throat. "And Marjorie obviously fits here. Between the two of us, she went through major trauma with her kids a while back. Her youngest had to be kicked out of the community when he was fifteen. He wouldn't listen to her. Or any of us. He became unstable."

"That's terrible." Then Lenna realizes something. "I thought it was a rule not to talk about people's pasts, though."

Rhiannon peers down the mountain. "There's no one around. Plus I thought it would be helpful for you to know what you're getting into. Don't tell, okay?"

Lenna is touched. She hates being out of control. That Rhiannon still recognizes this in her—she feels seen.

"Pinkie swear," she says.

They reach the top of the mountain. From this vantage, they can see north for miles, straight to the Catalina Mountains, dusky blue and far away. Hills of cacti jut here and there. Wisps of clouds float through the sparkling blue sky. Far in the distance, Lenna can see the haze of . . . a road, maybe. It's hard to imagine. This place feels like its own planet.

Lenna feels a buzz at her hip. It's her phone. When she pulls it out and looks at the screen, a bunch of emails have rolled in. Some voice mails, too. One is confirming a hair appointment Lenna forgot she made. Another is to tell her that her car is due for inspection. She thinks of it, inert, sitting in the garage. There are some missed calls from Daniel. Lenna notes the time stamps. He called after they talked a half hour ago. He hasn't left any messages, though.

"Yeah, you get actual cell service up here," Rhiannon explains, noticing Lenna checking her screen. "It's the only spot on the property where you're able to use a provider's plan. The Wi-Fi's good in other places around the property, though—Marjorie's installed a lot of hot spots."

At the top of the hill is a long, flat rock. Rhiannon sets the lunch bag on it, undoes the flaps, and pulls out a silicone baggie of homemade potato chips. Then she hands back Jacob. For a moment, Lenna is nervous about taking her own baby, and then immediately feels guilty. Lenna unclips her nursing bra and puts the baby to her chest, and after he sucks for a bit, he grows drowsy in the sun and the heat. She tries to feel relaxed, too. For him . . . but for herself. She can feel her hand clenching and unclenching.

She senses Rhiannon watching her. It's her same behavior from when they were friends.

"How's all that going?" Rhiannon asks gently. "Did having a baby make it worse?"

Lenna focuses on a nonexistent string on her sweatshirt so she doesn't have to meet Rhiannon's gaze. "Kind of."

"Are you still able to take medication?"

"Yeah. It takes the edge off."

Rhiannon cocks her head, looking at her more deeply. "I bet having a baby is hard without your mom, huh?"

Lenna feels tears in her eyes. "I miss her a lot. She'd love Jacob." She clears her throat. "What about you?"

A strange kind of startled expression settles over Rhiannon's features for a beat. "What *about* me?"

"I mean . . . you don't have your mom, either. Do you worry about the things you used to worry about, now that you're a mom yourself?" She clears her throat. "I remember you talking . . . you were afraid that you'd miss signs, the same signs she had—"

"I don't worry about that anymore," Rhiannon interrupts, her voice hard.

Lenna blinks. Pulls away. "Oh. Okay. Well, good."

Rhiannon's shoulders round inward. Yet again, Lenna can't

read her expression as she leans over Teddy, fiddling with a button on his shirt. Lenna feels the need to right things. Maybe clear the air entirely.

"Listen," she says, taking a breath. "You and me . . . I have a lot of questions. And some things to tell you."

Rhiannon straightens and turns to her as if to say *You go first.*

Say it, Lenna's mind urges. *Just talk to her about it.* "Do you remember . . . ?" she starts. But the words get caught in her throat. *Say her name,* Lenna's brain screams. *Say Gillian's name. Tell her what she said. Explain why you did what you did. Ask for the truth in return.*

But suddenly, Rhiannon turns away and sucks in a breath. *"Look."*

There's a flash of something far below in the ravine behind some twisted, dead-looking trees. Movement.

Lenna freezes. "What is that?"

The wind whistles. The sun shines in her eyes. Lenna stares down into the ravine, maybe seeing a shape that isn't there.

"Can people get on this property?" Lenna whispers.

Rhiannon frowns. "You saw the barbs on the fence."

"So you never have trespassers?"

"None that I've known about."

"Do you have any means of protection?"

"If you mean guns, no way." Rhiannon shakes her head. "We don't believe in them."

But then an animal, low to the ground, wide as it is long, appears around the rock. Lenna almost screams. Another materializes, and another, all of them appearing from around a corner. They are brown, heavy, with sharp tusks and snouts. There are too many for Lenna to count, all calmly scratching and milling about. There are even babies among the hooves, tiny creatures sticking close to the larger ones.

"Are those . . . pigs?" Lenna whispers.

Rhiannon nods. "Javelinas. Wild boars. They travel in packs. Just stay still, and they'll leave."

Lenna feels a wave of uneasiness. "Are they dangerous?"

"Not unless they feel threatened, or you're threatening their babies." Rhiannon nods at Lenna. "Same as what you're doing."

Lenna looks down. In a primal instinct, she is holding her son even closer than before. There's a sour taste in her mouth, too.

They stay still a few minutes longer until the boars drift away. Then Rhiannon turns back to her. "So what were you saying? Do I remember . . . what?"

Lenna slumps her shoulders, drained and cowardly. "Never mind," she says. "Can we go back? I've seen enough."

8

LENNA

That June, work was busy. They were putting out a double issue, the first of its kind, full of celebrity half stories and alleged tales that skirted the line between fact and fiction. (Lawyers on staff made sure they weren't constantly being sued.) Lenna reviewed page after page, barely having time for lunch. She had dreams of the actors and singers and influencers and other random rich people the magazine profiled, inserting herself on yachts and at parties and—her favorite dreams—on girls' trips. Rhiannon was always in those dreams, too. Lenna also dreamed of pitching in a little, writing-wise. A text box? A roundup of outrageous quotes? She didn't care. But in real life, Rhiannon said that Lenna was needed in copy at the moment—her hookup would come later. Lenna tried to be patient, she really did, but she felt she could do both. She tried to push down any resentment and frustration.

One morning, Lenna appeared in Rhiannon's doorway at work when Rhiannon was on the phone. Rhiannon had a look that was so guarded Lenna hurried away, flushed and embarrassed. She told herself she was being too needy, but later, Rhiannon stopped by her cubicle, repentant.

"Sorry about that. Work's just so stressful, you know? Everyone's breathing down my neck."

"No worries," Lenna replied.

Later that day, she asked if Rhiannon could see a movie with her or meet for drinks. She was feeling particularly lonely, and the idea of going back to her quiet apartment with its one dark window and the paltry take-out options depressed her. But Rhiannon shook her head and said, once again, that she couldn't. More work. Too much work. Disappointed, Lenna did something that surprised her: She emailed Frederick asking if he'd like to check out the movie instead.

They'd talked a little more by then. It was usually just passing pleasantries in the break room—Frederick, too, was busy with the double issue. But Lenna knew for a fact—she had copy edited his pieces—that his job on the issue was done, so he might have some free time.

She regretted the email the moment she hit send. What dork sends an email to someone who sits across the room? She should have just gotten up and asked him. Or, better yet, not asked at all. Lenna had never dated, not really. Certainly not in high school. A friend from yearbook asked her to prom, and they all went out to a mediocre steakhouse beforehand, but in the end he had barely paid any attention to her. There were random hookups with a boy who lived two doors down from her in her college dorms, but she'd always suspected she was the closest option, and willing, and he didn't even have to get out of bed. When her mom was sick, a hospital cafeteria manager asked her to drinks. William. He'd been nice. But she'd said no, the timing wasn't right.

And she'd certainly never *asked* anyone on a date. She started to panic. But then, a response came: *Sure. Give me ten.*

Lenna's heart banged giddily as she and Frederick rode the elevator down together. The movie theater was within walking distance—miraculous, for LA—so they didn't have to face the awkwardness of whose car they would take. Frederick was a bubbling fountain of conversation. He talked about behind-the-scenes stuff he'd done to get his stories at *City Gossip,* including calling up a star's assistant and pretending he was the star's distant cousin. "And they bought it!" he cried. "I got a ton of dirt from her about the actress. It was amazing." Then he stared down at himself. "God. Listen to me."

"Do you feel bad, lying like that?" Lenna asked.

"For that sort of story? Not really, honest. But for other things— yeah. It's why I never take the stories about people's breakups or their kids, I only do fluffy ones that don't really matter. Like what sorts of workouts influencers do, or if they ever fly commercial."

"I think that's where I'd have to draw the line, too," Lenna agreed, liking his answer. "Gossiping about something that could hurt someone—that seems like too much. Like what Rhiannon had to deal with, with her mom."

"What happened with Rhiannon's mom?" Frederick asked, a strange look crossing his face.

Lenna's chest fizzed. "Sorry, nothing."

She couldn't believe she'd nearly broken Rhiannon's confidence about her past. She'd never asked about it again, and Rhiannon never volunteered, not since that day she confessed.

Lenna had looked up the crash information just once. She swore Rhiannon said the story had been covered in the news, but she couldn't find the specific incident. There was a Google hit about a woman driving her children off a bridge and the dates matched up, but when she clicked on it, the local newspaper site said that story couldn't be found. Like someone had taken it down, maybe.

"You're friends with Rhiannon, huh?" Frederick added, breaking Lenna from her thoughts.

"Good friends," Lenna said, smiling. "She's the best."

But when she looked over at Frederick, she caught him grimacing. It almost seemed like he wanted to say something. But then they were at the theater. She decided to put it out of her mind.

As they stood in line to buy tickets and candy, Frederick glanced at her sheepishly. "So this is going to make me sound cheap, but I brought my own snacks from the office. Only . . . you might not find them at a concession stand."

Lenna asked what they were, and he opened his backpack to reveal dried squid from the Korean market down the street. Lenna laughed. "I love that, too, actually. But . . ."

". . . Worried we'll be caught . . ." He eyed the street. "We don't *have* to see the movie."

And so they left. They walked the empty streets, through West Hollywood and up to Sunset. They ate dried squid and laughed. Lenna felt like she was floating. Maybe this *was* a date. Who knew it could be so easy? Why hadn't she done this sooner? Why hadn't she and *Frederick* done this sooner?

Nothing happened between them that night—not exactly. There was the occasional brush of their hands, which made Lenna's heart rate spike each time it occurred. It was *fun,* though— and promising. And after they said their good-byes, Lenna was bursting to tell Rhiannon. But when she called her that night, Rhiannon didn't answer. The next day, Lenna dressed carefully for work, excited to see Frederick. She felt on top of the world.

When she got to the office, Frederick wasn't in. Lenna beelined to Rhiannon's office instead.

"Guess who I went out with last night because someone was busy?" she teased, swinging her hips back and forth.

Rhiannon looked up. Her expression was strange—weary, unnerved, distracted. There were circles under her eyes. "Who?"

"Frederick."

Rhiannon's skin grew ashy. *"Why?"*

"Because . . . I . . ." Lenna frowned. "I told you I kind of had a crush."

Rhiannon blinked hard. In the hallway, someone passed carrying a very pungent cup of chai. Lenna's friend grabbed her office pass. "Let's go for a walk."

Out on the street, Rhiannon walked with a hunch. Her phone kept pinging. "What's going on?" Lenna asked, feeling totally deflated. She thought Rhiannon would be excited for her. "What's wrong with Frederick? We had fun."

"He's not right for you."

"What? Why?"

Rhiannon stabbed at the walk button at the corner. Her mouth a tight line.

"I don't understand," Lenna said, heart sinking. "Why?"

"Just leave it alone," Rhiannon said. "Take my word for it."

"You can't tell me anything else?"

"Lenna . . ." Rhiannon rubbed her temples. "I'm exhausted right now, okay?"

They turned back for the office in silence. Lenna felt tears in her eyes that she didn't understand. When they were almost back to the building, it was like there was a pressure mounting inside her.

"I'm sorry, but this is really bothering me," she blurted. "You're being so weird. I thought you would be happy."

"Lenna." Rhiannon shut her eyes. "I can't deal with this right now."

Lenna slapped her sides in frustration. Rhiannon was speaking to her like she was a child. Was that how she saw her?

"Frederick knows editors at other magazines, too. He wants to help me get my foot in the door." She breathed in to say something else. She was terrified to say what she was really thinking, and yet she *wanted* to say it. She went for it, under her breath: "At least *someone* is making an effort."

Rhiannon rounded on her. "What's that supposed to mean? You don't think I have your back?"

"You always *say* it, but it certainly doesn't seem that way." Lenna's heart banged. "You keep saying you'll introduce me to the writers, but it's always tomorrow, and then tomorrow. Maybe you don't want me to write. I mean, I'm sure that's not what you're *intending,* but it's what it *feels* like sometimes."

Rhiannon's mouth dropped open. Lenna wondered if she'd gone too far. "Okay, first of all, I've never held you back from meeting other writers. If you want to talk to them, *talk to them.* Why do you need me? Don't accuse me of standing in your way or being manipulative."

"I'm not saying you *realize* you're doing it." Lenna felt her shoulders pulling in, her body getting smaller, taking up less space. "It's just . . . sometimes . . . I feel like you want everything to stay exactly the way it is now."

"I got you this *job,* Lenna. Does that mean nothing?"

"I know. A-and I'm grateful. But—you know, I thought it was going to be a writing job."

"It's not my fault they hired someone else the day before your interview!" Rhiannon cried. "Are you seriously mad about that?"

"I know it's not your fault. But . . . well, that's why I want to talk to some of the other writers. And I was excited about Frederick. And you just . . ." She took a breath. "I'm wondering why you took the wind out of my sails."

Rhiannon closed her eyes. Then her hands started to shake. Her breathing became sharp and labored.

"Hey," Lenna said. "Are you all right?"

Rhiannon shook her head, chin pointed down. "I just have to go."

And then she hurried off down the sidewalk in a half run. "Rhiannon! Hey!" Lenna cried. She started after her, but Rhiannon didn't stop.

Lenna hid in her cubicle for the rest of the day. Head down, marking up pages. At one point, she heard Frederick's boisterous laugh down the hall, but she ducked down, hoping he wouldn't see her. What had Rhiannon been so concerned about?

She texted Rhiannon again and again, saying she was sorry. Of course Rhiannon wasn't holding her back. She'd been a wonderful friend—Lenna owed her everything.

But Rhiannon didn't answer.

All night, Lenna tossed and turned. In her dreams, she and Rhiannon were going on a bike ride, just the two of them. At one point, the path diverged; Lenna wanted to take the road downhill, but Rhiannon told her not to. "Something bad will happen," she warned.

Dream Lenna got annoyed and did it anyway, but when she got to the bottom of the hill and turned back, Rhiannon was still at the top, and she was screaming. Something was *happening* to her—there were legs sprouting from the middle of her body, and her skin was turning an odd salmon shade. "I'm a bug!" she screamed, her body snapping, *Metamorphosis*-style, into the form of a giant salmon-colored cockroach. "A ginger bug! I told you not to go down that path, Lenna!"

Lenna shot up in bed, sweating.

The next morning, she dragged herself into the office, resolved to try again with Rhiannon. But when she arrived, Rhiannon wasn't at her desk.

"Says she's sick," Judy, the office manager, reported.

Lenna tried to call her friend, but she didn't answer. The next day, Rhiannon wasn't there, either. "Is she still sick?" she asked Judy.

But Judy didn't know.

A few days passed. Lenna kept trying to call her, but Rhiannon didn't answer. She almost considered calling the police to check on her—horror stories of people found dead in their apartments came to mind—but then she remembered that Rhiannon had spoken to Judy when she'd called in sick.

She could barely concentrate on work. Frederick messaged a few times, asking if she'd like to hang out, but she staved him off, Rhiannon's words ringing in her ears: *He's not right for you.* She couldn't move forward one way or another until she understood what that meant and where Rhiannon had gone.

Friday of the following week, Rich, Rhiannon's boss, stood at the entrance to Lenna's cubicle, a flustered look on his face. "Well, your friend has put us in a fine mess."

Lenna turned and looked at him. "What?"

"Taking leave like this. Says she'll be back in a month."

Lenna rolled back in her chair. Her heart was suddenly pounding. "Where did she go?"

"Oregon." Rich leaned against the cubicle wall. "She didn't tell you?"

The printer in the copy room let out a groan. Polly, the woman who occupied the cube next to Lenna's, was on the phone with some sort of furniture delivery company, explaining that her apartment didn't have an elevator, and they had to carry a couch she'd ordered up another way. Lenna could only focus on the brass buttons on Rich's blazer, not on his face. This made no sense. Rhiannon talked to Lenna before she ordered a pair of jeans online; she included her in her decision over what latte to choose from the Starbucks menu. Had Lenna's mistake been what caused Rhiannon to leave the state?

Lenna sent more texts. And emails. She left voice mails. She even went to Rhiannon's apartment building and rang the buzzer. No one answered. *What the hell was in Oregon?*

The weekend dragged. There was a pit in Lenna's stomach. Rhiannon still didn't answer her. *Fine,* she thought. A wall went up. But it was a thin shell; it immediately developed cracks and holes. What was so wrong with her that someone would just *vanish* on her? Or maybe it wasn't a friendship at all. Maybe she was just a distraction for Rhiannon.

Work held no joy. With Rhiannon out, one of the writers was temporarily promoted to her position; technically, there was an opening for someone new to take that writer's place. Lenna knew she should throw her hat in the ring. But she couldn't bring herself to summon the drive. The opening had come at too great a cost.

A week later, she was hurrying to work. It had started to rain, and she didn't have an umbrella. She pulled her jacket over her hair, but it was useless—she was getting soaked. She'd had another dream that Rhiannon turned into a bug. In this version, though, her mother appeared next to Rhiannon as the metamorphosis happened and held out her hand to help Rhiannon up. "Come on," she said. "We need to go now."

Lenna was flummoxed. Her mother was here, after so many years, and she didn't even want to say hi? "Wait!" Lenna cried, but Rhiannon and her mother both turned and flew away.

The dream rattled her so much that she called her dad the next day. "To what do I owe this honor?" he'd asked. They didn't speak on the phone much.

Lenna wished she wouldn't have to say it out loud—that he'd just *know*. She missed Mom. It was what she always said when she called him. Besides baseball, it was their only other point of conversation.

A woman's laugh tinkled in the background. A few years back, her dad had moved down the coast to an over-fifty community; his place was a tiny one-bedroom with a balcony that overlooked a man-made lagoon. It was never a move he would have made when Lenna's mother was alive—living in a "community" wouldn't have been her cup of tea—but he seemed happy about the change. Sometimes, he sent Lenna texts about how he'd gone Rollerblading, or played thirty-six holes of golf, and there was a members' club on the premises with a bar and restaurant and theme nights. She'd suspected he was dating someone, too, but she hadn't yet been introduced. Lenna didn't blame him for burying his grief and moving on. In a lot of ways, she wished she could, too.

Now, she heard footsteps behind her, and then someone called her name. When Lenna turned, she saw a petite woman around her age with round eyes and wavy, frizzy hair. She was smiling at Lenna expectantly, proffering a huge golf umbrella.

"Room enough for two," the woman offered.

Lenna blinked.

"Gillian," the woman reminded her. "Remember? The master with club soda? Got that wine out of your shoe?"

A fist clenched tightly around her heart. Gillian had also been there, in the background, the first day she and Rhiannon met. "Right," she mumbled.

They just stood there for a moment. Gillian shifted awkwardly. "Sorry. I'm so bad with meeting new people. It's a condition, actually. Social anxiety. I come off as this total weirdo. Or sometimes I lurk when I see someone I want to talk to, and I don't know what to say, and people think I'm stalking them. I'm not. It's just . . . I don't know, my mind goes blank."

Lenna looked at her with surprise. "That sometimes happens to me, too."

"Really? I wouldn't have guessed." Gillian looked relieved. And then, after a beat: "Want to try that yoga place that opened up down the street sometime? You and your friend—what's her name again? She seemed nice."

"My friend's, um, not in LA anymore," Lenna said. She could feel her mouth twitching.

"Oh." There was a wrinkle on Gillian's brow. "Well, just you and me, then? Or something else, maybe you hate yoga."

I do hate yoga, was Lenna's first instinct. But then she thought of her mother again. Not the woman in the dream, leading Rhiannon away, but the mother from childhood, encouraging her to come out of her shell.

"Actually," she said, turning back, "that would be great."

9

LENNA

When they start back down the mountain, Lenna feels like she's getting a sunburn. She'd liberally applied sunscreen to Jacob's head but had forgotten herself. She carries Jacob down, and on the last bit of trail, he wakes up but doesn't cry. He looks around solemnly.

"Look at him," Rhiannon breathes. "It's like he's about to make a proclamation."

"We call that his wise old man face," Lenna says, and then feels a pinch of sadness. It's one of the few sweet inside jokes about the baby she and Daniel came up with together. Then she glances at Rhiannon again. She's pissed she missed her window. Chickened out. She needs to say what she came here to say. It's literally weighing on her, heavier than her baby on her chest.

Back on the property again, the air feels thicker, dustier. A few paces from the door, Lenna's phone buzzes in her pocket. She pulls it out. Daniel has texted again.

I want to talk to this friend you're with.

Nerves streak through Lenna's stomach, and she sucks in her teeth. Rhiannon turns at the sound. "Everything okay?"

"Sure." Lenna shoots her a distracted smile and turns away to type.

I'm safe. I'm fine. I promise.

Dots pop up immediately. His reply appears, a huge block of text.

> This isn't like you at all. You don't go one whole state away because our baby is crying. You don't just jump on a plane to catch up with a friend. Forgive me for saying this, but since I've known you, you don't seem to have any friends, certainly not ones that are meaningful. I know you're stressed. The crying is a lot. You've had to deal with all of it. I haven't been helpful. I want to change that. But this seems completely out of nowhere, and I'm worried.

Lenna grits her teeth. Daniel isn't wrong. And yet . . .

"Lenna?" Rhiannon says, and she jumps. "Everything okay?"

"I just . . ." Lenna presses her phone to her chest. "Um . . ."

Rhiannon walks around to face her. "Who's texting you? Your husband?"

Lenna closes her eyes. But maybe this doesn't have to be difficult. "He wants to speak with you. To assure him we're fine . . ."

"Oh, Lenna." Rhiannon looks crestfallen. "I can't."

"What? Why?"

"It's a rule. No men on the property, and no communicating with men *while* on property. I'm so sorry."

Lenna stares at her. *"That's* a rule?"

"I told you when you got here. I'm sure I did."

Lenna tries to remember. Had she? Then she realizes something else. "So *I* can't even call him back, either?"

"Technically, no." Rhiannon put her hands on her hips. "You said you explained to him where you were going and that he was fine with it."

"I . . . did," Lenna lies. "But, well, he's a new father. He wants to know the baby is okay."

Rhiannon pulls in her bottom lip. "He should trust that he is. He should trust *you.*"

"He does, but . . ." *He doesn't really know who I am. At least the me that knew you.* "I didn't realize I couldn't check in with him at all."

"If you want to talk to him, you'll have to leave the property."

Lenna swallows hard. "You mean just go outside the gate? Could you unlock it for me?"

Again, Rhiannon looks conflicted. "I don't have access. Only Marjorie has the code."

Lenna's gaze darts to the gate, visible from where she's standing. There's a huge padlock holding it shut along with the keypad. Barbed wire hugs the top of the fence. Her stomach swoops, suddenly.

"And anyway, that's not really what I meant," Rhiannon goes on. "It isn't a matter of stepping outside the physical property. You'd have to go *home.*"

"Who wants to go home?"

Lenna whirls around. One of the twins, Melissa or Naomi, is coming toward them. She feels her muscles stiffen. What did she overhear?

"No one, Mel—all good," Rhiannon says. Then she holds out her forearms. "God, look at my skin! I've got a film of dust all over me."

"You look fine," Melissa says, winking at Lenna. Lenna's relieved it's the nice twin. "Though Lenna might be used to actual decent-smelling companions at dinner." She glances at Lenna and gives her a warm but concerned smile. "You ready for tonight?"

"What's tonight?" Lenna asks warily. She feels exhausted, suddenly.

Rhiannon turns to her. "A group dinner. We'd love for you to come, but if it's too much, I totally get it." She touches Lenna's arm again, and then adds, under her breath, "Get in touch with him when you're back in the room. Just this once. Tell him you're safe."

Lenna nods. She notices Melissa watching them carefully. She straightens and gives her a brave, guileless smile.

Then Rhiannon stretches, turning back to Melissa. "I want to see if Teddy will take a power nap before dinner. You'll be able to get to your room, Len?"

"Uh-huh." Lenna's voice sounds far away.

"See you, Ree," Melissa says. She turns and eyes Lenna, too. "Bye, honey."

Her voice cracks on the last word. Her smile twists. Lenna turns to go, but she glances over her shoulder at the last minute. Melissa is watching her.

It's not entirely welcome.

IN THE SAFETY OF HER ROOM, LENNA TEXTS DANIEL AGAIN. SHE doesn't know the repercussions of breaking the rules, but she doesn't want to get kicked out before she's made any headway with Rhiannon.

Talk to her. TALK to her. Lenna kicks herself for chickening out on the mountain. She vows to say something tonight.

Then she picks up her phone and starts to type.

> I'll explain everything when I'm back. I know what I'm doing, I promise.

She hits send. Daniel's response appears within half a minute.

> At the very least, you should have left the baby home. I don't trust this friend at all.

Jesus. Lenna blows out her cheeks. Don't be ridiculous, she writes back.

It was ridiculous. There's the fact that she's still nursing, the fact that Jacob *wants* to nurse, the fact that he needs her, loves her, *and* the fact that Daniel is totally and completely incapable.

The shared bathroom door is unlocked. Lenna brings the baby inside, closes the door again, and sets him on a towel on the floor to step into a quick shower. Jacob squirms and cries, but he settles when the room starts to steam. The hot water smells slightly sulfuric. Her brain feels jangled, too awake; at the same time, she feels mentally flattened. It's the combination of being thrilled to spend time with Rhiannon . . . but also feeling so on edge.

And it's not just about how she left Daniel so hastily, with no explanation. Something else needles at her, too. *Had* Rhiannon told her that she wouldn't be able to call Daniel while she was here? Lenna can't believe that she would have been so willing to come if she'd known about that rule in advance. Or was she so determined to spend time with Rhiannon that she didn't listen?

As Lenna dries her hair, the sound of bongos drifts from out-side. She peers out a small bathroom window. The sun is lower. Older kids race through the dirt, playing tag. A long, farmhouse-style table has been set. Some of the adult residents are already outside, too. Lenna spies Marjorie, Amy, and either Melissa or Naomi, though she can't tell which. Someone's laugh spirals.

She dresses again and returns to her room to put a fresh diaper on the baby. She's depleted her stores in the diaper bag, but she brought plenty in her suitcase. But when she turns to it in the corner, she notices the zipper is halfway open.

She frowns. She's had no reason to delve into the massive suit-case yet. Bending down, she unzips it the rest of the way and as-sesses the stacks of clothes. When she feels inside one of the pockets for the package of diapers, it isn't there. But that makes no sense. There's no way she would have forgotten diapers. Lying in bed next to Daniel last night, she'd mentally gone over everything she needed for the baby . . . had they fallen out on the plane, maybe? Had she left them in that bathroom in the airport? She'd been frazzled, but . . . no, that doesn't make sense. She hadn't gone into her suitcase at all.

She removes everything from the suitcase. Still no diapers. Her thoughts drift back to the way she'd found her bag, the zipper halfway undone. And then something else hits her: Lenna's suit-case has a four-digit passcode lock—Jacob's birthday. The dread chokes her now, makes her heart pound.

She has no choice but to leave Jacob in a dirty diaper tempo-rarily and head out to see the others for this dinner they've ar-ranged. At least she knows why he's crying. "It's okay, it's okay," she murmurs to Jacob as she walks down the hall. "We'll get you sorted."

Outside, the kids laugh as they bang on the drums. The way

the land is situated, the sound is amplified off the mountains. Everything echoes, actually. Marjorie and a few of the others laugh near an unlit fire pit, and their laughter reverberates on and on and on. It's eerie, kind of. Like the laughter keeps going even after their lips stop moving.

Marjorie probably hears the baby before she even sees Jacob and Lenna. She's already turned toward the door when Lenna comes out. Her brow crinkles when she sees Lenna's look of concern. "Everything okay?"

"I'm so sorry, but it seems I've misplaced my package of diapers," Lenna blurts. "Do you know if someone might have . . . put them somewhere?"

"Diapers?" Marjorie squints, confused. "I don't think so."

"It's just that my bag was unzipped, and . . ." Lenna trails off. Maybe it's unwise, accusing someone of rifling through her bag. "Never mind. I probably just forgot them. I hate to ask, but do you have any I can use?"

Marjorie nods. "Although—they're cloth." Her gaze goes to Jacob, and maybe Lenna is seeing things, but she seems to wrinkle her nose at the little plastic strip of his disposable diaper showing through his onesie. "Just put it in the laundry when it's time for a new one. I'll give you a whole stack." She gives Lenna a meaningful look. "Cloth really *is* best."

"Watch it with your indoctrinating, Marjorie!" a voice interrupts, and it's Naomi—definitely Naomi, because she has that same sly look on her face—playfully wagging a finger. "No judgment, no shame!"

"I'm not indoctrinating!" Marjorie cries. "It's Halcyon policy. That's all."

Lenna's cheeks blaze. "I didn't know. But I appreciate it. Thank you."

Behind her, someone snorts. Lenna turns and there's someone sitting in the shadows. Lenna squints. It's that quiet, refined woman—Gia. She's watching them like she's some sort of anthropologist. She thinks about what Rhiannon said: *Gia's okay. But I'd leave that situation alone.*

After Marjorie sorts Lenna out with a stack of cloth diapers and shows her how to use them, they're all back outside again. Lenna feels significantly more rattled—her palm hurts for how much she's squeezed it with her nails, and the color yellow isn't quite as soothing here as it is at home. If only she could just retreat to her room for the night with a tray of food. She isn't even sure she wants to get to know these women. She isn't even sure how long she'll be here. Jacob seems happier, which she supposes is a blessing. Maybe that's all it would take. Cloth diapers. Less stressing. Done.

Rhiannon emerges, freshly showered, hand in hand with her son. She spies Lenna and loops her arm around her elbow.

"You okay? Everything . . . *sorted out?*" She tucks her head slyly. She means Daniel.

Lenna shrugs. She wishes she could tell her friend what Daniel actually said in the text. He's not wrong. This *isn't* the Lenna he knows. To him, she isn't a person who feels pressured or influenced by the suggestions of a friend, no matter how treasured that friend might be. Is Lenna backsliding as a human, being here with Rhiannon? It's hard to parse the difference between the need to reconcile and the urge for Rhiannon's acceptance, no matter what.

She wants to tell Rhiannon about her missing diapers, too, but Rhiannon is already walking toward the table. Maybe it's silly. Maybe Lenna really *did* just forget diapers in her scramble for the flight this dark morning.

They head to the table. Rhiannon grabs the bottles of kombucha and wine and pours them each glasses of both. "You have to try the homemade bread," she says, gesturing at a basket in the center of the table.

Lenna selects a piece; it's warm in her hands and smells like rosemary and olive oil. The flavors ooze on her tongue. An intense wave of pleasure washes over her, so powerful that she has to sit down.

The other women settle in. Everyone talks at once, but it's a pleasant sort of chaos, and the echoes start to meld. A boy at the end of the table talks about a *Harry Potter* he's reading. A few of the little girls are chanting a song. Melissa gets the young children situated at a smaller table and tells the bigger kids to put their napkins on their laps. Marjorie settles herself at the head of the table and proudly beams. At one point, her gaze locks on Lenna's. She nods toward Lenna's glass.

"Drink up. We aren't trying to poison you, I promise."

As the sun sets, Coral returns with a large pot from the kitchen, and everyone cheers. The pot steams. When Coral lifts the lid, inside is a beautiful display of tamales. "My family grew up eating these," she says. "Everyone in Arizona does, it seems, even if you don't have Mexican roots. The peppers are from the greenhouse."

"So you grew up here?" Lenna asks.

Coral plunges tongs into the pot. "With my adopted family, yes."

She dishes out portions. After she's finished, she settles down with Matilda, Amy's teenager in the thick glasses. Their friendship is incongruous—Coral seems so much more responsible, and Matilda is still a child. It's hard to remember that Coral is nearly just as young. They sit close together, preening one another, laying their heads on each other's shoulders, eating off each other's plates. It fills Lenna with longing. It's a teenage friendship she wished she'd had: that draping laziness, those blurred boundaries. At one point, Coral looks up at her, catching her watching, and smiles. Coral's phone tweets again, that same birdcall. Lenna has never heard that ring before. She almost asks Coral where she might be able to find the same tone, but then Matilda grabs Coral's arm to tell her something.

Carefully balancing Jacob on her lap with one hand, Lenna loads up with fresh guacamole with the other. Maybe it's the desert air, but she's hungrier than she's been in a long time. When she takes her first bite, she closes her eyes and moans. The tamales are simple and perfect. Combined with the vibrant colors of the setting sun, it really is magical.

After some time, Rhiannon raises her half-empty wineglass. "To Lenna!" she calls. "Welcome, again!"

"To Lenna!" they all echo, raising glasses of various liquids, too. Lenna blushes. No one has ever toasted her before.

For a while, the only sounds echoing are the noises of their chewing. As the sky darkens, some sort of insect creature starts to chirp in earnest. It's so scrubby and wide-open out here, Lenna can't imagine where bugs might lurk. Maybe in plain sight. *Shake out your shoes.* Scorpions are probably here, too.

"Okay. Someone tell Lenna how amazing it is here and why she needs to join," Marjorie announces, mouth full of a bite. "Amy?"

Matilda's mother, Amy—the woman with the braids—stands. There's a warmth to her smile, a sort of honestness and straightforwardness that puts Lenna at ease. At least someone here isn't a total enigma.

Amy pauses dramatically, then stretches her arms out to encompass the sky and mountains. "It's *amazing,*" she states. "I hope to live here forever. And you should, too."

Everyone laughs.

"How do people find this place?" Lenna asks Amy.

"Referral," Marjorie interrupts, almost cutting Amy off. "People are called here for different reasons."

Amy clears her throat, then says that she was called here because after she got divorced, her daughter, Matilda, had health issues. Autoimmune problems, stomach pains, pain *everywhere.*

"Girl was miserable." Amy sighs. "Couldn't walk up a flight of stairs without getting winded. Everything hurt. Isn't that right, baby?"

Matilda nods. "I went to so many doctors. No one had answers."

"Which is why we came here," Amy says. "Matilda's health issues have really turned around. It's miraculous."

"That's amazing," Lenna breathes.

Marjorie swings her arm to Ann, the quiet, freckled woman who works with the animals. In fact, a dog has his head resting on her lap, like he's waiting for food. "Ann and I met shortly after I started the place. Think I was still living in the trailer back then."

"Yes," Ann says simply. She strokes the dog's head.

"When I told her I was starting a community in the desert but didn't know much about sustainability, I think a blood vessel popped in her forehead." Marjorie chuckles. "I suppose you could say I needed her as much as she needed me."

There's an awkward pause, a space perhaps for Ann to explain *why* she needed Marjorie. Ann instead says, in monotone, "She had a septic system that didn't work and a well that was dried up." There's something so morose about her. But also robotic.

"Ann got us not only composting more efficiently, but now we create very little garbage," Marjorie says.

Rhiannon turns to Lenna. "The whole community produces maybe one bag of trash a week. It's so gratifying to use so little."

"A week?" Lenna glances guiltily at her son's bottom. No *wonder* they don't believe in disposable diapers. And maybe someone *had* gone through her things?

"Melissa and Naomi?" Marjorie goads. "Want to share?"

Melissa sits up. "Well, we've always been close. And we were hoping for a different sort of life. And we desperately wanted to have children." She glances nervously at her sister, then touches her hand. "And we both *will*, eventually."

Naomi, Lenna notices, doesn't look back at her sister. Once again, Lenna wonders why they're a unit. And why Rhiannon said they might not be able to separate because the land won't *allow* it. She's been eyeing Naomi, too, almost waiting for her to make another snide remark about what she *did* to Rhiannon. Her choice of wording still rattles Lenna. So does the gleefully scandalized look that flashed across Naomi's face when she registered Lenna's reaction, as if to say *Ooh! What have I uncovered?*

Marjorie sits back expansively, glancing at Lenna. "It takes a village, you know. This is our village."

"Even the kids help," Melissa pipes up. "Even during the birth!"

"Really?" Lenna looks at the kids' table. Some of the kids are toddlers.

"They think it's magical. Years ago, people had babies in their homes. Children weren't shooed away. So now, we let them participate in all of our births. If they *want* to, anyway." Melissa nudges Lenna. "Your Rhiannon was a huge help with my birth."

Lenna tries to meet Rhiannon's gaze, but she's busy grabbing more food. It's interesting how much of an asset Rhiannon seems to be here. How open, giving, patient. *Tolerant.* She gulps more wine.

Then Lenna turns back to Naomi, wondering if she wants her own turn to speak, but Naomi is now busy talking to one of the kids. "So is anyone pregnant now?" she asks the group.

Marjorie smiles furtively. "Sarah—she's about eight weeks. We're all so thrilled. She has struggled a bit. She's still at the medical facility—they kept her to go through a few scans and genetic tests, but I hear it's all looking good. Baby's got a heartbeat."

Then someone else clears her throat. "I suppose you'd like to hear *my* story."

Gia is looking at Lenna pointedly, like she's trying to read Lenna's thoughts. Lenna bristles.

"Though I don't know if I *should*. Considering what happened last time."

"It's okay, Gia," Marjorie says. "It's better if it comes from you."

"You can trust Lenna," Rhiannon adds.

"What, um, happened last time?" Lenna asks slowly.

Marjorie sets down her fork. "We caught someone gossiping about Gia in a not-very-nice way. She's since left the community."

"A girl on educational exchange," Gia adds. "Carina."

Marjorie coughs. "Let's not name names."

"She wrote something about us, didn't she?" Matilda pipes up. "I heard something about—"

But Amy cuts her off, wagging her finger. "Now, now, no gossiping."

"My family is wealthy," Gia goes on. "The Civatellis?"

Lenna blinks. "I'm sorry . . . I don't . . ."

"My father's family owns a bunch of steel plants out east. I was a socialite. An heiress. Hated it. Didn't want to be part of their capitalist bullshit. So I came here and erased my past. Cut myself out of the family name, the will, all of it. I want nothing to do with that life." She waves her hand.

Lenna glances around the table, but everyone seems to be taking this in stride. They've heard it before, maybe. It's ironic, though. If Gia wants to erase her past, why is she so eager to talk about it?

"Wow," she says, because she feels she needs to say something. "Well, good for you for following your intuition."

Gia snorts, as if she doesn't believe in any of that bullshit.

"Hey, everyone, I know a joke," Matilda says, breaking the silence.

And then the conversation turns that way. Lenna's grateful. Her head is starting to feel light from all the stories and pasts. Or maybe it's the wine.

Matilda gets to the punch line, and everyone hoots with laughter. Coral shoves her friend playfully. Both young women look beautiful in the candlelight. *Real,* Lenna thinks. It must be such an experience to be a young woman here. Her teenage self would have never felt bold enough to tell a joke in front of a table of adults. Maybe her mom would have enjoyed a place like this, too. Maybe Halcyon could even have *healed* her neuroses, just like it healed Matilda.

The sun has sunk brilliantly into the horizon, dyeing the sky orange and pink. Casting the mountains into a shadow. The stars have come out, bright pinpricks against black, more visible than any sky she's ever seen in LA. Lenna thinks of the cabdriver from earlier, how he talked about the International Space Station. As she tilts her head upward, stars seem to explode in her vision. Comets, maybe. Shooting stars. Meteorites.

She gets a sudden burst of hope. She's glad Rhiannon brought her here, even for a little while. She's glad for how calm Jacob has been through this dinner—the company *is* helping. She needs to let go of her mistrust. She turns to Rhiannon suddenly, and is surprised to see that her chair is empty.

"She went inside," a voice says across the table. It's Naomi, staring straight at her, an unreadable expression on her face.

"Oh," Lenna says.

But she wants to find Rhiannon. And tell her—what? How much she missed her? How glad she is that they're reconnecting?

She rises and stumbles into the house, giggling. When was she last this tipsy? The hall is empty. Dark. Cool. Very, very quiet.

Then she hears whispers from the main room.

"She's here. Yes. This morning. But I'm not sure she's going to stay." And *"I know that. I'll do everything I can. I know we have an agreement. But it doesn't feel right."*

Lenna holds on to the wall for support. Rhiannon?

And then she sees her, in silhouette, her head tilted to one side, talking to someone. *". . . It's just,"* Rhiannon goes on. *"She . . ."*

Lenna's skin prickles. She can't hear another voice. Is Rhiannon on the phone, or is she speaking to someone just out of view? Then, when Lenna steps back, she bumps right into a small table, knocking it noisily against the wall.

Rhiannon spins around, her eyes wide. "Oh. Hey!" Her smile is twitchy. She isn't, Lenna notes, holding a phone. "Everything okay?"

"Yeah." Lenna swallows hard. "Were you, um, talking to someone just now?" Rhiannon's words echo in her mind. *It doesn't feel right.*

"Me?" Rhiannon shakes her head. "Nope. Just came in to use the bathroom. Why aren't you outside? Feeling okay? Do you want me to make you some tea?"

"I just didn't know where you were." The words spill out of Lenna's mouth almost in a sob, her good mood from earlier switching to anxiety and distrust. And then, before she can stop herself, she blurts, "What led you to this place, Rhiannon? I just don't get it."

She feels Rhiannon go still. Then she steps forward. Her arms stretch toward Lenna. "Does it matter?"

"I just . . . I don't . . . you leaving . . ."

"*Shhh,*" Rhiannon whispers, pulling her close. "I know you have questions. It's okay. We'll talk. We'll talk about all of it. Just not now."

And then she laces her arm through the crook of Lenna's elbow, just like she used to when they were both a little too drunk to walk on their own, and they head back outdoors.

10

LENNA

Gillian waited for Lenna outside the yoga studio. It was nice to have someone waiting, Lenna admitted to herself, but at the same time, Gillian wasn't Rhiannon.

Gillian brightened when she saw Lenna, and she held the door as they went inside, chattering about a work meeting she'd had to duck out from a little early to make the session. "My boss, Cordelia, wouldn't stop talking," Gillian said, rolling her eyes. "You heard her at the party, right?"

"What party?"

"The one at the bar where I fixed your shoe. God, Cordelia made a total fool out of herself. Went on and on, complaining about the shitty workers doing her eighty-thousand-dollar kitchen remodel—such a privileged Karen."

Lenna paused in pulling off a sock. "I thought it was just a *City Gossip* party."

Gillian cocked her head, her bangs falling into her eyes. "Then why would I have gone?" She laughed self-consciously. "With my anxieties, I would never go somewhere I wasn't invited. The party was for all the magazines. *Wellness,* too."

Ah. Rhiannon had it wrong, then. "So that's where you work? *Wellness?*"

"Yeah. I'm in editorial."

"It's a magazine about health, I guess?"

"I know, real original name, right? It's a little triggering—I mean, some of the articles are thinly veiled odes to disordered eating. Not that I write those."

"You get to write?"

Gillian bent over to stretch. She had a short torso and long, thin legs. "Sometimes. But I mostly fact-check. It's boring."

"I copy edit. Also boring."

"Two peas in a pod. But *you* get to write, don't you?" Gillian cocked her head. "I was under the impression everyone at *City Gossip* could write if they wanted to."

Lenna leaned back on the heels of her hands. "It's a little more complicated than that."

Gillian gave her a discerning look. "Really? Huh."

The instructor strode in, hitting a button on the thermostat to start the room's gradual temperature climb to 110 degrees. For the next hour, Lenna and Gillian downward dogged and pigeon posed, sweat dripping from their noses. It was fun, sharing something with someone else.

The next day in the office, Lenna's phone rang. The caller ID said *CALLER UNKNOWN.* She answered, thinking it was Rhiannon. She hated how her pulse spiked, how excited she felt. It was Gillian's voice on the other end.

"Where are you?" Lenna asked, looking at the caller ID screen again. Interbuilding calls always popped up on the caller ID. You didn't even have to dial a whole number, only an extension.

"Sorry, I'm in my car," Gillian said. "I lost my phone, but I think it's somewhere in my house, and I'm being cheap by using this random one temporarily."

"Have you tried the Find My Phone app?"

"It doesn't seem to work when your phone's dead. Anyway, I was wondering. Since you're having a hard time at *City Gossip,* would you like to write something for *Wellness*?"

Lenna blinked. "Seriously?"

"Sure. I think I can swing something with my boss." She coughed. "Also, do you want to go to this thing with me tonight? It's an open mic poetry reading. A little cheesy, but it's fun—and, you know, we could talk about your writing."

"Um . . ." Open mic poetry absolutely wasn't something Lenna was into, and going out with Gillian two times in one week felt kind of . . . fast? Intense?

But maybe she was serious about the writing offer. It wasn't like Lenna was getting anywhere at *City Gossip.* But Lenna couldn't bring herself to tell Rich she was interested. It was such a Pyrrhic victory.

Frederick was a dead end, too. After Rhiannon told her not to go out with him, Lenna hadn't responded to the jokey emails Frederick sent her and pretended not to notice when he tried to get her attention from across the office. She was so terrified he was going to confront her about why she'd done such an about-face—and she didn't know how to have that conversation—that whenever she saw him in the halls, she spun around and went the other direction. Soon enough, Frederick started to actively avoid her, too—she even caught him reversing direction when he spotted her, just as she did. And then, yesterday, she'd noticed Frederick hanging out with someone new they'd hired in the art department, a petite woman with blunt-cut, shiny black hair and an amazing shoe collection. So that was that.

Anyway. Gillian picked her up at the curb outside the building. Her car, a Prius, was filled with pictures taped to the dashboard. There were a few postcards from MoMA in New York, some pictures from a trip to Joshua Tree National Park, and a photo of Gillian arm in arm with an attractive woman with white-blond hair and thin lips.

"Your . . . partner?" Lenna asked.

"Nope. My best friend. Sadie."

"Oh."

Gillian let out a self-deprecating laugh. "I know. It's probably weird to have a picture of your friend in your car. Especially because we're in fights so much these days."

"What do you fight about?"

Gillian eased on the brake. "Dumb stuff. We're roommates. Well, technically, I'm crashing there for now. I'd never be able to afford half the mortgage. You should see her house. It's amazing. In the Hills!"

"Wow. Lucky."

"Sadie's a doctor." Gillian rolled her eyes. "Wish I'd been smart enough to do that, because she makes good money." She paused at another stoplight. "You got a roommate?"

Lenna laughed. "I'm in a studio. Having a roommate would be awful in somewhere so small."

"You dating anyone?"

Lenna shook her head. "You?"

"Nah." Gillian shut her eyes. "I'm thirty-three years old, and I swear I have the relationship IQ of a sixteen-year-old. That's when my last good relationship was." She said this somewhat cheerfully, but Lenna felt concerned.

"You've just been unlucky since then?" Lenna asked.

"Just haven't found the right person, I guess." Then she looked at Lenna again. "So you aren't dating that guy from your office? I saw you leaving with him a few weeks ago, and I thought . . ."

"Frederick? No." Lenna's cheeks flushed. It was weird, the notion of random people seeing them leaving together. Sometimes, she forgot how *visible* she was in the world. "I don't think that's going to turn into anything."

When Lenna didn't offer anything else, Gillian shrugged. "Well. Guys kinda suck anyway."

"Yeah." *And so do friends, sometimes,* Lenna added in her head.

As if reading her mind, Gillian cleared her throat. "If you don't mind me asking, where'd your buddy go? The woman, I mean. The redhead."

Lenna dared to look at her. "I don't really know."

Gillian frowned. "What's that mean?"

"She went to Oregon. But . . . I don't know why."

"But aren't you guys close?"

"I *thought* we were . . ."

Gillian concentrated on the road. "I don't want this to come out the wrong way, but she was kind of a bitch. I was always trying to be nice to her, but she was cold. Mean, even."

Lenna lowered her eyes. She thought about how Rhiannon said Gillian just wasn't her *vibe.* How her whole face closed when Gillian was around. She couldn't even stand it when Gillian was at that office party, all the way across the bar.

"She said you both didn't want me around," Gillian added.

Lenna looked at her. "Rhiannon spoke for *me*?"

"Yeah. She was like, *Please leave Lenna and me alone.* It was kind of my worst nightmare. I've really struggled with talking to people. The whole thing kind of gave me a panic attack."

"I'm sorry," Lenna said. "I don't know why she would say that. It isn't how I feel." Not exactly, anyway.

Lenna should have seen herself in Gillian. She suffered the same awkwardness, after all; sometimes it bordered on anxiety. What was Rhiannon's problem? It felt insensitive for Rhiannon to push someone away just for being nice. They should have given Gillian more grace.

Then Gillian pulled in a breath. "I'm guessing you don't know about her and that guy, either."

Lenna frowned. *"Guy?"*

"The guy you went on that date with. It was at that party, with your shoe? Before I saw you. But I feel really weird about saying this . . ."

Lenna's heart started pounding. "What are you talking about?"

Gillian blew out a breath. "I was in the back hallway, going to the women's room. And there's this extra little alcove behind the bathrooms—just wasted space. I heard people back there. I don't know what made me look, but your friend—she kind of lunged at him for a kiss. Frederick."

Lenna blinked hard. "What?"

"So I was kind of confused when you were going out with him a few days later. And when you said it didn't work out just now, I figured Rhiannon had something to do with it, but now, maybe . . ."

Lenna felt dizzy. Was this why Rhiannon told Lenna to leave him alone—*because she liked him, too?* Annoyance filled her, hot and thick. She'd told Rhiannon she liked Frederick before that party. If Rhiannon had feelings for him, too, she should have said so instead of secretly kissing him in a hallway. She felt bad for how she'd ignored Frederick, too—and maybe for no good reason.

"Sorry." Gillian's voice cracked. "I'm not trying to cause trouble. I just . . . sometimes, you don't know about people. You think they have your back, and then . . . they don't."

"Huh," Lenna said in a faraway voice. "Maybe that's true."

Even considering that about Rhiannon felt like a betrayal. And yet, as soon as the words left her lips, Lenna felt better. Validated, at least, and not so bereft in Rhiannon's absence.

A COUPLE DAYS LATER, LENNA PARKED AT A SMALL SIDE STREET meter just off Santa Monica. Gillian strode up to her, running shoes on her feet, sunglasses propped on her head.

"I love this neighborhood," she said, gesturing around. "I like to pretend I live here."

"Where are we?" Lenna asked, glancing up the street. It was named Canon. Had she heard of Canon?

Gillian looked at her and made an expression of mock surprise. "Beverly Hills, of course!"

"No, I know *that*." She'd passed the sign driving in. Dozens of tourists had been standing in front of it, posing.

"It's the Flats," Gillian said. She shook her head. "How can you live here for so long and not know about the Flats?"

Lenna shrugged. She wasn't a Beverly Hills kind of girl.

"I'm not really sure why I'm in LA at all, to be honest," she admitted. "I think I'd be better suited somewhere else. Quieter, maybe. Less flashy."

"Like Oregon?"

Lenna gave her a sidelong glance. Had Gillian said Oregon because Rhiannon was in Oregon? She wasn't sure how much she wanted to talk about Rhiannon anymore. Part of her needed someone to bounce the feelings off of. Another part of her didn't want their relationship just to be a long Rhiannon bitch session.

They started walking past the mansions. Lenna counted the number of Ferraris in driveways but stopped at four. The streets were broad, the front lawns perfectly pristine; a lot of the homes were hidden behind gates. For a block or so, Lenna didn't know what to say. This silence tended to happen when they got together. Gillian had told her she was a big advocate online for other people who had social anxiety; Lenna thought she'd found the account Gillian was talking about, but it was private, and Gillian hadn't yet accepted her friend request.

"That house there sold for eleven million," Gillian finally said, pointing at a Tudor on a corner. "And that one across the street sold for twenty-four."

"You're better than Zillow," Lenna joked.

Gillian shrugged. "I'm good at remembering numbers. And, okay, I memorized some of this stuff as conversation topics."

"It *is* interesting," Lenna said as what she was certain was a Rolls-Royce passed.

Gillian put her hands on her hips and appraised a Spanish-style home that looked to be at least ten thousand square feet. "Wouldn't you love to live there?"

"I have no idea how I would afford that."

"Come on, dream a little!" Gillian nudged her. "Maybe your writing will get you there."

"Uh, I have to *publish* something first," Lenna said, hoping that at least this was a segue. As promised, Gillian had assigned Lenna a piece for her magazine, *Wellness,* about celeb-exclusive drug rehab programs. Lenna enjoyed the research, calling up various facilities and hearing about all of their amenities. This morning, she'd turned in a draft to Gillian's email, and Gillian wanted to talk to her about next steps. Her heart was pounding. It had been so long since she'd put herself on the line like this—probably not since the journalism program she hadn't been able to attend.

"I think your piece is great," Gillian said. "Really well done. My boss will love it."

Lenna breathed out. "Really? You're sure?"

"You're a great writer. I have no idea why they don't use you for *City Gossip*."

Lenna couldn't help but grin. It was happening. She was finally writing.

They talked through some revisions, which Lenna was pretty sure she could turn around quickly. She made a mental note to double-check quotes with her sources, too. The sun shone brightly in stripes across the road. The houses gleamed from their emerald lawns. Finally, finally she was going somewhere. Moving forward.

"I just don't understand why they didn't throw you some pieces at *City Gossip*," Gillian said again as they rounded up another street. "Rhiannon had a higher position than I do. She could have."

"She said I needed to take that up with the writers," Lenna explained carefully. "That I should try and shadow them when they were reporting a story, and then hopefully share a byline. Although . . ." She stared at the sidewalk. Here was this fine line again.

"We had an argument about it, before Rhiannon left. I thought she was holding me back. She acted like she didn't know what I was talking about. Like it was out of her control."

Gillian made a face. "It was absolutely in her control. You know what? I bet she felt threatened by you."

Lenna blinked hard and then laughed. "I don't *think* so."

"Don't be so sure. I bet she worried you'd realize how good you were and go somewhere else. Somewhere much more high profile. And she'd still be stuck at a gossip magazine."

Lenna mulled this over.

"She kissed a guy I said I liked," Lenna said slowly, partly to herself. "And she also stood in the way of me getting writing assignments. Why would she do that?"

"I think some people like the control."

"And that's what you think Rhiannon was trying to do? Control me?"

"Well, she certainly didn't want you to be *better* than she was. Or gain an advantage."

"She got me my job. She used that in the argument, actually. Like she *saved* me."

"It's like you were her project. Like she was going to make you better. But instead, she just kept you down."

"She's had a hard life, though," Lenna protested, trying to walk the conversation back.

"Everyone has had a hard life!" Gillian railed. "We can't all go around using that excuse!"

A lump formed in Lenna's throat. Gillian was right. Lenna never used her mother's death to justify *her* bad behavior. She thought about when Rhiannon chose to disclose her past, too—right before she told her that Lenna's ideal job had been filled. Was there intention behind this? Had she made herself vulnerable to Lenna to soften her up emotionally, so that Lenna would say yes to anything, even something that was a little bit beneath her goals? She felt her hand form a fist.

"Rhiannon's mother killed her brother," Lenna blurted. "And set out to kill her, too. In a car crash, off a bridge." She explained, too, about the moment Rhiannon chose to tell her this, and maybe her motive.

But Gillian stopped and gave Lenna a strange look. "That didn't happen."

Lenna felt shaken. "Are you saying she's *lying*?"

"I'm saying she's way too well-adjusted to have survived something like that."

"Yeah, but . . ." Lenna couldn't fathom Rhiannon making that up.

Gillian stared into the middle distance. "It's pretty amazing what people will lie about." Then she shrugged. "But whatever.

Maybe it is true! My point is, it's still no excuse to be a controlling dick." She took a breath. "Sorry. I'm not trying to turn you against her. I'm just trying to get you to see clearly. I care about you. I feel like we really get each other."

"Yeah," Lenna said softly. Because Gillian did get her. She saw Lenna's awkwardness. She saw Lenna's hunger. She saw the true Lenna more than Rhiannon did, in a lot of ways.

With that, she felt a burst of magnanimousness. Lenna wanted to be as good a listener to Gillian as Gillian was to her. "So!" she said. "Let's change the subject. What's going on with you? I've been blathering on about all of my stuff."

Gillian sighed. "Things with Sadie are really going downhill."

"You're still fighting?"

"All the time."

"Just about house stuff, or . . . ?"

For a few moments, the only sounds were their sneakers on the asphalt. Then Gillian said, "Sadie wants to have a baby."

Lenna stared at her shoes, trying to figure out which questions to ask. Gillian filled in the blanks. "On her own. Through fertility treatments. She's ready, but it complicates her and me. Since I live with her and all." She made a face. "Not sure I want a baby around, you know?"

"You'll have to move, I guess."

Gillian's face clouded. "I *realize* that." Then she sighed. "If only the procedure, like, somehow didn't work. Like if our refrigerator went on the fritz and the medications went bad, or if there was a mistake and they were somehow filled with water instead of actual drugs."

Lenna turned to her. "But if she really wants a baby . . ."

"I *know*," Gillian said sharply, suddenly. "God. I'm just talking out loud. And . . . I just want things to go back to the way they were, you know?"

Lenna did know. She cleared her throat. "I'm sorry. It sucks. You feel like she's abandoning you."

"Totally," Gillian said miserably.

They passed a woman walking three little dogs. Then Gillian shifted awkwardly. "What's going to happen when Rhiannon comes back?"

"What do you mean?"

"I probably won't be able to hang out with you anymore, seeing that she hates me."

"She doesn't . . ." Lenna started, and then sighed. Would Rhiannon want to talk to Lenna at all? She still hadn't replied to a single text.

Having Rhiannon in the office again might be beyond awkward. And knowing what she now knew about Rhiannon's sneakiness with Frederick and possibly keeping Lenna from writing . . .

She spoke all this aloud to Gillian as they walked. "Maybe I should just resign. I mean, if you could give me some more freelance pieces and I found writing work elsewhere, maybe I would be okay, financially."

Gillian's expression hardened. "*She* should be the one who shouldn't come back to the office. Why should you have to rearrange your life?"

"Yeah, I can't make her quit."

"Maybe not." Gillian's eyes were suddenly gleaming. She pointed at Lenna, raising an eyebrow. "But maybe there's another option."

It took Lenna a moment to realize what Gillian meant. But then she did. Maybe there was something she could do.

[Image description: A young woman with wavy brown hair and bright pink lipstick holds a sunflower in one hand and a sign in the other hand that reads, "Whole new me."]

♡   ◯   ◁   ◻

Guys. So much has changed. Well, I mean, I'm still me. I still have two cavities on my right molars that I'm too afraid to get filled, and I still have nice-looking eyebrows and—duh-duh-duh-DUH!—debilitating social anxiety. But recently, a window opened. An opportunity. And instead of receding back into the shadows like I always do, I climbed through.

And now, without further ado, a soft launch. Can you do that, with a friendship? Welp, I've just coined a thing. I am soft launching my new friend. Her name is L. She's one half of the girls I was talking about before—and we're soulmates. Total sisters. And also, I think I saved her just as much as she saved me. Her other friend, the other woman I wanted to talk to first? Total dud. A flake, but also kind of a bitch, and totally untrustworthy. I didn't even want to say anything to L, but before the other woman took some sort of "break" from

LA or whatever, she came up to me and flat-out said that I was "weird." Weird! Hello, does she even realize how OFFENSIVE that is?

So L is much better off without her. And she's had these amazing revelations now that she isn't around her old friend anymore—isn't it amazing how new friendships can do that? It's like getting out of a shitty relationship and suddenly realizing, wait, it doesn't have to BE like that. It's just like how things fell apart between me and S. I'm so glad I finally have someone in my life who gets it. (Speaking of S, her passive-aggressiveness is just getting worse and worse. I swear she's going to blow her top one of these days, and she's going to take it out on me. I'm not sure she should be practicing medicine, TBH.)

But most of my day, I'm on cloud nine. Me and L, we're going to be togetha foreva. I got her back, and she has mine. And everyone else is in our rearview. See ya!

TOP COMMENTS:

@anxious_jackieggg: So excited to hear this news! You're a beacon of hope for the rest of us!

@allibgbgbp9: You and L seem really well suited. So glad you've put yourself out there.

@cort44xx8: Can you tell us the name S uses professionally? I want to make sure she isn't my doctor! (Who I'm not sure should be practicing medicine, either!)

@lonely_girlRZ4540: You rock. 🙂

II

LENNA

When Lenna wakes the next morning, she shoots up in bed, startled. The horrible dreams at the canyon—she didn't have them. She slept the whole night through. She stares at her palms, her legs underneath the sheet. That hasn't happened in two years. Since . . . *before.*

She props herself up on her elbows and glances at the baby through the slats in the crib. He *never* sleeps this long, either. And the wine—she doesn't even feel hungover.

Memories of the previous day flood back. She swore she'd heard Rhiannon talking to someone. *She's here.* And then Rhiannon saying they'd talk about everything soon . . . not that they'd talked about *anything* so far.

She breathes out and rummages under the sheets for her phone. She wants to report her night's sleep to Daniel, anyway—it feels like a win. There are no new texts from him. Maybe he's listening to her, pulling back.

Sadness floods her. She misses him, suddenly. His silliness, his voice ringing through the house, his routines. She wants to go home. She will talk to Rhiannon today and get some actual answers. She makes the promise to herself.

Jacob wakes gently and spends a few minutes just looking around. Lenna holds her breath, waiting for him to erupt into sobs, but aside from a few whimpers, he's tranquil. "Look at you," she coos softly. "Maybe you could be like this all the time?"

After nursing him, she dresses him for the day—the pins for the cloth diapers are driving her crazy—and heads into the kitchen. Her head feels a little fuzzy. She prays coffee is allowed here.

Kids chatter at the table, eating oatmeal and fruit. Amy, a shovel propped on her shoulder, crosses the room for the fridge. Ann writes something on the chore board, her fingers covered in chalk. Once again, the lazy retriever waits by her side like an extension of her skeleton. Coral stands at the stove, shaking a pan full of chopped onions. Matilda is next to her, whispering in her ear.

"Those two," murmurs a voice.

Lenna turns. One of the twins—Melissa? Naomi?—has sidled next to her, crossing her arms. "Sometimes I think they're a little *too* close."

Lenna studies the woman, trying to figure out which one she is. "What do you mean?"

"I just think they should branch out. There are other people here, a few other teens. But hey, I guess it's human nature to want to make a best friend." She smiles at Lenna. "Want coffee? I made some." She points at a restaurant-grade coffee urn in the corner. "It's one of our luxuries, one of the few things we get off property."

"*Yes,*" Lenna says, holding her hands out for a mug. And then she spies a square on the chore chart: *Coffee: Melissa.*

Melissa pours Lenna a cup, then claps her hands and announces to the little kids that it's school time. Dutifully, the kids rise and follow her into a back hall.

A moment later, Marjorie bangs in from outside, stripping off a pair of gardening gloves. Sweat pours down her face. "Okay, let's go over what we need to do for the day," she calls out.

Everyone who remains settles at the table, which is still cluttered with the kids' breakfast dishes. The sight of congealed oatmeal and thready orange peels turns Lenna's stomach; she resists the urge to grab everything and stack it neatly in the sink. She glances around, looking for Rhiannon—and there she is, coming through the doorway. When she spies Lenna, she smiles and drifts over.

"I looked for you in your room. Didn't realize you were already up."

"Just came out." Lenna holds up her coffee cup. "So glad for this."

"You didn't sleep well?" She touches the baby's cheek. "He certainly seems to be in a good mood."

"We slept amazingly, actually." Lenna laughs. "Almost *too* good. Am I still dreaming?"

Rhiannon waves her hand. "It's our dark, cold rooms. They make for really restful sleep cycles."

Behind them, someone snorts. Lenna turns around, not sure who it was. Ann is fixing something on the dog's collar. Coral and Matilda don't seem to be listening.

Marjorie consults the chore board and picks up a piece of chalk. "Okay, so Ann's nearly done. Started before dawn." She tallies a score next to Ann's name. "Naomi, you've got the greenhouse." Lenna follows Marjorie's gaze—and there is Naomi, leaning in the doorway to the outside, peeling an orange. "Rhiannon, how about you start on the laundry?"

"On it," Rhiannon says.

"And Amy." Marjorie leans back and assesses the board. "You're on goats. Why don't you take Lenna?"

Amy, who is at the head of the table, peers around the women until she finds Lenna. She gives her a thumbs-up. Lenna feels a surge of panic. She turns to Rhiannon.

"Can't I do laundry with you?"

Rhiannon makes a face. "The kids' clothes are disgusting. And dirty diapers? Blegh."

"But . . ."

"Seriously. Goats with Amy is super fun. You'll love it."

Rhiannon pats Lenna's shoulder, then turns and heads out of the room. Lenna rests on her heels, the taste of coffee acidic in her mouth. Is Rhiannon avoiding her? She thinks again about that strange, whispered conversation . . . and also the questions Lenna forced on her. *We'll talk about all of it. Just not now.*

"Ready?" Amy asks.

Lenna jumps. "Um." She watches as Coral brushes around her and starts stacking the breakfast dishes. At least that's being taken care of, anyway. Then she glances one more time toward the door through which Rhiannon disappeared. It seems she has no choice.

"Sure," she says, turning back to Amy. "Let's go."

THE MOUNTAINS GLOW THIS MORNING. THEY PASS A SPRAY OF SUC-culents on their way to the goat pen; some of them have colorful flowers jutting out the tops among their jagged spines. A field of saguaros waits quietly, in silhouette, their arms poking, backlit by the sun. They're beautiful in their starkness. They pass lemon trees, too, planted on a small patch of scrub grass.

"Those smell delicious," Lenna admits, breathing in the scent of the lemons as they pass. A few have fallen to the ground, their juices spilling. A fly buzzes lazily around.

"Nothing cleaner than the smell of a lemon," Amy says happily as she unlatches the goat pen. Immediately, the animals wander over, gently butting their heads into Amy's side.

"Lookie!" Lenna murmurs to Jacob, trying to point him toward the goats. He stares at them with interest, wearing his same serious baby expression. She wonders what he's seeing.

"This one's Jamie, and she's Colonel Saunders," Amy says, petting a white goat and a large brown one with floppy ears. "We'll milk them." She glances at Jacob in his sling. "You take him everywhere, huh?"

"I like having him with me. Plus, I mean, I don't want to stick him with any of you. I know, I know, you've all said it's fine—it's a me problem."

"Doesn't it hurt your back?"

"Not really."

Though actually, Amy is right. Her back *kills* today. She hadn't realized how sedentary she is in her normal life, how much time she and Jacob spend on the couch.

Amy retrieves a pail from a small shed and brings it over. "You know, when I first got here with Matilda and realized that I didn't have to be watching her every second, it really opened me up. I'd been so laser focused, with her illness, and once I realized I didn't have to be that anymore . . . it was a relief."

"I can't believe she was just *cured*," Lenna gushes. "What was she diagnosed with, exactly?"

"We don't like giving it a name these days. We've already wasted too much time on it."

"But she doesn't need medications, doctor's appointments?"

"She's better."

"And how long did it take for her to feel better?"

Amy goes still. "It's not like I kept a meticulous diary. I just let this place do its thing."

"Oh. Of course." There's an edge to Amy's voice. Lenna feels like she's misstepped. "I just thought . . . if this place can heal so well, you should tell the whole world. It's a miracle."

Amy softens again. "I suppose you're right. My hope, of course, is that Matilda stays here forever. She's healthiest here. Anywhere else . . . it's a crapshoot."

"Does she like it here?"

"Sure. She's doing great. Really learning life skills, and she and Coral are two peas in a pod. So devoted to each other."

Like me and Rhiannon, Lenna thinks. But thoughts of Rhiannon are like a pebble in her shoe.

Amy squats down beneath Colonel Saunders and casually starts milking her. The goat just stands there placidly. "Do you think being here has made you a better mother?" Lenna asks.

"I think I kind of let go of the good-mother-or-bad-mother dichotomy a long time ago. But sure. I found a cure for my baby. I feel like I've won." Milk squirts into the bucket. It makes a tinny sound as it lands. "Is that something you worry about? Being a good mother?"

"Well, yeah." There's a lump in her throat. "I mean, the crying . . . it feels directed at *me.*"

"All babies cry. Some more than others. It isn't your fault."

"When will it stop feeling like it is?"

"Maybe never." Amy smiles sadly. "But I'll put it this way: We aren't judging you."

Lenna shuts her eyes. "I also feel like if I was a better person, I'd be a better mother."

"C'mon. All babies really need is food and warmth and love." Amy stops milking and looks at Jacob. "Seems he's getting all three."

Lenna looks away. "I hope so."

Squirt, squirt, squirt. "Man, did you even carry the baby to the outhouses?" Amy asks out of nowhere, gesturing to the baby. "That couldn't have been fun."

". . . Outhouses?"

Amy pauses, then frowns. "Didn't Marjorie tell you? Septic's down. We're supposed to be using the toilets outside. They're over there." Amy points around the other side of the house, near the kitchen. "Someone should have said something."

Lenna pulls in her bottom lip. "I used the bathroom this morning. And last night. When were we supposed to stop?"

Amy releases her grip on the goat's teat, and the animal trots away. "Marjorie told us before dinner. Oh, I think you were getting changed." Then she waves a hand. "Don't worry. It's more to keep all the kids from using the bathrooms, flushing seven thousand times, throwing weird stuff down there. The toilets are sensitive." She looks up at Lenna and points to the other goat. "Can you hold this lady steady while I milk her?"

Lenna holds the sides of Jamie the goat. Her fur is spinier than Lenna expected. She isn't sure if she's actually ever touched a goat before. Then something occurs to her. "Wait, Marjorie told you guys about the outhouses *before* dinner?"

"Uh-huh." Amy's fingers gently pull down as she squeezes.

But that doesn't make sense. When Lenna came inside and heard Rhiannon talking, Rhiannon told her she had just come in to use the bathroom. Only, Rhiannon had been in the living area, which was on the east side of the house. The kitchen—and the outhouses—is all the way on the west.

It both surprises her and doesn't, how quickly the certainty that Rhiannon isn't telling her the whole truth rushes in. Lenna tries to remember what Rhiannon was saying. Something about Lenna having come yesterday morning. Something about an agreement. An agreement to *what*?

Amy pats the head of one of the goats. She speaks to him in a soft voice, murmuring niceties Lenna can't hear. There's such a gentleness to her. A trustworthiness. Lenna clears her throat.

"Did Rhiannon . . . say anything about me, before I came?" she blurts.

Amy raises her head. "No . . ." she says after a beat. "Actually, I didn't even know she was bringing anyone until you showed up."

"Is that . . . normal?"

"Not really. But no matter. We're happy to have you. We don't get a lot of new people."

The uneasiness feels palpable, pressing against her skin from beneath, trying to wriggle free. "Do you know why Rhiannon came to Halcyon? Did she, um, tell you anything about her past?"

Almost imperceptibly, Amy moves away from her. "I don't really like talking about people when they aren't here."

"I get it. I don't want you to betray her trust—it's just . . ."

When Amy looks up, her eyes are sympathetic. "I think you and Rhiannon have some things to work out. And it's good that you're here."

Lenna's mouth drops open. "Did she *say* we had things to work out?"

Amy's expression is pained—like she wants to say something but knows she should hold back. Then she opens her arms. "You look like you need a hug."

Lenna stares at the woman's outstretched limbs. A hug isn't really what she needs, but she moves forward all the same. Amy is warm, and her arms grip her tightly, though she's mindful of Jacob's little body between them. Amy's compassion sends a shudder through Lenna's bones. It's like the past is just *here,* knotted up in front of her, everything true, or maybe nothing at all, and she doesn't have the capabilities to tell which is which. She doesn't want to think what Gillian said about Rhiannon was true, considering who Gillian turned out to be. But maybe it's all *absolutely* true, regardless. And maybe Lenna was foolish to come here, foolish to believe that Rhiannon had forgiven her and was letting the past drift away.

She lets out a sob.

"It's okay," Amy murmurs. "Let it out."

"I just feel so lost," she says into Amy's shoulder. "I don't know what's what anymore. I don't know what I'm doing. I wish I had my mom. I wish she was still here."

"Shhh. You'll find your way."

"I'm not sure I will. The thing is, I . . . I *did* something. To Rhiannon. And I wonder if she knows and is still mad at me for it. One of the reasons I wanted to come is so we could reconnect—and figure things out, maybe? There are so many gaps in our story. I want to set it straight."

"You *can.* I think that's a wonderful idea."

"But also . . ." Lenna gulps in a breath. "It's not just what I did to her. It's what all of it led to. Which has nothing to do with her, but . . ." Another gulped-in breath. Her head spins. "I did something bad. I'm not a good person. And it's haunting me. It's affecting my parenting, I think. I'm not a good example for my baby."

"It's *okay,*" Amy insists. "You aren't the first person who has come here feeling haunted. But whatever you did—it can't be as bad as you think."

But Lenna shakes her head. That's the problem. It *is* that bad.

It's the very worst.

12

LENNA

Lenna thought long and hard about what she could write to Rich in order to make sure Rhiannon didn't return to *City Gossip*. That conversation with Gillian in Beverly Hills had slipped into every cell of her body. She'd reviewed every talk she'd had with Rhiannon, every choice, all their friendship dynamics. Maybe Rhiannon *had* chosen her as a friend not because of who Lenna was, but because she was someone Rhiannon could manipulate, like a doll.

Lenna felt humiliated. And also naïve—Gillian had spotted it so easily. Lenna had never gotten revenge on anyone, never *dreamed* of it, but it felt like poetic justice to manipulate Rhiannon's career just like Rhiannon had manipulated hers.

And, well, Gillian kept egging her on. She didn't bring it up just that one time, but dropped little hints whenever they got together. It got to the point where Lenna almost felt like if she *didn't* do something to ensure Rhiannon couldn't return, she'd look like a pushover, a fool.

Making allegations about Rhiannon and Frederick wouldn't fly—Lenna hadn't seen the kiss firsthand, and it wasn't like couples weren't allowed in the office. Nor did she have real proof that Rhiannon was preventing her from writing. Rhiannon's attitude toward Gillian, especially considering Gillian's anxieties, was problematic, but maybe not enough, either.

But then she thought of the Valium that Rhiannon sometimes took when she was having bad days. Lenna had witnessed it more than just that one time before her interview—often, if Rhiannon felt stressed or annoyed, or if she had to give a presentation or an interview, she popped a pill like it was a Tic Tac. She slipped some to other coworkers, too, sometimes in exchange for cash. So that was what she went with, in an anonymous email, both to Rich's account and the head of HR. She knew how it would look. She knew the company policy. She knew Rhiannon would get in trouble.

She wrote the email quickly, from a throwaway Gmail account. She sent it off before thinking too hard about it. Then she spent about fifteen minutes lying on her bed and staring at the ceiling, feeling like shit. She thought of her mom, as she inevitably did when she felt she'd made a bad decision. She wished her mom could give her advice right now. Then again, she couldn't imagine her mom ever getting into this kind of situation. The only friend her mom had—*really* had, looking back on it—was Lenna.

That Monday was Independence Day observed, so she had the day off. But she was too afraid to go in on Tuesday. She pictured that if Rich took the email seriously—would he?—the company would likely search Rhiannon's office and question her coworkers. They'd probably question Lenna, too. She feared that her expression or mannerisms would give away that she'd been the one to turn Rhiannon in.

On Wednesday, when she returned to work, she got her answer. There were whispers that Rhiannon had been fired. No one knew why. There was no ceremonial packing of her things and security leading her out—because Rhiannon was already on leave, she simply didn't return. Rich didn't say anything to anyone about a note, though. Part of Lenna hoped maybe it *wasn't* because of her anonymous email and maybe some other reason . . . but she also knew that would be an awfully big coincidence.

And that was that. Lenna was sickened. It didn't feel as validating as she'd thought it would. Did Rhiannon even *deserve* this? Lenna felt full of doubt.

"Stop that," Gillian insisted. "You did the right thing. I mean, pills? Don't beat yourself up."

"I just would feel so bad if she ever found out I was the one who reported her," Lenna moaned.

Gillian scoffed. "Like you're ever going to see her again?"

Probably not, Lenna thought with a dull ache. Maybe Gillian was right.

TWO WEEKS PASSED. THINGS WERE EERILY CALM. LENNA HADN'T heard from Rhiannon, but she also hadn't received any hate mail or suspicious packages. Rhiannon didn't appear to know that Lenna was the person who'd told on her, but then again, she never came back to *City Gossip*, not even to collect her belongings.

Lenna kept thinking she might run into her old friend—because surely she'd come back to LA by now—and they could have a conversation about it. In a perverse way, she *hoped* to run into Rhiannon . . . and maybe that Rhiannon would even know what she'd done. At least then she'd get to apologize. But a run-in never happened.

There were bright spots: Rich approached Lenna and asked if she wanted to write a piece about a young starlet who had a jewelry line at a local Pilates studio. "It's only three hundred words," he warned. "And we can't pay you." Regardless, Lenna jumped on it. Here was an assignment, falling in her lap. Maybe all she'd needed was for Rhiannon to move out of the way. She had Gillian's piece, too. According to Gillian, it was going to be a two-page feature in the magazine.

Two mornings later, Lenna's head was swimming with edits from Gillian as she walked into work. She was so distracted, she didn't realize someone was standing in the entrance. The woman was talking to Honey, the friendly guard at the security desk. Lenna realized she knew her—it was Sadie, Gillian's friend. The roommate she was fighting with. Lenna remembered the picture Gillian had taped up on her dashboard.

"Oh!" Lenna said. "Are you here for Gillian?"

Sadie spun around. Her eyes were red-rimmed, like she'd been crying. Her hands were trembling. "I'm Lenna. I'm at *City Gossip,*" Lenna explained.

"Lenna!" Sadie nodded. "Yes! Gillian's mentioned you! She works here, right? Do you know which floor she's on?"

At that very moment, Gillian strode up from down the sidewalk. She had a laptop bag slung over her shoulder. When she saw Sadie and Lenna together, she paled.

"Hey!" Gillian practically sprinted to them. "What are you doing here?"

"I wanted to talk to you," Sadie said gently, sadly. Her gaze darted into the lobby. "But when I talked to the guard—"

"Come on, babe," Gillian said abruptly, taking her arm. "Let's get coffee."

She steered Sadie back down the street, glancing at Lenna just once over her shoulder with a reassuring—and eye-rolling—smile.

Later, Gillian texted Lenna. The number always came up scrambled—Gillian said she *still* couldn't find her regular cell phone—but she had some telltale texting quirks that made her easily identifiable. For example: She swore a lot, but she often didn't bother to fix the autocorrect. *Fucking* was always *ducking*. It softened Gillian's frustration.

Sorry I had to run, but shit hit the ducking fan, Gillian texted. Sadie's IVF failed. She didn't get a single viable ducking embryo.

Lenna's fingers wavered over the keyboard. She didn't really know the technicalities of fertility treatments. Also, this felt so personal—she wasn't sure Gillian should have shared it.

Gillian blasted off another text. She blames me. She's pissed. We had a fight.

And then another text.

I ducking need to get out of here, Gillian texted. Are you free?

Lenna sat back, thinking about it. The last thing she needed was to get embroiled in someone else's drama. At the same time, Gillian had been her shoulder to cry on about Rhiannon. It seemed only fair.

She met Gillian at Barney's, which she'd never set foot in before because she presumed—rightly so—that everything was too expensive. They perused the shoe floor. Gillian kept picking up shoes and putting them down. Her cheeks had high circles of pink. She breathed, bull-like, through her nostrils.

"I should buy something," she said miserably. "Make myself feel better."

Lenna eyed the price tag on the bottom of the shoe. Twelve hundred dollars! "Did she take it out on you, or something?" she asked tentatively. Wouldn't *Sadie* need to buy herself something to make herself feel better? She wasn't sure where Gillian figured into all of this.

Gillian picked up another pair of shoes. "She's crushed. She can't believe it happened."

"But why is she mad at *you,* exactly?"

"Because that's just how she is. Everything's always my fault."

Lenna's phone beeped loudly in her pocket. The contact that came up was so startling she nearly dropped the device.

Rhiannon.

Something in Lenna's expression made Gillian notice right away. "Who's that?"

Lenna's mouth was dry. "Um." She tried to hide the screen without it looking like she was hiding the screen. She tapped the alert to open the text. Hey, Rhiannon had written. How are you?

Her mind spun. She'd wanted this for so long, but now that it was here, she felt paralyzed as to what to do next.

She didn't hear Gillian sneak around behind her, but suddenly she was there. She scoffed. "You aren't going to write back, are you?"

Lenna slipped her phone in her pocket, feeling embarrassed. "I mean . . ."

"I don't think it's a good idea."

The memory of the phone screen blurred before Lenna's eyes. "You're right."

Gillian slung an arm around Lenna's shoulder. "Let's get a drink. Seems like we *both* need to de-stress."

That night, alcohol barely touched Lenna. Maybe it was because she was already so dazed, her mind already so scattered. Gillian kept talking about Sadie and her "weird quest to have a baby." She'd become so shrill, all of a sudden. Lenna tried to stay present, but she kept thinking about Rhiannon.

Gillian's voice rose higher and higher. "And, I mean, every time I walked into the kitchen, Sadie was shooting a needle in her belly. Her meds were always just sitting there. The tops open. Sometimes she left this huge mess on the table. Anything could have spilled into those vials, accidentally."

Lenna hadn't been fully paying attention, but suddenly she was present again. Gillian's voice was playful, sly. "Wait, *did* something get into her meds?"

Gillian blinked innocently. "Of course not."

Lenna made it through the rest of the night without looking at Rhiannon's text. Yet with every drink Gillian ordered, her patience felt more and more frayed. Finally, when she said she wanted to go home, Gillian grabbed her arm and begged her to stay for just one more.

"I'm so tired," Lenna protested.

"Come on," Gillian whined. "All the times I've listened when you've bitched, the least you can do is listen to me."

Lenna stood, not liking Gillian's tone. "I think we both should just get some sleep."

Gillian pouted. "But that means I have to go back and maybe face Sadie."

There was a pause then. Lenna suddenly wondered what Gillian was hinting at. "Oh, Gillian, my apartment is tiny. I don't think—"

"I wasn't asking if I could stay with you," Gillian interrupted sulkily. Her shoulders drooped. "Forget it."

This was the awkward part of friendships Lenna never knew how to navigate. When someone was emotional and erratic like this, what could you say to pull them out of it? All she wanted to do was retreat. Not deal with this sort of thing.

"Okay," she said eventually. "So . . . I'm going to go . . ."

"Actually, hang on." Gillian's head whipped up. There were tears in her eyes. "I need to tell you something. I know I've been really weird tonight. I'm sorry. It's just . . . I've been really triggered by Sadie's baby thing."

Lenna frowned. "Why?"

Gillian tipped onto the bar, then hiccuped. "It was really, really hard. I had to go through it all alone. And then I had to pretend it was all good."

"What are you talking about?"

Gillian's eyes were closing. She put her cheek on the bar. Lenna looked around, wishing someone else would help.

Then Gillian stood. "I'll go home," she mumbled, stumbling off the chair, tripping over someone else's purse. "I'm fine."

Lenna walked her to the curb and called her an Uber. When the car arrived, Gillian fell inside. The door slammed shut. Lenna watched the car through several traffic lights, something gnawing at her gut.

She was grateful to be alone back in her own apartment. The evening had unnerved her. Maybe this was the simple truth: Lenna was someone who couldn't really be there for friendships when things got tough. The moment she was needed emotionally, she left.

She picked up her phone. There sat Rhiannon's text: Hey. How are you?

Lenna wanted Gillian to be right about leaving Rhiannon alone, she really did. But at the same time, the pull to reply to her was undeniable. She pictured Rhiannon on the other end of the phone, waiting for Lenna to respond. Hurting that she hadn't.

Finally, she gave in. Doing okay. You?

Dots appeared immediately on Rhiannon's end. And then disappeared. And then appeared again. Lenna swallowed.

Is everything okay? Lenna wrote.

The dots appeared again. A text popped up. Not really.

Traffic hummed. Lenna repositioned herself on the bed. She composed a dozen replies, but deleted them. *Where are you? Do you need help? Are you mad?* She wanted to ask outright how Rhiannon felt about being fired from *City Gossip* . . . and if she knew *why.* She also wanted to know why Rhiannon went to Oregon, and if what Gillian had speculated about her was true.

But in the moment, with Rhiannon on the other end, *paying attention to her,* some of her anger faded. How much did that stuff matter?

Have you been watching The Bachelor? she chose to write instead.

They watched the show, sometimes; the latest season had aired earlier in the year, but Lenna and Rhiannon had been catching up on the episodes together before Rhiannon took off. In fact, Rhiannon had left mid-season, when things were just getting interesting. Lenna felt like it was a safe enough topic.

Rhiannon answered that she hadn't watched any more episodes. When Lenna said she'd gone ahead and watched a few new ones, Rhiannon asked Lenna to catch her up. She filled up text bubbles, her fingers moving so fast, her body full of so much *joy.*

There were other things she needed to tell Rhiannon. Important things, *good* things, like how she could now do a headstand in hot yoga, or that she'd been given an assignment at work, or that she had a new friend. But she didn't write about Gillian or work, because Gillian and work seemed way too close to a conversation about harder truths.

It was late when Lenna ran out of things to write. Rhiannon typed back she should probably go to sleep. Oh, how Lenna ached to ask something as simple as *Sleep where, exactly?* But finally, she got up the nerve to type something real.

I hate how things were left between us.

She sent it off and squeezed her eyes shut. When she opened them, there were no little dots indicating Rhiannon was replying.

Ten minutes passed. Still no answer. An hour. Well, that was that, then.

Finally, Lenna went to bed. She slept fitfully. She dreamed she and Rhiannon were very old, stooped and wrinkled, walking side by side around a lake in Iceland. Lenna had never been to Iceland, and yet this dream was telling her that it was in Iceland and nowhere else. All at once, all of the geese on the lake took off at the same time. The sky was filled with them, flying elsewhere, and then the lake was empty. Then Rhiannon turned to her. Except it wasn't Rhiannon at all. It was a baby's face.

"Boo," the baby said.

The dream rocked her awake. On her bedside table, her phone was blinking. She grabbed for it. The alert on the screen was from Gillian, not Rhiannon.

Can you talk?

It was six A.M. Lenna groaned. She navigated back to her last text to Rhiannon from last night. She'd fallen asleep, but Rhiannon wrote back hours later, at nearly four in the morning.

Agreed, was all Rhiannon had said.

Lenna clutched the phone hard and started to type. Sorry I didn't see this. Call me. Anytime. Let's talk through it.

The text made a *bloop* as it disappeared into the ether. A chime announcing that a new text had arrived sounded moments later. Rhiannon, again. Lenna stared at the new bubble that had appeared even though it made no sense.

This number has been blocked.

A glitch, she figured. She composed another text. The same error message appeared. She tried again. Same result.

Her heart started to pound. Why would Rhiannon block her after accepting text upon text about *The Bachelor* all night?

A *ping.* Up soared her heart, until she saw Gillian's name. SOS.

Lenna rubbed her eyes with the heels of her hands. The room seemed to have darkened instead of lightened, time moving backward. She was exhausted, suddenly, like she hadn't slept at all.

The phone rang. Gillian's number. Lenna didn't want to answer. She wanted to dive under the covers and start the morning over. She ignored the call, but Gillian called again. Finally, Lenna hit the green button, saying through gritted teeth, "It's so early."

"Sadie's being weird," Gillian sobbed. "Can I come over? Can you meet me?"

"This early?" Lenna said blearily. "Can't it wait a few hours?"

"I really need you, Lenna. I'm spiraling."

"Is it because of what you told me? At the bar?"

A pause. ". . . What did I tell you?"

"I'm not sure. You started telling me that Sadie wanting a baby is triggering. But then you . . . well, you were pretty drunk."

Another silence. Gillian cleared her throat. "Okay, can you come here, then? Maybe you can talk some sense into Sadie."

"Me?" Lenna felt confused. "I don't know Sadie. I don't think that's my place."

"Fine, then come after she leaves." Gillian sounded annoyed. "She's heading out soon anyway. She has to see a patient, I think."

Lenna's head spun from how many times Gillian was changing her mind. All she could think of was the *blocked* message from Rhiannon's number. Why did she reach out to her only to block her? Maybe she did know Lenna was the one who sabotaged her. Or . . . or maybe she'd found out last night?

"Lenna?" Gillian's voice was sharp. She'd been talking, but Lenna missed what she said. "Hel-*lo*?"

"Sorry," Lenna said vaguely. "I have to go. There's, um, someone at my door."

"What? Who?"

She hung up. She was halfway to actually walking to her door before she realized that she didn't have to actually pretend to answer it. It wasn't like Gillian could see.

She bent over the kitchen counter. The sheen on the surface, silver with dim morning sun, made her think of the glassy lake in her dream. All those geese leaving—and then Rhiannon turning into that baby. What did it symbolize? What sort of sign should she read from it?

She looked at her texts again. A person didn't cry out for help and then block you. She scrolled all the way down, looking for what, she wasn't sure. Then, in the upper left corner, she noticed a tappable word that read *Edit.* One of the options was *Show Recently Deleted.* As in texts?

She tapped it, and sure enough, some of the texts she'd deleted previously came up—junk spam, all of it, or huge image files. But there was something strange. In this folder was a text she'd apparently sent to Rhiannon, except it was sent SMS instead of iMessage. The bubbles came up green and not blue. It was dated early this morning—shortly before four A.M., right about the time Rhiannon replied to the *other* chain, that she hated how things were left between them.

> Too fucking late. Lose this number.

Lenna gasped. She never would have written that! How had this gotten here? Had someone hacked her phone? But beneath that text, also deleted, Rhiannon had sent a response.

> Got it. Sorry.

And then . . . she'd blocked her.

Lenna clutched her phone and composed a new message under

this strange, mistaken, deleted thread. Rhiannon! I didn't write that text. My phone got hacked, I think. I'm so sorry.

She sent it off. *Bloop.* The number had been blocked.

She let out a groan. How did you get someone to unblock you? How could you claim a text you wrote wasn't from you even though it came from your phone? She could call Rhiannon from another phone, she supposed. She rooted in her bedside drawer for a pad to copy down Rhiannon's number. Suddenly, something caught in her mind. She picked up her phone again.

The deleted text she swore she hadn't written was in all caps. TOO FUCKING LATE, it read, which was something Lenna would never say.

But there was something else. It didn't actually say *fucking*. It said *ducking*.

Her hand fluttered to her mouth.

As if on cue, Gillian's number appeared on her screen. Who was at the door?

Lenna gripped her phone hard, wanting to hurl it across the room. Gillian's text seemed to taunt her. *Call her,* Lenna's mind screamed.

But this was a face-to-face conversation.

Instagram post from @GillianAnxietyBabe

July 22

[Image description: A young woman with wavy brown hair stares into a mirror without expression. Only half of her face is shown. The room is dark. There are shadows across her face.]

♡ ◯ ◁   ⊓

First of all, a total caveat, I'm a TEENSY bit tipsy tonite. We all know how alcohol helps us loosen up, but I may have gone overboard just a little. Purely out of stress. And here's why.

I'm SO worried about L. I think she's still in touch with R. It really does feel like a bad boyfriend sitch. It breaks my heart. It's like, I can see the future of how this is all going to go, all based on the fact that S and me are a few steps ahead. (Btw, S is getting more and more hysterical. I caught her following me to work. She made up an excuse, but I felt really unsettled. I really, really need to move, friends. That much is clear.)

But back to L: I can really tell she's still thinking about her ex-friend. It seems so obsessive. R isn't even that great. I wish there was something I could do. L means so much to me. I've told her all my secrets, even the biggest, scariest ones I wouldn't tell anyone. Or I'm getting there, anyway. I can trust her. I want to continue to trust her. I don't want R to ruin that. Ruin her.

What would you do if you were me? Would you let her make her own mistakes? Or would you do a teensy little thing to just sort of nudge the boat back out to sea?

TOP COMMENTS:

@BBach5truth: You gotta go with your gut, honey! This is your bestie you're talking about!   ♡

@anxiouskitten23: Totally agree. You gotta keep those toxic ex-friends away.   ♡

@RTGz69: You should totally report S. Major stalker. What's her problem?   ♡

@mimi_has_troubleZ: S is probably jealous of your new friendship. Watch out!   ♡

@lonely_girlRZ4540: I hope everything is okay.   ♡

13

LENNA

OCTOBER
PRESENT DAY

After Lenna and Amy milk the goats, they return to the house. Lenna heads straight to the laundry room, where Rhiannon is supposedly working. But the room is empty. The washers, two of them, stand open. The drying racks and lines are bare, too, the clothespins waiting.

Out in the kitchen, Coral stands at a cutting board, chopping peppers. Lenna realizes that besides the table, she's never seen Coral anywhere else. "Have you seen Rhiannon?" she asks.

Coral looks up. "I don't think so. I'll tell her you're looking for her?"

Ann parades through the door, a stream of dogs following in her wake like some sort of pied piper situation. She heads for Lenna. "Ready for the dogs?"

Lenna looks down at the leashes Ann holds loosely in her hand. "Huh?"

"You're with me on the chore list for this afternoon."

"But I didn't sign up for dog walking."

A tiny smirk appears on Ann's lips. "We don't really *sign up* for stuff. Marjorie tells us what to do, and we do it."

"I . . ." Lenna swallows hard. "I just really need to talk to Rhiannon, is all. Maybe after?"

"Actually, Rhiannon was the one who suggested you help me." Ann searches her face. "Is there a problem?"

Lenna sinks onto the long bench that runs the length of the kitchen table. She can feel that Coral has turned from her chopping and is watching. "Where is Rhiannon now?"

"She took a four-wheeler to the perimeter," Marjorie says from the doorway. Lenna swivels around. How long has she been standing there, listening? "To make sure no animals are trying to get inside. Everything okay, Lenna?"

Lenna's mouth feels dry. "Um, sure. It's fine."

"As long as you're our guest, we do like you to help."

"I know." Lenna's cheeks blaze. "Sorry. It's just . . ." It feels like her chances of talking to Rhiannon—and maybe getting out of here today—are slipping away. Rhiannon is definitely avoiding her, probably because of her questions from last night. Lenna has no doubt.

She looks at Ann, feeling she has no choice. "I'll be out in a minute."

Ann nods. Then she nods at Marjorie, though the nod is slightly different—more deferential, just a little. Then she whistles. A few dogs come running. They wait while she pulls more leashes down from hooks by the door.

When Lenna turns back, Marjorie is still watching. She points at the baby. "Want me to take this guy while you go out with the pups?"

God, Lenna is getting tired of people asking her that. And yet her back is literally screaming in pain. And he *is* so much calmer today. . . .

"It's all right. I've had two of my own. Boys, even." A melancholy look crosses Marjorie's features. "So long ago."

"Right." Lenna nods. "Rhiannon told me they grew up here."

"They did. They were the pioneer kids, before any other kids arrived."

"Did they like it?"

Marjorie glances behind her. The kitchen is empty—even Coral has vacated her chopping station. "There's magic in this place. But if you're not open to that, it won't help you. Wherever you go, you're still the same person, deep down."

"Right," Lenna says, wondering where Marjorie's going with this.

"I think the key is recognizing you're bringing your baggage with you at all times," Marjorie adds. "Only once you drop your baggage can you change." She looks at Lenna hard, like something unspoken is passing between them. "I meant it when I said you are here for a reason. I can tell. And I don't think you should go quite yet."

Lenna's lips part. Is it that obvious that she wants to leave?

Marjorie rises and bends. A joint cracks in her back. "Ann's waiting. I can take your baby. It's the least I can do."

Lenna undoes the straps of the carrier carefully. Her back releases the moment Jacob's weight lifts away. When she hands him over to Marjorie, for a moment, her fingers don't want to let go. But then they do. Jacob recently ate. He was recently changed. He'll be *fine*.

Marjorie carries Jacob out of the room. To Lenna's surprise, her baby doesn't cry at the notion of being separated.

The door bangs, and they are gone, and she is alone. But she still feels someone watching. She peers into the pantry; no one is there. Nor is anyone hiding behind the island or in the doorway. But when she looks into the hall, she almost doesn't notice Gia through an open doorway off the kitchen until she's right next to her. The room is dark, but she can see the globes of Gia's eyes staring out, watching silently.

"Oh!" Lenna cries, jumping backward.

Gia sits at a tiny desk. A banker's lamp illuminates the space. A laptop screen plays against her features, making distinct shadows under her eyes and around her mouth.

"Welcome to my dungeon," Gia says. "It's where they keep the dragon all day."

"Wh-what are you doing?"

"I'm the place's bookkeeper. Money, money, money. There's never enough."

Gia is impeccably dressed. Her hair smooth and sharp, her skin flawless, her silk shirt tucked into crisp black trousers. Everything she wears looks expensive—but also impractical for doing any heavy labor or even venturing into the heat.

She glances toward the kitchen. "I heard Marjorie giving you her magic speech. It's bonkers, right?"

"Well . . ." Lenna shifts to one hip.

"Her children totally resented her for bringing them here. Their behavior become worse and worse, and then one of them drugged her and escaped."

"Drugged her? With what?"

Gia's smile is crocodilian. "We've grown valerian root in the greenhouse since who knows when. People still use it in tea. Guess Marjorie's boy gave her a little too much. Knocked her out—and he ran into the desert alone. I heard it was a shit show. Nearly got eaten by something out there. She sent him away to live with his father. And the other son—he's got problems, too."

Lenna turns back toward the door, a streak of worry coursing through her for way too many reasons. *Tea.* Someone—Melissa?—had made *her* tea. First when she arrived, and then Rhiannon gave her more before bed.

"You still grow valerian root, you said?" she asks.

"Well, not me. But some people think it's great for sleep. I use stronger stuff. Pick it up at the nearest pharmacy every month. Marjorie hates it, but she's always asking for some. For someone who claims this place is serene, she certainly likes to be medicated." Gia looks at her steadily, one corner of her mouth curved.

"But Marjorie's okay now, right?" Lenna asks. "I just left my baby with her."

"Oh sure. She takes care of all the babies here and there, as long as she doesn't have to get up with them at night. But it's certainly why *I'm* not having any children at this place. Kids need more than six other people their own age around. By the way." She reaches for something under her desk. "These belong to you?"

To Lenna's horror, Gia is holding a package of diapers. Size 2 diapers, Mickey Mouse print.

"Where did you find these?" It comes out of her mouth before Lenna can think straight.

"I just found them." Gia scoffs. "Figured they were yours. No one else uses disposable around here."

"Where did you find them?" Lenna whispers.

Gia looks guilty. "I don't want to make trouble." But then she drops her hands to the table in a giving-up sort of way. "Okay, fine. Rhiannon had them."

For a moment, Lenna doesn't speak. "She . . . *did*?"

"They were in this laundry tote she carries around. I went into the laundry room because something of mine was in the wash that I needed to hand-clean, and that's when I saw them in there."

"This was . . . today?" Lenna's mind spins. "But why?"

"Maybe because they aren't allowed. Maybe she didn't want

you to get in trouble." Gia shrugs. "Maybe she was trying to be a good friend."

A shiver dances down Lenna's spine. Something about Gia's tone makes her think Gia means the opposite. Not a good friend at all.

Gia flicks an imaginary piece of lint off her pants, then ceremoniously hands Lenna back the package of diapers. They feel so much heavier than Lenna remembers. "Totally don't blame you for bringing these, by the way," she says. "Those cloth things seem like a pain in the fucking ass."

LENNA CAN'T WALK DOGS. NOT YET. SO SHE GOES TO HER ROOM. LET Ann wait. Or let Ann go without her.

She sits on the edge of her bed, restless. Is it possible Gia accused Rhiannon of something she didn't do? Gia could have taken those diapers and is just trying to make trouble. Maybe there's some sort of bad blood between Gia and Rhiannon. After all, Rhiannon told her to leave Gia alone.

But what if Gia is telling the truth? What she said about the tea . . . and valerian root . . . rattles Lenna, too. She'd slept like a rock last night. Jacob was positively soporific today, which isn't like him at all. Did Rhiannon drug her—and Jacob? Only . . . why? To make Jacob stop crying? To make Lenna too woozy to leave?

When she stands back up, her head swims, which only heightens her anxiety. The panic presses against her temples. *Squeeze, squeeze, squeeze,* and she fixates on the yellow onesie neatly folded on her dresser. *Jacob's* onesie—he'd worn it yesterday. It was freshly laundered—*by Rhiannon.* The idea that she'd slipped in here and touched Lenna's things *again* suddenly makes her uncomfortable. What else did Rhiannon touch in here? The mug with tea is gone. What else did Rhiannon discover in here? Did she see Lenna's phone? Lenna turns to it and wakes up the screen.

This is silly. She's making herself crazy. Her friend *wants* her here. No one is trying to gaslight her. In fact, forget about walking the dogs, forget about Marjorie—she'll march out to the fence line right now and *find* Rhiannon. Talk to her point-blank. The air needs to be cleared immediately.

On go her shoes. On goes sunscreen. She heads back down the hall and out into the main room, trying to get her bearings. Marjorie said Rhiannon took a four-wheeler to the perimeter fence. Which is . . . everywhere?

Wheels roll on gravel outside. Lenna's hopes soar—maybe Rhiannon is back early. Perhaps she even realized her mistake with the dogs and she's come back.

Lenna heads toward the front door. Her hand is almost on the knob when she hears a car door slam—*not* Rhiannon, then.

Another door slams. Another. Lenna hasn't heard this much car activity since she's arrived. Voices rise. People say hello. She hears Coral, and then Amy. They're chirping about someone in the car.

"Sarah!" Amy calls.

Lenna licks her lips. Right. That woman at the OB appointments out of town. Lenna forgot about her, and she's not in the mood to meet anyone new. She wants to wait until the residents go inside or move around to the back before she heads out to look for Rhiannon. Fewer questions, less fuss.

As she bides her time, hiding in the shadows, her gaze drifts to the walls. To her right is the group photo that she'd noticed the first day she came. It's covered with a fine sheen of dust, but when she wipes it away, she can just make out Rhiannon, holding a tiny Teddy in her arms.

God, she thinks, and her suspicions rise up again. *How* did

Rhiannon get pregnant? Who is the father? Why won't she answer Lenna's questions?

Her gaze moves to the center: Marjorie looks maternal and proud. Then she spots Amy and Melissa, Ann and Coral, and even Gia in the back, wearing the same silk blouse Lenna saw her wear the first day. They look no different than they do now, for the most part.

She spies another woman, too—a dirty-blond woman off to the side, set a little apart from the others, her hands shoved into her pockets. She isn't one of the kids, but she's barely an adult. Someone who has left, maybe. Her mind catches on a gossipy story Gia told last night. Something about a woman who crossed her. Karen? Carmel?

Then she spies another blond woman at the other side of the photo. She's pretty. *Really* pretty. Lenna leans back, something twanging in her brain. She *knows* this face.

"How *was* it, Sarah?" Coral chirps through only a thick wall of adobe. "How's the baby?"

And then this new person, this Sarah, answers: "It was great. Baby's doing really well. A strong heartbeat!"

A chill runs up Lenna's spine. She knows the face, and she thinks she knows the voice outside, too. Except in her mind, that voice didn't belong to someone named Sarah. She went by another name.

She hurries over to the window. The Suburban sits at the front of the house, two of its doors wide open. Coral hefts some luggage. Two other women stand at the front of the vehicle, chatting excitedly. One is Amy, who seems so delighted that she's holding the other woman's thin, pale forearms. The other woman is the person in the group photo. But she's also the woman in a dashboard picture. The woman who appeared outside Lenna's office building, wrecked when her fertility treatment failed. The woman who knocked on Lenna's door after Gillian went missing.

Lenna's heart starts to pound. She can't quite feel her feet.

Out the window, Amy leans in to give Sarah a hug. Coral reaches down to pick up Sarah's bags. But Lenna doesn't know her as Sarah. She knows her as Sadie. Gillian's roommate and friend.

The one person who might know the terrible thing Lenna did.

14

LENNA

Lenna had a general idea of where Gillian lived: She'd shown Lenna the house online several times. The bungalow was along the Runyon Canyon path. Her roommate had gotten it for a steal, Gillian said, at least by LA standards. Inheriting some money for a hefty down payment helped.

Getting there was a straight walk uphill through the park, and she wasn't in the mindset to do that in the early morning or the icky weather. So she drove and parked her car a few streets away from the house, nearly blocking someone's driveway, telling herself that this wouldn't take long.

It was an unusually miserable morning for July in LA. The temperature was in the sixties, bizarre for that time of year, and the spitting rain made it seem even chillier. Twice on the walk to the house, she stopped in her tracks, telling herself she should go back. Confrontation wasn't her thing.

But then she was there. The house glowed, perched on the edge of the cliff. Gillian's Prius sat to one side of the slanted driveway.

The garage door was closed. Lenna shifted from foot to foot, unsure. She really didn't want to have an intervention with another
person around. But she was pretty sure Gillian said Sadie left early.

The front door opened, and Lenna ducked behind a tree, watching Gillian step out. She wore a quilted, hooded vest, long tights,
running shoes. After popping wireless headphones into her ears
and pulling her hood tight against her head, she headed down a
side street toward the entrance to the canyon trail.

So Lenna followed.

She had to jog to keep up, and after a few minutes she called
Gillian's name. Gillian turned. Pulled the earbuds from her ears.

"Lenna!" She looked confused but happy. "You came after all!"

Gillian was so *chipper*. But Lenna felt the phone in her pocket.
She thought of the word *ducking*. And *Lose this number*.

"I have to clear my head," Gillian said, gesturing toward the
trail. "I don't usually run in this kind of weather, but—"

"Did you text her as me?" Lenna interrupted.

The smile faded from Gillian's lips. She looked caught, and
then annoyed.

"Did you?" Lenna demanded. "Did you tell her to lose my number last night?"

"Lenna, she's not good for you," Gillian said. She sounded
empty. "She makes you crazy. It kills me."

Lenna felt sick. "So you did clone my phone? You've been reading all my texts—my emails?"

"She's just going to hurt you again. I'm trying to keep that from
happening."

Lenna's gaze searched Gillian's face, which had gone blank.
"Talking to her or not talking to her is *my* decision," she spluttered.
"Not yours."

"Yeah, but I'm your friend *now*."

"I get to choose who I am friends with. Not you."

"Even after everything you've realized about her? After how shitty she was to you?"

Lenna shook her head. "Can you just undo that text? Explain that I wasn't the one who sent it?"

Gillian stared down at the ground. "Why does she have such a hold over you? It's like you're obsessed."

"She doesn't have a hold on me."

"You just can't see it. She only cares about herself, she doesn't care about you. Mark my words."

Lenna backed up. Who *was* this person?

Then something else occurred to her. She leaned back, making a guess. "Did you even see her kissing Frederick that night, or did you just say it because you knew it would get me riled up about her?"

Gillian's nose wrinkled. "She was the one who was weird to you about staying away from him, not me."

"But maybe that's why you don't want me talking to her now. Because you know I'd ask her, and you know she'd say that never happened—that you made it all up." And then Lenna kept going. "And did she actually say that *I* didn't want to talk to you? Or did you make that up, too? Did you make a total case for getting her fired based on lies?"

Gillian blinked innocently. "You didn't *have* to send that email to get her fired. I didn't twist your arm. You were ready to hate her. And I don't blame you." Then she put her hands on her hips. "Oh, and by the way, she knows what you did."

Lenna's stomach dropped. "What do you mean?"

"I thought she deserved to know. So I forwarded your email to her. It was easy to find your login credentials. You keep them in that little book in your purse."

Lenna clapped her hand over her mouth. She couldn't breathe.

"You want her back so badly, but you also did something terrible to her," Gillian said in a sad voice. "You're a bad friend, Lenna."

Her bottom lip stuck out in an almost childish pout. This was a person, Lenna thought, that she'd never see again. She could already feel it in her bones, her fingers, her heart. Even if she had to quit *City Gossip.* Even if she had to move away from LA entirely.

"Get her to unblock me," Lenna said again.

"What's the point? She won't want to talk to you anyway."

"Get her to unblock me . . . or I'll tell Sadie."

Gillian cocked her head. "Tell Sadie *what*?"

"How you were *happy* when her IVF failed. And . . . and that thing you said about the meds, too. About something being *wrong* with them." Fear struck her. "Oh God, you tampered with her medicine, didn't you? *You* made that treatment fail."

Gillian's eyes blazed. "Of course not!"

But Lenna didn't believe that. "I'll tell Sadie." Lenna held up her phone. "I'll tell her everything. Unless you get Rhiannon to unblock me."

A beat passed. Finally, Gillian sighed. "Fine." She reached out and took Lenna's phone.

Lenna breathed out. "Thank you."

But in the next moment, the phone slipped from Gillian's fingers . . . accidentally, perhaps, but probably on purpose. It flipped once, twice, banging against the guardrail. Time moved achingly slow. Lenna watched helplessly as the phone disappeared into the canyon. Even Gillian's eyes widened like she hadn't expected that to happen.

"Fuck!" Lenna cried, hurrying over to the railing. The light was so dim, but she swore she could see her device careening over the rock. "Gillian, what the hell?" She ran to the edge, her feet sliding on the wet ground. She felt someone tugging her shirt from behind, and Gillian pulled her backward. Lenna's whole body tensed. Letting out a wail, only wanting to be free from Gillian's grip, she elbowed her hard in the stomach.

"You bitch!" Gillian cried. "I was trying to save you from falling!" She stood, lip quivering. "You don't care about me at all, do you?"

And then Gillian leapt on her. Lenna wasn't sure what was happening, only that the other woman had grabbed her and was holding her waist. Lenna gasped. Her feet slipped on wet leaves on the path. She kicked to get away from Gillian. Clawed. But Gillian was stronger. She was edging Lenna toward the canyon's edge.

Lenna didn't know what to do, but she needed to save herself. She sank her teeth into Gillian's shoulder. Gillian reared back, her fingers releasing their grip. Lenna fell to the concrete hard on her hip, the back of her head knocking against the guardrail. When she looked up, Gillian was on her feet again, coming toward her, her fingers outstretched, her eyes mad.

And then—it got blurry here, but Lenna found herself on her feet, ducking out of Gillian's lunge, but she leapt, the weight of her body pressed against Lenna's back, her arms around Lenna's throat. Lenna screamed. She tried to shake Gillian off, but Gillian was too heavy. Finally, with all her might, Lenna sort of lunged to the side, flinging Gillian into the guardrail. That's what she told herself, anyway, afterward, when she put it all together—she was just trying to get Gillian *off* her, and that was all. But then she saw Gillian's feet skidding in the wrong direction, and the top half of her tilted forward, her balance lost. The canyon howled. Gillian howled, too. Lenna was so overwhelmed and disoriented, and her legs suddenly went numb.

And then, everything was black.

THE NEXT THING SHE KNEW, SHE WAS LYING ON A BENCH. SHE wasn't sure how she'd gotten there. She was soaked through, and her head was pounding, and she was alone. It took her a moment to realize where she was. Runyon Canyon. At the trail entrance near Gillian's house. Low clouds hung over the city, obscuring the view.

It was daytime, but no one was hiking because of the rain. How had she slept through this? Lenna stared into the canyon. Brown mud. Rock. She remembered Gillian throwing her phone over the side. *Fuck.*

And where was Gillian? She sort of remembered fighting with her, but the details were blurry, and eventually, everything faded out entirely, and her memory was a black hole. Had Gillian tossed her phone into the canyon, or did she dream that? She felt in her pockets. Her phone really was gone. She glanced down the ravine.

She trudged from the trail to her car, grateful it hadn't been towed, grateful, too, that her keys were still in the zipped pocket of her jacket. She felt like some primordial creature that had crawled out of a swamp. It was three hours since she'd left, but it felt like days. Something had happened between then and now, something she didn't understand.

Later, she didn't remember actually driving home or unlocking her front door. The next memory was of how badly her fingers were shaking as she turned on the taps for the shower. As the spray hit her, more details from the night before started to come back. The incident with Gillian was like a fever dream—she couldn't imagine having fought with her like that, except what else would explain her muddy, soaked-through clothes? What were these scratches on her arms? And the argument—when what was said returned to Lenna's mind, she winced in disgust. It was sickening that Gillian had access to her phone. She'd read every single text Lenna wrote . . . for *what*? She felt so violated. It made her hate herself, too—because she'd trusted Gillian, maybe more than she'd even trusted Rhiannon.

And how did they leave things? It felt like something happened. The detail crouched in her memory in shadow, teasingly out of reach. She couldn't grab on to the details.

Speaking of Rhiannon, Lenna still had her old friend's number written down. She could call it with a new phone number, she supposed, and straighten everything out herself. As much as she didn't want to make herself the victim, maybe she could explain that Gillian tricked her and lied about things Rhiannon said and did. (Or *were* they lies? Lenna's mind went in circles. She didn't know what to believe.) But she was too chilled and shaky to do anything. She checked the emails on her laptop, marveling over the fact that she couldn't tell that Gillian had even *looked* at her Gmail account. It was eerie. Were people just doing this all the time? It made her feel like she was in a bad movie.

She felt fluish, her skin hot and then cold. It was like someone had slipped her something. She slept most of the afternoon, her dreams spiked with restlessness.

The next morning, a local news alert popped up on her computer as she woke. *Runyon Canyon Accident.* She blinked at the screen, unsure of what she was seeing. Then she read the words. Police were speculating that the day before, a woman had fallen into Runyon Canyon. Her name was Gillian Winters.

Lenna's knees went out from under her.

She made herself read the story. Gillian's roommate, Sadie, had reported her missing yesterday evening. The location of the home where she lived was mentioned. Then, early this morning, a jogger farther down the trail found a woman's down vest snagged on a twig over the canyon's edge. Gillian's name and address were inscribed on the tag.

Lenna's hand flew to her throat. This was impossible. Was this . . . was this because of their fight? She searched, *scraped* her memory for some sort of evidence, but there wasn't any.

She couldn't have done something to Gillian, could she? There was no way. She wouldn't.

But she *did*. She could feel it, almost see it. They were fighting.

Lenna was scrambling to get away. And she was angry. *So* angry. She could see her arms pushing, maybe, and Gillian tumbling over the side. It was possible, and she'd blocked it out because it was too terrible to face head-on.

Horror struck her. What if someone found Lenna's phone? Or what if someone saw them arguing, or ID'd Lenna's car? Those links would be far too clean. She'd be a suspect for sure. The police would connect them because they both worked in the same building. Someone would know they were friends—Sadie, who'd reported Gillian missing. And Lenna was writing a *story* for Gillian. They'd talk to Gillian's editors.

A strange mix of feelings rose in her throat. Her feelings sickened her—on one hand, she was relieved Gillian was gone, because it meant Lenna wouldn't have to face her ever again. On the other hand, maybe with her socially awkward ways, Gillian truly thought she was doing a *good* thing, saving Lenna from Rhiannon. Gillian was always talking about how she was a work in progress, navigating the world of social experiences because they didn't come innately, and that even missteps were learning opportunities. Gillian could have learned a *lot* from this situation.

Except now she wouldn't have the chance.

Lenna was too superstitious to read or watch the news. Should she turn herself in? Explain herself, her innocence, her lack of memory or action? But all those things Gillian did to her. The way they yelled at each other at that canyon's edge. Someone might have heard—they would point fingers at Lenna, say she was making it all up, that she'd *meant* to do it. That she was a horrible person.

A few hours after she'd read the story, a knock came. Lenna shot up from the couch, but she was too petrified to move. She heard the neighbors bickering next door like they always did. Maybe they'd just knocked against a wall?

But then a voice called out. "Hello?" A *woman's* voice—and not like the woman's who lived in the next apartment over. There was no announcement. Didn't the police have to identify themselves? After a few minutes, whoever it was walked away.

Lenna slunk to the window, heart in her mouth. When she looked out, she suppressed a scream. Sadie's blond head moved across the sidewalk to the parking lot, but she was walking away. Maybe to the police?

The next few days passed in abject terror. Lenna fielded an email from Rich—she'd handed in her three-hundred-word piece about the Pilates studio and now he had a new assignment. Lenna couldn't fathom writing anything, so she said she was really sick and would have to pass. She wondered about the article Gillian had assigned her. Gillian had never given her another editor's name at *Wellness*; she didn't even know who to get in touch with. Maybe better, though, that she didn't associate herself with Gillian at the moment. She didn't dare go to work because she knew the police had to be swarming the building, and she didn't want to jog anyone's memory that she and Gillian were friends.

She did go out to purchase a new phone (with a new number), but the whole time she was in the store, handing over her ID, swiping her credit card, she waited for the police to descend. It was bizarre when they didn't. With the new phone, she finally called into work and spoke to Judy, the office manager, to see if she could send her copy editing work home to her. Not that she had the wherewithal to do *that*, either, but she had to make money.

"Seems something's going around," Judy replied when Lenna told her she'd been sick. "Hey, did you hear about that woman who hung around the office? You knew her, right—Gillian? She fell into Runyon!"

"I . . . did hear that." Lenna felt nauseated. There was something off-putting about Judy's glee. Something odd, too, about the way Judy had phrased Gillian's situation. Lenna backtracked. "Wait, what do you mean, she *hung around* the office?"

"So apparently, she was just pretending like she worked for one of the other magazines. They never let her in the building, but she just went around telling everyone she worked here."

"She *what*?" Bile rose in her throat. Gillian never worked at *Wellness*? Gillian used a Gmail account for their *Wellness* discussions. Lenna hadn't thought much of it; some of the writers at *City Gossip* used their Gmail accounts, too. Something to do with easier access on cell phones.

But it made sense—Gillian used Gmail because she didn't have an actual *Wellness* email address. Lenna had never actually seen Gillian's desk or even the *Wellness* floor. Gillian always found *her,* usually downstairs or in the lobby. She was always calling Lenna during the workday, from her car or the street. Just as Judy said, Lenna had never actually seen her in the building.

What a fool she was.

And the article Gillian assigned her. Gillian had just . . . made up that assignment. How would Lenna get paid? What a dumb thought: Of course she wouldn't get paid. But Jesus, Lenna had sent her an invoice!

"Anyway, it's all so terrible," Judy was saying. "They're questioning her roommate."

"What?" Lenna nearly dropped the phone, thinking of Sadie's shadow in her doorway.

"I don't know. She's some doctor? I guess she was letting that Gillian woman live rent-free, but she wanted to have a baby on her own so she was trying to get Gillian to move out, or something? Oh, and Gillian had this blog talking all about how weird her roommate was getting. This anonymous tip came in, backing the whole thing up."

Lenna's head was spinning. It took her a moment to realize they were questioning Sadie because they thought Sadie was a suspect. But surely Sadie would steer them to Lenna. Lenna recalled Gillian having an Instagram page about social anxiety. But unlike everyone else Lenna's age, social media wasn't really her thing.

And an anonymous tip from whom, saying *what*?

"Was her roommate . . . arrested?" she asked, coming up for air.

"I think she's just a person of interest at the moment. But I'm not really sure. Hey, I gotta run. Rich is calling."

Lenna put her head between her knees. She could picture it. Sadie was in an interrogation room right now, swearing her innocence, probably providing an alibi, and then probably providing a list of people they should question next. Which absolutely would include Lenna. All their emails and texts together. And Gillian's social media pages—Lenna cursed herself for never looking into it.

With shaking hands, she typed in Gillian's page on Instagram. The account was still private. Gillian still hadn't given Lenna access. Now she never would.

Friday turned to a weekend. The police still didn't come. Lenna dared to read the news; it said that Dr. Sarah "Sadie" Wasserman, who ran a private concierge practice specializing in geriatric medicine, had been released from questioning but was still a person of interest in Gillian's death. The scandal had caused her to step away from her medical practice. Gillian had told Lenna how much Sadie loved being a doctor. She had to be out for blood, Lenna figured, to have that taken away from her. Surely Sadie was looking for someone who really *did* do this, so she could clear her name and get on with her life.

On Monday, Lenna begged off sick again, trying to figure out what to do. By Wednesday, Rich wasn't quite as understanding, saying she'd used up all her sick days and he'd have to dock her pay. "We need a copy editor," he said. "If you can't get here by Friday, I'm going to have to look for someone else."

Friday came, but she just couldn't get out of bed. And that was that.

Rent was a week past due. Lenna could pay it, but her savings would run out soon. She couldn't live here with no job. Where would she go? Her father's felt like a last resort. For one thing, he didn't have room in his little condo. For another, she wasn't sure he wanted her there.

A few days later, an alert flashed. More of Gillian's belongings were found farther in the canyon, including one of her shoes. The police were still searching for her body. A message came on the screen: *If anyone has any information, please come forward.*

Lenna pressed her hands over her eyes.

Later in the day, she was walking back to her apartment from an unavoidable mission to the grocery store, despairing. She had to come up with a plan. But she was so despondent. Everything felt impossible. She had no friends. No money. She stared at the street before her, a four-lane boulevard filled with whizzing cars. What would it be like if she stepped off the curb?

Experimentally, she placed a foot on the pavement.

Someone grabbed her from behind and pulled her back. When she turned, a sandy-haired man wearing a gray suit stared at her in shock. "Whoa. You okay?"

The sharp grind of metal on metal had brought Lenna back to the present. She started to shake.

"They almost hit you," the man said, gently touching her arm. He had kind, hazel-colored eyes. "Drivers around here are nuts."

Lenna turned to the street. One car had T-boned the other and sent a sedan flipping across the boulevard. The sedan still lay upside down, the driver trapped inside. A few people had rushed over; someone was calling 911. Sirens rang through the air.

Lenna burst into tears.

"Shit," the man said, his face falling. He wrapped his arm

around her. "Hey. It's okay. I know. It was awful to see that, and be so close to them hitting you . . ."

But that wasn't why she was crying. The accident was just the icing on the cake. That driver, Lenna felt, had crashed because of *her*. She'd seen him glance at her walking into the road. Their eyes had met; maybe he'd noticed the steely resignation in her eyes. He'd wrenched the wheel and torn across the midline of the road just to avoid her. She knew it.

She seethed with self-loathing.

"It's okay," the man said again. He was still hugging her. But he was a stranger. Strangers didn't hug people like Lenna. And yet it was exactly what she needed. She sobbed into his shoulder, more vulnerable than she'd felt in forever.

Finally, the man stepped back and looked at her. "Do you need medical attention? Maybe I could buy you a coffee? Or at least drop you somewhere. My name's Daniel, by the way. I don't feel right leaving you like this."

At first, she demurred on coffee. But he persisted. He got her number, saying he wanted to check up on her, make sure she was okay. He asked if she'd take a rain check and get a drink with him the next day. Lenna wasn't sure. She didn't deserve to date someone, especially someone who seemed kind and decent.

But Daniel pushed gently. He wanted to make sure she was all right. Lenna needed someone; she let him care for her. At first, they kept their outings strictly as friends: movies, bowling excursions, hikes. Daniel planned it all. He picked her up in his sporty little BMW, which he'd bought with his tech salary. He was an adult with a job, not a weirdo who'd been fucked up by two friends and now had a murder on her conscience. He had a condo south of the city in Orange County, far enough away that it felt like another planet. Lenna liked going there. She didn't recognize a soul, and no one recognized her. She felt safe. When the lease on her apartment ran out and she had no money to pay the next month's rent, Daniel said she could stay with him officially. "As friends!" he said quickly.

When Lenna moved in, Daniel showed her the spare room he'd gotten ready for her. The bed was covered in a new weighted blanket—he'd bought it for her because she'd said she'd thought about getting one for her anxiety but hadn't been able to justify spending that much money. "It's yours, really," he said gently. "You can keep it."

It broke her. Lenna turned to him, unbelievably touched and sad and grateful, and kissed him, and of course he kissed her back.

It felt too easy after that. There was a part of her that figured that Daniel would eventually realize Lenna was deeply messed up. But amazingly, Daniel seemed to see something in her that she certainly didn't. And unlike with Rhiannon, Lenna hadn't felt like she had to be the best version of herself at all times. Nor did she ever feel like she had to walk on eggshells, as she did with Gillian. It was just . . . *uncomplicated.* He showed up to their apartment with dinners. He bought her thoughtful gifts. He read the piece about the Pilates studio that had published just as the whole Gillian mess was going down and said it was great. He even got her a gig freelance copy editing for his friend's tech magazine, which at least brought her a little money. The work was boring, but she needed boring. And it had nothing to do with celebrity gossip or anyone who worked in that world, and that was even better.

The first time she was alone in Daniel's condo, she ransacked the place, looking for a red flag. A weird fetish. Bodies in a closet. A wife and a family. His niceness made her put her guard up. Rhiannon and Gillian had been nice, too—and look how that had turned out.

But Daniel's house held no mysteries. He didn't have a manipulative bone in his body. He was steady, dorky, lovable, dependable. He didn't have the radiance that Rhiannon had, or the incessant love-bombing tendencies that Gillian did, but maybe that was okay. This was what she needed. Something less intense. Something that wouldn't drain her.

She tried to forget what happened. During the day, she was okay. But lying next to Daniel at night—because, at that point, she was in his bed, not the spare room—all she saw when she closed her eyes was Gillian's twisted mouth and terrified eyes as Lenna pushed her sideways. She was plagued with dreams of deep, deep holes in the ocean. She was a diver, finning toward them, her breaths loud inside her helmet. The flashlight she held bounced on something solid and pale. She drew back, realizing it was Gillian's skinny arm. A lock of her frizzy-wavy hair drifted past.

Eventually, Gillian's case dried up. Sadie was no longer a person of interest, though Lenna didn't know the particulars, only that there were no charges filed. The very last story she read was something about how a body that might be hers had been pulled from the Runyon Canyon ravine. It was badly decomposed from the elements, and it had been found a ways from the running trail, but it *might* be a match to Gillian. That was all the story said. Nothing about a cause of death or previous assault. No reports on a cell phone that had also been found at the bottom of the ravine that matched the number for Lenna's, a *real* employee in the *City Gossip* building. No speculation had been made on why Gillian was faking her employment, either—Lenna would love to know *that* most of all. Ironic: It would actually be a great article, a twisted tale gone wrong. Lenna could probably pitch it to *Vanity Fair.* But instead, she made herself actively stop thinking about it altogether. She had to. It was swallowing her.

Except for this: A few months into their relationship, Lenna and Daniel had dinner with some of Daniel's friends from high school. One of them was a park ranger in the city; the topic of Runyon Canyon came up, and Lenna went cold. The ranger said people dropped so many things down its depths. "We've found all kinds of weird shit down there, stuff people don't want to find," Daniel's friend said. "Money. Jewelry. Teeth. Dildos."

"Cell phones?" Lenna blurted.

The guy didn't even blink. "Tons. But they're all smashed to pieces."

It hit a sad place, dark and deep. Lenna pictured all her texts with Rhiannon—the funny ones, the vague ones, the stressed ones, and even Gillian's fake one—smashed and ruined in that canyon somewhere. Gone for good. As hard as she tried not to think of Rhiannon, she thought of her all the time. Where she was. Why she'd floated back to Lenna in the night. How crushed she must have felt when she learned Lenna had been the one who got her fired. Rhiannon was gone for good. She'd never returned Lenna's text stating her new number. That was okay, though. It had to be. Lenna took solace in the fact that the story had vanished. She'd gotten away with it. No one knew.

Except maybe someone did.

15

LENNA

OCTOBER
PRESENT DAY

Upon hearing Sarah's voice, Lenna snatches Jacob back from Marjorie, mumbling an excuse that she needs to nurse. Then she's in her room, haphazardly throwing items into the suitcase. Jacob lies on a play mat on the floor. Several soft items dangle above him, and he swats at them, trying to roll over. His sweet oblivion and cheerful mood are a relief.

Her brain feels electrocuted. Sadie is here. Or Sarah. Whatever she goes by now, she is *a resident of Halcyon Ranch*. This cannot be a coincidence.

A knock comes, and Lenna whips around. It's Rhiannon. "Hey!" she calls brightly. "How was the morning with Amy?" She stops, her gaze falling to the open suitcase and Lenna's frenzied expression. "What's the matter?"

"Get away from me," Lenna whispers, her voice low and ragged.

Rhiannon's eyes widen. "Wh-what happened?"

"I have to go. I shouldn't have come here."

"Lenna." Rhiannon takes a few steps into the room. "What are you talking about?"

"Don't come in here!" Lenna hisses. Everything she's learned—the diapers Rhiannon stole from her room, the whispers, and now Sadie being here—it's not a coincidence. "Are you two working together? Is that it?"

"Huh?" Rhiannon looks around. "What do you mean? What the hell are you talking about?"

"I heard you whispering to someone last night. I heard about the outhouses. You lied about using the bathroom. And you broke into my suitcase and stole diapers to . . . to what?"

"Diapers? I . . ."

"And what about the tea? Did you drug me? Drug my baby?"

"Lenna!" Rhiannon's eyes go round. "I don't—"

"You were talking to *her,* right? You're both angry at me, and now you have me where you want me?"

Rhiannon takes a deep breath before saying, "Lenna. I think you're having some kind of episode . . ."

She tries to touch Lenna's shoulder, but Lenna wrenches away. "If you come any closer, I'll scream."

Rhiannon takes a beat. "Okay. *Okay.* I admit, I noticed that Jacob was wearing disposable diapers when you came. So I went into your suitcase—I guessed the code—and took the diapers because I was trying to *help* you. Marjorie is so weird about disposables—I was going to talk to you. I shouldn't have just taken them, though, and I shouldn't have gone into your things. I'm sorry." She searches Lenna's face. "That's why you're upset?"

Rhiannon looks so bewildered, but it's a ploy. It's got to be. She has to know Sadie is here, and that it all connects. Perhaps Sadie has been looking for her all this time. Lenna vanished so soon after that all went down. Moved in with Daniel. Cut off all ties to *City Gossip* and her LA life.

"How did you find me? How did you know I was still in Southern California?" Lenna demands.

Rhiannon looks confused. "I looked for you online."

"I'm *not* online. I took myself off all social media. I had to."

"You had to . . . ?" But after silence, Rhiannon shrugs in exasperation. "Your dad has a Facebook page. There are pictures of you—and the baby. You're not tagged, but that's how I found you, okay?"

Her father. She didn't realize her father even knew how to *work* Facebook. But of course. Everyone in his apartment complex probably has Facebook, posting photos of their grandchildren.

"And I still had your cell phone number in my contacts. You sent me a text, way back when. I saved it."

At least, Lenna thinks, she was right about *that* piece of the puzzle. "Well, I have to hand it to you. I fell right into your trap. I thought you wanted me here so I could get some help and we could be friends again. What a fucking fool I am!"

Rhiannon searches her face. "That *is* why I want you here!"

Lenna laughs mirthlessly. "Would you drop the act? You've trapped me here. With *her.*"

"*Who?* And . . . why would I want to trap you?"

Jesus, does she have to say it outright? But maybe this is what Rhiannon wants, too. For Lenna to face her guilt. "Because of that email I sent, Rhiannon. The one that got you fired from *CG.*"

Rhiannon's eyes widen. "Wait. *You* got me fired?"

Lenna glares.

"I have . . . I have no idea what you're talking about." Rhiannon pushes a hand through her hair. She looks rattled. "Let's get some air, okay?"

"I'm not leaving this room. She'll *see* me. Then again, she probably already knows I'm here, right?"

"Lenna. *Who?*"

Lenna stares at her friend. Rhiannon must be playing her. Of course she knows it's someone here. "Did you keep me from writing pieces for *City Gossip*?"

Rhiannon looks at her like she's lost her mind. "Huh?"

"And did you make out with Frederick at a bar? After I said I liked him? That's why you told me to stay away from him?" An uneasy sickness is starting to fill her. She's there on that canyon trail again, all of the lies Gillian told her starting to unravel. "Did you randomly take off to Oregon because of our argument about you not supporting me?"

"I . . . no. That's not why."

"So why did you leave, then? Why didn't you answer any of my texts? Why did you act like I did something to piss you off?"

Rhiannon pinches the bridge of her nose. "Your questions . . . from last night . . . I get why you're curious. But I . . . I don't have the right words. But I *did* reach out, and then you told me to lose your number!"

Lenna presses her hands over her face. "I didn't write that text. Someone else did."

"Who?" Rhiannon sounds skeptical. "And wait, can we go back? You *got* me fired? As I remember it, Rich just called me and said they were restructuring and that my position had been eliminated."

Lenna stares at her. "Didn't he say something about an email?"

"What email?"

"I . . . I sent an email from this throwaway Gmail account, but I was told it was forwarded to you after the fact. And you'd figured out that I was the one behind it." The words feel lodged in her throat, nearly impossible to extract.

"I have no idea what you're talking about." Rhiannon puts her hands on her hips. "What did the email say?"

Lenna looks away. Now she wishes she hadn't said anything. "The email was to Rich. About you, and the Valium. I said you distributed it, sold it to other people in the office. That's why they let you go."

Rhiannon's mouth hangs open. "But I wasn't an addict. *Or* a dealer. You wrote to him making it out like I was both? Jesus, it's a good thing I didn't try and get another job somewhere else! I'm probably on some sort of Do Not Hire list!"

"I'm sorry." Lenna squeezes her eyes shut. "I was angry. You'd cut me off. And I thought . . . I don't know, I thought you were try-ing to sabotage me, even keeping Frederick from me."

"Why would you believe that?"

"Because we had that weird talk after my date, and then you were just . . . *gone.* I just thought . . . I don't know. I figured we were never really friends. That I didn't mean much to you."

"Jesus." Rhiannon rubs her eyes. "Okay, the Frederick thing? He cornered *me* at the party. I should have said something . . . I just got scared."

Lenna turns away. A likely story. "Someone said they saw you make the first move."

Rhiannon swallows hard. "I didn't. I'm *sorry,* okay? I really was trying to protect you. And I never kept you from writing. Or . . ." She trails off, looks to the ceiling. "I don't know. I was immature. Maybe I did, subconsciously. It's probably why I overreacted when we fought. You were right, though. I left without explaining. And I'm sorry."

Lenna bites down hard on the inside of her cheek, feeling a pinch of remorse and forgiveness . . . until the present comes rush-ing back.

"I planned on coming back," Rhiannon goes on. "But then my job was gone, so I didn't. And I thought you'd reach out, but when I didn't hear from you . . . you hurt me, too, Lenna. *Lose this number?*"

"I told you, I didn't write that."

"How was I supposed to know?"

A lump forms in Lenna's throat. She can't tell if Rhiannon is the world's best actress or if she's sincere. She struggles to put herself in Rhiannon's place. "Where did you go? And *why?*"

Rhiannon's eyes lower. "I had to . . . I had to take care of something."

"*What?* Why won't you tell me?"

Rhiannon shuts her eyes. It takes her a while to speak again. "I just don't understand this. If you thought I was so terrible, why did you agree to come to Halcyon?"

"Because I didn't *want* to believe you were terrible, obviously. I wanted to fix things. You've always meant so much to me." She laughs self-consciously. "She always did say you had a strange hold on me. I guess it's true."

"Who said that?"

Lenna eyes her. "Gillian," she says quietly.

Rhiannon straightens up like the name is electrified. *"Who?"*

Lenna just stares blankly. She still doesn't quite buy that Rhiannon doesn't know about the past and is playing dumb.

"Gillian, as in that creepy woman around the office?" Rhiannon thinks aloud. "You talked to her? What, after I left?"

Lenna just shrugs.

Then Rhiannon jolts as if something physical has struck her. "Wait a minute. Sarah had a friend named Gillian, too. But she died. Fell in a canyon, or something. It was tragic . . ." She squints, putting pieces together. An uncomfortable expression rolls across her features. "Is this the *same* Gillian?" she sounds out.

Lenna studies the woman across from her. It doesn't make sense that she'd be just piecing this together.

"Is it?" Rhiannon repeats. "And are you afraid of Sarah, for some reason?"

Lenna wants to shake her. "You *knew* that."

"I swear, Lenna, I *swear,* I had no idea." She puts her hands on her hips. "You really think I'd invite you here if I knew there was a complicated person from your past already here as a resident?"

"Maybe."

"I'm sorry you'd think of me like that." Rhiannon clears her throat. "Tell me what happened. Maybe I can help you."

Lenna shakes her head. She can't do this. "I need to go." She tries to step around Rhiannon. "Get out of my way."

"Wait, Lenna." Rhiannon grabs her arm. "It's not that easy. The gate. It's locked."

"So?"

"I mean, I . . . I could get the code. But I don't have permission to use the car, and neither do you."

Permission? "Fine. Then I'll walk."

"It's miles to the highway. And even if you *do* get there, you might not encounter a car for a long time. And there's all kinds of creepy stuff out here. That house we passed? That guy has lots of guns. It's why we have that huge barbed-wire fence."

Lenna crosses her arms. "You told me the fence was to keep out animals. Not people."

"It's . . . both."

Just then, something makes a noise outside the door. Maybe a footstep. Maybe a breath. Lenna freezes. Rhiannon's eyes widen. They wait a few seconds. No new sounds come. But Lenna's heart is pounding.

Rhiannon inches closer. "If you really need to leave, I'll help you. But you have to hang on just a little longer."

"For how long?"

"We'll go tonight. That's when the car's free."

"*Tonight?* Why not sooner?"

"Because . . . I can't, okay? I need to speak to Marjorie first. She's the only one who knows the gate code."

"Is that safe that only one person knows the code?"

Rhiannon clenches her jaw. "There are so many kids here. We don't want anyone to get out and wander around the open desert."

Lenna feels faint. "Is this really the only option?"

"Please, please trust me," Rhiannon begs. "I will help you."

There are new crinkles around Rhiannon's eyes. Her cheeks are flushed, which Lenna remembers used to happen when Rhiannon became overwrought. On one hand, Rhiannon is the last person she wants help from. On the other hand, Rhiannon is the person Lenna knows best at Halcyon. Lenna wants to break into sobs. Daniel was right about Rhiannon. She never should have come.

"What am I supposed to do until you sort this out?" she asks, resigned.

"Stay in your room. The doors have locks, if you really want. We'll leave tonight, I promise. Sarah won't even know you're here." She looks uncomfortable. "You can trust me."

Lenna sits down on the bed and puts her head in her hands. There is definitely something Rhiannon isn't telling her.

But Rhiannon also looks caught unaware—especially about Lenna getting her fired. Is it possible Gillian never forwarded her that email? Maybe she just said it to rile Lenna up. And also, if Rhiannon intends to hurt her, Lenna realizes with sickening clarity, she would have maybe done so already.

"Okay," Lenna says reluctantly. "Fine. I'll wait."

And then she peers out the window. The yard is empty save for the kids on the playground. But in the distance, by the rocks, for a brief second, she thinks she sees multiple figures, a whole bunch of shining wild-animal eyes watching from behind a tree.

But then, in a blink, she sees nothing. Whatever it is has gone.

RHIANNON PROMISES THAT SHE'LL TELL MARJORIE AND THE OTHERS that Lenna isn't feeling well and is going to rest all afternoon. Once her door is closed, Lenna picks up a pillow and presses it into her face, letting out a long, muffled scream.

Once that is over, she reaches for her phone and the charger. She plugs the phone in, and a wave of relief washes over her. She did what she came to do. She told Rhiannon the truth.

And now she can't wait to get out of here.

She sends Daniel a quick text: Coming home. He writes back immediately: Thank God. When?

Soon. Hopefully tomorrow morning.

Late afternoon, she dozes alongside the baby. Her sleep is restless.

Gillian's face shimmers in her mind. That photo with Sadie on Gillian's dashboard is etched in her brain. She thinks, too, of the top of Sadie's head as she left Lenna's apartment building once Gillian was missing. Why had she come, and why didn't she come back, especially after she'd been brought in as a person of interest? Why had she never named Lenna as someone the police should look into?

The plan is that they'll leave around eleven P.M.—it's a good time because most of the residents will be asleep. Rhiannon can only drive Lenna to the turnoff, no farther. A cab will be waiting to take Lenna to the nearest motel. Rhiannon will make the arrangements.

"Do you still have an ATM card?" Rhiannon asks through the crack in Lenna's door when she brings her dinner. "I'll book your room. I know of a good place."

"What if a man answers?" Lenna challenges.

Rhiannon frowns, caught off guard. "I think we can bend the rules. Anyway, I'll wait for you outside, next to the Suburban. Though . . . I really don't think you should leave." Her eyes search Lenna's. "Why won't you tell me what's going on?"

Lenna just shakes her head.

Eventually, Rhiannon leaves. It's amazing that Lenna is able to fall asleep, but she places Jacob in his little crib for what she hopes is the last time, shuts her eyes, and sinks into restless dreams. One of them is about the morning she found out Rhiannon blocked her texts; in it, she tries again and again to retrieve them on her phone, but the screen keeps frosting over, obscuring the letters. In another dream, she wakes on a cold canyon bench to see Gillian rising from the rocky depths like a sea monster. In a third dream, Jacob is crying. She rises to retrieve him from the crib only to see an enormous snake at the corner of the mattress, creeping toward Jacob's bare foot. She shrieks and grabs for him, but someone yanks her from behind and spins her around. It's Daniel. How did *he* get here? "We need to help the baby," Lenna protests, pointing toward the crib. But Daniel shakes his head. "It's too late. What's done is done. You should never have come. You should have seen the writing on the wall."

Except in her muddled brain, he doesn't say *writing on the wall*. He says the writing on the *blog*.

This jars her awake. She's sweating so profusely that the pillow is soaked through. She leaps to check the crib; there are no snakes. The sheets are white and smooth, perfect. But there's a rattling sound somewhere. Lenna whirls around. It's the doorknob. It's . . . *twisting*. Someone is trying to open it.

Lenna's hand flies to her mouth. The rattling stops. She waits. Her ears ring. The doorknob doesn't move. In the dark, she reaches for her phone on the bedside table, wanting to call someone. Her fingers automatically dial Daniel's number, but then she doesn't go through with it. Even if she confessed she was scared, even if she confessed she and her baby were in danger, he'd want answers. And what can she tell him?

A few minutes before the designated meeting time, she quietly straps the baby to her chest, hefts her luggage in both arms, and heads down to the garage to wait for Rhiannon. The door creaks loudly, and she freezes, wincing, certain someone has heard.

Silence. She presses on.

The night is stippled with stars. Crickets chirp madly. Lenna has never been somewhere so remote. The air is unbelievably still. The mountains are out there, but because of the darkness, she can't see them. She thinks about all the other things she can't see. At every *crack*, every tiny *whoosh,* she stiffens, certain it's something that might bite her—or worse.

Lenna crunches through the dirt until she reaches the same big Suburban that Rhiannon had driven to retrieve her. Rhiannon isn't there yet. She checks her watch. The minute hand edges up on eleven thirty. She pictures the cab at the turnoff point. How long will it wait?

She dials Rhiannon's number and lets it ring once, then hangs up because the ring seems so *loud*. She watches for a light to snap on, but nothing happens.

Come on, Rhiannon. Let's get this over with.

Another minute passes. Something shuffles in the distance, and Lenna swings around again. It's foolish being out here alone.

She looks at her phone again. Dials the same number. This time, she lets it ring. She doesn't hear it ringing inside the house.

It rings so many times that it eventually goes to voice mail. It isn't Rhiannon's voice on the automated message but a computerized woman, rattling off the digits.

"Where *are* you?" Lenna whispers into the phone after the beep. She can't control the blame in her voice. And then something hits her. Everything Lenna told her friend might have stewed in Rhiannon's mind all day, crystallizing into a grudge. She'd confessed to wrecking Rhiannon's life. She'd accused Rhiannon of being a terrible friend. The guile of Lenna, Rhiannon might be thinking, to surmise that Rhiannon had brought her to this sacred space, this hallowed community, for any motive other than love.

Maybe Lenna should have held her tongue.

She holds the phone between her palms, feeling her pulse in her fingertips. The fence surrounding the property gleams under moonlight. Lenna walks toward it and looks at the security panel at the gate. Just waving her fingers over it makes the keypad glow. Did Rhiannon punch in four numbers, or six? She hesitates before guessing something, worried that if she gets it wrong—which she surely will—an alarm will sound.

She walks to the gate itself. Pulls at the latch. It doesn't give. She loops her hand through the wire and tugs. The metal clangs noisily. She steps back, her heart pounding. There has to be another way out.

There's a *snap* behind her, and she freezes. The wind shifts. The moon has gone behind a cloud, and the sky is so much darker. Out of the corner of her eye, she sees a flicker of something. Some*one.*

"Hello?" she cries, whipping around. "Rhiannon?"

Footsteps crunch. Someone walks toward her, but it's too dark to see who it is.

"Hello?" Lenna calls again. "Rhiannon?"

"Nope," says a voice.

A shadow appears on the other side of the picnic table as though by magic. She's tall and slight, and her eyes gleam in the darkness. As she steps into the light, a chill zooms through Lenna's veins.

"So it *is* you," she says.

"Oh," Lenna whispers, backing up.

"I didn't want to believe it," Sadie—*Sarah*—says. And then she walks straight up to Lenna and the baby, her face twisted with fury, her fingers wrapped around something silver and sharp.

A knife.

PART
TWO

16

SARAH

The first time Dr. Sarah "Sadie" Wasserman heard that Gillian had made a new friend, she was crouched on the rug in Mrs. Rosen's living room. Mrs. Rosen was her patient. She had a stethoscope pressed to the old woman's chest.

"Breathe in," Sadie instructed. "Now out. Good."

The woman smelled like baby powder. Two Limoges teacups sat on a heavy wooden side table. A matching teapot was next to them. Mrs. Rosen always insisted on using the good tea set, and she always insisted on pouring, no matter how badly her hands shook.

"What do you hear?" Mrs. Rosen asked. "Is it okay?"

"Not *too* bad."

There was a small crackling sound in her lungs. She'd developed lung scarring from either a virus or a lifetime of cigarette smoking, it was difficult to tell which. Sadie worried that Mrs. Rosen had a progressive condition. That would be the pulmonologist's job to judge—Sadie was just her GP, advising on blood pressure and such—but she'd have to put a call in. Mrs. Rosen had had such a hard life, anyway. A lot of Sadie's private patients had been through hardship, but Mrs. Rosen had been a child in Germany during the Holocaust and spent time in one of the concentration camps before the war ended, which seemed like a different echelon of hardship altogether. Her heart went out to her.

Sadie's empathy wasn't confined just to her patients. She sought to find homes for stray cats, gave food to people she encountered in the long line of trailers parked on some of the side streets, and she couldn't bear to watch any commercial having to do with any sort of call for charity donations for children's hospitals for fear she'd burst into tears. It just was who she was, aware of and concerned for everyone's struggles, generous with her time and money. Certainly it was why she became a doctor, though there were moments when her patients broke her heart.

She sat back and let the woman button her blouse. Mrs. Rosen's living room had floor-to-ceiling bookshelves, matching Chippendale chairs, and a large oil painting over the mantel. Outside the bay window, Sunset Boulevard twinkled in the distance. An ambulance raced in the direction of the Chateau Marmont. "Any more questions before I go?"

"Will you play a quick game of Scrabble?" Mrs. Rosen asked, making puppy-dog eyes.

"Sure," Sadie said, checking her watch. "I think I have time." She didn't, but she knew how happy it made Mrs. Rosen to play.

As Mrs. Rosen set up the game board, Sadie's phone rang. She reached for it eagerly, thinking it might be the nurse from the IVF clinic. But maybe it was too early for them to call with news—her egg retrieval had been three days ago, and she was pretty sure they only reported on the embryos on day five, to see how many had made it to blastocyst. She'd been on high alert since the procedure.

How many embryos would she get? Should she PGS test them or just transfer them untested? Should she transfer one or two? It was such a mindfuck, first deciding to be a single parent by choice and then going through all this fertility shit. Sadie wanted a baby, though, and she wasn't getting any younger. She'd foolishly thought she and Jordan would have children—over the course of their nearly ten-year relationship she kept asking and asking and he kept putting her off, *later later later,* until she realized there would never *be* a later. After Jordan was a string of bad dates, and then a really *scary* date, and then no dating at all ever again . . . but the desire for a child remained. It seemed easier—safer—to go this route. Right, too.

But it was her friend Gillian's name on the screen. Sadie felt a pinch of dread. Months before, she'd finally told Gillian not to call her during the workday. Gillian used to a lot, in the early days of their friendship, always needing something, and Sadie—being Sadie—always came to her rescue. But Sadie had to put her foot down. She simply didn't have the time to react to twenty texts when she was working. She was too busy with patients. When she'd told Gillian, Gillian had gotten defensive. "I didn't realize I had to schedule things with you," Gillian said tightly. "But fine. I'll leave you alone."

Sadie answered the phone now. "Hey," she said, slightly terse. "Everything okay?"

"I'm so excited for tonight, Len," Gillian rushed in. Her voice was frothy and light. "I'm going to be so happy to get out of my prison."

"Sorry?" Sadie frowned. "What prison?"

There was silence. The Scrabble tiles clicked together as Mrs. Rosen got the velvet bag ready.

"Gillian, it's me." Sadie switched the phone to the other ear.

"Sadie. Did you call me by mistake? Were you calling someone named . . . Len?"

"Yeah, my *friend*. Lenna." Gillian gave the word *friend* weight. As if Sadie was *not* her friend.

"And . . . where's your prison?" Sadie pressed. "Work?"

"Just . . . never mind." Gillian sounded flustered. "I gotta go, Sadie. I'm *busy*."

She hung up. Sadie stared at the phone. "You called *me*," she whispered.

Out the window, traffic on Sunset had come to a standstill. Sadie rubbed her eyes.

Gillian did this sometimes. When she felt insecure, she passive-aggressively insisted that she didn't need Sadie at all. And things had been tense between them lately. She suspected that her pregnancy journey rattled Gillian. It was a boundary she'd drawn, an impending change. The more Gillian panicked—and lashed out at Sadie—the more resentful Sadie felt. Sometimes, Gillian just felt like an anchor.

"Dr. Wasserman?"

Mrs. Rosen had set up the Scrabble board. With a shaking hand, she held out the velvet bag so Sadie could pick her tiles. Sadie put the strange call out of her mind. A huge part of this job—maybe the *biggest* part—was attentive bedside manner. Making sure the patient felt heard and seen, loved, and cared for. She felt like a mother to hundreds sometimes.

SADIE HAD MET GILLIAN AT A PARTY LAST YEAR, AFTER SHE'D BRO-ken up with Jordan and also after she'd had the terrifying experience on one of the canyon roads with the man that put her off dating, period. The party was thrown by someone she'd known as a resident in med school. Sadie hadn't really wanted to go, but she didn't have anything else to do that night, and it had been ages since she'd socialized.

She and Gillian happened to be at the snack table at the same time. Gillian caught her attention by looking around at everyone in the room and saying, in a very low voice, "What do you think the odds are that any of these men know where a woman's clitoris is?"

"*Pardon?*" Sadie cried.

Gillian's mouth twitched. Her cheeks flared. "Shit. Sorry. Sorry. Sometimes I just . . . *say* stuff."

"No, wait!" Sadie said before she could scurry away. "You're totally right. Guys strut around like they rule the world. But it's like most of us are too afraid to tell them they've got it all wrong."

Gillian's smile was tentative, like she wasn't sure if Sadie was joking. "Have you dated a lot of awful guys?" she asked.

"You could say that."

She described Jordan—who, to be fair, wasn't *awful,* just immature. Then Gillian—Sadie had to encourage her to talk, insisting that she was completely fine that a total stranger had come up to her talking about clitorises, and no, that wasn't totally inappropriate—also spoke of a series of bad dates that had gone nowhere. "I blame my anxiety," she said. "I swear the last decent boyfriend I had was when I was sixteen. He was a dream."

"Oh yeah? Maybe you should call him up," Sadie said.

But Gillian looked away. "Nah. He's probably moved on."

Then she backtracked and introduced herself, clunking herself on the forehead because that's typically what people do *first,* right? She lived down the hall; she didn't know the couple throwing the party particularly well, but she and the guy were at the mailboxes at the same time, and he'd invited her. She'd debated over coming. "Me, too," Sadie admitted.

Gillian said she posted regularly on an Instagram account about her terrible dating life. "Well, technically, it's more about my social anxiety—there's a whole community of us out there—but there's dating stuff in there, too."

"Like social anxiety awareness, or something?" Sadie asked.

"And support," Gillian said. "I have almost eleven thousand followers suffering with the same things I do. We're there for each other. It's a private group, though."

"Can I join?" Sadie asked. Gillian said she could, but Sadie never got around to sending a friend request.

Still, once she let down her guard, Gillian was fun to talk to. Smart, and good at analyzing people at the party with her startlingly accurate observations. The woman over by the chips and dips clearly had a drinking problem, as she kept pouring vodka into a water bottle when her husband wasn't near. Sadie knew this to be true: The husband, another man she'd gone to med school with, had expressed worry himself. And a couple by the window was on the verge of breaking up; you could tell by their body language. This was also correct: Sadie knew this couple, and her whole circle was pretty convinced their relationship was doomed.

"I'm good at observing," Gillian admitted. "Mostly because I'm usually hiding in the shadows, hah. And people aren't that hard to figure out, when it comes down to it. You just have to know what to look for."

What really roped Sadie in, though, was the fact that Gillian was just another one of those lost birds Sadie couldn't help but scoop up and coddle. Gillian wore her anxiety on her sleeve; it seemed to debilitate her, but at the same time, she flew it like a flag. They continued to talk after the party; every time, Gillian consulted Sadie as though she were some sort of social etiquette expert, recounting every little conversation she had with people at the place she worked, as she was sure everything she said was mortifying or just plain wrong. Sadie took it upon herself to dive deeper with Gillian into *why* she felt so scared of social situations—did something happen in her childhood? It was in Sadie's nature to home in on the thing that was broken and attempt to fix it.

"My childhood was fine," Gillian said. "Idyllic, really. This is just how I'm wired."

Sadie had taken this at face value—and felt relieved by it, actually. Little did she know it was a lie. That Gillian lied about *everything*.

One morning, when she and Sadie met at a coffee joint between Sadie's appointments, Gillian announced that her current roommate wanted her to move. "She wants her boyfriend to move in. It sucks—I've gotten used to her, I'm comfortable around her, and now I have to start all over again with someone new, and that's so scary. Is it hot in here?" She looked around the coffee shop. "I think I'm having a heart attack."

"You're okay," Sadie said. "It's just anxiety. Try to breathe."

"No, this has happened to me before. It's something to do with my heart. I need to go to the ER. I can go myself, don't worry about me."

"Gillian, *I'm* a doctor," Sadie reminded her. "And I sometimes get panic attacks, too. I know what they look like."

Gillian wiped her eyes. "Why do *you* get panic attacks?"

Sadie looked around the busy coffee shop. Was this a safe space? She took a breath. "I was sexually assaulted last year. He was a Tinder date—it was going well—but I was stupid and got into his car to go to another bar. Instead of going to the bar, he drove into the hills, and stopped the car on this deserted stretch of road, and . . . you know."

Gillian's eyes were round. "Shit. Did you report him?"

"No. I should have. I *know* I should have. And then when I got myself together, afterward, I realized he'd given me a fake name and his Tinder profile had been deleted. I had no idea who he was or how to find him."

It was hard to admit. It wasn't even just about what he did but also what he said when he was doing it. He called Sadie a dried-up bitch and ugly as fuck. He said no one would ever love her. He said this *as* he was penetrating her—like it was part of the kink. In therapy, after, she expressed that she understood she shouldn't take the words personally, but she still kind of did. It was the words that sent her into the panic more than the memory of the assault, actually. She worried they were true.

"Oh, Sadie," Gillian whispered, taking her hands. "This makes my stupid roommate problems seem so small."

"That's not why I told you." And then she added, for reasons she still questioned, "Why don't you come stay with me for a little while? So you won't have to jump into a strange new roommate situation so soon. I have the space."

Gillian pulled her hands away. Her breathing slowed. "Really?"

"Sure," she said, figuring it would be temporary. "It'll be fun."

It was fun . . . for a little while.

TWO DAYS AFTER GILLIAN'S MYSTERIOUS CALL ABOUT "LEN," SADIE was leaving another house call. Her phone rang again. This time it really was the fertility clinic, calling with the results. She stared at the number, her heart rising to her throat. *Here we go.*

"Dr. Wasserman." It was her doctor's voice. "How are you this morning?" His tone was steady, giving nothing away.

"Fine?" Sadie said shakily. She was on the 10 in the middle lane of traffic. Not even on Bluetooth, instead holding the phone up to her ear. Cars shimmered in her peripheral vision.

"Well." He sighed. Sadie's throat started to close at his foreboding tone. "I'm afraid I have some bad news. You had a few eggs fertilize, but none of the embryos have made it to blast."

"Oh no," Sadie whispered.

She knew what that meant. The IVF round had failed. They wouldn't be injecting an embryo inside her in hopes it would become a fetus. They hadn't even gotten that far.

The doctor was now saying something about trying a different protocol, vitamins, hormones. Sadie couldn't hear. She felt numb. How dumb was she for not anticipating this outcome? But she figured she'd get at least *one* embryo to try.

"Or maybe it's the sperm donor that's the problem," the doctor was saying.

Sadie thought of the donor she had chosen from the mind-numbingly vast database: tall, blond, Swedish, good at math. He also played the flute. She didn't want to go through that process again.

She thanked the doctor and hung up. There was almost an hour until her next appointment; she'd been driving to the neighborhood early because there was a smoothie place she liked nearby, but now she couldn't imagine eating. This, she realized, was maybe a reason some people chose to have children with another person. So when there was bad news, they could bounce it off someone else. So they could be sad together.

On a whim, she got off the exit that took her to Gillian's office in Hollywood. Sadie was close with a lot of people from med school still, but most of them were partnered off; everyone was in their own bubble. Perhaps because she was single—and also because she was Sadie's roommate—Gillian was the only person with whom she'd shared, so far, the details of the fertility journey. Sadie regretted this now. She had other friends she should have gone to first. Plus Gillian wasn't even being supportive about it.

"What does this mean for us?" Gillian had asked stiffly, the day Sadie said she had made an appointment with the fertility clinic and had decided to get pregnant.

"Nothing, as friends," Sadie said carefully. She'd learned by then that some topics needed to be approached *carefully* with Gillian. "But I guess you'd have to get used to a baby around. I mean you'll probably want to look for somewhere else to live." Then she laughed. "Babies are quite annoying!"

Gillian's bottom lip quivered. "You're kicking me out?"

"No!" Sadie said. "Of course not!"

But she kind of was. It felt like she was breaking the news to a partner. Sometimes she wondered if Gillian *did* love her. Whenever she took stock of her friendship with Gillian, she realized that it wasn't very healthy. Yet Sadie felt a strange sense of responsibility for Gillian in ways she didn't quite understand. She'd assumed Gillian would only stay with her until she found something else, but nearly six months had passed, and she was still here. She wasn't paying rent. Sadie had brought that up a few times, delicately, but Gillian had become emotional, saying again that finding a roommate was so overwhelming, and she would help out with expenses soon, she *promised.* And she'd recently gotten a new job at a magazine about health and wellness, apparently. Sadie was glad for her. Gillian said it was her dream job.

It wasn't even about the money. Sadie just wanted her space back. And yet, if she just dropped Gillian, what if she had a hard time? Could she rely on her family? Gillian said her childhood was great, but she never mentioned her parents. What about other friends? Sadie hadn't heard her talk about anybody. Gillian's social anxiety was so debilitating, she found meeting people difficult. And the more Sadie got to know Gillian, the more it also became clear why she had a hard time holding on to people.

Actually, that wasn't true. Sadie *had* heard Gillian talk about someone. Len. Lenna. Her new friend. So maybe that was something.

But right now, Sadie wasn't sure who else she could talk to. She drove through the streets, following the GPS to the building where Gillian's magazine's office was located. The building was a nondescript high-rise near Hollywood and Highland. It was by far the nicest place her friend had ever worked—before this, Gillian had been at a copy shop. She felt a burst of hopefulness for Gillian, suddenly.

She walked up to the security desk in the lobby. Employees swished through, showing their ID badges.

"I'm looking for *Wellness*?" she asked the guard, a smiling woman with a name tag that read *Honey*.

"Who are you here to see?" Honey asked, reaching for the telephone to call up.

"Gillian Winters."

Honey scanned a list, then frowned. "Huh. Not seeing her on my list."

People walked past Sadie to the elevators, swinging totes, carrying sacks full of lunch. Sadie wrapped her arms around her waist. She wondered if people could tell how fragile she felt.

"Maybe I have the wrong magazine," she said. "Can you search building-wide?"

The guard typed something into her computer. "No Gillian Winters anywhere. Maybe she's in an office down the street? People mix up these buildings all the time."

"Maybe . . ." This was odd. Gillian had bragged about her new job. Talked about parties she went to for the office. Sadie swore she said she worked for a place called *Wellness.*

At that moment, a tall woman with a long face, dark hair, and a diligent expression stepped through the revolving doors. She stopped short when she saw Sadie, seemingly recognizing her.

"Oh!" the woman said. "Are you here for Gillian?"

Relief washed through Sadie's veins. Someone knew Gillian. Sadie wasn't losing her mind.

The woman smiled bashfully. "I'm Lenna. I'm at *City Gossip.*"

"Lenna!" Sadie smiled brightly. "Yes! Gillian's mentioned you! She works here, right? Do you know which floor she's on?"

Lenna looked over Sadie's shoulder, noticing someone. "There she is."

Sadie swung around, too. Up walked Gillian with a laptop bag slung over her shoulder. The moment Gillian saw her, she looked like she wanted to dive into traffic. Then she started running toward them like they were both on fire.

"Hey! What are you doing here?" Gillian demanded.

"I wanted to talk to you," Sadie felt like she was tripping over her words. "But when I talked to the guard—"

Gillian frowned. "Come on, babe. Let's get coffee." Immediately, she steered her away from the building. "It's so stuffy up there," she said. "Your allergies would go crazy."

They headed toward a coffee place. Sadie glanced over her shoulder. Lenna had disappeared into the building.

"Why aren't you on the office employee list?" Sadie blurted.

Gillian's jaw tightened. "Excuse me?"

Sadie explained the guard not having her name on her roster. Spots formed on Gillian's cheeks. "Well, obviously it was some kind of mistake. What, you think I'm lying about working there?"

"I wasn't saying that . . ." Sadie looked at her. She felt so discombobulated, the last thing she wanted to do was fight. "Look, I came here because I need to talk to you. Something happened."

Gillian's expression changed. "What's wrong?"

"It's the embryos." Sadie's voice cracked. "Or, well. The *lack* of them." She explained the results.

"Oh shit," Gillian whispered. "I'm so sorry. So, *so* sorry." And then she threw her arms around her and squeezed tight.

There, then. Gillian was coming through for her. She'd put aside her feelings and was focusing on how Sadie felt for once. Should Sadie have noticed the false note in her tone? The *relief,* even? Should she have known that actually, Gillian was a liar through and through, someone she absolutely didn't want in her life?

Easy to be sure of that in hindsight, she supposed. If she lived her life backward, she'd do everything right. Everyone would.

SADIE JUST DIDN'T UNDERSTAND HOW NONE OF THE EMBRYOS MADE it. Her bloodwork was good. Her uterine lining excellent. Her donor was in perfect health. Such calamities were possible, of course—she was on enough message boards and support groups— but she never thought she'd be one of the unlucky ones.

It was evening that same night. Sadie sat in the living room in the dark, looking out the blinds to the sloping street that overlooked the canyon. Where was Gillian? She'd been so supportive when Sadie gave her the bad news and promised to come home so they could order takeout as soon as she was done with work. Gillian's company was better than nothing. Sadie really, *really* didn't want to be alone. Her doomed thoughts were getting the best of her.

She dialed Gillian to see what the holdup was. Voice mail. She dialed again. This time, voice mail picked up before it even rang.

She frowned and lay down on the couch, her heart twisting. What felt like a lark, a fun little experiment, even a few months ago was now suddenly something she desperately wanted. *Needed.* Her life felt so stalled, suddenly. Now that she'd decided to have a child on her own, she wanted immediacy, progress.

She tried Gillian again. Still nothing. After the beep, she cleared her throat. "Um, can you come home?" she said in a small voice. "I'm having a hard time being alone. My thoughts are spiraling."

She waited for Gillian to call, but she didn't. What *was* that all about today at Gillian's office? Gillian had been twitchy the rest of the time they'd been together, like she couldn't wait to leave.

Sadie opened her laptop. Navigating to her Gmail, she pulled up an email Gillian had sent to her from her official address at *Wellness* magazine. At the bottom was an official-looking logo and signature. *Gillian Winters, Assistant to Cordelia Logan, Editor in Chief.*

But then she noticed something strange. Gillian's email ended in .net. Sadie navigated to the *Wellness* website, which provided a few free articles from that month's issue—including a letter from the editor in chief . . . whose name wasn't Cordelia Logan. It was someone named Stacey Ross. Cordelia was the *old* editor in chief; she'd moved on to another magazine several months earlier.

Puzzled, Sadie scrolled to the bottom of Stacey's letter, which included Stacey's email address at the magazine in case anyone had questions or comments. Stacey's email at *Wellness* ended with .com.

Sadie sat back, jiggling her legs.

A moment later, the key turned in the lock. When the door opened, Sadie rose from the couch and watched as Gillian stepped inside. "Where were you?"

"I got sucked into this work thing," Gillian said, pulling off her jacket.

Sadie caught a whiff of Gillian's breath and drew back. "Are you drunk?"

"Are you my mother?" Gillian walked back to the bedroom. She was buried in her phone. She'd barely looked up since she'd come in.

"You said you were going to come back hours ago," Sadie said in a small voice. "We were going to have dinner, watch some TV . . ."

Gillian's eyes darted to her for a moment. "I tried to call you. You didn't pick up."

"I had my phone on the whole time. There was no call."

"Well, I did. An hour ago. I had an awful day at work."

Gillian whipped around so forcefully that she banged her hip on a console table in the hallway. She let out a shriek and then stared murderously at the table, seizing a small bird made of felted wool that served as decoration. She squeezed the bird between her palms, let out an *ugh* from the back of her throat, and then dropped the bird to the floor in fury.

Sadie bit down hard on her lip. It was her bird; the felt was crushed inward from where Gillian had squeezed, right at the bird's wings.

"You okay?" Sadie asked.

"Yeah, fine," Gillian said gruffly. She stood in her bedroom doorway now. "Just tired." She finally looked at Sadie for the first time since she'd come home. "What's up with you?"

Something inside Sadie snapped. "What's up with *me*? Oh, I don't know, I found out I wasted twenty thousand dollars on a procedure that didn't work, and I'm probably not going to be a mother, but it's all good!" She almost added that she'd discovered that Gillian was possibly faking her job at *Wellness*, but all of a sudden, she felt too tired to get into it.

Gillian looked at her with a beat of pity. But then her phone beeped, and her attention flagged once more. Sadie clenched her jaw. She was tired of this person, this friendship. Something solidified in her mind.

She needed to stop feeling bad. This friendship had run its course.

Instagram post from @GillianAnxietyBabe

July 22

[Image description: A figure of a young woman in silhouette. The woman sits on a bare floor, her knees to her chest, her head on her knees. Her hair around her face. She looks to be in despair. The lighting is soft and shadowed.]

♡ ◯ ◁   ◻

Hi friends.

Same me. Same tipsy night. Two posts in one day! Aren't you lucky?

Not only am I so worried about L and her toxic friend, but things are now really, really falling apart with S and me. S caught me in a lie tonight. She thinks it makes her all high and mighty. It's hard for me to make her get why I lied. But maybe you guys will understand.

See, I told her I worked at this place, but I actually don't. But it doesn't sound as bonkers as you think. I really did go in for the interview. Honest. I wanted to work there. I was ready to kick ass. It's hard living with S. She just has it so . . .

together. She's a freaking doctor who owns her own home! I just wanted to show her I could accomplish stuff, too. I wondered if maybe I wasn't enough for her to keep around. Like maybe that was why she wanted a baby: because all she had to show for herself and her life was her amazing job. I thought if maybe I became less of a loser friend, she wouldn't be so ready to drop me.

Anyway, I went in for this interview. All of us are writers, right? All of us with communities here. And it was just an assistant position. What could go wrong?

But in the waiting room, they forgot about me for forty-five minutes. It made my anxiety go haywire. Then, the guy who was doing the interview was a decade younger than me. Even worse, he told me the salary—I swear it was below minimum wage. He smiled like he was doing me a favor. Like lots of women in LA would kill to work there.

And then, and this is the worst part, he made me take what's called an "editing test." I had never seen one before and surprises are not good for my mental health. I was given a story and had to make it sound better. There were marks on the page I couldn't make heads or tails of. I asked him what they were, and he made this lemon-sucking face and asked why I was even here.

But here's where it all comes together, friends. As I was leaving, there was this woman in front of me going out the regular door to the side of the revolving doors. I saw the badge around her neck, where she worked. And I did something I never do: I told her I liked her necklace. She

seemed really flattered. And then the security guard, who'd
been so nice before my interview, asked me if I got the job. I
don't know what made me say it, but it was maybe the cool
girl standing right there, and me wanting her to like me, but I
said that I had. The security guard congratulated me. And the
cool girl looked at me and said, "Cool, good for you. So see
ya around, then." Her smile was truly accepting, because I'd
been let into the club.

So, okay, I just sort of went with that. It wasn't like I had
anything else to do with my days. I fell into this . . . current, I
guess, imagining myself in that sort of life for real. I mean, it's
not like I really hurt anyone by saying I worked somewhere
I didn't. It was just a nice alternative reality for a while.
A way to take my mind off of how my life was crumbling
to shit.

And I thought, too, that maybe something good would come
out of the weird lie I was telling: At least maybe I'd get to
know this woman more. The woman who smiled at me. The
potential friend. New friends can change your life, you know.
And you can probably already guess, ladies, who that friend
ended up being.

TOP COMMENTS:

@anxiouskitten23: Oh G. I'm so sorry to hear this. ♡
Thank you for being honest with us, though. Thank you
for being AUTHENTIC.

@RTGz69: My heart goes out for you, honey. It's so ♡
hard. Of course you want to hold on to your friend. Of

course you want to make your life look as good as hers does. We are HERE for you!

@mimi_has_troubleZ: Such a jerk with the editing test. ♡
F him!

@lonely_girlRZ4540: Can I send you a DM? I have a ♡
question. Xo

17

LENNA

Sadie—Sarah—wears a flowered, empire-waist dress and delicate brown sandals. Her blond hair hangs straight down her back—not styled as the last time Lenna saw her, outside the *City Gossip* and *Wellness* offices, but still thick and pretty. Her stomach is flat, but she carries herself a bit swaybacked as if already straining under pregnancy weight. And she holds a knife in her hand. A kitchen knife, from the block Lenna saw inside.

The automatic lights over the fence snap off, bathing them in shadows. Lenna glances over her shoulder. *Where* is Rhiannon?

"I can't believe it," Sarah repeats. "I *know* you."

Lenna places her hand protectively around Jacob's body. "Don't hurt us." Tears dot her eyes, blurring her vision. She could try to run for it, but she wouldn't get far with the baby weighing her down.

"What are you doing here? How did you *find* me? What are you going to do?"

A line of spiny plants grows along the fence line; Lenna can feel a few of the needles stabbing her bare legs. She doesn't understand the question.

"I'm trying to leave." Lenna is hyperventilating, barely able to get the words out. "I had no idea you were here—I never would have come. Just let me leave, okay? For my son's sake. I talked to Rhiannon—"

Sarah stiffens. "What did you tell Rhiannon?"

"Just that I want to go home. I came here by accident, I swear. Rhiannon's on her way down." She's shaking so badly. "I'm sorry. I should have . . . I never meant to . . . i-it was such a mess. I didn't *mean* for it to happen. And the way it impacted *you* . . . just don't hurt me, okay? Don't hurt *us*." *Rhiannon,* she mentally screams.

Sarah lowers the knife an inch. Her eyes dart. "You really expect me to believe that you had no idea I was here?"

Lenna blinks. "Why would I have come if I knew you were here? And you go by Sarah. Not Sadie. I had no idea. And like I said, I would have *never* come if I knew you were here. It's why I . . . disappeared, pretty much."

"No, *I* disappeared."

They stare at each other.

Lenna feels confused, too. Then, something catches in her mind. *What are you going to do?* Sarah had said. Like she's *afraid* of Lenna.

There's a prickly sensation in her brain. She's felt this same kind of uneasiness before—the only other time Sarah sought her out, that time at Lenna's apartment. Why had Sarah done that?

She asks now. Sarah looks at Lenna as though it's beside the point—and then as though it is a stupid question. "Because I wanted to talk to you."

"But why come all the way over to my apartment? You could have just called me. It would have been much easier."

"Because . . ." But then Sarah puts her hands on her hips and glares.

"Did you know I didn't have a phone at the moment?" Lenna asks, her heart pounding. "Did you know it had gone missing?"

Sarah squints at her like she's trying to figure her out. "I mean, yeah," she finally says. "Obviously."

The knife stays raised in her hand, immobile. But Lenna's mind is exploding. That morning, Gillian said Sarah had already left for work, but had she? It wasn't like she'd checked for herself.

"You were there," Lenna whispers. "On . . . on the trail? When I confronted her?"

Sarah raises her chin. Her lips are mashed together, trembling.

Lenna's heart races for a new reason. "You were. You saw us, didn't you? You saw . . . *everything.*"

18

SARAH

A half hour after Gillian returned home and had her colossal fit, she knocked on Sadie's bedroom door, apologetic to the point of tears. "You're totally going through this awful thing and I've been a total shit." She clasped her hands. "Sometimes I don't know how to handle someone else's big feelings. But I care. I really do. Do you want to talk about it?"

No, Sadie thought. In fact, she'd been sitting on her bed, trying to figure out how she could tactfully kick Gillian out. One idea was to put the house up for sale and move out of LA altogether.

"It's okay. I'm feeling better," she lied.

"Seriously, I'm here for you," Gillian said. But then her phone pinged. Gillian glanced at her phone and made a face.

"Lot of stuff going on, huh?" Sadie mused.

"Just work stuff."

"*Work stuff,* huh?" She said it with a tinge of sarcasm.

Gillian looked at her sharply. "Why did you snoop at my office building? I felt so awkward in front of Lenna."

Sadie's mouth fell open. Why was she even bothering? "I came because I was sad and wanted to talk to my friend." Then she crossed her arms and decided to try another tack. In her best physician's tone, she said, "Look, Gillian, I know you've felt a little . . . wayward, lately. This has been a big time of transition for you—for us. But you don't have to pretend. And I hope you're not making things up just to get people to like you." *Like that Lenna person,* she thought.

Gillian raised her chin. Sadie thought she detected fear in her eyes. "What do you think I'm pretending about?"

Sadie stared. Gillian stared back. Was Gillian delusional, or was this deliberate? How long had this been going on, too? Before she started with the magazine—well, so she said—Gillian was at Sadie's house a lot, always on her phone or computer. But Sadie didn't know what she was up to—looking for a job, Gillian always said, but was that true? Maybe they weren't even friends—maybe Gillian was just using her. She was a stranger, essentially—Sadie wasn't sure about Gillian's real life at *all.* And sure, lots of people had strangers as roommates or boarders, but typically, the roommates and boarders *contributed.*

"Never mind. Forget it." Sadie was so tired. The day had been terrible. "I'm going to bed." She would deal with kicking Gillian out tomorrow.

With the help of a Xanax, Sadie fell asleep fast. But at three A.M., Sadie's eyes popped open again. The first things she thought of were the embryos. Despair swarmed her. The second thing she thought of was Gillian. Was this neglectful, letting Gillian get away with such duplicity? Gillian's behavior had to be a cry for help of some sort, and maybe it was Sadie's duty, as a doctor, to help her. She was possibly enabling some sort of mental health crisis. And what if Gillian's lies were affecting someone else?

She slipped out of bed for some water. It wasn't until she got to the doorway that she realized that Gillian's bedroom light was on. A ball lodged in her throat. Maybe she could talk to Gillian now.

She tiptoed down the hall; the door was open just enough. Gillian was *still* looking at her phone. Not typing. Not swiping, not anything. Just looking at something, her gaze unblinking. Was she . . . *reading* something? Sadie wasn't sure.

Sadie backed away, a sour feeling welling in her gut. She climbed back into bed, but she didn't fall asleep. Names of psychiatrists she knew drifted through her mind. She would call one of them in the morning. Get their take. She cared about Gillian, she did, but something was very off, ready to tumble.

The next morning, she got up and made coffee even though it was so early and she didn't have any appointments until midmorning. After a few minutes, Gillian appeared in the hall dressed in running gear.

"Hey," Sadie said quietly. "You're going running in this weather?"

Gillian shrugged.

"Maybe we could talk first?"

Gillian gave her a weird look. "Later." She turned for the door. "See you in a bit."

"Wait!" Sadie cried.

Gillian turned back. She looked annoyed. Combative. All the words Sadie planned to say jammed in her throat.

"Be careful," she said.

Gillian nodded and shut the door. Sadie stood there, irritated. All of a sudden she felt like she needed to confront Gillian. Now. She needed to take her life back.

She stepped out onto the slick, steep driveway. Sadie glanced toward the gray street, frowning at the rain. She saw Gillian jogging toward the street's dead end, heading for the trailhead. Sadie started to follow.

But then she noticed someone else was following Gillian, too.

The figure was hunched. When Gillian turned toward the canyon path, the figure turned with her.

Gillian reached the entrance to the trail. There was a little railing with an overlook to the winding trail below. Sadie didn't like peering over the railing, as it offered a view straight down the rocks. The trail wound down into the canyon; the people below—when there *were* people, on a nicer day—looked like ants.

"Gillian," whoever it was called out.

Gillian stopped. Turned. She stepped toward whoever it was, relief flooding her face.

The other person turned, too, catching the tiniest bit of light. It was that woman from the *Wellness* lobby. Lenna.

Lenna stood, arms crossed, her face a mask of discomfort. She was saying something about Gillian cloning her phone. Reading her texts. Lenna's posture seemed stiff and uncomfortable.

"Talking to her or not talking to her is *my* decision. Not yours," Lenna was saying.

The rain pelted Sadie's forehead, blurring her vision. She was starting to shiver, but she didn't dare leave her spot to go back inside. It was probably time to intervene. Despite all that they had been through, Sadie felt protective of Gillian.

Sadie squared her shoulders, ready to step forward.

But then Lenna said, "Get her to unblock me . . . or I'll tell Sadie."

Sadie froze at the sound of her own name.

Gillian looked amused. "Tell Sadie *what*?"

"How you were *happy* when her IVF failed."

Something got caught in Sadie's throat. The world went still.

"And . . . and that thing you said about the meds, too. About something being *wrong* with them. Oh God, you tampered with her medicine, didn't you? *You* made that treatment fail."

"Of course not!" Gillian cried.

But Sadie's knees buckled. She pictured those vials of medicine she'd kept in the fridge. Pulling them out every day, inserting a new needle into the top, drawing out the proper amount, injecting them into her abdomen. Sometimes leaving the tops off. Sometimes tending to other things before she put them away. She stored them in the fridge, in plain view, next to Gillian's oat milk.

Then Gillian grabbed Lenna's phone. A moment later—Sadie couldn't see quite how—it was flying through the air into the canyon. A beat of silent horror stretched long. It was anticlimactic, actually—no sounds of plastic hitting rocks because of the splattering rain.

"Fuck!" Lenna said, rushing to the railing. "Gillian, what the hell?"

Gillian grabbed her shirt, hard. Lenna jerked backward and rounded on Gillian, an accusing look on her face. Gillian blubbered that she was trying to *save* Lenna, not hurt her, but from where Sadie was standing, she wasn't so sure. Especially because right after that, Gillian grabbed Lenna around the waist and pushed her toward the edge again. Sadie clapped her hand over her mouth as Lenna's feet slid on the wet ground. Lenna tried to fight back, but Gillian had a good grip on her. Her hands circled Lenna's neck.

Because of this secret? Sadie thought with horror. So it *was* true?

Suddenly, she didn't want to just stand there anymore.

At her feet was a thick, heavy branch that had fallen from the storm. She grabbed it with both hands and stepped forward, straining under its weight, and she raised the branch over her head. Lenna didn't even have time to turn around before Sadie clocked her on the temple—hard, but not *that* hard. Just enough to keep her quiet for a little while.

The tall woman crumpled easily, falling almost gracefully to the ground. When Sadie looked up, Gillian was gaping at her, blinking stupidly through the rain.

"Sadie?" Her gaze shifted to Lenna and then back. "Thank God you're here. She's . . . she's unhinged. She just *ran* for me. Thank you for saving me from her."

"I can't believe you," Sadie whispered. "You know how much I wanted a baby."

She stepped forward, still holding the heavy branch. Gillian blinked hard. "Wait. Hold on. I didn't do that. Don't believe her."

"You're lying about everything. Who you are. Your *job.* You're really going to make *me* feel crazy for doubting you now?"

Gillian pinched a spot between her eyes. It took a while for her to speak. "What does it matter? I know you, Sadie, you can't have a baby with your life right now. People try, but something gives."

Sadie was stunned. "So you *did* tamper with my meds?"

Gillian shrugged. "It probably wouldn't have worked anyway. What is it they say? Fifty percent of pregnancies end in miscarriage."

It was the most asinine thing Sadie had ever heard. The worst part was that Gillian looked so *earnest,* like she actually believed what she was saying—that she was being helpful.

"Who *are* you, even?" Sadie hissed. "I want you out of my house. Now."

"I know." Gillian didn't miss a beat. "But you'd better watch it. I'll tell everyone you just clubbed an innocent woman with a tree branch." She pointed at Sadie. "You'll lose your license. Maybe even lose the right to have a child."

Sadie's chest burned with fury. "You wouldn't."

Gillian put her hands on her hips. "You know, it's clear we were never friends. I know I'm just your pity case. Just someone to fill the void because you're so fucking unlovable. Isn't that what that date said to you that time?" Her smile was teasing.

Sadie's mouth dropped open. It felt like Gillian had kicked her. Who *was* this person? How on earth was she part of Sadie's life?

Something inside her snapped. Her hands shot out. She pushed

Gillian hard, square at her chest. Gillian's face registered surprise. Her feet went out from under her, and her arms wheeled. She was over that pathetic little railing instantly. There was nothing she'd be able to grab on to—the rocks were so slippery in the rain, and the branches were mere twigs. As Gillian fell, Sadie screamed out her name and tried to grab her. But her fingers caught air. Gillian didn't answer.

Sadie stood there a long time, her hand clapped over her mouth. Then, with a groan, she turned to the right and puked all over the trail. It was like her stomach wouldn't stop emptying. She gagged and coughed and then sobbed for a good few minutes, so hard that her mouth tasted like salt. "Fuck," she groaned, hugging herself. "Oh fuck, oh *fuck*."

Then she turned to Lenna. The woman lay on the path, unconscious. Sadie considered dragging her to the house, but Lenna would ask questions when she awoke. Lenna would turn on *her*, maybe. It might be better to get out of here. She didn't know what Lenna had seen, but maybe, when she woke up, she wouldn't remember.

With shaking fingers, Sadie leaned down and took Lenna's pulse. It was steady and strong. The rain was cold and dreary, but the air temperature was around sixty if not warmer. It was unlikely the woman would suffer hypothermia. She'd wake up soon enough.

Did she feel bad, leaving her there? She felt terrible. But at that moment, she was only looking to save herself. Her future baby. The only thing, she realized even more that day, that she really wanted.

SHE HAD TO STAY CALM. SHE HAD TO THINK THIS THROUGH. SHE channeled her most worried, distraught self when making the call to the police that Gillian was missing. She wanted to do it *immedi-ately,* but she knew that would look strange and telling. So she waited until that evening—even went to work. She couldn't remember a single patient she saw or a single thing she said. All she could think of was Gillian's startled, angry face as she fell.

The cops asked Sadie all kinds of questions: when she'd last seen her friend (before running); if Gillian seemed upset (maybe a little distracted); if they'd been having issues (not particularly); if she knew anyone Gillian was arguing with (nope); if she was in trouble at work. Where she was working *in general.*

Where do I start? Sadie thought miserably. But maybe it was better to keep quiet about what she'd discovered about all the things Gillian was making up. Better to play the clueless friend who had no idea about anything Gillian was up to. As for Gillian's phone, she reported that Gillian was using cheapo temporary phones because she was sure she'd lost her expensive device somewhere in the house and was too stubborn to buy a replacement—she had no idea what the phone number was, because it always came up unlisted. The strangeness of Gillian never having a permanent phone had occurred to her before, but she'd thought it was maybe a money issue, Gillian finding it too overwhelming to budget for a regular monthly plan. But maybe she'd underestimated Gillian. The burner phones helped perpetuate her lies. Burners were harder to trace.

Then she told the cops what Gillian had told her about her job at *Wellness.* Let the cops unwind the lie for themselves. They'd come back to Sadie, surely, asking if she'd had an inkling, and Sadie would say, sure, she'd gone to Gillian's building the day before and they didn't have her listed in the system, but she thought it was a mistake, and then they'd chalk it up to an accident. Hopefully.

The story made the news. Thankfully, Sadie's name did not—only Gillian's. Sadie expected people to flock to LA for search parties. Gillian's family, certainly. Old friends. And yet no one showed up. Sadie didn't even know how to reach her family. They weren't online friends—Sadie wasn't online much to begin with, having removed a lot of her profiles after the assault. When she googled Gillian, she couldn't find a Facebook account. She rifled through Gillian's desk for an address book, a letter from her mom, a post-card from an old friend. There was nothing. She thought of the online social anxiety community Gillian mentioned. If only she'd sent a request to join the group like she said she would. At the time, she'd been sort of resentful of Gillian's neediness and didn't want to, but now it might give her a clue about who Gillian was close to and what went on in her head.

The cops went to *Wellness,* and the *Wellness* staff reported that Gillian had never worked there. As her picture was passed around, people started to say that yeah, they recognized her—lurking outside, sometimes even in the lobby. Proprietors reported seeing Gillian at lunch spots, things like that. As for other employers in the area, no one came forward to say Gillian was working for them, either. In fact, no one really seemed to know her or have any idea what she was up to *instead* of working.

Sadie was careful not to tell the cops about Lenna—for they would go to Lenna and ask her questions, and Lenna would point them right back to Sadie.

Where *was* Lenna, though? Why wasn't she coming forward, telling her side of the story?

The cops asked Sadie if she could verify where she was the day Gillian disappeared. Sadie blurted out something about seeing Mrs. Rosen early that morning, the only time there was an actual hole in her alibi—the rest of the day, she really *was* with patients. "She likes to meet early," she said, even though this wasn't necessarily true.

"Mrs. Rosen," the cop said, writing down her name. His name tag read *DIAZ.*

Diaz asked for Mrs. Rosen's phone number. "Just trying to be thorough. We're going to talk to the neighbors, too. See if they saw anything."

Sadie recited Mrs. Rosen's number only because she had to. She barely held it together until the cops left. Once the door closed, she slid down the wall and started to weep. What the fuck was she going to do?

Maybe she needed to talk to Lenna. Figure out what she knew. Maybe she could convince her not to say anything. They were both there. They were both guilty of . . . something, anyway. Maybe they could keep quiet together?

Not that she had any idea where Lenna lived. Calling the office building and asking might be suspicious. Even if she had Gillian's phone—which she didn't, as it had probably gone into the canyon with her—she wouldn't be able to get into her contacts. Instead, she turned on Gillian's laptop. It was an old model, so it didn't have a password to log in. The email program did, though. Gillian's password wasn't saved. Sadie clicked on the Google Chrome app, thinking that the pages Gillian had been looking at before shutting down the program might reload. But they didn't. Nor did she save cookies or browsing history.

Then her gaze drifted to a file off to the left. *Lenna invoice,* it read. She clicked it, and lo and behold, it was an invoice for a payment Lenna was requesting through Wellness Inc. for the first draft of a writing piece.

Sadie squinted. Was Gillian fake-assigning stories for her fake job at the magazine? In the upper right-hand corner was Lenna's home address. She even listed her social security number. Sadie felt sort of sorry for her, as sorry as she felt for herself. Hastily, she trashed this file, too, and then emptied the recycle bin.

Lenna lived in an apartment building in Hollywood, which sounded far more fancy than it actually was. The parking lot had broken glass everywhere. Someone was sleeping on the front steps to the lobby. Loud television sounds echoed from the unit next to Lenna's; two people were bickering.

She knocked on Lenna's door. No answer. She waited, shifting her weight, her heart pounding because suddenly she had no idea what she was going to say. What if Lenna wasn't home, but instead was at the hospital? What if Sadie had killed *two* people?

She said, "Hello?" Still nothing. Eventually, the two people who'd been bickering next door came onto the landing; Sadie jumped when they opened their door. One of them was a woman in a pink tracksuit and giant earrings. The other was a reedy man with tattoos on his forearms. They both stared at Sadie as though she was unwelcome.

There was no way Sadie could stand there with the two of them watching her. She apologized to the woman and went back down the echoing metal stairs.

When she came back to her house, there were police cars in the driveway. Her heart leapt to her throat. Someone had seen her, then. She considered turning around, but the cops had already spied her. There was no choice but to get out of the car. She tried to smile as she walked toward two detectives, including Diaz.

"Did you find Gillian?" she asked hopefully.

"Ms. Wasserman," Diaz said sternly, and Sadie could suddenly tell how it was going to go.

They brought her to the station for some questions. Two things had come to light: First, they'd unlocked Gillian's Instagram page. She was active in the mental health community, the cop explained; she wrote vulnerable, diary-entry-style Instagram posts, that sort of thing. He asked if Sadie knew about this.

"I did, but I didn't have access," Sadie admitted. "And I asked to see it, but she never let me in."

The cop nodded thoughtfully. Perhaps, he said, that was because

Gillian was quite brutally honest on the account. Often, Gillian talked about *her*. Apparently, Gillian said Sadie acted erratically.

"Erratically?" Sadie blinked hard.

"Can you think of what she might mean?" Diaz asked.

Sadie swore up and down that she always treated Gillian kindly, but it didn't matter. Because there was a second piece of evidence: An anonymous call had come in; someone had seen Gillian on the trail that morning . . . and Sadie, too.

"Me?" Sadie squeaked. "Who said that?"

Diaz smirked. "There's a reason it's called 'anonymous.'"

Lenna. So she'd come forward after all.

Still, she swore she wasn't there. She reiterated her alibi about Mrs. Rosen—not because she thought it was a good alibi, but because it was what she had blurted out at first, and maybe it would be worse if she changed her story now. But because of this, she demanded a lawyer. She didn't know if that made her look guilty, but she feared saying something she'd regret or getting caught up in twisted questioning.

The deck seemed stacked against her when she finally gained access to Gillian's private posts, too. It had been a fluke, discovering a way into the account: Gillian had a little book in her desk where she wrote down a whole bunch of passwords to accounts; miraculously, the Instagram password for @GillianAnxietyBabe was there. Sadie figured logging in to Gillian's Instagram on her own phone would raise some flags. She questioned if there was some IT expert at the police station watching and waiting for *anyone* to sign in to the account, thinking it might be a lead. But she took the gamble anyway, buying a burner phone at Walmart and entering Gillian's credentials. When she was in, no alarms sounded, and no one came for her.

But the posts didn't give her any peace. Gillian wrote to her followers that Sadie was unstable and unhinged. She said she threw shoes at her—which had *never* happened. She said Sadie wanted her out of her life—which, okay, was definitely her mind-set that last night, but Gillian implied that Sadie hated her from the get-go. A reaction to her baby decision, surely. But still . . .

There were so many posts that Sadie couldn't wade through all of them. She had to assume the account was a lie . . . but then Gillian admitted, on the page, to faking her job. She also truly did have eleven thousand followers. They actively commented on Gillian's posts, cheering her on and expressing sympathy. They also sent her a lot of DMs, quite a few of them unread. It was too much for Sarah to weed through. On both her second-to-last and last posts, the comment sections were jammed with people begging for an update, puzzled about why she hadn't posted again. Then, someone leaked the news that Gillian was missing. Then there were a barrage of sympathetic comments once people learned the news—as well as suspicious ones. *Does anyone else think it's weird that S caught her in a lie and now she's missing?* And *Justice for @GillianAnxietyBabe!* And *Cops need to talk to S. She's hiding something.*

They weren't wrong.

The commenters—and the police—were also interested in two other people Gillian's posts made reference to: L and R. It seemed she desperately wanted to befriend them. *Someone needs to question them, too,* one person wrote. *This poor girl was all alone—people were treating her like shit, even those she thought were friends!* One of the women might be Lenna, Sadie figured. But who was the other? She told the cops she didn't know.

"But I thought you were roommates," Diaz said.

"We didn't tell each other everything." Wasn't *that* the truth.

"The way she puts it, you two disagreed about something," Diaz pushed, again and again. "Was it about L and R? What lie did you catch her in? Are you *sure* you weren't on that trail?"

Her lawyer told her not to answer. Sadie thought about the fight, the triggers. Had Gillian *actually* tampered with her meds? Because the more she thought about it, the more she wasn't sure Gillian could have. After she gave herself the shots, she sometimes would slip into the bathroom for a moment, leaving the meds unattended—but only a moment. When she came out of the bathroom, it wasn't like the meds had been moved, and it wasn't like Gillian was standing over them or something. She couldn't think of an instance where Gillian was even near the kitchen when this all went down. Had Gillian just blurted something out the way she sometimes did, not really thinking through the consequences, just to get a rise out of her, a messy way of stating how hurt she felt?

Except then she'd taken it one step further. She'd also said that nasty comment about Sadie's assailant. And *laughed* about it. She'd found Sadie's most open, festering wound . . . and plunged in the knife. Sadie wasn't sure she could square that part in her mind.

She was released from the station while the cops gathered more evidence on the case, but for a few weeks, she was a person of interest. Her lawyer didn't seem interested in whether Sadie had actually killed Gillian—in fact, he asked that she not even *tell* him. All he was looking for was someone else they might be able to pin it on.

"These friends, L and R," he said. "I'd love to find them." He held up his phone; Gillian's account was on the screen. "Even her Instagram friends have theories that they were behind it."

Right around this same time, the boss at the hospital group Sadie's practice was affiliated with called. Sadie didn't even know being implicated in a crime could threaten one's license, but all of a sudden, she was asked to transfer her patients to one of the other doctors in the practice. Just for visibility reasons, it was said, until this blew over. Sadie was crushed, and then angry. What *else* would Gillian take?

It was Tuesday morning. Over three weeks after that morning at the canyon. Sadie felt like she was drowning. If she had no job for much longer, she wouldn't be able to afford her house. And forget fertility treatments. Tears streamed down her face. She felt so freaking *alone.* It only occurred to her after Gillian was gone how much time they actually spent together; Gillian had become the only person Sadie really saw when she wasn't working.

As she stepped into the bathroom, a number popped up from the LAPD. Bile rose in her throat. Her voice cracked when she answered hello.

"Checks out," a man's voice said on the line.

"Excuse me?"

"Oh, sorry, Ms. Wasserman—it's Detective Diaz. I mean your alibi. We finally talked to Mrs. Rosen—she was out of town with her daughter and hadn't really turned on her phone. She vouched for you on that morning, and there's no video evidence putting you at the scene at the canyon."

Sadie nearly dropped the phone. She stared at her slack face in the steamy mirror. *Mrs. Rosen vouched for me?* she thought.

"So the case against you is dropped. To be honest, I don't think this was foul play anyway. Some of your friend's items were found in the canyon: a key chain you described, an earring matching ones she was wearing in an online post . . ."

"Oh," Sadie whispered.

"It was wet out that morning." He sighed. "Lotta people slipping on trails. Mudslides everywhere."

She got her job back. She was able to drop the lawyer, though she didn't get back a lot of the retainer she paid him. But still, she felt vulnerable. As much as she could stand it, she perused Gillian's Instagram page—well, only the posts about her—trying to figure out why Gillian said such terrible, untrue things about Sadie. Had she ever really been Sadie's friend at all? It was her turn to feel slighted. Despite everything, she and Gillian were close once. It hurt to think Gillian was painting a very different picture of her online. Almost setting her up to be a suspect in her own murder, macabre as that was.

A few weeks later, Sadie was walking in Beverly Hills when she saw a woman with a coat-hanger shoulder slump coming toward her. Her whole body shut down. Was that *Lenna?* Sadie ducked behind a post, her heart pounding. She couldn't allow Lenna to see her. On one hand, she suspected that Lenna was the anonymous tipster. Who else could it be? Strange that she'd come forward anonymously, but maybe she didn't want to get in the middle of things. She was probably disappointed that Sadie had been set free. She *knew* what Sadie did.

The woman passed. Her features were thicker. She spoke on the phone in a jocular voice. Sadie was almost disappointed. As much as she didn't want to face Lenna, it felt like this was the only other person in the world, besides her, who had a personal connection to Gillian. Who actually *cared.* Ironic, then, that they'd both been there on the day of her death. That Gillian had betrayed both of them so completely.

It was harder than Sadie expected to go back into work. Her patients were wary of her; seemingly all of them had heard the news. She blamed Gillian. She blamed herself. She even blamed Lenna. Should Sadie confess? Maybe she deserved punishment. Of course she did. She hated herself.

But then. Then, she met the woman who would bring her *here.* The person who reminded her about the thing she really wanted: a child. A child who would save her. And at this place, that felt possible. She would have purpose again. She would be redeemed.

Until now.

19

LENNA

OCTOBER
PRESENT DAY

You were there," Lenna whispers, shielding her baby at her chest. "On that trail. You heard what I said to her. You saw when she threw my phone into the canyon. Right?"

A muscle twitches in Sarah's cheek. She still hasn't dropped the knife. Nor has the door opened from inside, nor have any lights been flicked on, even. It breaks Lenna's heart that Rhiannon could be inside, purposefully deciding *not* to help her and her baby.

"Why didn't you tell anyone?" Lenna asks. "After it happened— why didn't you say something?"

Sarah's brow furrows. And then, in one swift movement, she pushes Lenna into the garage through the creaky open door.

"What are you talking about?" Sarah growls.

"Please," Lenna whimpers, tears gathering behind her eyes. The small space is dark and hot and smells like gasoline. Several four-wheeler vehicles crowd the space. Jacob lets out a whimper, too.

"What did you just say?" Sarah repeats.

Lenna swallows hard. She can feel the tip of the knife's blade touching her skin. "I . . . I said wh-why didn't you tell them what you saw?"

"Why would I do that?"

"It would have gotten you off the hook." She looks away. "You could have told them what I did."

Sarah shifts her weight. Finally, the knife falls a few inches to her side. She looks like someone has spun her around and she isn't sure which way is up.

"What you . . . did?" Sarah says. She steps back. "What *you* did," she repeats. She looks like she's just regained consciousness. A strange smile spreads across her face.

And suddenly, another new idea glimmers inside Lenna. There's something about the woman's expression, her *energy,* that opens another door.

The notion explodes, fanning out like ripples in water. Could it be that Sarah's attack on her is not in self-defense?

Sarah is holding the knife because Lenna knows something dangerous about *her.*

"Wait a minute," Lenna whispers. "You . . . you didn't *want* them to know you were there. I wasn't the one who pushed her . . . you did?"

"Shut *up,*" Sarah snaps. "You knew it was me. You told on me in the first place. And it's why you're here now. Are you, like, some kind of vigilante?"

"*No.*" Lenna shakes her head desperately. "I just . . . I just figured it out right now." Her heart is thrumming. "Is this why you're afraid? You think I've come here to . . . *find* you?"

It all makes sense. When she woke up on the bench, her head had throbbed. She figured it was from her fight with Gillian, but maybe not.

"You hit me on the head," she realizes. "You left me on a bench, wet and cold and afraid!"

"I wasn't thinking clearly." Sarah's mouth forms a line. "Though when I left, you weren't on a bench. You were on the ground."

"That's supposed to make me feel better?" Lenna asks.

Sarah shrugs. She looks baffled. "You really had *no idea* I was there until right now?"

Lenna shakes her head. Oh, how she wished she had. It would have changed the course of her life. Though she doubts she would have done anything differently. Because she understands, instantly, Sarah's rage, especially if she overheard the part about Gillian tampering with her embryos. Gillian manipulated people's lives. It was infuriating.

But she would have lived her life differently. The past two years, she wouldn't have been so paranoid and afraid.

"You heard that stuff about the embryos, is that it?"

Sarah winces. A look of great pain crosses her features. "I did."

Lenna blows out her cheeks. "She got hurt so easily. She thought she was losing me as a friend. She was acting really erratically, especially that last day. I tried to give her a wide berth. I let a lot of things go. I tried to ignore a lot of what she said."

"Same. And she was having a hard time with losing me as well."

Lenna takes a breath. "You knew she was faking her job?"

"I figured it out before. The day you saw me, actually, at the office."

"I had no idea she wasn't working there. And when I met her in the canyon, I wasn't angry. Well, I *was,* but I certainly didn't intend to hurt her."

"I didn't intend that, either," Sarah whispers. "I was just so . . ." She shakes her head. "That whole thing about the embryos, and then she made this reference to this thing that happened in my past . . ." She bursts into tears and covers her face.

"Hey," Lenna says, though she isn't sure she wants to comfort

Sarah. Ironic, though: In those few minutes at the trailhead, both of them discovered just how duplicitous this person they cared about was. The curtain was ripped away in one fell swoop.

Lenna clears her throat. "She hurt us both so badly. I'm so, so sorry for what she might have done to you. But I'm not going to hurt you. I won't tell. I'm leaving, I swear. Can you please move the knife away from my baby? *Please?*"

The knife trembles. After a few seconds, Sarah wilts to the floor, the knife clattering beside her onto the ground. She shuts her eyes and buries her face in her hands. "This is all so fucked up," she says.

Lenna stands there, considering. *Now* should she run? But Sarah seems so weak and vulnerable. She kneels down slowly. Sarah lets out a groan.

"I hate her," Sarah mutters. "So fucking much."

Lenna nods. Maybe there were signs she should have seen as well. "I bought her lies easily, too. I accepted that things were a certain way just because she said so. It's like . . . I *wanted* to believe them. I wanted to think she had a good job and was looking out for my best interests. There's a part of me that is still like, *was* she being a good friend, deep down? In her own twisted way? She was there when I really needed someone."

"But who sabotages a woman's embryos?" Sarah shakes her head. "Not that I'm even certain she did."

"I wish I had warned you," Lenna realizes. "She joked about it to me, but I never believed she'd do it."

Sarah shrugs. "It's over with." Then she eyes her. "I was sure you saw me on the trail. So you weren't the one who sent the anonymous tip to the cops?"

Lenna shakes her head. "No, but I heard about it."

"I wonder who it was, then?"

Tension is still vibrating inside Lenna. It's the same way she felt in those days after Gillian went missing, certain that the police would add up all the pieces and find her. But . . . she *didn't* do anything. She isn't the killer. It's weird, realizing that, finally. Everything she thought was true isn't. She waits for relief to come, but it doesn't. The trauma, the sadness, the fear, the disappointment—all of it remains.

"How did they end up dropping the case against you?" Lenna asks. Because it hits her then—Sarah actually *did* do it.

"A patient vouched for me." Sarah looks away. "I never really got to thank her, that's the shittiest part. She died shortly after all this went down." Her gaze flicks to Jacob again. "And you had a baby, huh?"

Lenna nods, touching Jacob's cheek. "I hoped he'd save me."

"And has he?"

"Yes," Lenna answers. "But . . . also no. I mean, I'm still me. It still happened."

Sarah looks at her belly. "Yeah. Huh."

They share a comfortable, silent moment. It fills Lenna with uncanny companionship. Here is the one person in the world who maybe understands her best. Odd that it's the person she feared most.

"You really didn't follow me here?" Sarah asks. "Track me down?"

"Of course not. I mean, I did come because I thought being here would help me get over what happened. But as soon as I realized you were . . . *you,* I tried to escape." Lenna points at the Suburban out the little garage window.

"Who brought you in here?"

"Rhiannon." Lenna looks toward the door again, as if Rhiannon will step outside, finally, on cue.

"Really?" Sarah cocks her head. "How do you know her?"

"She's one of my closest friends. From LA. She's the one I was fighting about with Gillian at the canyon, actually. Did you hear that part? Gillian was texting Rhiannon from my phone's account. Gillian knew both of us, but then Rhiannon left. I actually thought she somehow orchestrated us getting together, or was working with you in some sort of revenge, though she swears she wasn't . . ." Lenna trails off and looks at Sarah. "What?"

Sarah's face is pale. "*Rhiannon* is R?"

". . . Who's R?"

Sarah clutches the side of her head. "This is bad."

"Why?"

"Because," Sarah whispers. "Rhiannon was the one who re-cruited *me* to come here, too."

20

SARAH

A few months after Gillian's accident, Sadie still felt like she was being followed. She never saw anyone tailing her. It was more of a premonition.

She was slogging through life. She woke writhing in the dead of night. She kept seeing Gillian's wide eyes as she fell. She felt rain on the back of her neck. She saw Lenna lying there, too, inert, unconscious, all because Sadie had hit her. She couldn't focus. Some days she couldn't eat. She just needed to start over, to *change,* to *forget,* but she didn't know where or how.

It was September. The weather was hotter than Sadie ever remembered. She stopped into a coffee shop on Santa Monica Boulevard for a shot of espresso. As she was waiting for her turn, the bells chimed, and another woman stepped in line. Sadie wasn't sure how, but she could tell the new woman who'd just come into the café was here for her. Her gaze seemed to bore pointedly and meaningfully into Sadie's back.

Sadie ordered and hurried over to the counter for some napkins. Just as she predicted, the woman took her place next to her, reaching for a sugar packet. For a split second, Sadie worried it was Lenna. The fact that Lenna had dropped off the face of the earth and hadn't come forward when Sadie was no longer a suspect just didn't add up. Sadie was waiting for her to reemerge.

It was a woman with auburn curls instead. "Are you Sadie?" she asked quietly. "Sadie, um, Wasserman?"

Her skin prickled. "Do I know you?"

"No." She glanced at the tables. "Can we sit? Just for a minute?"

Sadie stiffened. "What's this about?"

The woman's smile was unassuming. "Really, it would be better if we just sat down."

Sadie didn't know why she indulged her. They sat by the window, watching cars stream by. The woman pulled the lid off her coffee and blew on the liquid. She glanced up guiltily. "I heard you had a friend who died."

The hair on the back of Sadie's neck stood on end. "Where did you hear that?"

"The news."

"I wasn't *on* the news."

"No, sorry, I meant from around the neighborhood, really. I recognized you, just now. It's a terrible thing." She shuddered. "I'm really sorry. I've had weird tragic stuff in my life, too—I know how it feels."

Sadie's stomach did a flip. "Who are you? What do you want?"

"Sorry. I'm just someone who cares."

Someone who cares? Sadie stood. "I should be going."

"Look, you can absolutely tell me if I'm out of line," the woman said hurriedly. "But I think I might be able to help you get past this."

"I doubt it." Sadie reached for her bag. "Thanks, though."

"Are you grasping for something you can't find? Do you need things that you just can't get? I went through some trouble a while ago. I lived in LA, too, once upon a time, but I had to leave abruptly. And for a while, I was at my wit's end. But then I found this community. Of women. We live together, work together, but we're all a little . . . *broken,* I think? Like, we've been through stuff. I've been there for a little while now, and I have to say, it's wonderful."

Sadie blinked at this woman. And this had to do with her *why*?

"Halcyon is women-only. Well, and children, too, but no adult men. I have a baby, and I have tons of help." She leaned in closer. "It is a *game-changer.*"

The woman had an open, expectant face, but her eyes were gleaming in a way Sadie didn't trust. "Good for you," Sadie said diplomatically.

"We're tasked with finding other women who might benefit from the community—and who might fit into the lifestyle. You're from Washington State, right? You participated in 4-H club, county fairs? So you know what it's like to farm."

Sadie's heart seized. "How did you know that?"

The woman raised her palms. "Here I come, barging into your life while you're grieving. I'm sorry. It's just—I thought this sort of thing might help you. Joining us for a weekend, I mean. Do you ever just wish you could get away? Have time to really think, really breathe? Do you ever think, if you just had the space and time, everything would be better and you'd know what you wanted?"

"Really, I'm not interested." Sadie was relieved. This was just some hippie following her around, trying to recruit her for her cult.

"No problem!" the woman said brightly. "Totally get it. Just—in case you change your mind, here." She slipped Sadie a piece of paper with some scrawl, including her name. "It really is a healing place—and, no pressure, but highly difficult to get into. And we have interesting initiatives for women. Including a fertility collective."

"A what?"

"We contribute money to an IVF fund. Most women there are mothers, but some people who move in are still trying. We want to facilitate that process. This one woman, Melissa? She's had two children through the fund. We're all helping to raise these kids. It's a godsend, especially for women who want more than anything to be mothers." She smiled. "Do you have kids?"

Sadie couldn't keep her hands from trembling. "I have to go."

"It might be good for you to escape!" the woman called after her. "Because of what you did?"

Sadie turned slowly. "*What* did you say?"

The woman smiled guilelessly. "It's a really good escape. For mothers and kids."

The coffee shop bustled. Someone clinked a spoon against a ceramic mug. Sadie's brain was just playing tricks. That was all.

"Good luck," she mumbled to the woman, walking backward out the door. It was only when she was outside that she looked at the card. *Rhiannon Cook,* she'd written. *Halcyon Ranch.* And then a phone number.

What-fucking-ever.

21

LENNA

W *hat?*" Lenna whispers.

"Rhiannon recruited me to come here," Sarah repeats. "Meaning . . . she brought *both* of us here. And now she's in Gillian's life, too?"

She walks Lenna through how Rhiannon tracked her down about six weeks after Gillian disappeared. At the first meeting, she says, Sarah wanted nothing to do with Rhiannon's proposal to come to Halcyon. "But . . . after she left, I couldn't stop thinking about it. A fertility collective. Maybe I'd get to have my baby. I felt afraid to try again. I wasn't sure if I could do it by myself."

"When was this?" Lenna whispers.

"September."

Lenna does the quick math—she had left LA by then to live with Daniel outside the city. So Rhiannon was already *here*, at Halcyon, recruiting people?

"Rhiannon said nothing about knowing me when she talked to you?" Lenna asks.

Sarah shakes her head. "But you two worked together, is that right? And Gillian was . . . trying to horn in on your friendship, I guess?"

"Did Gillian tell you that?"

"No. I read it on Gillian's Instagram way after the fact, after she died. Gillian talks about two friends she wanted to get to know, L and R. I'm assuming you're L."

"And Rhiannon is R?"

"According to Gillian, Rhiannon was the reason she faked having that job. She wanted to get close to Rhiannon. But then Rhiannon rejected her, and Gillian never got over it. She could hold a grudge."

Lenna nods. She remembers that grudge. "But this is so strange. Did Rhiannon know what happened to Gillian when you guys met?"

"I have no idea. She made it out like it was all happenstance. Like she'd . . . read about me, or asked a neighbor, just knew I was suffering but maybe not why. Certainly not that she *knew* you or Gillian or had any personal stake in what happened." Then she pauses. "Although . . . she did say this one weird thing. Like she knew what I'd done. Or at least that's what I *heard,* I thought, but then I just told myself I was going crazy." She shudders. "But . . . maybe I wasn't."

Lenna sinks to an overturned milk crate. Jacob's legs hang limply between her own. He has passed out against her chest. "Do you think she *knows*?"

"I have no idea," Sarah murmurs. "What about when Rhiannon invited *you* here? Did she make any references to Gillian? Or me?"

Lenna glances at the house once more. It would be so much easier if Rhiannon were with them to explain herself. "I mean, she mentioned your name, said you were pregnant . . . but I knew you as Sadie. Sarah's a common name."

Sarah looks down. "I changed it, after I came. On the news, I was called Dr. Sadie Wasserman. Not Sarah. It concealed me, a little."

"Do you think Rhiannon knew more than she was letting on?" Lenna thinks about the shock on Rhiannon's face earlier today, when Lenna said she hung out with Gillian after Rhiannon left. *Sarah had a friend named Gillian, too,* she'd said. *But she died.* Did she really not know they were the same person when she'd been the one to recruit both Lenna and Sarah?

"Has Rhiannon given you any indication while you've been here that she knows more about you than she let on?" Lenna asks next.

Sarah shrugs. "Not really. We aren't particularly close, but she's always been fine. Grateful, actually, that I joined. I always wondered if she got a cut of my community buy-in fees or something. And she's been supportive about the IVF stuff. That's why this doesn't make sense that she'd be . . . I don't know, *conspiring* in some way."

Lenna chews on a thumbnail. "I think *something* is going on with her." She mentions the whispered phone call. The lies she's caught Rhiannon in. How sleepy she and Jacob have felt, maybe from the tea. Even the fact that Rhiannon promised to help her tonight . . . but she still hasn't shown up.

Sarah crosses her arms. "Let's go find her. Together. We need to figure out what's going on."

She drops her bags and starts off toward the house. Lenna hefts the baby higher in the sling as she follows, not knowing what else to do. They're halfway through the door when they hear the scream.

It's a child's voice from inside one of the rooms. Lenna's nerves snap. She starts to run down the hall as lights switch on and doors fly open. Lenna hears the name *Rhiannon,* and her stomach flips.

The kitchen is empty. She rounds the corner and heads down

the hall. Rhiannon's door is open. Melissa stands just inside, blinking groggily. Teddy is pressed into her waist, sobbing.

"What is it?" Lenna cries. "What happened?"

Marjorie steps out of Rhiannon's room, raising her palms. Gia follows her with a shrug, and Lenna bristles at her presence. Lenna peeks inside Rhiannon's tiny space.

The wood floor is bare. A table lamp casts shadows across the furniture. The only sounds are Teddy's whimpers.

"What's going on?" Lenna asks the group. "Where's Rhiannon?"

Gia turns to Lenna. For the briefest of moments, surprise registers on her face when she sees Sarah. But maybe Lenna imagines it, because in the next instant, Gia straightens. "Rhiannon's gone."

22

LENNA

one?" Lenna cries. "Gone where?" And then Jacob, perhaps sensing her stress, wakes up and starts crying, too.

Melissa turns to Teddy, giving him a brave, protective smile. "It's okay. Your mommy's probably just on a walk. Let's go back to sleepies. I'll stay with you."

Teddy sniffs. He looks exhausted, and he accepts Melissa's hug. "Good boy," Melissa murmurs, guiding him back toward his bed. "That's it . . ."

More doors open in the hall. Footsteps sound. A few of the older kids creep to Rhiannon's doorway. "What's going on?" one of them asks, shooting daggers at crying Jacob. "Did I hear a scream?"

"Teddy had a bad dream, and it woke up the baby," Marjorie says quickly, walking toward them. "Go back to bed."

Lenna turns to the others. Marjorie is rubbing her eyes. She looks annoyed that her sleep was interrupted. Lenna bobbles Jacob, shushing him. No one will get back to sleep at this rate.

"Marjorie," Sarah says, "where could she be?"

Marjorie's shoulders fall, and she lets out a long sigh. "Let's check outside."

She heads to the door. Lenna goes after her, and Sarah does, too. A few women follow. One of them is Gia. She glances over her shoulder, her gaze landing on Sarah and Lenna together.

"I see you two have met," she says smoothly, almost like she's holding in a snicker.

Lenna's hands ball into fists. What does *that* mean?

They walk into the yard. The sky is inky, and something about the topography of the canyons makes Jacob's screams echo hauntingly. Finally, Lenna reaches for the emergency bottle she'd prepared for the cab ride, tucked into her backpack. Screw Marjorie and her breast-is-best philosophy. She guides it into her baby's mouth, and he's instantly soothed.

After a cursory check around the yard, they determine Rhiannon isn't nearby.

Marjorie stifles a yawn. "Has anyone tried calling her?"

Lenna isn't sure whether she should volunteer what she knows.

Gia taps her phone. "Trying her now." She waits a moment, then glances at the others. "Voice mail."

"Was anyone else on the property today?" Lenna asks. "Like, beyond just us?"

Marjorie gives her a peculiar look. "No."

"There's no way someone can get in? Does anyone have access? The gate code?"

Something flickers across Marjorie's face, but then disappears. "We all take night walks from time to time. I'm sure that's all this is."

"But . . ." Lenna bites down so hard on the inside of her cheek. She can feel Gia waiting. She doesn't want to ask this with Gia here, but she has no choice. "Didn't Rhiannon speak with you? About . . . me?"

Marjorie frowns. "What about you?"

The contents of Lenna's stomach start to swirl. "I had planned to leave. Rhiannon was going to drive me to the turnoff. We planned to meet about a half hour ago."

"Leaving so soon, Lenna?" Gia asks, head cocked.

Marjorie shakes her head. "She didn't say a thing about this. Why do you need to go?"

Lenna's heart pounds harder. "It's my husband," she says, thinking quickly. "I need to go back, talk with him. I know there's a policy that we can't have phone conversations with men while on the property." Maybe if she mentions a rule she *does* follow, it will earn her some brownie points. "Rhiannon was going to help me get to the road. So her vanishing right now . . . when she said she was going to drive me . . . it doesn't make sense."

Marjorie shrugs. "Rhiannon never asked for the gate code *or* to use the car. It seems there were some crossed wires."

"Maybe she bailed on you," Gia says. Her tone is flat. When Lenna glances at her, Gia stares back, unblinking.

"She'll turn up." Marjorie pats Lenna's shoulder. "Once, I went on a three-day hike. Camped on the property. Perhaps Rhiannon caught that same whim."

"I can walk around the perimeter," Amy volunteers. "As long as you don't mind checking on my kids. I'm already up—might as well."

"Take the antivenom kit," Marjorie tells her. "But thank you. Good idea."

Amy nods and starts toward the back of the house. Marjorie follows. "Wait," Lenna squeaks, and Marjorie turns. "Um, about me leaving. Is that possible? Someone else can drive me tomorrow morning, maybe?"

Marjorie sinks into one hip. "The desert calls us here, Lenna. Do you think the desert is ready for you to leave?"

"Yes," Lenna blurts.

Marjorie shrugs. "Well, I don't think tomorrow will work. We have a full schedule with the car. Can it wait another few days?"

Lenna is vibrating. Another few *days*? "But the turnoff isn't even *far*. I can walk."

"With a baby?" Marjorie raises her chin. "In the heat? And even if you make it to the road, it sometimes takes car services hours to get out this way." She shrugs. "Had you mentioned this earlier, we could have worked something out. But don't worry. We'll get you there. Okay?"

Lenna lets her arms fall to her sides. Marjorie heads back in. Gia hangs back a moment, eyeing Lenna, her lips parted as if she intends to speak.

"What?" Lenna snaps, her patience worn thin.

"Nothing," Gia says, almost like a tease. "Hope everything works out with your hubby." She turns on her heel and heads inside, too.

The door finally closes. Sarah lets out a breath. "Jesus. *That* one."

"Gia?" Lenna dares to ask. "You think she's . . ."

". . . Odd? Shady? Sneaky? Making it impossible to figure out what the hell she's even doing here? Yes. All of the above."

"Oh my God, *thank you*." Lenna wants to hug her. "I felt that the moment I got here, but I've felt bad saying so."

"Marjorie expects us to turn into saints when we get here, but human nature is human nature." Sarah leans in closer. "I don't know why Marjorie even let her be a resident."

"Same," Lenna cries. "And what do you think about Marjorie not letting me leave?"

"Marjorie doesn't like when the status quo is disrupted. When I was out of town for my appointments? She called me *all the time*. Kept asking what I was doing at any given moment. Wanted to know exactly when I was coming back. I think she feared I was going to bolt."

"Do you think Rhiannon never asked Marjorie for the code tonight?" Lenna whispers. "Or do you think Marjorie is lying?"

"If given the choice of trusting Marjorie or Rhiannon, I'd probably trust Marjorie." Sarah looks around. "Because where is Rhiannon *now*?"

"I just can't think she'd leave Teddy for a night hike," Lenna muses.

"Could she have left?" Sarah wonders. "Maybe she climbed the fence."

Lenna thinks of Gia's story about Marjorie's son getting out back in the day. Maybe it was possible. "But, again—Teddy?"

Sarah shrugs. "Maybe she was sick of this place. It happens."

A thought hits Lenna, suddenly. She pats at her pocket. "*Shit.* Rhiannon still has my ATM card. I completely forgot."

Sarah stares at her. "Why'd you give her your ATM card?"

Then Lenna remembers something. "She . . . she said she was going to book me a hotel for the night. And then I'd get a flight the next morning." She covers her face with her hands. Her ATM card was the only money she brought with her, besides some cash. Now she doesn't have enough to get a hotel room on her own *or* a flight.

Her phone beeps. It's an email, picked up by the Wi-Fi service. Lenna squints at the sender's name, then draws in a breath.

"What?" Sarah asks sharply.

"It's . . . from *Rhiannon,*" Lenna whispers.

Sarah moves closer. Lenna taps the email notification. The body of the message contains no text, only an audio file. All kinds of possibilities zoom through her mind.

With a shaking finger, she presses on the file, and the file slowly loads, flickering against her and Sarah's faces.

PART
THREE

23

RHIANNON

When Rhiannon Cook received the message that would change her life, she was in her office at work. She was so surprised, she dropped her phone into her trash can, which happened to be right beneath where she was sitting at her desk.

When she fished it out, she stared in amazement at the note on the screen. Her heart banged hard in terror and confusion. But it also soared with hope.

"Hey!"

Rhiannon jolted up. Her friend Lenna leaned in the doorway. But then her face fell. "Oh. Sorry. Am I interrupting?"

Rhiannon looked again at her phone, trying to appear neutral. "Just lots of work."

Lenna nodded, but she didn't leave right away. "So I was thinking of seeing a movie. Maybe around six?"

Rhiannon shook her head. "Can't, love. Sorry."

Lenna sighed, but then she left the office. When Rhiannon was sure she was alone, she stared at her phone again. There really *was* a message.

From *her.*

The new message seemed to almost glow radioactively. Rhiannon couldn't concentrate on anything else. She slipped her phone into her pocket and hurried down the building's stairs to avoid Lenna seeing. She felt guilty, deceiving her friend, but she needed time to process this. It wasn't really something she could explain.

She pushed open the door to the lobby. It was empty, save for one person, who spotted her right away.

"Rhiannon! Hey!" that overbearing—and, let's face it, creepy—woman Gillian said, her smile broadening.

Rhiannon's whole body tensed. "Hey," she said in monotone, and kept walking.

Gillian fell in step. "How are things? You busy?"

"Yes. Very."

"God, me, too. *Wellness* is running me in circles."

Wellness. Right. That was where she worked. Rhiannon didn't reply.

"So I was wondering if you wanted to get lunch? You and—Lenna, is it?"

Rhiannon's head throbbed. Why did this woman seem so fascinated with her? She'd noticed her watching them so many times. Finally, at the revolving doors, Rhiannon stopped short and looked at her. "I don't think so. Not with me, and not with Lenna, either."

Gillian looked like Rhiannon had kicked her. "Oh." She licked her lips. There were tears in her eyes, actual tears. "Okay. Sorry." She started to walk away, but then she turned back, jaw trembling, her hands balled into fists. "You know, I have a really hard time talking to people. You don't have to be such a bitch."

Oh, how Rhiannon was not in the mood. "You don't have to be so weird," Rhiannon said under her breath.

Then she walked away. She didn't feel sorry for saying it. Not one bit. Because here was the thing: She'd always been able to spot a liar. And Gillian was most definitely a liar. About what, Rhiannon wasn't sure.

Then she thought of the message that had popped up on her phone moments before.

Hi baby, it read. *It's me. Your mom. Wondering if you wanted to come for a visit. It's been a long time.*

Of course Rhiannon knew Gillian was a liar. Liars knew their own kind. That was because Rhiannon was a liar, too.

Instagram post from @GillianAnxietyBabe

June 8

[Image description: A young woman with brown wavy hair stands against a pale background. Her hands cover most of her face so only her eyes are visible. Her brow is furrowed. She looks distraught. She stares straight into the camera.]

♡ ◯ ◁   ◨

Friends, I've never been so humiliated. I went to shoot my shot, and I crashed and burned. I want to curl up in a ball and cry. This is where anxiety stems from. People who just cut you down. People who are unkind. Let's just say I failed. Colossally.

I just don't get it. I wanted answers from her—more than she gave me, anyway, which was just a simple "No, I don't think so" and a mutter under her breath that I was weird. WEIRD! Are you even allowed to say that anymore?

I did follow her for a little bit, mustering up the courage to ask what her deal was. I thought I deserved that much. I kept my distance, though. I didn't want her to think I was stalking her or something. She got on the phone with someone pretty quickly. She was being secretive about the conversation, and at first I thought she was talking to L—about me. But then I heard her ask someone if they needed her to make the trip now. Work was busy, she said. It wasn't a good time to drop everything. So I supposed it wasn't L, then. She waited a minute, and then she was like, "I'll come. But I can't come for iong."

And then she hung up and swung around—almost like she saw me. I ducked into a doorway like some kind of spy. I really wished that wherever she was going, she wouldn't come back. I wished there was a way I could make that happen.

I know, friends. That's mean. I'm not a mean person. I only wrote that because my feelings are hurt. You know that, right? Of course you do. I can always depend on my community for support. Thanks for letting me vent. Love ya!

TOP COMMENTS:

@anxiouskitten23: Ugh. It never stops hurting. Here for you, babe.

@RTGz69: Good for you for confronting! Ignore that bitch!

@mimi_has_troubleZ: Just circling back to this post to comment and say that I MISS GILLIAN SO MUCH. It sucks that no answers were ever found about what happened to her. Right @anxiouskitten23 @coolkat33 @yellomello00_0 @theresesociallyawk?

@anxiouskitten23: I KNOW! Justice for AnxietyBabe! WHY did the police mess up so badly?

@coolkat33: I swear something is fishy here. AnxietyBabe had GOALS. She was on a good path. She wouldn't throw it all away.

@yellomello00_0: Why hasn't someone questioned L and R more? And what about S? It's like there's one article about G and that's it.

@theresesociallyawk: Wait, what happened to G? Did I miss something?

@coolkat33: Oh, @theresesociallyawk, horrible story that she went missing and some of her belongings were found in this canyon in LA. Horrible, but also SUSPECT.

@theresesociallyawk: OMG @coolkat33, totally bawling right now. This is unacceptable. Why are there no answers? #JusticeForGillianAnxietyBabe!

@rrbbaskklo9: Wait WHAT? I wondered what happened to her but thought she got tired of posting!

@moonfa_9_mine: Saddest. Story. Ever. Love G. My money's on S. She was UNHINGED.

@rrbbaskklo9: right, @moonfa_9_mine? Or what about L and R? What happened to THEM?

@lonely_girlRZ4540: Hey, everyone, you don't know me, but I love this page, too. And I'm trying to find answers about all of this. And I promise you, I think I'm getting close.

24

LENNA

Lenna listens to the voice memo from Rhiannon that has just downloaded on her phone. The sound is shaky. Someone breathes heavily against the microphone. It's ragged, short sips punctuated by whimpers. Someone sounds terrified.

And then a voice—Rhiannon's voice. *Hey!* She screams. After that, the audio cuts out.

Sarah's mouth hangs open after it's finished. "That's disturbing."

She leans over Lenna and taps the play button again. The file starts up again—that breathy voice. That *scream.*

"Do you think it's recent?" Sarah asks.

Lenna looks at the data on the file. "It's dated now. So she is still on the property, then? Connected to the Wi-Fi? How else could she have sent an email?" She doubts the Wi-Fi could extend beyond the property boundaries very far. "We need to look for her."

Lenna rises to leave, but Sarah catches her arm. "Okay, maybe this makes me an asshole, but isn't it better just to leave it alone?

There's something up with her. She could be *dangerous*." She glances at her belly. An anguished look crosses her features.

"So you think we should just ignore it? She could be dying in the desert. A snake might have bitten her."

"Or maybe she's hoping we *do* look for her, and this is a decoy, sending us off to a place she isn't. She lied to us. We have no way of knowing her or trusting her."

"But Teddy. She wouldn't leave him." Then Lenna thinks of something else. "Doesn't it strike you as odd that the moment Rhiannon was about to get me off the property, she suddenly vanishes into thin air?"

Sarah cocks her head, not following.

"Maybe someone needs to make sure we stay. Rhiannon was going to help me leave. Someone needed to stop that."

"Someone *else*?" Sarah looks skeptical. "That all seems kind of far-fetched. Besides, Rhiannon never asked Marjorie for the key code. Why would someone else need to punish her if she wasn't actually going to help you in the first place?"

Lenna isn't sure. She isn't sure about anything. But there's a rising panic in her all the same. A sense that this isn't adding up. She reaches for the doorknob to the house. "We should play this for Marjorie."

"Wait." Sarah grabs her arm. "What if she decides it *is* a cry for help?"

"That's good. She'll know where to look."

"Or she'll bring the police out, Lenna. And . . . and they'll ask questions—of all of us. They'll look into our backgrounds. I can't afford to leave; I've sunk most of my money into this place."

"Really?"

Sarah nods. "It's a requirement for living here. A big sum of cash that goes into the pool. I don't make the rules." She clutches Lenna's hands. "I really can't believe someone in this house hurt

Rhiannon. Rhiannon's the person we shouldn't trust. It's the simplest solution. She's probably playing us."

"But . . . she's my *friend*," Lenna says reluctantly. "I can't just ignore this message."

"Your friend who ran off with your money, you mean."

Lenna raises a finger. "The ATM card! We can track that."

On her phone, she calls up the website for her bank and enters her username and password. Within seconds, her account data is on her screen.

"Well?" Sarah asks.

"Okay. The only new charge is a hold for the Sunrise Hotel in Green Valley, Arizona." Lenna's heart starts to thump. "She really did make a reservation for me, I think."

Lenna looks up the number for the Sunrise Hotel. Her nerves jump as the phone rings. A sleepy attendant answers, and Lenna asks in her steadiest voice if a reservation has been made for Lenna Schmidt.

"Uh-huh, for one night," the desk clerk says. Lenna's heart lifts.

"And what about Rhiannon Cook? Is there a reservation in that name?"

There's some typing. "Nope. Sorry."

Lenna cancels her reservation, then hangs up. Sarah chews on her lips. "Fine. But that doesn't prove she didn't run."

"I have this weird feeling. Like, maybe Rhiannon got in the middle of our secret, somehow. I know it sounds crazy, but we should consider it." Lenna thinks again about how someone rattled her doorknob earlier this evening. "Have you ever felt on edge here? Like someone moved your things, or tried to get into your room at night? Like someone was . . . watching you?"

A look of worry crosses Sarah's face, but then she shakes it off.

"What?" Lenna asks. "*Have* you?"

Sarah takes a breath. "I mean, okay, sometimes it all feels kind of too good to be true. But if I'm hiding something from everyone, maybe other people are hiding things, too."

Lenna shivers. "Like Gia, maybe."

Sarah looks uncomfortable. "I hate to think that." She looks down at her midsection. Lenna can work out what she's thinking. This is the place that facilitated the child growing inside her. She doesn't want to do anything to jeopardize that.

"Just try to see it my way," Lenna whispers. "We both could be in danger. We should at least try and figure out if this message is real."

Sarah takes a deep breath, rolls back her shoulders. "Fine. We'll do some investigating. *Quietly*. We'll have to be very, very careful."

IT'S TOO QUIET IN THE HOUSE IN THE MIDDLE OF THE NIGHT, SO THEY decide to meet first thing in the morning, once everyone else is up and starting on their chores. Exhaustion hits Lenna hard and fast. She places Jacob carefully in his crib, so as not to disturb him, and then falls into her own bed for a few hours of restless sleep.

At seven A.M., the smell of coffee wafts from the kitchen, along with the shouts of footsteps, slammed doors, murmurs, and children's whines. Lenna decides to take a calculated risk. In the kitchen, she finds Amy and clears her throat.

"Would you mind taking Jacob, just for a little bit?" she blurts. "I, um, need a few minutes to myself. In the bathroom."

"Of course," Amy says, holding out her arms. If Lenna and Sarah are going to poke around, it might be better to do it without a crying Jacob giving them away. Anyway, she trusts Amy more than anyone here.

She hopes.

"I'll just be ten minutes," Lenna tells Amy, which she hopes is enough time. She kisses her baby on the top of his head, praying that leaving him isn't a mistake.

She finds Sarah at Rhiannon's door, which is farther toward the back of the house. As she approaches, Sarah looks at her and shakes her head. Lenna thinks she can sense what Sarah is thinking. Bizarre, the difference a few hours can make. Yesterday, running into Sarah again was a fate worse than death. Now, they're working together.

Rhiannon's door is ajar. The lights are all off. Lenna peeks inside. The covers to Teddy's little bed are thrown back, and his pillow is on the floor. He'd been taken into someone else's room to sleep last night; she wonders how he's doing this morning. A few toy trucks are on the floor, and a drawer is open, though she can see it contains messily folded kid-sized T-shirts. A miniature potty sits in the corner, though it looks unused; a stack of folded cloth diapers rests on the floor.

The diapers. Lenna thinks of the pilfered diapers from her own room, how Gia gave them back to her, saying she found them among Rhiannon's things. *Had* she, or had Gia taken them herself and then blamed Rhiannon to seed her distrust?

"We need to establish if Rhiannon intentionally left." Sarah turns to the neatly made bed. "She had the presence of mind to tidy up. Meaning she wasn't, say, kidnapped kicking and screaming."

"She couldn't have gone willingly," Lenna says quietly, looking at Teddy's bed. "She wouldn't leave her kid."

"Maybe she thinks he'll be better off. How do you really know?"

"I think I *do*, though. She's really concerned about being a good mother." Lenna breathes in. "When Rhiannon was young, her mother drove her and her brother off a cliff. Her brother died. Rhiannon and her mom lived, but she never saw her again. It messed her up about having kids. She's so afraid she'd screw something up the way her mom did."

Sarah looks appalled. Unconsciously, her hands go to her belly. "She never said a word of that to anyone here."

"That's not surprising. It's not something she likes to talk about. I think she told me only because my mother also passed away—it was something we shared. But I just can't believe she'd willingly leave her child. Even if she has some sort of vendetta against someone, she wants to do right by Teddy."

Sarah puts her hands on her hips. "Okay, so what *did* happen?"

Lenna walks to Rhiannon's desk. A writing journal rests on top. Lenna hesitates, then opens it. The binding crackles. The pages are blank.

She lets the book fall back on the desk and opens a drawer next. It's full of a few pens and pencils, and then a receipt from a 7-Eleven in Bend, Oregon. She studies it awhile. It's dated June 10, two years before. At the time, Lenna had still thought Rhiannon was out sick and fully intended to return to work. Turns out, she hadn't even been in the state.

Reaching in the back of the drawer, Lenna feels for anything that might be hiding. There's nothing. Next, she opens Rhiannon's bureau; the drawers are stuffed with clothes. There's also a drawer of old baby bottles, some books, a stamp pad, a pair of headphones, some batteries. A top drawer reveals mismatched socks.

Sarah walks over to a drawer that's open. "Besides Teddy, what else would she take if she knew she was leaving? Can you think of anything really important? Because if we find it here, it might prove your theory that she either left in a hurry—or she didn't know she was leaving at all."

Lenna nods. "Her phone, I guess, but she did take that, because she sent the audio file." She opens another drawer. This one holds jeans, sweatpants. If there are any clothes missing, Lenna wouldn't know.

"Wait," she says, standing straighter. "She's got a locket."

"What?"

"She was always wearing it . . . I think it was from her brother? Before he died?" She pulls open a top drawer but only finds socks. "If she knew she was leaving, she might have grabbed it . . ."

Sarah inspects a small table by Teddy's bed and looks around for any jewelry. Lenna heads to Rhiannon's dresser. On top of it is a little cloth box that might hold small items like a locket. Lenna lifts it, certain she's going to find what she's looking for, but there is nothing there except for a small beaded bracelet. She clacks the beads together, moving them through her fingers. It looks like the same one Coral was wearing. She gets down on her hands and knees and checks under the bed. All she finds is dust.

"Inside a pocket?" Sarah points to a pile of dirty clothes in a woven laundry bin.

"Maybe," Lenna says, but she doesn't move. There is something intimate about touching her friend's dirty clothes. She spies the T-shirt Rhiannon wore the other day when she picked Lenna up at the side of the road. Just looking at the stuff brings unexpected tears to her eyes. She'd had so much hope about this place, about *Rhiannon.*

She pads over to a few articles of clothing draped over the chair, perhaps to be hand-washed. One is a bra. She picks it up by the straps. She's about to toss it down—handling it doesn't feel right—but then something about the left cup is stiff in an usual way, certainly not like normal padding. She runs her hand along the fabric. The seam is sewn shut, but there's something hard and unwavering between the pad and the underwire. Like something has been stuffed in there.

On Rhiannon's dresser is a nail clipper; she grabs it and starts making tiny cuts at the seam. Sarah notices. "What are you doing?"

"It feels like there's something stuck in here."

She frees enough of the cup that she can push her fingers

inside. There *is* something there. Something folded flat. She twists and wriggles it so that it fits through the inch-sized hole.

It's a color printout of a photo, pasted on a torn piece of paper. Lenna brings it to the light. A middle-aged woman smiles straight into the lens. She has a sharp jaw, thin lips, downturned eyes. Her face sags a little—she looks nearly fifty—and her hair is a shiny reddish brown, the same color hair as Rhiannon's. Same eyes, too.

When she looks at the other person in the picture, it's Rhiannon herself. And it's a *recent* Rhiannon, a grown-up Rhiannon, with her bouncy curls. The shirt she's wearing is a sleeveless Old Navy plaid button-down that Lenna distinctly remembers.

The women look caught off guard, like they didn't plan on someone snapping a photo. Rhiannon is thinner than she is now, her jeans hanging off her hips, her bare arms sinewy. But the other woman, the older Rhiannon clone, has a T-shirt stretched across her midsection. It takes Lenna a moment to realize that it isn't just a beer belly.

She turns the photo over, blinking hard at the half-smeared poetic scrawl in black pen.

Mama and her babies: one inside, one where we can see.
You might be fooling some, but you're not fooling me.

25

RHIANNON

Rhiannon stomped on the sidewalk stars on the Walk of Fame, glaring at the text she'd just received. She was agitated. Gillian's little sob story had interrupted her, thrown her off. Also, seeing Gillian felt like bad luck. She reminded Rhiannon about her own lies. One of which was, ironically, staring her in the face right now, in the form of a friendly text message.

> Hi baby. It's me. Your mom. Wondering if you wanted to come for a visit. It's been a long time.

After all these years? Where was this *coming* from?

It wasn't like Rhiannon was lying completely. Her mother, Joanna, was a shitty person—that much was very true. Addicted to pills—not that Rhiannon knew about that when she was young. Back then, there were some days when she'd extend her arms wide for Rhiannon to fall into. Other days, she hid behind closed doors, or else she'd be all fangs and horns, raging at Rhiannon and her brother, throwing things at them, bemoaning the fact that she had children at all. They had to make their own meals on those days— if, that was, there was food in the house. One winter day, a pipe burst in their bathroom from a freeze, and water started flooding the floor. No matter how hard Rhiannon pounded on Joanna's door, her mother couldn't be bothered to come out to do anything about it. Eventually, Rhiannon had to run over to the neighbor's, but she felt so much shame when the man came into the house and saw the dirty dishes, the filthy floor, the neglect. She still could picture the guy's look of disgust.

Rhiannon's father wasn't much help; he worked long shifts at a local wastewater plant, and even when he was around, he was just a slumped presence at the edges. It was kind of amazing he was even in the picture, considering how young he and Joanna had gotten together—one baby when she was sixteen, a second one at eighteen. Granted, he was a little older . . . but not much.

For as many pills as her mother took, her father drank as many beers. Dad was not, however, an angry drunk—he'd never laid a finger on Rhiannon or her brother, Carey, which wasn't the same as she could say for their mom. There was also a window between stressed and comatose where Dad was shining and mellow and gracious with his time; he liked when Rhiannon curled up next to him and read him stories—it was how she practiced learning to read. He sat with his eyes closed like he was listening to a symphony; she liked that she could give that to him. Though half the time, her reading just made him doze off.

She knew this wasn't really a family. Or, rather, not the kind of family *she* wanted. When she drew pictures, she drew a family portrait but with other parents. Taller. Different hair color. They ate ice cream cones. They paddled a canoe. She doubted her parents would ever take her and Carey to paddle a canoe.

On the last day Rhiannon ever saw Joanna, her mother sat

listlessly on the couch. It seemed to hurt her to blink. When Carey, who was nine at the time, spoke to Joanna, she startled like she'd been sleeping with her eyes open. Rhiannon wasn't sure what to do. Their father had told them if anything seemed wrong, they should call him at work, but she didn't want to admit anything was wrong.

She suggested they rent a movie at the video store that had opened up down the road. Their father had just brought home a used DVD player someone had given him at the plant. It would be fun!

Carey nudged her. "We should stay here until Dad comes home."

But then their mother's eyes snapped open. "It's okay. Let's go."

"See?" Rhiannon said to Carey, her body deflating with relief.

Except Joanna didn't know where the car keys were. Her movements were slow, messy. Rhiannon did—she'd stumbled upon the extra set in a coffee can on her father's workbench in the basement when she'd been looking for some shiny things she could use as jewelry for her dolls. Funny place for him to mislay the keys. Never did it occur to her that it was a hiding spot.

In the car, Joanna gripped the wheel hard. She leaned over the dashboard like an old lady. Several times, she lingered too long at red lights; cars behind her honked. "Go, Mommy!" Rhiannon cried, trying to sound lively. The car jerked forward. Carey chomped on his fingernails like they were made of Swedish Fish.

In the video store parking lot, Rhiannon bounded out and headed toward the front door. Inside, she perused the DVD cases, trying to figure out which one would be best. Something they'd never seen? Or maybe something familiar?

The store's front door beeped, indicating it had opened. Carey glanced over his shoulder. His mouth made a flat line. He took off. "Mom?" he called out. "Mom!"

Carey made a beeline to the front door just as their mother's car squealed out of the parking lot. Rhiannon got out there just in time, though she wished she'd missed it. She would never forget her mother's blank look behind the windshield. Joanna saw them, but she didn't hit the brakes and turn back. The car lurched forward, and she turned onto the road, driving fast.

There was a halfhearted search for Joanna, but she didn't want to be found. Based on hints their father gave, Joanna had pretty much said she was going to do this. Which filled Rhiannon with guilt. She never would have made the video store suggestion. She never would have fetched those keys from the coffee can.

Joanna ended up resurfacing: first in Utah, where she'd met a man, and then in Denver, with another man. Every few years, it was another place, another guy. She'd call them, sometimes—at first, Rhiannon looked forward to the calls, thinking Joanna was going to tell them she was coming home. But she never did. Their conversations were always light and evasive and always, *always* cut short on Joanna's terms. A few years after she started calling, Rhiannon refused to speak to her anymore. Not long after that, the calls stopped.

Rhiannon grew to hate Joanna. There wasn't even a good story to explain her mother's absence. It was humiliating to say *Yeah, she just didn't care enough about us, so she left.*

Around this time, a story broke that a car had crashed over a nearby bridge and plummeted into the water, killing a child. The driver was a mother named Jackie Cook—same last name as Rhiannon's. Jackie lived, and so did her daughter, who was also in the car—and who was also right around Rhiannon's age.

She pored over the story. People were up in arms about Jackie Cook's negligence, and those poor children, and *How could a mother do such a thing?* The little girl who'd survived the crash was never featured in the news, but Rhiannon had to think she was being pitied, coddled, cared for by people in her town. Yet no one pampered Rhiannon because of what *her* mother did. And was it really that different?

For high school, Rhiannon was accepted into a private academy across the river, all tuition paid. There was no way she would have been able to go otherwise—her dad still worked, but they didn't have *that* kind of money. In his lucid moments—he hit the bottle even harder after Joanna left and had become increasingly weepier, though never angry—he encouraged her to go. There was nothing in this town for her, he said. If she had the chance to get out, she should take it.

The school was small, and no one she knew attended. Everyone there had something that made them stand out; she was loath to start another year being her same old self, motherless and inadequate and broken. If she was going to be broken, she'd rather be broken with some style. The first time she told someone that she was the daughter of Jackie Cook, the mother who drove her children off the bridge . . . well, it felt good. The reactions. And then the pity. And then the understanding—it was understanding she *deserved,* for hadn't her mother done essentially the same thing? It made her stand out, too. People remembered her for it. They made exceptions for her, scholastically and socially, exceptions Rhiannon believed were completely deserved.

Eventually, Carey heard what she was going around saying. He was furious. "Why would you say Mom is the woman who drove her kids over a bridge?" he cried. "And are you telling people I'm the dead brother?"

But Rhiannon felt that Joanna Cook and Jackie Cook were the same person, more or less. Her brother didn't see it that way. He thought Rhiannon was sick. It changed their relationship, going forward—they were still in touch, though sporadically, and Carey had the grace not to ever mention it to Rhiannon's father, who she tried to check in with once a week. Rhiannon doubted Carey would be proud if he knew she was still telling that story. And to important people, too—friends. Lenna.

And Lenna was right—it was absolutely why she wanted to join an intentional community if she ever was financially stable enough. She didn't want to go forever—she also wanted a career— but at least for a little bit, just to see what it was like to live in a house and function . . . well, like a family. With support. Kindness. Predictability. Was it terrible to want a do-over?

Now, she bubbled with rage. How dare her mother drop back in like this and interrupt her calm life! But even so, she stabbed the contact information in the text. It was like an invisible hand was forcing her to do it.

The phone started to ring. A voice answered. Her mother's voice. "Rhiannon!" her mother gasped. "Oh my God. Is it you?"

Rhiannon stopped walking. It was a hand reaching out from the long, dark tunnel of her past. This was a voice she dreamed about. Tried to re-create. Still out there. Still alive. Saying her name.

"Hi," she croaked.

"You got my text, then. I'm so glad. So I was wondering if you'd like to visit," Joanna went on. "I'm in Oregon. You're still in Cali, right? So not so far. How's your father, by the way? He still kickin'?"

Get off the phone, Rhiannon's rational mind screamed. "It's actually not a great time," she said. "To visit, I mean. I'm in the middle of all this work stuff . . ."

"It's just . . . I regret things, baby girl. I know that doesn't make up for anything, but I'd really like to see your face. And say I'm sorry."

Rhiannon's feet had carried her to a crosswalk. She stared emptily at cars whizzing past. Even when the light flashed that she could cross, she didn't move.

"And also, I need you," Joanna said in a small voice. "I need your help with something."

"What?" Rhiannon asked suspiciously.

"Life stuff. I'll explain when you get here. Really, honey, I'm not sure who else to turn to."

Oh, it was so manipulative. Rhiannon knew it. But then a random memory came to her. Joanna, on a good day, taking her to Goodwill for new pants. The pants they found in her size were worn but fine; after adding a few T-shirts to the pile, they went to the register. Rhiannon dragged her feet. Goodwill was never much fun. Kids could always sense when you wore used stuff.

Then, Joanna selected two pairs of dangling earrings from a rack and plopped them on top of the pile. "Every girl needs some sparkle," she said.

"But I don't have my ears pierced," Rhiannon said.

"I know. But we'll go do that next. Surprise!"

And they did. It didn't hurt. They shared a soft pretzel at Auntie Anne's. There was no slurring, no sadness, just two girls together. She shut her eyes. Why couldn't her mother have been like that always?

"I mean, maybe I could get away for a day or two, if it's really necessary," she mumbled.

"Oh, baby. That's wonderful." She sounded choked up. Rhiannon tried not to feel moved. She tried not to feel anything. She told herself it was just a brief road trip to help her mother out, that was all. Nothing more. Certainly not the beginning of a relationship.

BUT LENNA. HOW TO EXPLAIN TO LENNA? IT WAS A BIZARRE LIE; Rhiannon knew that. She wasn't so far afield, morally, that she didn't understand how deranged it was to tell people your mother had driven you and your brother off a cliff when such a thing never happened. She wished she'd never told Lenna at all. It had been years since she'd trotted out that lie. But it was hard, hearing about how much Lenna adored her mother, how pure their relationship had been; it was the way a mother and daughter *should* be.

She couldn't tell Lenna she'd lied. She *couldn't*. Lenna might not forgive her. Maybe she could just . . . slip away for a little. This trip wouldn't amount to anything; she'd go, her mom would say whatever she needed to say, and then she'd be back. Afterward, she'd explain to Lenna she just needed a few days in the mountains or at the ocean. Oregon had both of those, right?

She took off the next day, in late afternoon. During the drive, Rhiannon flipped from radio station to radio station, but she couldn't concentrate on music or talk. She didn't know why her mother was choosing *now*. Rhiannon was twenty-nine years old; over twenty years had passed and not a word had come from Joanna before. When had her father last heard from her? He was still working at the same plant, but he'd finally gotten sober. It felt like he was always teetering on the edge, though—Joanna reappearing might cause a relapse. And had Joanna contacted Carey, too? Carey probably had the good sense to tell her to fuck off. He was living in Nevada, where he'd earned his medical degree. He'd done it all on his own—was an attending endocrinologist at a big hospital there. But they'd barely talked after Carey discovered she'd killed him off in her narrative about their mother. She didn't blame him for putting distance between them. Still, Rhiannon wondered if she should have called him before coming. They could have gone together, maybe. And . . . what? Or should she have called her dad? It felt harrowing, navigating this alone.

She was usually so prepared for anything, especially when it came to people. Rhiannon rarely had problems talking to anyone or winning people over—she often flirted with people to get them to do what she wanted. A skill she learned from her mom. Not that Rhiannon had any idea what to do with someone once they were interested in her. It wasn't as if she'd had a model of a stable, normal relationship in her parents, growing up.

Her flirtatiousness was probably what made Frederick think he could kiss her in that bathroom hallway at that party. She wasn't the type of woman who kissed someone her friend was interested in, but she should have said no a teeny tiny bit sooner than she had. She thought it was right to warn Lenna away from the guy—he'd slept with a lot of women in the office. But maybe it was because of a little more than that, too, something she avoided thinking about. Lenna's eyes had been so sparkly when she said that she and Frederick went on that date, and a streak of jealousy had gone through Rhiannon, hot and furious. A future scenario unfolded: Lenna spending all of her time with Frederick instead. Lenna *happy*.

Was she a terrible friend?

Lenna and her mother were the reason Rhiannon was on the way to Oregon. She wanted that maternal closeness, she realized. A lot. It was one of those things she didn't even realize she wanted so much until she was in the car, her foot on the pedal, following the freeway signs for Oregon, not turning back. She'd white-knuckled her way through childhood, grinning and bearing it with this absent parent looming over her; it was time to move on.

At a rest stop, she walked to a dead patch of grass and waited for her stomach to stop churning. The smell of funnel cake wafted into her nostrils. A child ran out of the rest stop, inexplicably carrying a red balloon. The setting sun glinted off it. She took a breath and got back into the car.

Hours later, she started to see signs for the state border. She drove all the way past the city and into the suburbs, the land flattening out, the traffic sparse. Finally, she came to a small house on a grassy patch of lawn at the end of a street that matched the address on her phone. The house was small, and there were weeds in the yard, and some of the siding looked like it was starting to rot. There weren't any lights on, but a pickup truck was parked in the driveway. Rhiannon couldn't fathom her mother driving a pickup truck—in her mind, she thought her mom still might be driving the Buick she'd peeled away in at the video store.

Her legs felt boneless as she walked up the front steps with her overnight bag slung under one arm. There was a rocking chair on the porch. A metal mailbox, emptied of mail. How bad could things be if the residents were regularly checking their mail? There was a little jute rug by the door with a picture of a dog on it. These things all felt like clues, but to *what*, Rhiannon wasn't sure.

She rang the bell and waited. She heard footsteps and braced herself, and then reassured herself—she'd been *asked* to come— and then braced herself again because her mother had implied there was *danger*, and what if that danger was another person?

The door opened a few inches. And there she was: the woman in Rhiannon's memories. Her hair was shorter and fluffier. Her eyes seemed greener. There were lines around her mouth and eyes, though perhaps that was because she was frowning. Something occurred to Rhiannon: Her mother didn't recognize her.

"Mom." Her voice cracked. "It's me."

Joanna's expression broke. "I know."

She clutched Rhiannon's hands then. Despite the soul-searching realization that she probably, *absolutely* shouldn't be here, Rhiannon fell into her arms. A split second later, her senses took stock of the rest of her mother's body. She was so surprised, she let out an *eep*. Joanna looked down at the swelling in her belly. Then she peered back up at Rhiannon sheepishly—and playfully, as if to say *Can you believe it?*

"H-how far along are you?" Rhiannon managed to ask.

Her mother grinned. "Thirty-three already. It's almost time."

26

LENNA

enna and Sarah read the words written on the back of the photo together. *Mama and her babies: one inside, one where we can see. You might be fooling some, but you're not fooling me.*

"So this is . . ." She points at the woman next to Rhiannon.

"Not her mom," Lenna says in a small voice. "That's impossible."

But she notices something blurry in the background of the photo. Rhiannon and this woman are standing in a parking lot of a roadhouse of sorts. There's an old-fashioned placard near the curb bearing a schedule: *Live Music Fri and Sat.* There were some dates: *6/18: Four Finger Willy's.* At least that's what she thinks it says. There are dates for musical acts on June nineteenth and twentieth as well.

June. That's when Rhiannon left. And Teddy is almost two and a half now.

She stares at the second person. She really does resemble an older version of Rhiannon. A sister? But Rhiannon said she didn't have a sister, only a brother. A *dead* brother. *Could* it be her mother?

Perhaps Rhiannon changed her mind about reconciling with her mom. Maybe she decided to forgive her.

Then Lenna notices the name tag hanging limply off the shirt the pregnant woman is wearing. It's emblazoned with the logo of a popular pharmacy, and below it is the name *Joanna*.

"Joanna?" she repeats to herself.

"What?" Sarah asks.

It takes Lenna a moment to realize what's wrong. "I looked up the accident involving Rhiannon's mother once. Rhiannon's name wasn't listed, but the mother who'd crashed the car was. Her last name was Cook, just like Rhiannon's. I don't remember her first name, but it wasn't Joanna."

"So this woman is an aunt, maybe?" Sarah asks.

But Lenna looks at the odd little poem again. *Mama and her babies: one inside, one where we can see. You might be fooling some, but you're not fooling me.*

A strange falling sensation fills her. She thinks of what Gillian declared during that walk in the Beverly Hills Flats. *That didn't happen,* in response to the story Lenna told her about Rhiannon's mom. Could Gillian have been right?

"Gillian could be very accurate when it came to understanding people," Sarah said when Lenna voiced this aloud. "It was such a weird trait—on one hand, she couldn't relate to people at all, but on the other, it was like she knew people's weaknesses."

Lenna sits down on the bed, the picture still in her hands. "Say this is Rhiannon's mother. At the moment, whether or not she is the Cook woman who drove her kids off a bridge is irrelevant, actually. What's more important is that in June two years ago, Rhiannon went to see this woman in Oregon, maybe because she was pregnant. And then, somehow, Rhiannon ended up here, at Halcyon, with a baby. A baby whose chronological age matches with when this woman is pregnant in the picture."

Sarah crosses her arms. "Maybe I'm right in saying that people are running from things, coming here. Look at me. Look at you, even."

"So Rhiannon . . . *kidnapped* Teddy?" Lenna whispers. "From this person who is possibly her mother?"

"That's what whoever wrote this note seems to think." Then Sarah's eyes narrow. "Maybe whoever wrote it knows something about where Rhiannon is now. Maybe your theory is right."

"But who would that be?" Lenna whispers. "Her mother? The baby's father?" She isn't sure that makes sense. If Teddy's parents dared to come on this property, she'd think they'd take *Teddy,* not Rhiannon. Wouldn't they care more about their missing child?

Then Sarah widens her eyes at the note. "What?" Lenna asks.

"See where it's torn, here? The image at the edge, here—this note was written on an old spreadsheet."

"Okay . . ."

"I think it's Halcyon's accounts. As members, we can review where the money goes. I recognize these abbreviations Marjorie made up. OG is for organic grocery. GF is for goat feed."

Lenna sees what Sarah means. A shiver goes through her. "So if this paper comes from the property, then someone on the property wrote this?"

"Maybe."

"*Gia* does the accounting," Lenna whispers.

Sarah looked puzzled. "But how could she have found out Rhiannon's secret? Was it on the news?"

Lenna isn't sure. There have been times, through the years, when she's searched Rhiannon's name. Nothing like this has ever come up. Or maybe she just isn't looking in the right places?

She reaches for her phone. Her fingers shake as she navigates the search engine. She types in *kidnapped baby, Oregon,* and Rhiannon's name just in case. She presses enter. After a moment, a window comes up saying that the website Lenna is trying to access is blocked.

She hits the back button and tries another search, this time using Rhiannon's first and last name and just *Oregon*. Again, the same blocked message appears.

Sarah notices. "Maybe there's something wrong with your phone." She tries on her own phone, but the same error message appears.

Lenna hits the back button to try again. This time, she types just *Oregon* and accidentally hits enter before she can key in the other search words. But a millisecond later, results appear. Oregon .gov. The Oregon Wikipedia page. Commonly asked questions like *What is Oregon best known for?* and *Is Oregon a friendly state?* Her phone is working, then. Lenna hits the back button once more. This time, she types in *Rhiannon Cook*.

There's that error message again.

"Weird," she whispers. "It's like my phone is rigged to prevent me from looking up anything about Rhiannon."

Sarah seems puzzled. "Maybe Rhiannon blocked searches for herself? You can do that, I believe, within a closed network."

Lenna is about to shake her head—that sounds so paranoid—but maybe it's not such a crazy idea. If Rhiannon *did* steal a baby, of course she wouldn't want people here to know. It's precisely why Sarah doesn't go by *Sadie* anymore: so people are less likely to find out she'd been accused of killing Gillian.

She types Sarah's name into the Google search. But to her bewilderment, the same error message appears. *Access Denied.*

Frowning, she types in her name next. Same message. She types in Amy's name, and Melissa's, and Gia's, and Coral's. But when she types in a *random* name—her father's name, and then Judy's from the office, and then Daniel's—Google works just fine.

Uneasiness settles over her, crawling across her skin like tiny mites.

She shows the screen to Sarah. "Rhiannon's isn't the only name that's blocked. We *all* are. No one here can look up anything about *any* of us."

27

RHIANNON

Joanna Cook opened the door wider for Rhiannon to step inside. Did she want coffee? Something to eat? She had completely brushed over the fact that she was having a baby. But Rhiannon needed to rewind.

"Hang on," she said, gesturing toward her mother's swollen midsection. "How did this happen?"

Joanna smiled wryly. "I'm assuming you've taken sex ed."

"But you're . . ."

"Old? Age is only a number."

She was forty-seven, though. It wasn't impossible, Rhiannon supposed—but unlikely. But she wasn't even only asking that. She had lost track of Joanna's romantic situation.

"Is the baby . . . you know, healthy?" she asked instead.

"Think so." Joanna shrugged. Then she clutched Rhiannon's hands and pulled her into a hug. "I'm so glad you came. It's good we're finally doing this."

At first, Rhiannon's disappointment startled her. She searched for the meaning behind it. The weirdness of her mother having a baby. Or maybe it was how she'd said *It's almost time,* like she'd been called here not just because her mother missed her, but because of something else.

"Almost time for what?" she asked.

"Huh?" Joanna paused mid-waddle as she led them into an old-fashioned kitchen: chipped cabinets with grimy hinges, a butter-colored refrigerator that made ominous groaning sounds, suspicious stains on the tile floor.

"You said, before, that it was almost time. For what? Is this what you wanted me to help you with?" She pointed at Joanna's belly, the dread rising. It was. It had to be.

The back door banged before Joanna could answer. A man in a workman's jumpsuit and heavy boots stepped into the kitchen, his brow furrowed in surprise when he noticed Rhiannon there. He had a good head of frizzy graying hair, a goatee, squinty eyes, and leathery skin.

Joanna's smile was fluttery. "John. This is my daughter. Rhiannon."

John's eyes bulged. He slapped his thighs dramatically. "You look too old to be her daughter!"

"Well, I mean, I *am,* kind of," Rhiannon said under her breath.

"Aren't you sweet." Joanna smiled shyly. "Rhiannon, this is Johnny."

Johnny shook her hand. His palm was warm, and he smelled, nauseatingly, like tobacco. Rhiannon had always hated the odor. She thought about her own father, who might have smelled like booze half his life but at least never smelled like cigarettes.

Johnny said he worked at a Mercedes car dealership up the road—maintenance, not a bad gig. He had grown adult children, too—two sons, both in their late twenties. Pieces of shit, they both were—though in the next moment, he grinned. "I'm kidding."

Rhiannon inspected him stealthily, looking for shaking hands, dilated pupils.

Coffee mugs in hand, Johnny and Joanna sat down on an old plaid couch to chat. It all felt very awkward. Joanna's leg looped over Johnny's knee. Joanna kept glancing at Johnny for approval.

Joanna asked Rhiannon what she was up to. Rhiannon tried to answer her questions, but her life felt so far away. She was more interested in her mother, especially the blank space between when Joanna had left her old family and now. How much did this Johnny person know about that? Had he been with her all along? Was he an addict, too?

What was frustrating was that Joanna didn't seem that interested in filling in the blanks. She only wanted to talk about their present day—the luxury vehicles Johnny sometimes brought home for them to drive for the weekend, loaners from the dealership. And she complained about her job at the Walgreens up the road. "Just customer service," she said. "And I work the photo kiosks, too. You should *see* what some people want printed. It's like, don't they realize there are people on the other end, putting their shots of their private parts into envelopes?"

Rhiannon felt the sudden urge to call Carey. Maybe this woman *was* the woman who'd plunged her children off a bridge, and Rhiannon had been a victim of that, and she'd been fooling herself all these years, thinking it was a dream.

"So," Joanna said, hopping up. "Would you like to see a picture?"

At first, Rhiannon thought her mother was going to show her a picture of *them,* Joanna and Rhiannon and Carey, when they were young. But then she walked to a dresser on the other side of the small room and pulled open a drawer, extracting a flimsy set of photos in an accordion and placing it, in a jumble, on Rhiannon's lap. It was the first sonogram Rhiannon had ever seen besides posts on Facebook.

"There's the head," Joanna explained, pointing to a blob among the blackness. "And in this one, there's the feet. Oh, it's a boy, by the way. Look, he's giving us the finger."

"So this was planned, then?" Rhiannon blurted. "This baby?"

Her mother's palm flattened over the ultrasound photos. A look passed between her and Johnny. "A bit of a surprise." Her voice had risen in pitch. "When is a child ever *planned,* really?"

Rhiannon's gaze landed on the photos. All at once, she could see a baby's hand through the black murk, clear as day. And Joanna was right. Kid *was* giving the finger.

AFTER THEY WENT TO SLEEP, RHIANNON SEARCHED THE HOUSE. First the guest bedroom, then the kitchen, the den, the half bath, the full bath, the finished part of the basement (with, of course, a pool table), the *unfinished* part of the basement, and the garage— for bottles of any kind. Medications. Even chemicals you could huff. There were cartons of cigarettes, there was a huge stash of Diet Coke, but neither of them seemed addicted to anything stronger.

She supposed they might keep all of their supplies in their bedroom, but the next day, she learned that Johnny was in AA and rigorous about it. Had a sponsor, sometimes sponsored others. It made Rhiannon feel better. He also knew Joanna had once been an addict, too. "Muddling through it together," he told her. "Every day's a challenge, even still."

Rhiannon was glad to see her mother was stable and with someone who was working on himself. But she kept waiting for some sort of moment between her and Joanna. A big conversation, maybe, a reason Joanna had summoned her, the *help* she needed. Acknowledgment from Joanna that what she'd done to Rhiannon had been incredibly damaging would be nice, too.

Rhiannon was too stubborn to break the ice, though. She wanted Joanna to do the work, for once in her life.

But even after weeks passed, no revelation came. Johnny and Joanna favored a smoky dive bar on the side of the road that sometimes played loud music. Rhiannon accompanied them two times. She was dying for a stiff drink, but Johnny and her mother never drank anything harder than Dr Pepper, and she didn't want to be a bad influence. Just standing in the dark, musty bar, she felt like she'd dropped into another life. She was using up all her work vacation time. For this.

"C'mon, girls," Johnny said on the second night they went, once they picked up Joanna from her shift at Walgreens. She was still wearing her name tag. "Smush together. Smile."

It was weird, having her picture taken with her mother. Rhiannon wondered if it might be the only memento for the rest of her life. It made her sad.

"Can you send it to me?" Rhiannon asked, and in a moment, it landed in her inbox. That night, she studied the photo, marveling at how similar she and Joanna looked as adults, feeling queasy, still, at her mother's pregnant belly.

Another day passed. Rhiannon started to feel antsy. She needed to get back to her real life. Whatever she had come looking for, she wasn't going to get it. Lenna had called multiple times, and Rhiannon needed to clear the air. Maybe she should even tell her the truth of why she was here.

Finally, an email landed in her inbox. Apparently, *City Gossip* was going through a reorganizational period. Rhiannon's position had been made redundant. He was very sorry.

Rhiannon was stunned. She called Rich, begging that he

reconsider, but he said, in a somewhat clipped voice, that the decision had been made. She felt like she'd been slapped. She'd worked so hard there, and this was how they left things?

She expected, too, for Lenna to reach out after this news. Strange when she didn't. Their argument floated back to her—all those accusations Lenna hurled her way. *Had* Rhiannon stood in the way of Lenna writing? *Had* it always been about Rhiannon?

Maybe Lenna was really and truly mad. And maybe she deserved to be. Rhiannon missed Lenna fiercely, suddenly. She'd been so shortsighted. All this time, she'd dreamed of joining a community, yearning for a family—but wasn't Lenna both those things? Had the family she'd been looking for been right in front of her all along?

Over a month into her stay, she'd had enough. Nothing was going to be said here. Nothing was going to improve. "I need to go back home," she told her mother and Johnny at dinner.

Joanna and Johnny exchanged a glance. "But we're enjoying having you."

Were they? "I can't stay any longer," Rhiannon said. "I'm sure I've outstayed my welcome anyway. Thanks for having me."

And then she got up to pack her things. A few minutes later, Joanna knocked on her door. Rhiannon was staying in the tiny guest room, on a pullout sofa bed; also stuffed in the room were a bunch of unopened Amazon boxes, milk crates full of DVDs, and other odds and ends. Anywhere she stepped, she feared knocking something over.

"Honey," Joanna said, her eyes full of sorrow. "Can I be honest?"

Rhiannon paused in her packing. Here it was, maybe. The apology, at long last.

Joanna breathed out. "Johnny's a little mad at me. I don't want to set him off. Having you here . . . it's been a nice buffer."

It took Rhiannon a moment to regroup. So this was the help

Joanna needed, then. She grew wary. "A buffer? And what do you mean, *set him off*? He's not—"

"He's *not*," Joanna interrupted, as if anticipating what she was going to say. "Man wouldn't hurt a fly. But . . ." She sighed. "It's this." She touched her belly. "He thinks we're too old. But I couldn't go through with . . . you know. The alternative." She glanced defensively at Rhiannon. "He's a good man. Lots of other guys would have kicked me out or left me in this condition."

"That's your standard?" Rhiannon spluttered. "Because he didn't abandon you, he's a model husband?"

Joanna looked like Rhiannon had just kicked her in her uterus. It was, by all accounts, the first time Rhiannon had said anything honest to her. It felt good. "When you're married, you'll see," Joanna said self-righteously. "You just don't understand."

"There's a lot about you I don't understand."

Joanna's eyes widened. The statement hung between them. But then she blew her bangs into the air and rolled her eyes. "Well, I guess Johnny will get used to it. You go. Live your life."

After Joanna left, Rhiannon fought back tears. How dare she make Rhiannon feel bad in this scenario! Did Joanna just forget what had happened to her *first* batch of kids?

Rhiannon couldn't understand why she couldn't say those words. Why wasn't she brave in this flimsy little house? Why did she feel so withered and small? It had been a mistake to come. Her mother hadn't made her feel loved or wanted. She'd brought her here to . . . to who knows what. But Rhiannon had had enough.

She turned her phone on and pulled up a new text to Lenna. Hey. How are you? was all she wrote.

When she saw Lenna's name—Doing okay. You?—her heart soared. Maybe all wasn't lost. And yet, she was so ashamed. She'd just . . . *left*. She'd totally neglected Lenna's feelings—which were totally valid, of course they were, even if they weren't totally right.

Lenna did most of the talking, all about *The Bachelor*. It seemed Lenna felt as awkward reconnecting as Rhiannon did, and she remained in their comfort zone. But it was nice. Oh, how Rhiannon missed those evenings on the couch, dissecting the contestants. But then, a while into the conversation, Lenna said she hated how things had been left between them.

It gave Rhiannon pause. She wanted to be in her old apartment instead of this thin-walled room for a child neither parent seemed to want. She wanted to explain all of this to Lenna, but it all felt too heavy to talk about over text. She considered calling her, telling her everything, but she feared her mother might hear what she was saying. Then, a few hours in, she felt foolish. Lenna was her best friend. She should just tell her. Even if she risked Lenna getting mad. She needed *someone*.

Agreed, she finally texted.

A reply pinged shortly. Rhiannon blinked at the words. TOO DUCKING LATE. LOSE THIS NUMBER.

Rhiannon gawked. A sour taste welled in her throat, and tears dotted her eyes. She let the phone fall from her fingers. Numbness overtook her. Then anger. *Fine,* she thought, and blocked Lenna's number. After a beat, she deleted it altogether.

"Hello?"

The door creaked open. Rhiannon shot up in the dark. Her mother peered inside.

"Thought I heard you up," Joanna whispered. She padded into the room. "You okay?"

"Just, um, watching something," Rhiannon muttered, turning her phone over on the mattress.

Joanna sat on the edge of the little bed. Rhiannon curled her feet away. But Joanna didn't look like she wanted to comfort her anyway. She fidgeted with her fingers in her lap.

"Are *you* okay?" Rhiannon asked.

"*No,*" Joanna blurted. Her eyes were wet.

Rhiannon thought, for a moment, her mom was sad because she was leaving. But then she noticed Joanna was staring regretfully at her belly. Rhiannon shifted.

"You have to see it from my perspective, honey. I'm nearly fifty. This . . . it's kind of . . . crazy."

"But you've had a long time to think about it."

"I know. But I just held on to the idea that he was meant to be, you know? Meant to exist. I believe in that, I do."

Rhiannon crossed her arms. "So what are you going to do?"

Joanna picked at a string on the bedspread. "I was wondering if you might want him."

"*Me?*" Rhiannon laughed. "No. No way."

"You're so much younger. You'd be good at it. Better than me."

That did it. "You were a *terrible* mother!" Rhiannon exploded.

Joanna lowered her eyes, but Rhiannon didn't feel bad. She absolutely wasn't going to apologize.

"I'm sorry, but you can't ask this of me," Rhiannon went on.

Joanna's chin wobbled. "I can't leave Johnny. He got me off drugs."

Unceremoniously, here was the elephant, making his presence known. Rhiannon swallowed hard. "And do you think if you left him, you'd feel the urge to go back to . . . drugs?"

"A baby might trigger me. It's fucking *hard,* hon."

Rhiannon nearly swallowed her tongue. The rage she'd been trying to suppress bubbled to the surface. "You don't think I *know* that?"

Her mother peeked up at her through a curtain of hair. "Ree . . ."

"I was seven when you disappeared. You just . . . *walked out.*"

Her mother blew out a breath and started to stand. "I didn't come in here to fight."

"Then don't put me in this position," Rhiannon growled. She stood, too. "You could have tried a little harder for your children. You could be trying a little harder now, with the one who isn't born yet."

Joanna's gaze narrowed.

"Look, I get that addiction is addiction. But . . . but maybe you shouldn't have gotten pregnant in the first place." It hurt, saying this, though it was true. With this baby . . . or with Rhiannon herself.

But that didn't feel like it stung enough. So then she said the other thing, the worst thing. "Do you know what I used to tell people when they asked why we weren't in touch? People who didn't know me as a kid, I mean. I used to tell them you were Jackie Cook. The woman who drove the kids off the bridge. That you tried to kill me."

Joanna's lips parted.

Rhiannon held up her hand. "My whole life, I never wanted kids—because of you. I was afraid that what happened to you would happen to me. But now I realize it probably won't. I'm better than you. I'd never do that to a child." She felt Joanna go still beside her. Maybe hopeful. "But I'm not taking your baby. And after tonight, I don't want you to ever contact me again."

Joanna still didn't speak as Rhiannon stood, shaking. There was a dust ball in the corner that Rhiannon had neglected to sweep in the deep clean she'd done since moving in. She stared at it then, thinking about how dust was actually a mingling of human hair and cells and dirt.

Finally, her mother breathed in. "I knew, actually."

Rhiannon turned. "Sorry?"

"I knew that's how you described me. Carey told me. Said it just like that, actually, same way you did."

It was the first time Joanna had mentioned Carey's name since she'd come. But nothing she'd said made sense. "Carey said he talked to you."

"It was only once."

The dim shadows danced over her mother's features, sharpening the lines in her face. She looked so small, almost shrunken. Rhiannon didn't want to feel sorry for her. She didn't want to feel anything regarding her mother anymore. Now she felt saddled with a bunch of new emotions, including exasperation. "If you knew that, why did you still ask for my help?"

Joanna raised a shoulder but didn't answer. Instead, she slipped out of the room and closed the door.

THE NEXT MORNING, BEFORE RHIANNON LEFT, SHE ASSEMBLED A Pack 'n Play she found in a box in the room where she was sleeping. She opened the diapers and sorted them by size. She arranged a few stuffed animals she'd bought at Target on the windowsill.

She left before her mother woke. She supposed she'd go back to LA, but she still felt so directionless. Lenna wanted nothing to do with her anymore. And neither did her mother, not really.

In the driver's seat, her chin started to wobble. What did she expect? Of course Joanna wanted something taken *off* her hands instead of wanting Rhiannon to be part of her life. And she'd brought Rhiannon here with the full knowledge of what Rhiannon thought of her! Joanna had to be scraping the bottom of the barrel, out of other options. This visit couldn't actually be because Rhiannon was her daughter, and Joanna wanted to finally have a relationship with her—or, God forbid, she actually *was* looking out for the welfare of her unborn child.

When she was at the end of the block, her phone rang. It was her mother. Rhiannon considered not answering, but something made her pick up the phone.

"My water broke," Joanna said, frantic.

———————————

JOANNA'S LABOR WAS SWIFT; SHE BARELY MADE IT TO THE HOSPITAL in time. The moment the baby arrived in the world, first pale and gasping and then screaming his head off, Rhiannon turned away. Her half brother. The child of some dude that smelled like cigarettes. And yet the baby was so small and helpless, his arms and legs splayed out, his little mouth opening and closing like a fish out of water.

The nurses whisked him away to weigh him, clean him off, and test his reflexes. Rhiannon drifted over to survey what they were doing; she didn't want to face her mom. Leaving again would be awkward. She had to at least wait until Johnny got there. They'd tried to call him on the way to the hospital but his phone was off—Joanna said that he didn't check it when he was working. A coworker said he'd pass on the message, but Johnny still hadn't shown up.

The nurses placed the baby under a warming lamp, but they said Rhiannon could move closer and touch him. She felt like declining would seem rude—it wasn't like Joanna was making any moves to go over there—so she stepped in front of the lamp to say hello. The baby was still wiggling, and his eyes were closed. She touched the edge of his hand with one finger. So quickly, the baby's little hand closed around it. Hard.

Rhiannon stared down, struck dumb. Then he opened his eyes and looked at her. Really *looked* at her. Rhiannon looked back. There was a person in there. A little soul.

Her insides wobbled. She didn't want kids. She *didn't*. Or . . . did she not want them simply because of what she'd gone through? She believed what she'd told Joanna about how she thought she was a better person. She'd never be the sort of woman her mother was. And yet, if she left this kid here, with Joanna and Johnny . . .

She shut her eyes, took a long, slow breath in, and then let it out again.

THERE WOULD BE PAPERWORK. ADOPTION FORMS. LEGAL FEES. SHE needed to start that process. Reality began to dawn on Rhiannon. She didn't want to make a life here and see her mother or Johnny on a regular basis. But LA didn't seem like an option, either. She didn't even have a job there anymore, her closest friend wanted nothing to do with her, and even *if* Rhiannon wanted to call Lenna, she didn't have her number anymore, and she was too proud to go hunting for it.

A commune, Rhiannon thought wistfully. It suddenly felt like the perfect idea. It wasn't like she had anything to lose. But were communities open to babies? Did that exist? Along with compiling the paperwork she'd need to start the adoption process, she would look into communities, too.

The day turned to evening. Joanna looked exhausted. Labor had taken everything out of her. Rhiannon figured she should let her rest, so she told the nurses to take the baby to the nursery and went downstairs to the cafeteria for coffee. She felt a rush of excitement. She would give this baby—*Teddy,* the name formed in her mind—a wonderful life.

After an hour, she returned to her mother's room, figuring she'd given her mother enough time to rest. But Joanna wasn't in her bed.

"Joanna?" she called. She'd never gotten used to calling her *Mom*. "Hello?"

The sheets were mussed. There was still a foam cup of ice on the little tray. Rhiannon thought her mother might just be in the shower, but when she went to check, the bathroom was empty. Her mother's purse was gone. A strange, gnawing feeling began to worm its way through her gut.

One of the nurses brought Teddy back into the room. "Ready for a feed," she cooed, and then looked at the empty bed in surprise. "Oh. Where's Mom?"

"Um, in the bathroom," Rhiannon blurted, her heart hammering. She pointed at the en suite bathroom in the corner. "She'll be out in a sec. I'll do it."

She took the bottle the nurse had prepared and settled into the chair. She'd never fed a baby before; the nurse had to show her how. As the baby drank the bottle, Rhiannon looked around. She would call Joanna, she knew, but she had a sinking feeling Joanna wouldn't answer. And then what? Would she tell the nurses? She hadn't even called the lawyer yet.

Rhiannon knew the legality of things. The delivery had moved so quickly that they hadn't even explained to the staff that Joanna wouldn't be caring for the baby. The staff would never give Rhiannon permission to walk out of here with Teddy. A terrible thought crossed her mind: What if they took the baby away from Joanna ... *and* Rhiannon? A mother abandoning her child was irresponsible. Child Protective Services would deem Joanna unfit. But Rhiannon doubted they'd just cede the baby to her.

She bundled Teddy up, took as many diapers and sample bottles of formula from the room as she could fit in her tote, and left. She took the stairs. No alarms blared. But when she saw how many security guards stood in the lobby, she panicked. She couldn't let them see her walking out with a baby. There were probably protocol measures in place. Her gaze fell on an emergency exit. An alarm would sound if she went through that door, but it was the risk she had to take.

She dove through the door. As she expected, the alarm blared, but she was in the parking garage before she heard shouts. It was an old hospital; she wasn't sure how many cameras were on doors or in garages anyway. She got to her car and stopped, realizing she hadn't installed a car seat. Of course she hadn't. She hadn't banked on having a newborn here.

She opened the door and sat gingerly in the driver's seat. In the footwell on the passenger side was a cardboard box; the baby fit perfectly inside. It was an insane solution, illegal in so many ways, but it felt like the only choice. Shakily, she backed out and fell in line behind another car heading for the exit. No one searched them. She stuck her ticket in the pay console, fed the machine a dollar, and the gate lifted for her to leave.

She started to drive. There was a Walmart close by; she stopped in and bought a car seat, blankets, bottles, formula, all the while with the baby cradled in her coat. *What else, what else?* Her mind was spinning. She was a fugitive. She had a baby who was less than a day old.

She kept going. The first few nights, she stayed at a motel outside town, unsure what to do next. She didn't know where she could go. What had she done? How would she keep this baby alive? Every time she stepped into a store to buy more formula or diapers, she felt marked. And surely he needed to see a doctor?

And then, two weeks after she'd fled the hospital, two weeks of going from hotel to hotel, a miracle came from out of the blue: a private response to a general query she'd put on Reddit in the hazy hours after she realized her mother wasn't taking the baby, asking if there existed an intentional community that would take in a woman and an infant. There was a place for Rhiannon and the baby at a community in southern Arizona, the message said—a few people just left, and some space opened up. Normally, the community only brought people in through word of mouth. *But we feel for you. We are all about creating a safe place for women—a "mommune," of sorts. And also a refuge. A home.*

It was signed *Marjorie Clark.*

28

LENNA

The room feels too small and hot. Lenna and Sarah look at the blocked searches once more. Then they look at each other.

"Marjorie," Sarah whispers.

"Yes," Lenna agrees. They need answers. This has gone too far. Something is very wrong here. And there are children in this house. *Babies.* And a mother is missing, possibly dead.

Jacob. She bolts into the corridor, terrified she's made a mistake leaving him with Amy. But to her relief, Amy is coming down from the other direction, Jacob in her arms. She frowns when she sees Lenna. "Is Rhiannon back?"

Lenna glances at Rhiannon's name on the placard on the bedroom door. "I needed something for Teddy in here," she lies. She takes Jacob back. She wants to hold him forever, never let him go. "Was he okay? Did he cry?"

Amy waves a hand. "He was fine. Was just grabbing something from my room." She brushes past them but gives Lenna a lingering look. Then Rhiannon's room. Finally, she moves on. When she's turned, Lenna and Sarah exchange a doomed glance.

The corridor is dark and cool as they head toward the front door. Lenna's head pounds with a mixture of dehydration and fear. *Why are our Google searches blocked?* Is it so they don't learn the truth about each other? Maybe it's just because of what's in Rhiannon's past, but Lenna doesn't understand why someone would block information on *all* of them. Maybe it's just a Halcyon policy, an extra layer of protection along with not talking about people behind their backs?

But what if it's something more sinister?

"Who's good with tech stuff?" Lenna whispers to Sarah as they tiptoe down the hall, hefting Jacob higher onto her chest.

"I have no idea," Sarah admits. "The only people I really see on computers are the kids."

Surely someone set up the Wi-Fi, though. Gia has her own computer, in that little office. And if she really is the community's accountant, she creates spreadsheets.

Suddenly, Sarah stops short in front of her just before the front door. "Oh," Lenna hears her say. "Hey, Coral. Matilda."

The two girls are parked in front of the door in folding chairs, playing cards.

"Hey, guys," Coral says. "How were your appointments, Sarah? How's the baby?"

"Baby's fine. Can we get past?" Sarah says impatiently. "We need to talk to Marjorie. She's outside, right?"

Coral's gaze dances from Sarah's face to Lenna's and back again. "There's a dust storm coming. We're rounding everyone up."

Sarah stiffens. "A dust storm? Yeah, right."

"What about Rhiannon?" Lenna says at the same time. "She's still out there, somewhere."

Matilda looks worried. "I know."

"Did someone put you up to this?" Sarah growls. "Are we being *forced* to stay inside?"

Coral shifts awkwardly. "We don't want anyone to get hurt." She turns to Lenna and Jacob. "You do *not* want to be out in a dust storm. It's like . . . the apocalypse. Stuff flies everywhere. The dust is bad for kids' lungs . . ."

Red creeps into Sarah's cheeks. When she wheels around, cords stand out in her neck. "Come on," she says through clenched teeth to Lenna, stomping back down the hall.

She leads Lenna into her bedroom and slams the door. It's the first time Lenna's been in Sarah's room, and she looks around warily. Her bed is the same as Lenna's, down to the quilted comforter. There's an old dresser with a broken drawer in the corner.

"This is bullshit," Sarah whispers, pacing around angrily.

"You don't think there's really a dust storm?"

"Look at the sky!" She points to the window. She's right. The sky is clear. Cloudless.

"So Coral's lying?" Lenna asks. "Matilda? They're probably just doing what they're told."

"What Marjorie wants them to do, you mean. No one wants to cross her. Oh, it might *seem* like this place is egalitarian, but Marjorie is the leader, full stop."

"So . . . *Marjorie* doesn't want us to leave?" She looks at Sarah skeptically. "You think . . . *she's* the person who's behind all of this?" A chill runs down her spine. She thinks of Daniel back in California, waiting for her. She looks down at Jacob in her arms, and her heart twists.

"Maybe we need to call the police," Lenna decides. "This has gone far enough. Rhiannon's missing. And if there truly *is* a dust storm, that's really dangerous."

"No." Sarah steps back. "We can't."

Sarah curls her fingers over the window sash. Lenna can see the knobs of her spine through her T-shirt.

"I get how much you want to protect your baby. But you might be in more danger staying here than you would with the police. Something is wrong here. We both have children to protect."

Sarah has her eyes squeezed shut. But after a moment, she nods. "Fine. But you talk. I can't do it."

Lenna feels focused. Still. *Calm.* This is what they should have done from the very start.

She wakes up her screen and hits the phone icon. Her fingers slide on the keypad, and it takes her two tries to key in the three numbers correctly. She touches the round, green button at the bottom of the screen to make the call. Another window appears, announcing that the call is being made.

But then . . . nothing.

A red *X* appears on Lenna's screen. *Call failed,* it reads. She tries again. *Call failed.*

"It's not working." Her vision is starting to narrow. *"Why is it not working?"*

"It should work on the Wi-Fi," Sarah says, but then pauses, eyes wide. "Unless . . . unless someone has blocked outgoing calls?"

"You can *do* that?" Her hands start to shake. "Okay. *Okay.* We can just get out of this Wi-Fi bubble and into actual cell phone range. Then we'll have service, right?"

"Presumably. But that would mean we'd have to leave the ranch. And what are we supposed to do, climb the barbed wire?"

For the second time in a span of a few minutes, Lenna hits on the answer. "Chiricahua Peak," she whispers. "I had service at the top. *Real* service."

Sarah nods. "We have to get up there."

29

LENNA

Sarah throws sweatshirts into a backpack in case they're stuck on the mountain for hours. When the sun goes down, the temperature drops—though hopefully it won't come to that. Lenna fills up water bottles and laces up her shoes. She brings extra sunscreen, diapers, a hat for the baby, a hoodie. Her cell phone is only a quarter charged, but it will have to do.

Coral has left her post at the door to prepare some food, but Matilda is still sitting in the same spot, laying out cards for Solitaire on the floor. The rest of the women, including Amy, are back inside.

Marjorie sweeps through the living area, announcing that it's almost time for midmorning yoga. Before Lenna knows what's happening, Marjorie sidles next to her.

"I'm very sorry, again, about not being able to get you out of here today," she says. "And of course, with the dust storm, that will set us back a little further. But if you'd like to join us for yoga, I'm going to lead us in a practice right now."

Lenna's mouth wobbles. *Are you trapping us?* she wants to ask. But she can't make sense of why. All she wants is to get out of this house.

"Wait," Sarah whispers when Marjorie heads toward the yoga studio. "That's it."

"What?" Lenna asks.

"They'll be distracted. No one will be watching the door."

"During *yoga*? Are you serious?"

But sure enough, when Marjorie bangs the gong to announce that yoga is beginning, Matilda rises from her chair and drifts down the hall. Lenna exchanges a look with Sarah. Could it be that easy?

"Ladies?" Marjorie pops her head into the hall. She's staring at them. "Coming?" She smiles at Lenna. "The baby is welcome, too."

Lenna looks at Sarah. Sarah gives her a tiny nod as if to say *Just follow my lead.*

They head into the studio. Ann, Amy, Naomi, and Melissa are already sitting on mats. Gia comes in, too, wearing a linen tunic and slippery-looking leggings. Her makeup is perfect, her hair is smooth. Her gaze darts to Lenna and Sarah, but then she looks away. Lenna's stomach twists. Every cell in her body is screaming at her to jump up and demand to know where Rhiannon is. Only, what if it *isn't* Gia? Then she'd give away to whoever is the real perpetrator that she's on to them.

Sarah nudges her to grab a mat. Before sitting, she lays Jacob on a blanket on the floor. He lets out a cry, and she thinks that's that, but then he seems to focus on the whirring ceiling fan and calms down. Still, Lenna hates the idea of him even breathing the same air as the traitor who is keeping them hostage. She stares at the crisscrossed tank top Amy wears, the messy braid in Melissa's hair, the easy way Matilda bends forward and her glasses slip to the tip of her nose. Maybe it's all of them. Maybe it's none of them.

"Lie back," Marjorie orders. "Let your body feel heavy. Close your eyes. Shut off all outside distractions."

Reluctantly, Lenna lies on her mat, listening to the noisy air-conditioning unit in the window. She doesn't dare close her eyes for even a second. The children settle, including some of the littlest. She eyes Teddy lying next to Melissa, his hands splayed out at his sides like he's done this plenty of times.

Then she feels Sarah's hand on her wrist. Sarah is already on her feet, glancing to the door. Lenna rises and scoops up Jacob, praying with all her might that he doesn't make a sound. Besides a tiny coo, he stays quiet, almost like he knows. She takes a few steps, leaving her mat behind. This seems risky. Impossible. Ridiculous. They are all right *here,* next to her feet, and while the air conditioner drowns out some sounds, she can't believe they aren't reacting more. *Shut off all outside distractions,* indeed. Gia's hands rest by her sides so vulnerably. It's strange to see her in repose. Marjorie's chin is tilted upward, and her eyes are squeezed closed. And then, Lenna sees it. Matilda's eyes are open. She lifts her neck and stares straight at Lenna, Jacob, and Sarah.

Lenna freezes. Matilda stares blankly, like some other entity has taken residence inside her. Lenna swallows hard and takes a small step backward. Any moment now, Matilda will call out. She'll tell the others. Marjorie.

But then, miraculously, Matilda's eyes flutter closed. Lenna hurries out before anyone else can see—or, for that matter, before Jacob's good mood shatters.

They grab the backpacks and walk to the exit. When Lenna pushes on the door, it isn't locked, and an alarm doesn't sound. Her heart thrums as she puts distance between herself and the house. She hasn't even strapped her baby into his carrier all the way; his weight droops to one side.

"This way," Sarah whispers, leading them through a maze of

cacti. Lenna glances over her shoulder, afraid they're making tracks in the sand.

At the goat pen, the animals eye them suspiciously. Gnats sting at Lenna's legs. It must be a hundred degrees out, and Jacob makes a note of protest. It's too hot for him, but with Jacob strapped to her chest and the backpack on her back, for her it's even worse.

A twig snaps. Lenna's heart jumps in her throat, terrified someone is following. When she turns, it's one of Ann's little dogs, Cosmo. He must have slipped out with them, and now he's trotting along, his eyes eager and hopeful.

"Go home," Lenna hisses.

The dog doesn't move. "Cosmo," Sarah repeats, swishing her hands. "Seriously. *Go.*"

The dog whimpers. Jacob, however, has quieted again, staring contemplatively at the dog. He calmed down when he saw Cosmo another time, too. "I'm afraid that if we put him inside, Jacob will start crying," she whispers.

Sarah shuts her eyes, exasperated. "We could just let him tag along, I guess. He's probably been on hikes before." She pats her thigh. Cosmo marches over, tail wagging. And, thankfully, Jacob stays quiet.

They traverse the ravine, out of sight of the house. It calms Lenna—at least they won't be able to see them the moment they look out the window. For a while, the only sounds are the wind, Cosmo's panting, their footsteps, and Jacob's little feet flopping against her torso. When Lenna checks her watch, she's surprised to see that fifteen minutes have already passed.

They push on toward the mountain. "We can't go up the easy way," Sarah says, squinting straight into the sun. "It's too visible. We'll have to go up the back. Over the rocks. Think you can with the baby?"

She points to the treacherous boulders, and Lenna's heart does a flip. Maneuvering over them with a baby strapped to her front seems next to impossible. She looks at Sarah, too. "*You're* pregnant. You shouldn't risk it, either."

"I'll be fine. Or I could just go up alone . . ."

"No." Lenna doesn't like the idea of separating.

Lenna crawls up the first rock, cradling Jacob at her chest to protect his head. Sarah watches her warily. Lenna heaves her body to the next rock, and then to the next. Her feet slip multiple times. She curses herself for not choosing better shoes. For having to do this in the first place.

After a few minutes, though, the rocks become flatter, the foot-holds more secure. Lenna feels drained. Every muscle aches. There is a stabbing feeling between her eyes. And Jacob is all-out crying. She fears the sound will carry back to the house.

"Shh, honey nut," she urges, bouncing him. "This will be over soon. And we'll see Daddy again. And it's getting dark. No more mean sun."

But as soon as she says this, something catches in her brain. It's too early for it to be dark. And yet it is.

She stares at the sky, startled at the change. All the blue is gone, and the world has turned a yellow-brown. The wind has picked up, too, bending the flimsy branches on the mesquite trees and scrub bushes. A gust smacks into Lenna, stinging her eyes. Jacob's lungs fill with new wails. Cosmo the dog lets out a low growl.

"Lenna!" Sarah is higher up the rocks, taking shelter in a small outcropping. "Get up here! Out of this wind!"

Lenna's arms and legs ache as she climbs. The wind blows so hard it stings against her face. Jacob is really losing his mind. But somehow, she, Jacob, and the dog make it up the next boulder and squeeze in next to Sarah. The nook provides a little shelter, but Lenna is horrified at how the weather has transformed. The sky is apocalyptic, so fraught with dust Lenna can only see a few inches in front of her face.

She turns to Sarah in horror. "So . . . they were telling the truth about the storm?"

"I . . . don't know." Then Sarah looks down at her phone, and her eyes widen. "I have service!"

Sure enough, there is a single bar in the upper right-hand corner. Lenna reaches into her own pocket, extracting her phone. She, too, has minimal service—but it's something.

"I'm calling," Sarah murmurs.

Lenna watches as her fingers tap the screen. But when she puts the phone to her ear, she grits her teeth. "Still not going through."

"Try again!"

Still no luck. Sarah glares at her phone like she wants to smash it to pieces. Lenna tries to call as well, but the call remains in a holding pattern, the connection not made.

"We need to go higher," Sarah says.

"In this weather?"

Suddenly, a news alert pops up on her phone—a wildfire is happening south of Los Angeles.

A news alert means that at least the data part of her service is connecting. Now that she's not on Wi-Fi, the search engine restrictions will be gone. Maybe they can find out *something*. But who to look up first? *Gia.*

With sweaty fingers, Lenna types in Gia's name. The page takes forever to load. At one point, Lenna's screen is totally white, and she wonders if she's lost connection completely. But finally, results for Gia Civatelli pop up. Lenna stares.

"What are you looking at?" Sarah asks. "Are you getting service?"

Just as she suspected, using regular service without any sort of restrictions, several images appear in a line across the top of the screen. The photos are of a woman with the same obsidian hair as Gia's. That same cheeky smile. Lenna's gaze falls to the tabloid headlines. *Gia Civatelli, Philadelphia Society Best Dressed. Gia Civatelli, chair, Barnes Foundation.*

"Huh," Lenna murmurs. "Gia is who she says."

"So?"

The wind whips again, sending stinging rocks against their faces. Lenna shields her son from the onslaught. She can only skim through an article or two, but there's no news about Gia having, say, a police record, or even a history of erratic behavior.

Jacob is crying so hard now, he's made himself hoarse. "Baby," Lenna cries, cradling him. "Just hang on a little longer."

She types in Rhiannon's name next. Up pop some articles from *City Gossip.* There are old social media pages, headshots, Getty images of Rhiannon at a magazine-sponsored fundraiser. All of these are things Lenna has seen before. Even when she scrolls to the third page of results, she finds nothing about Rhiannon being a suspect in kidnapping her mother's kid. She even tries spelling Rhiannon's name incorrectly. She searches Oregon kidnappings. Still no results.

None of this is making sense. If there's no information about them on the Internet, how could someone from within have figured any of this out? Who would even *care* to?

Then she has a thought.

The sky has turned from day to night. Lenna can taste dust on her tongue. Somewhere far, far in the distance, a siren wails. Cosmo's ears prick at the sound. Lenna types in one more name on her phone. It doesn't take long for results about Marjorie Clark to come up. Like Lenna's search on the other women besides Gia, there isn't much. Except a Reddit post catches her eye. *Avoid Halcyon. Marjorie Clark is a scammer.*

Lenna's blood turns cold. She shows Sarah the post title. Sarah squints at the username. "CarinaBird07. I wonder if that's . . . Carina? The girl who lived here?"

The name comes to Lenna's mind like a dart. "The girl who was kicked out?"

"Yeah. Marjorie says she caught her stealing."

Lenna shakes her head. "Really? I heard she was asked to leave because she was caught gossiping."

She clicks the actual post. *Last year, I joined a WWOOF program,* CarinaBird07 writes. *It's where you volunteer at various farms and communities and help with labor and chores in exchange for room and board. I was excited to do it. It was a gap year for college, and my boyfriend and I were taking a little break.*

More dust blows past them. Lenna covers her head and shields Jacob's body.

When I found Halcyon Ranch, the woman I connected with, Marjorie, was lovely. Said it's a community of women empowering women. Mothers empowering mothers. I loved that idea. I also love Arizona, so it felt like a good fit.

When I got there, I felt so seen. People were open. I felt so relaxed and free that I told them things about my family. Things I hadn't told a lot of people before. I had no idea it was going to be used against me.

Lenna blinks hard.

About a few weeks into my stay, the leader, Marjorie, started pressuring me to become an official resident. But I wasn't sure the lifestyle was for me. I'd become a little uncertain about the residents. One woman seemed to be faking her daughter's illness to get whatever she wanted. There were these two sisters who hated each other but also seemed codependent. This one woman seemed like Marjorie's soldier, like she owed Marjorie something. And there was this heiress who acted like a total snot—she claimed she didn't want her inheritance, but she had to be in hiding because of something. I think she might have killed someone.

I told Marjorie that I wouldn't be committing or paying the fees. I got ready to leave. But she got really weird. Said that I was making a huge mistake. Then she said she'd call my family and tell them the things I said about them. She said she actually recorded me, at times. She even wrote me this note saying she had guns stored, and she wasn't afraid to use them.

It got really ugly. I had to literally run away—through the desert.

Lenna lowers her phone. "Have you ever read this?"

"No . . ." Sarah shakes her head. "Though I've kind of *heard* about it. Just that Carina wrote some mean things—as far as I know, no one ever found it. And Carina was kicked out not long after I arrived."

Lenna wonders if Marjorie blocked the data. Deleted it from their servers, somehow. "And *guns*? Rhiannon told me the community is against them."

"We *are*."

Lenna keeps reading. *I didn't know what to do. I left anyway. She never sent the video,* the post goes on. *But I felt traumatized. And here's the thing—I think a lot of people there are traumatized. It wasn't just Marjorie—I think there were quite a few bad apples. Or maybe not bad—maybe that's the wrong word. Damaged. They needed help, and they were expected just to be "better" by working hard and doing chores and feeling the "magic" of the land. I wish something that simple could heal us. But in the end, I didn't notice it healing anyone.*

Lenna reads the last few sentences aloud. "How many people have left Halcyon?" Sarah asks. "Do we even know?"

"And does Marjorie know about *us*, somehow? Is this . . . ammunition to keep us here?" Lenna stares into the distance. "Marjorie threatened to use Carina's secrets against her unless she stayed.

Maybe she intends to do the same with us—she already kind of has, simply by putting us together. And she *already* did that to Rhiannon—and whatever she knows about the baby."

Sarah looks puzzled. "So you think Marjorie brought us here specifically because she knew we have secrets? Like, she targeted us to fund her community?"

"You said you sank a lot of money into this place. It's a strange sort of fundraising, but who knows? But I still can't figure out how Marjorie knew about what happened. With me . . . with you . . . with Gillian . . ." What is Lenna not seeing clearly? Does Marjorie have a connection to *City Gossip*? *Is* Rhiannon a spy, somehow in on the whole thing? But why would Rhiannon be missing, then?

Dust swirls in the sky. Lenna considers the people in that house with Marjorie. Innocents. Trapped there under the weight of their secrets. She and Sarah need to climb higher. Call 911.

Her phone buzzes, and she looks down, startled. A call is coming through. Lenna doesn't recognize the number on the screen.

"Who is it?" Sarah cries.

Lenna just stares. It can't be someone from the outside. It must be someone from inside the house. Finally, Sarah reaches over and presses the green button, putting the call on speaker.

"Lenna?" a voice crackles. "I-Is that you?"

"Who is this?" Lenna screams.

"Lenna. Jesus. I've been calling and calling. It's Marjorie. Tell me where you are. It's not safe out there. I'm coming to find you."

30

RHIANNON

The quiet and desolation of southern Arizona was a comfort to Rhiannon after she ran off with Teddy. And there was really something maternal about Marjorie, the woman who'd brought her there. Halcyon hadn't even been one of the communities Rhiannon reached out to. It was like Marjorie just *knew*.

She picked her up at the turnoff, took the baby in her arms, and comforted Rhiannon when she burst into tears.

"There, there," Marjorie cooed. "It's okay. It's all going to be okay. We've all been through this. We all know pain. And you've come home, my love. We're going to help you. You're safe."

It wasn't that Rhiannon feared her mother finding her. That was part of what made her cry so hard—she knew she *wouldn't*. Even more troubling, if Rhiannon *hadn't* returned to Joanna's hospital room, where would the baby be now?

She sobbed as Marjorie drove up the dusty road and unlocked the cattle gate. She sobbed as Marjorie took Teddy and carried him toward the rambling house with the bizarrely painted exterior. A few children stared, wide-eyed. Rhiannon took in the cluttered room. There were books everywhere, food scraps, dusty corners.

Rhiannon was led into a tiny bedroom, and sat on the bed. She cried more. So did the baby. He screamed all night. The other residents seemed unnerved; they kept their distance. Rhiannon paced back and forth in the room that first night, shushing Teddy, coaxing him to take bottles, weeping with relief when he finally drifted off to fitful sleep.

But as time wore on, the women grew kind. They took turns holding Teddy. They taught Rhiannon how to burp him and treat his cradle cap. They said nothing at how clueless she seemed, how tentative. She learned their names: Melissa, Naomi, Amy. Ann. Gia. They all seemed a little broken, too. Maybe it was why they never asked her for details—they didn't want to share their own. The favor went both ways.

Rhiannon never told anyone the truth. Surely they'd report a kidnapping—only, *was* that what she'd done? Her mother gave her permission to take Teddy. It was possible the hospital didn't report the baby being gone because the parents had left, too. Maybe they let the incident go.

The fact that Halcyon dissuaded others from prying into someone's past acted as a protection. If people suspected there was something off about Rhiannon and her baby, they didn't question it, nor did she feel they were gossiping about it when she wasn't around.

Within a few days of coming to the ranch, Teddy was crying much less and feeding well. Rhiannon was grateful for the respite. The community grew on her. The food was good, the people were kind, the world was quiet and secluded. She felt *safe* here.

When she told Marjorie she wanted to stay permanently, she figured Marjorie would be welcoming. But instead, she was cautious. "I'm all for you joining the family. But do you think you can come up with the funds for the buy-in fees?"

Rhiannon shifted. When she asked Marjorie how much the fees were, the amount was staggering. She had no idea how she'd come up with that kind of money.

"Do you have any, like, scholarships?"

"Sadly, not at this time," Marjorie said. "The upkeep of this place—we do it on a shoestring, but it's not nothing." She said she could float Rhiannon's fees for a few months, but that was pushing it.

Rhiannon swaddled Teddy and sat on her bed and stared at the glorious sunset. The mountain peak jutted up in the center of the community like a lighthouse. She thought of all the people she'd left behind. Her mother. Johnny. Lenna. People at the office. She thought of the one conversation Carey had had with their mother, allegedly—when he told Joanna that Rhiannon was going around saying she was the mother who drove her children off a bridge. It felt like validation, that Carey had stood up for her. She almost wanted to call him and thank him. Only, how would she explain the baby?

But it felt like those people existed on another planet now—a planet that, frankly, she didn't want to return to. Her heart was broken, and she wasn't sure if she'd ever be able to put it back together after what had happened. But Marjorie's nurturing ways, the rhythms of the place, even Teddy's emerging placidness—she just *needed* this. Just until the cracks healed a little.

Who could she ask for money? She had no one.

One night in November, her phone rang. It was two A.M. She didn't recognize the number on the screen.

"Is this Rhiannon Cook?" There was something unusual about the person's voice—it had a computerized buzz in spots, though that was probably just the connection.

"It . . . is," Rhiannon said hesitantly. She worried she'd made a mistake in answering.

"I've received word that you're a woman who's struggling."

"Wh-what?" Rhiannon sat up in the darkness. "Who is this?"

"They make it hard, sometimes, with those fees. But I can help you."

"How did you get this number?"

"I'm someone who cares. Someone invested in the success of these communities. Most importantly, I'm a feminist. I believe in women helping women. And I believe that there should be no privilege hierarchy in these places. If you want to be there, then you should be there."

"H-how do you know I need money?" Rhiannon pictured her mother on the other end. But that made no sense. Why wouldn't she just identify herself? "Are you here? In the house?"

"I can help you. We can help each other."

"How?"

"I'll pay your buy-in money. *If* you do something for me."

Rhiannon's chest tightened. "What?"

"I want you to be my pigeon. Do you know what pigeons do?"

A full moon appeared from behind a cloud. "No . . ."

"They carry messages. The ancient Greeks used pigeons to carry the names of the winners in the Olympic games to other cities. In the 1800s, stockbrokers used pigeons to transmit stock quotations from Paris all the way to London, can you imagine?"

"You want me to carry a message to someone?"

"I want you to carry the message of the ranch. That's how this is done. But only to a select few. Just like a carrier pigeon, you'll have a destination. And you'll bring them back here."

Rhiannon felt uneasy.

The voice continued. "There are other women just like you. Suffering. In need of the ranch, but not knowing the ranch is an option. You might even know someone, if you think hard enough. So I want you to be my carrier pigeon. Bring them into the fold. Get them to buy into the program. Get them to join the family. You don't even have to figure out what to say. I have a whole speech for you."

"But I can't leave."

"Whatever you're worried about," the voice said, "you'll be fine."

"How do *you* know?"

"It would only be a day trip. And you'll always be driving. I'll give you the instructions about what you need to do."

"Is this Marjorie?" Rhiannon blurted. It had to be. When the voice didn't confirm or deny, she added, "Is this really the only way? What about Teddy?"

"He'll be cared for. Say you're having a medical procedure. Something that was booked ahead of time. You'll take a taxi to the airport parking lot. I'll leave a car for you. Space 52A, in the long-term parking."

"I don't have money for gas."

"The money will be there. You'll have another ID. No one will know it's you."

Rhiannon pinched the bridge of her nose. This seemed insane. And yet she wanted to stay here. She had nowhere else to go.

"How many people do you want me to . . . bring the message to?" she asked.

"Two, maybe three at the most."

"Three," Rhiannon repeated. "I'm pretty sure I don't know three people who'd want to give up their lives for this place."

"Don't worry. I have some ideas. I'd appreciate if you kept this between us. The others might feel a little slighted if they found out someone was getting a chance to circumnavigate the fees. But you are my scholar, Rhiannon. You have a quality the others don't have—and believe me, I've gotten to know all of them."

"I do?"

"You do. You have the ability to inspire. To really *reach* people."

She didn't want to feel flattered. But when had someone last called her a scholar? An *inspiration*?

"Okay," she said. "I'll do it."

"Atta girl, Pigeon. I've got the first name of someone to look into. I've done some research on her. She's endured a tragedy. *Desperate* to have a baby. Hang on. I'm going to text it to you."

A moment later, Rhiannon's phone beeped. A name appeared in the window: Dr. Sarah Wasserman. Listed was her address in Los Angeles and some extra details: Goes by Sadie. Hurting. Recently lost a good friend to a terrible accident. Wants a child.

Rhiannon began to make the arrangements to take a trip.

31

LENNA

OCTOBER
PRESENT DAY

enna!" Marjorie shouts through the phone. "Where *are* you? There's a dust storm! Find shelter, *now*! It can be very dangerous!"

"I know everything, Marjorie," Lenna says in a low voice. "And I know you did something to Rhiannon."

"Huh?" Marjorie shouts. "I can't hear you!"

"You know things about us. You're threatening us. Holding our lives hostage. Did you do something to Rhiannon? Tell me where she is."

There's a pause. The wind smacks against Lenna's side. The dog whimpers. "Lenna," Marjorie pleads. "Look, whatever you think— I just want you safe. I care about you. I have no idea where Rhiannon is. I promise."

Lenna exchanges a glance with Sarah. A likely story. "You blocked outside web searches about everyone to confuse us. If you had only blocked yourself, that wouldn't have been suspicious. But block *all* of us . . ."

"What are you talking about? I didn't block any searches."

"Yes, you did. In the house. On the Wi-Fi."

"No. I'm serious. I don't even know *how* to do that."

"Did Rhiannon find Carina's post?" Lenna presses. "Is that it? And did she confront you about it? You sent her that photo with the note, didn't you? The one of her and her mother?"

"Lenna, can we please, *please* have this conversation later? You shouldn't be out there in this storm."

"What about the guns?" Sarah breaks in.

"Guns?" Marjorie scoffs. "There aren't any guns here."

"You told Carina you had an arsenal and weren't afraid to use it."

"Wha . . ." Marjorie sounds perplexed. There's a long pause. "That's not true. I swear. And I didn't send any notes or threats. I have no idea what you're talking about."

Lenna glances at Sarah. Likely story.

"Please," Marjorie says desperately. "The weather—dust storms kill people. And I can't call 911. We just tried. The number is blocked."

"Yeah, we know. *You* blocked it."

"*Me?* I wouldn't do that. There are children! You have to believe me. Look, what happened with Carina was wrong. I admit that, freely. I pushed her to stay. Pushed her hard. Said things I shouldn't have. I even spread misinformation about her within the group because . . . I knew I fucked up, and I was too afraid to admit it. But I swear—this isn't a trend. I'm just trying to build a nice community here. I believe in this place. I didn't write her any letters, and there aren't any guns. And if Rhiannon is missing—I want to help. You shouldn't be afraid. I'm on your side."

"Lenna," Sarah suddenly says, tugging Lenna's sleeve.

Lenna shakes her off. "But you know things about us. And Rhiannon. You're keeping us locked in here. You're withholding the car, withholding freedoms."

"That's for your safety!"

"*Lenna*," Sarah says, poking her again.

"Where are you?" Marjorie shouts. "We'll come. Just tell us."

Lenna chews on her lip. Will she help, or is this a trap?

But before she can decide, the call goes dead. Dust swirls into their little nook, and Lenna shuts her eyes.

"Lenna," Sarah urges one more time. Now the dog is growling, too.

Lenna finally turns to face her. Sarah's gaze is on something down the ravine. The color has drained from her cheeks. "Someone's down there."

"What? Who? Marjorie?"

"N-no." She turns to Lenna with haunted eyes. "Someone else."

32

RHIANNON

Rhiannon's hand trembled as she dialed the number to make a reservation for Lenna at the motel up north. A woman answered, and she repeated back Lenna's ATM card number.

"And, oh," Rhiannon added, "do you have a crib?"

Afterward, she hung up and tried to breathe as she walked, searching for Marjorie. The heat was suffocating. She was tramping halfway up Chiricahua Peak, thinking it would give her a good vantage. This property stretched for miles, and the desert all looked the same.

She was also still trying to process what Lenna had told her. The fear in her friend's eyes.

Lenna was afraid of Sarah. It was like Lenna had *done* something to her. Sarah wasn't a very open person, but she never mentioned abuse or assault. The only thing Rhiannon really knew that had happened to Sarah was that her friend had died in a terrible accident. That was the only information the voice on the phone gave her. Before she left to talk to Sarah, Rhiannon had tried to look into it. But she hadn't found any details.

The sun beat down on her head as she walked. Her phone barely had a signal, but she typed in the search anyway—*death, Runyon Canyon, hiker.* To her surprise, stories popped up that she swore she hadn't seen before when she'd searched at the house. One story caught her eye. Of the four accidents that had happened in Runyon Canyon in 2021, one of the women who'd fallen was named Gillian Winters. The person to report her missing was Dr. Sarah Wasserman.

"Oh fuck," Rhiannon whispered, stopping short.

Gillian. The same Gillian. The woman Lenna had become friends with, the one Rhiannon had blocked from becoming friends with them. She was dead. In fact, for a little while, it looked like the police suspected she'd been murdered—and Sarah was a suspect. But then it was deemed an accident. A wet morning, a terrible fall.

She's trembling now. Whatever Lenna was afraid of, did it have to do with this? But Sarah was a suspect, not Lenna.

And now they were both here. *Rhiannon* had been tricked into bringing them. Of course Lenna had reasons to distrust Rhiannon if she was culpable. She cursed herself for following the voice's rules without question. Thinking that she was helping Lenna and Sarah, leading them into paradise—all because *she* needed money. She should have asked more questions of the voice. Why didn't she? And if the voice was Marjorie, how did Marjorie know about Gillian's death? And why on earth would she bring these two women together?

Rhiannon felt like such a pawn.

She tried to think back. Rhiannon found Sarah in that café in November. Sarah reached out to Rhiannon with questions about Halcyon by December, and little by little, she seemed more interested in seeing the place. By February, Sarah decided to visit; by March, she wanted to stay. After that, the calls from the voice stopped for a while. Rhiannon's massive buy-in payment to the community hit the account, and just like that, she was an official resident. Marjorie was pleased—and she didn't question where the money came from. She had to be the voice. Why she'd disguised herself to get Rhiannon to recruit was kind of baffling ... but then, Marjorie was kind of unorthodox in general. She truly believed the land was magical and *spoke* to her sometimes, telling her what to do. The canyons had a voice, and so did the mountains, the insects, and even the desert dirt.

Still, things were great. Rhiannon and Teddy thrived. If there was an investigation into a child who'd gone missing from that hospital, Rhiannon never heard about it. And she hadn't heard from Joanna, but Rhiannon figured that was what Joanna wanted.

But then, seven months into her official stay, the calls began again.

"Seems like your recruit is settling in nicely, Pigeon. Good work. But what about *you*? Do you have anyone at the ranch you really jell with? To whom you'd like to tell your deepest thoughts and wishes?"

"That doesn't really matter," Rhiannon admitted.

"Come on. You don't want a friend? Maybe someone you were close to in the past? There's got to be someone."

The only *someone* was Lenna. And while Rhiannon would love to have her in her life again, there was absolutely no way. Besides, she didn't want to bring anyone else. The first time, going out into the world, had made her nervous enough. She'd technically committed a crime. "I live here now. These are my people."

"It's one thing to live in a community of *people*. It's another to live in a community of *friends*. When I was growing up, my sister and I fantasized about running away from our boring lives in the suburbs. Bringing our friends, maybe living in a hut on the beach somewhere. It was a decadent idea—always being around people you loved, always having company. You ever wish for that?"

Rhiannon dwelled on this now, as she walked higher up the peak. According to what Marjorie told all of them, she'd grown up in intentional communities. *Not* the suburbs.

So maybe the voice wasn't Marjorie. Maybe it was someone else.

"I can't do this," she pushed to the voice on the phone.

"I told you. You have to do two, maybe three."

"Isn't there some other way?"

"You should think it over. I wouldn't want you to have to leave Halcyon."

When Rhiannon hung up, she'd felt sick. She didn't want to leave, either. But this didn't feel totally legitimate.

The next morning, she was getting Teddy out of bed and dressing him for the day. She noticed something strange sticking under her door that hadn't been there last night. It was an envelope: white, rectangular, nondescript. Rhiannon picked it up and sliced it open. Inside was a piece of paper; pasted to it was the picture of her and Joanna standing in the parking lot of that dive bar. "Smush together. Smile," Johnny had said, aiming his phone at them.

Rhiannon's heart fluttered. The photo had been in her possession when she came. She'd forgotten about it, this one vestige of her strange interlude with Johnny and her mother. Then she turned the paper over. Someone had written a message on the back. An awful poem. A *teasing* poem.

Someone knew.

Bile rose in her throat. She tried to rip the photo to shreds, but her fingers were shaking too badly. She shoved the picture into a drawer and slammed it tight, but that didn't feel hidden enough. She looked around. With scissors, she cut a hole in one of the cups of her favorite bra and smashed it in. There. Now it would always be on her. Safe, next to her chest.

It had to be the voice's doing. It was a threat. Incentive so Rhiannon did whatever the voice wanted. But also . . . this was a physical object, the photo. She'd brought it with her. And the threat was *slipped under her door.* The voice was here, then. One of them. And the voice was saying, *Unless you do what I ask, I'll make everyone know exactly what you did.*

Powerless, Rhiannon did some digging on Lenna. There was barely anything about her online. Finally, she thought to check Lenna's dad's Facebook page. On it, she found a few photographs of him and a newborn baby. He looked so pleased. Grandfatherly. Lenna was an only child.

Rhiannon flipped through a few pictures of her old friend. An ache welled up inside her. She really, *really* missed Lenna. She hated that she hadn't appreciated her fully when they were friends. She hated that they'd just stopped speaking. The words *Too ducking late. Lose this number* flashed in her mind, and she squeezed her eyes shut. Lenna clearly hated her, but she'd give anything to talk to her again. The voice was right. She would love to have Lenna here—Lenna *specifically.* Even if Lenna said no, it would be nice to see her one more time.

When the voice called again the next day, there was no talk of the photo, but Rhiannon understood it was the underlying ultimatum. She told the voice about hitting up Lenna as a potential recruit. "But I think she's married. She has a kid."

"You never know until you try," the voice said. "You really have no idea what people are hiding, or what they want, or what they need. You should reach out. At least get her to visit. Maybe, once she comes, she'll want to commit after all. Marriages have cracks. Maybe she'll see that."

"Who are you?" Rhiannon whispered, one last try.

The voice just laughed. "Don't worry, Pigeon. I'll keep your se-crets, as long as you do what I ask."

Rhiannon couldn't believe it when Lenna agreed to meet her at the café. She'd played it cool, like there was no history between them—bringing up the past, she figured, might harden Lenna, make her less malleable to the idea of Halcyon. Lenna was awk-ward at first. She'd danced around questions about Rhiannon's disappearance that Rhiannon wished she could answer. But then she'd have to admit her terrible lie. That felt like starting off on the wrong foot, too.

She'd told Lenna about Halcyon and how amazing it was, giv-ing the speech the voice had provided. *Maybe you're stuck.* Rhian-non knew it by heart. Lenna seemed a little unnerved about that, too, and certainly not up for upending her life and marriage and making a change. Asking her to come felt much harder than ask-ing Sarah, who'd been a stranger. She truly believed in what she'd told Lenna about Halcyon, but she didn't like the pretenses of why she was trying to get her to come. This wasn't the way to start over as friends. Rhiannon was almost hoping Lenna *wouldn't* say she'd come—even though that would have spelled disaster for her and Teddy.

But then, a few days after they parted ways, Lenna reached out late at night and said that she'd try it out at least for a visit. Could she come tomorrow, if she could find a flight? Rhiannon felt con-flicted. Overjoyed . . . relieved . . . but also guilty. She tried to tell herself that maybe Lenna really did need to come to Halcyon—maybe not permanently, but at least for a little while. She decided to see it as divine providence, the universe pushing them back to-gether, rooting for their friendship to reignite. She wasn't doing anything wrong.

Rhiannon had tried to believe that. She shoved down the

feeling of guilt she felt, too, when the voice called her just last night, after Lenna arrived, asking how it was all going. Even when Lenna nearly caught her on the call.

"She's here," Rhiannon told the voice.

"You picked her up?"

"Yes. This morning. But I'm not sure she's going to stay."

"Get her to give it a few days. I asked that of you."

"I know that," Rhiannon argued, but she felt annoyed, because Lenna was married, and she didn't even seem that unhappy. "I'll do everything I can."

But she must not have sounded very convincing. "We have an agreement," the voice nudged.

"I know we have an agreement," Rhiannon said wearily. "But it doesn't feel right."

"I'm sure you can do something to convince her that there's magic to the place. The baby cries, yes? Maybe something to get him to stop crying? Something to help her rest, too?"

Rhiannon licked her lips. She didn't like what the voice was asking. But she'd done it. She felt she had to. It pained her to mix the herbs into the tea, but what did every mother want, after all? Sleep, and lots of it.

And now, it was clear there was something much bigger at play—a grand manipulation much more serious than she'd ever imagined. If Lenna and Sarah were strangers, Rhiannon would only see all of this as a campaign to bring in money. But maybe it wasn't about money at all. Someone wanted Lenna and Sarah *specifically* trapped here. The voice wanted Lenna to stay a few more days, and . . . *what*? The Gillian link was a smoking gun, connecting both women. Clearly it was something the voice didn't want Rhiannon to know. It scared Rhiannon, too, this anonymous voice holding all these secrets—*including hers.*

Her phone rang, startling her. It was the unknown number. She steeled herself. *Speak of the devil.* But actually, she wanted to talk to the voice. She had questions.

"Hello," she said coolly.

"Hi, Pigeon. Just checking in again. You cut me off last night."

She was so *livid,* suddenly. It felt like sparks were flying from her fingers. She felt guilty and ashamed and like such a fucking dupe, bringing her friend into a situation that was potentially dangerous. Fuck this voice, whoever she was.

"You baited me," she exploded. "You made me think it was *my* idea, and now I've brought Lenna into some kind of . . . *trap.* I'm done, okay? I'm done with ruining people's already broken lives."

"My my, Pigeon!" The voice laughed. "Okay, fine. I did know a thing or two about your recruits. So what? What did Lenna tell you? Did she give you a sob story? That she's scared? And you fell for it—what, because she's an old friend? Because you told some nasty lies that you feel guilty about?"

Rhiannon swallowed. "I mean . . ."

The voice cut her off. "Your friend is smarter than you think. She's more in control of her destiny than she lets on. Just like *you* are, Rhiannon. You brought Lenna here because you wanted her here. And she came because she couldn't live without you. You didn't have to follow my instructions."

"You would have made me leave. And you sent me that photo. You *know.*"

"You still could have walked away."

Fear streaked through Rhiannon. The voice was basically admitting she'd slipped Rhiannon that photo. That she'd *threatened* her.

She was halfway up the peak. She stared into the valley, at the house. It looked so tiny. "Who are you?"

The voice chuckled. "I think you need to get off that rock. Call me back when you're more levelheaded, okay?"

There was a *click.*

Rhiannon stood still for a while, the sun baking into her scalp. She felt like she might explode. *I think you need to get off that rock.* The voice knew where she was.

She had to get out of here.

Rhiannon scurried down the peak and flew back into the house. As usual, Coral was hunched at the stove. When Rhiannon burst through the door, she wheeled around, her birdlike face full of fright. Everything spooked Coral. The slightest sound made her squeak like a little mouse.

"Is Marjorie back?" Rhiannon demanded.

Coral frowned. "Think she's still out on the four-wheeler."

Rhiannon bit down hard on her lip. She stormed into the next room; Ann was brushing one of the dogs. When she saw Rhiannon, she withered. It was so obvious being around other people drained her. But other people were the whole purpose of Halcyon. Why *come,* if you'd rather have solitude?

"Do you know the gate code?" Rhiannon demanded.

Ann gave her a strange look. "No. Why?"

Rhiannon called through the open door into the kitchen. "Do you, Coral?"

"Me?" Coral laughed. "They don't give me any responsibility around here."

Behind Rhiannon, someone snickered. Gia typed on her laptop at the table. There was a stack of spreadsheets next to her. Naomi stood on a chair, changing a light bulb. Neither of them looked at her.

The children had eaten early; she saw signs of their dishes stacked in the kitchen sink. To Rhiannon's relief, tonight wasn't a communal meal—Coral had left some grab-and-go veggie-stuffed pitas on the table. Rhiannon took one and shoved it into her mouth, practically forcing it down just to get in some sustenance.

Teddy was playing with some of the kids in the main room; Rhiannon swooped in and picked him up. "Bedtime," she announced, kissing him on the top of his head.

When she looked up, Amy was giving her a curious smile at the other end of the hall. A chill went through her, and suddenly she couldn't trust her, either.

She lugged Teddy down the hall. Rushed through bedtime, skipping pages in his favorite book, turning off the light fast. She needed her child ensconced in the safety of sleep.

Then she lay on top of the covers, staring at the ceiling in the darkness. She kept her ear trained for Marjorie coming back from wherever she'd been. Her mind felt scattered, and she had no idea what she would say to get Marjorie to relinquish the gate code— even if Marjorie *wasn't* the voice, she was very particular about people coming and going. Then again, before, when she'd recruited Sarah and Lenna, she'd said she needed medical tests for a preexisting condition; Marjorie hadn't questioned that. Could she say Lenna needed medical care? Or her baby? She had to get Lenna out of here. She owed her that.

The pillow was cool and soft. The sky outside had turned a dusty purple. There were sounds from down the hall—dice rattling in a cup. Game night. So freaking *innocent,* and yet there was a wolf lurking.

She stifled a sob. It wasn't fair. To any of them. All these kids . . .

Something shifted in the corner, almost imperceptibly, shadow upon shadow. Rhiannon bolted awake, but she didn't dare move. She peered behind the chair. Something was lurking behind her mountain of clothes. *Someone.* In her room.

The figure stood. She moved through the darkness like a ribbon, like she had all the time in the world, somehow knowing that Rhiannon would be too petrified to scream. Rhiannon remained still as she slithered over to her bed until they were just inches away from each other.

"Hello, Pigeon," the voice whispered.

There was something very familiar about this voice—not just because she knew it from the phone call, but from real life, too. Before Rhiannon could say a word, before she could even *breathe,* there was a hand over her mouth and something sharp was piercing the inside of her arm. She swung around, and for a split second, she saw the face of the person who was hurting her.

She couldn't believe who it was.

33

LENNA

A person?" There is dust in Lenna's eyes. Dust in her throat. "Where?"

"*There,*" Sarah says. "Oh shit. Get behind me."

She yanks Lenna to the right. The dog seems to rise up like he's going to bark.

"Shh," Sarah warns, snapping her fingers at him. "Cosmo, *quiet.*"

Lenna tries to peer in the direction of Sarah's gaze. The rocks block her view. "What should we do?"

"I don't know. Maybe you should have told Marjorie where we were. Safety in numbers? They could have come for us."

"But I have no idea if she was being genuine. We *still* don't know."

Sarah's gaze is on something down the rocks. Lenna strains to hear anything over the wind. Then, Sarah stands straighter. Despite the heat, the color drains from her face.

"Fuck," she says.

"Who is it?"

She glances at Lenna again. Her eyes have turned dark and

haunted. "This always lurked at the back of my mind, but . . . but I never thought it was a real possibility."

"What?"

Sarah runs a trembling hand through her hair. "It's really never occurred to you that she might still be alive?"

"*Who?*"

"You know. *Gillian.*"

A ringing sound begins in Lenna's ears. "Wh-what?"

"They never actually found her body," Sarah whispers. "Only some of her personal effects. But it was never actually official, and—"

"What the *fuck* are you talking about?" Lenna shrieks.

Sarah claps a hand over Lenna's mouth. "You have to keep it down."

Lenna peers around Sarah to look into the barren ravine. If it's Gillian, then she wants to see for herself. But all she sees are rocks. Cacti. Swirls of stirred-up sand. Twisted trees half bent over from the storm. Branches snapped off.

She looks at Sarah. "What did you see?"

"A woman." Sarah's voice is shaking. "Someone with her hair."

"Why didn't you tell me sooner you didn't think Gillian was dead?"

Sarah looks distraught. "Because I didn't want to *believe* it. But think about it. We both wronged her. No matter how things ended up that day, she couldn't have returned to a normal life."

Lenna swallows a lump in her throat. She thinks of Gillian charging for her on that cliff. Gillian somehow pretending she was Lenna and texting Rhiannon. Gillian faking that she worked at that magazine and who knows where else.

"Rhiannon, too," Lenna whispers. "Gillian hated her. She was jealous of me being friends with her."

"She holds grudges, Lenna. She wrote them down on that Instagram page."

Lenna is sobbing now. "*No.* Gillian fell into a canyon. Her family never even showed up when she went missing. She had no support."

"Are we sure she fell? Do you know for certain?" Sarah looks pained. "*Someone* is looking for us, and someone did something to Rhiannon. It all connects."

Lenna's mind reels. She needs to sit down, but there's nowhere to sit. Images dance back into her brain. She hates how tidy this all is.

But *fake her death*? *Could* she have? Maybe Gillian tumbled over the canyon but fully knew she'd get a foothold and be okay. Maybe she threw her things deeper into the canyon to make it look like she died. A chill comes over Lenna. Maybe *Gillian* was the one who'd made that anonymous tip about Sarah that got her in trouble. Only, why hadn't she tipped them off about Lenna, too? And why had she brought them all here? To get them together to punish them at once? All three women . . . *and their children*?

Sarah stares at Jacob on Lenna's chest, maybe thinking the same things. "We have to hide." She starts back down the mountain. "This way."

"The phone service! 911!" Every step they take down the mountain means less of a cell signal.

But Sarah is already heading down the winding path, the dregs of the windstorm sweeping against her ankles. Lenna doesn't know what else to do but follow. The dog is quickly at her heels, clearly not wanting to be left alone. Barbed plants claw at her ankles. Jacob stares at her with drowsy eyes; his lips are cracked, possibly from dehydration. Lenna needs to get her baby out of the desert. It could be life-threatening.

Desert rocks jut up haphazardly; one wrong step, and Lenna will careen into a sharp cactus. She follows Sarah, Jacob bouncing, as she heads to the backside of the mountain. There, they find an outcropping of rock that makes a natural awning, almost a little cave. Sarah stops under it to catch her breath. Jacob is wailing again, and though Lenna tries to silence him—his voice echoes worryingly—he is so worked up, probably overtired, certainly done with this journey, that he can't be calmed. *Please,* Lenna thinks as she slicks back his hair, wanting to cry, too. *Please, just hang on a little longer.*

From their spot, they have a good view of the land. Sarah points to the right. "If she's still there, at least now we'll see her." She pulls out her phone. "I'll call someone at the house. I bet the Wi-Fi signal is back."

"Are you *sure*?" Lenna feels a stab of trepidation. "What if they're all working together? What if they're all in on this?"

Sarah gives her a look that seems to say she hasn't considered this. She shakes her head. "I don't want to believe that. We have to take the chance."

Sarah taps her phone. On the screen, Lenna can see that the Wi-Fi signal is indeed back. "I'll call Ann," Sarah says. "The woman who works with animals. Have you met her?"

"She wouldn't be my first choice," Lenna says.

"Why? Okay, Melissa, then?"

Lenna chews on her lip. What if they called Melissa but got Naomi? What if Naomi was *pretending* to be Melissa all this time? She isn't sure Naomi would want to rescue them on a rock.

"Amy?" she suggests. "Matilda's mom? She'd come."

"You're not calling anyone," says a voice behind them.

Lenna's limbs turn to steel. She whips around, searching for the voice, but the desert is playing tricks. All she sees is shimmering dirt. Sarah seems equally confused. But in the very next moment, there's a small, flat *smack*. Something hard hits her leg. A stinging insect? A cactus needle? Lenna yelps and bends down, touching something unfamiliar protruding from her calf.

"What the . . . ?" Sarah whispers. There's one in her leg, too. When she pulls it out, it looks to be a tiny dart. Sarah stares at Lenna in horror. The dog starts to bark.

"Oh my God," Sarah whispers, dropping the pointed end to the dirt. "Lenna. *Lenna.* Pull it out! Pull it out *now*!"

"I'm trying," Lenna says. Her fingers are shaking too badly. Her knees start to buckle. *Jacob.* The dog's bark rises in pitch. But she can't tell what he's barking at.

She gets on her knees, knowing she's about to fall forward, desperate not to cause any injury to her baby. Footsteps sound close—heavy boots on the dirt. Her limbs are liquid. *Jacob.* Her shoulder hits the ground. It brings the baby down, too, his body still strapped to her. *No,* she wills her body. She needs to protect him. She can't let this happen.

But whatever was injected into her bloodstream is too powerful. Lenna can barely open her eyes. Her ears still function, and she hears the footsteps come closer and then someone's hands click the baby carrier's latch free from her waist. Weight releases from her—the carrier, and Jacob, too. *No,* Lenna tries to scream, but her mouth won't open properly, and her body won't move. She curls her hands into fists.

A figure looms over her, gently lifting Jacob up. "There, there," a voice says over the sound of the barks. A woman's voice. *Gillian.*

"Please," Lenna croaks, but her mouth feels like it's welded shut. *Her baby.*

"Please," she says, trying to speak more clearly. In her head it sounds clear enough, but on her lips it's something else. *"Please."*

Jacob fusses. Struggling hard against the exhaustion, she forces her eyes open. Every cell in her body screams at the sight of Jacob's chubby, sweet, *innocent* body in this person's arms—someone blurry, but just like Sarah said, with Gillian's wavy hair like a halo around her head. Jacob is twisting around, his gaze staring down at Lenna as if he knows what's happening. The figure—blurry, growing blurrier by the second—is staring down at her, too.

Lenna's lips part. She wants to scream out. But before she can, her ears thunder with echoing sound. And the world goes black.

34

LENNA

When Lenna opens her eyes again, the world smells like rot and sweat. There is only darkness and murk. She hears someone close to her gasping, sucking air through a straw.

She experiments with moving her fingers, then her arms. It comes back to her: the tranquilizer in her leg. *Gillian.*

And then: *Jacob.*

That thought jolts her fully awake. Pain shoots through her all the way to the roots of her teeth and palms of her hands as she tries to sit. "Jacob!" she screams. At least her voice works. *"Jacob!"* Her baby is no longer in her arms.

Nothing. No sounds at all, really, except for that ragged, sucking breathing from somewhere in the darkness. Tears prick Lenna's eyes. Her heart is pounding so hard, she's afraid it might seize. She thinks of Daniel, safe at home, thinking they're coming back soon. She wishes she could scream for him.

She needs her baby. She tries to move forward, but something is clamped on her ankle. Her fingers fly there, touching plastic. It's a zip tie. She's attached to what seems like some sort of metal clamp bolted into the ground. She scrabbles at it, but it doesn't give.

She lets her fingers fall dejectedly. Her mouth is dry with thirst. Her heart twists.

"*Jacob,*" she whispers. And then, "Sarah? *Anyone?*" Then she notices a pair of eyes gleaming in the darkness. Cosmo. He's still here. He's panting heavily; she wonders if he was drugged, too.

"Cosmo," she wails. "Where did they go?"

"*Shhh,*" calls a voice.

Lenna turns her head, alert. "Who's that?"

A moan. "Sarah."

"Are you okay?"

"I think so. Are you?"

"Yeah. Where *are* we?"

There's a long pause. "It looks like a cave, but I can't really see."

Lenna feels around on the floor. It's warm. Earthy. Moist. Rock. She can sense, without actually seeing, that the ceiling is low.

She curls into herself. *A cave.* She thinks of the terrifying things that lurk in these caves. Snakes. Spiders. Bats. Death.

"How long have we been here?" Sarah's voice pierces through the darkness.

Lenna glances at her watch, but it's too dark to see the face. Then she remembers her phone. Miraculously, it's still in her pocket. The battery is on red, but the screen wakes when she presses the side button. The clock reads 8:54 P.M.

"Over an hour," she reports.

Her heart splits in two. *Where is Jacob?* She can't remember when she last fed him. Should she scream more? Maybe someone will hear? Tears blur her vision. She can't breathe. *Her baby.*

"Is your phone still working?" Sarah calls.

Lenna consults the screen. "It hasn't run out of battery. But I'm not getting any service. No Wi-Fi."

"So that means we're not within the range of the router, nor are we up high. But maybe we're still on the property. Not that that's particularly helpful, considering how big the property is."

"Should we scream?" Lenna asks her. "Do you think they'll hear us?"

"We can try."

On the count of three they scream, ravaging Lenna's throat. When they finish, their voices echo on the cave's walls. They wait. A coyote howls, somewhere, but that's all. The wind has died down, the dust storm over, but it still seems like the cave has absorbed the noise.

Tears stream down Lenna's cheeks. How could no one have heard them? Is this *it*?

Then her foot brushes against something soft and skin-like. She lurches back, mortified. *Sarah?* But Sarah's voice comes from farther away. "Hello?" she says. "Wh-who's there?"

No answer. Lenna squints. She's able to make out a head, shoulders, a mound of hip. It's . . . a *person,* lying on her side. She shifts closer. And then, she sees it: a few locks of that wild, curly hair, splayed out on the dingy floor, barely visible. *Rhiannon.*

"Rhiannon!" Lenna cries. "Jesus, Sarah, Rhiannon's next to me!"

"What?" There's scrabbling. "Are you *sure*?"

She stretches, just able to touch the edge of Rhiannon's shoulder. It's cold, and Lenna recoils, beginning to hyperventilate.

Rhiannon moans. Lenna's heart bursts with joy. With the tips of her fingers, she touches Rhiannon's side. "Rhiannon! It's Lenna! And Sarah! Are you okay? Where are we?"

"Mmmm." Rhiannon sounds woozy. Her lips smack dryly. "Wha-?"

"Holy shit," Sarah whispers. "Is it really her?"

"Lenna? What the . . ." Rhiannon's words are garbled and slurred. "Y-you can't be here. Where's Teddy?"

Teddy. "He's back at the house. Safe. I think. I *hope.*" Guilt slams into her. Not only has she lost her child, but she's put Rhiannon's in danger, potentially.

"We were looking for you," she goes on.

"*Both* of you?" Rhiannon sounds heartbroken. "No. *No.* Why?"

"Because . . ." Lenna's voice breaks. She's surprised Rhiannon doesn't sound pleased. "How did this happen? How did she find you? She has Jacob, Rhiannon. She's going to hurt him. We have to get to him!"

"You shouldn't be here," Rhiannon moans. "You were supposed to get help."

"I didn't understand. How did she find you?"

"You need to leave. This isn't safe."

"Too late for *that,*" Sarah says, deadpan.

"Do you know where we are?" Lenna asks Rhiannon.

"No clue. I tried to call, but she took my phone."

"After you sent that audio file?" Lenna asks. "You were calling for help?"

There's a pause. "I only had service for a second. It was before she came back. It was my one shot."

Lenna shuts her eyes.

"It's why we were looking for you. Only . . ." Lenna takes a breath. "We didn't know who to trust. And we couldn't call 911, and we were looking for higher ground . . ."

". . . but then she drugged us," Sarah adds. "How did she get on the property, anyway?"

Rhiannon pauses. "What do you mean?"

"Does Marjorie know her?" Lenna whispers. "Did she let her in? How else would she know the gate code? But why haven't we seen her before now?"

Rhiannon shifts her weight, swallows. "I don't know what you mean. Of course we've seen her."

Lenna stares into the darkness. "What are you . . . ?" Rhiannon must be delirious. Gillian isn't a member of the community. That, Lenna knows for sure.

A tiny, electronic *ping* sounds from outside the cave. Lenna stiffens. *She's there.* And Gillian has cell phone service—how?

"It's *Gillian*," Lenna whispers. "Sarah and I both know her. I can explain later, but she's *here*."

Rhiannon makes a small, strange noise at the back of her throat. "Lenna. *No.* The person . . . she . . . it's not Gillian."

"Of course it is," Lenna insists. "It has to be."

The cell phone bleeps again. The ringtone is a curious choice, a melancholy but familiar birdcall. It takes Lenna a moment to remember what sort of bird it is. A mourning dove. That sweet, sad coo. But the tone sticks out. She heard that ringtone recently—considered using it as her own ringer, actually. She thinks of a phone ringing inside a young woman's sweater pocket.

But . . . *no.* It must be just a coincidence.

A footstep sounds. Lenna clamps her lips shut. She glances down at her phone. It, too, suddenly has a bar of Wi-Fi. There's one way to prove her theory. She has all of the women's phone numbers, and they all have hers.

She pulls up the number she'd tried earlier, when she and Sarah were still on the mountain. They'd called everyone in the house, after all. No one had answered.

The call goes through. On Lenna's end, she hears it ring once, twice. And then, from outside the cave, comes that same curious little tweeting ringtone. Lenna's heart does a somersault. And then, at the mouth of the cave, Lenna notices a shadow of a woman in profile: a short, thin silhouette, turning toward the mouth of the cave, one hand on her hip. Weakly, Cosmo starts to whimper.

"Lenna," Coral says as she puts the phone to her ear. Her voice is calm, easy—and Lenna hears it in two places: through the receiver, and through rock, mere feet away. "Nice to hear from you."

35

RHIANNON

Rhiannon woke up in darkness. Her arms were bound. Her legs were chained. She was desperately thirsty.

Then she heard footsteps. Coral stomped into the cave, weighed down by a backpack. She was sweating like she'd been running. Rhiannon blinked in surprise. She thought she'd imagined Coral's face in her bedroom. It didn't seem possible.

Coral stood over her, snickering, looking much older than her years. "Oh, Pigeon. Oh, Pigeon, how you got it all right, but how you got it all wrong."

Rhiannon took in the young woman's features. It was so incredibly confounding.

"*You're* the recruiter?" She blinked up at her silhouette. "But . . . *why*?"

Coral smiled sadly. "You couldn't afford the financial commitments to stay here. And I mean, where else were you going to go? You'd lose the baby. People would find out. You could say I'm just trying to support healthy parent relationships."

Rhiannon felt a lump in her throat. "I don't understand how you knew anything about me. You didn't come here until *after* I did."

"I knew who you were when you came. I've been tracking you for a while. And I needed to keep you here until I could come, too—*and* until I could round up the others." She clucked her tongue. "It also took some real arm-twisting with Marjorie to accept me as a resident. But you know how it is—she only likes people who are damaged. Who, like, *need* this place. Clearly I couldn't show my hand in that department, so I just sort of fudged it. But lucky for me, I had a lot of cash. My adoptive parents are loaded. And I had to promise that I'd cook all of the meals for the whole place in exchange. You think that's fun, cooking for all of you? Half the time, you don't even appreciate it."

Rhiannon had no idea what she was talking about. "What do you want?" she whispered. "Why are you doing this?"

"Because I want you to do what I ask. So far, you have. But you got a piece of the puzzle a little too early. You started to ask too many questions."

"About . . . Lenna?" Something else occurred to her. "*You* sent me that photo? Of my mother and me? How did you know about that?"

"I found it on your phone." Coyly, Coral put her finger to her lips. "I'm a pretty good hacker. It runs in the family."

Then she knocked Rhiannon out.

36

LENNA

Lenna's phone trembles in her hands. She lowers it from her ear, gasping in the darkness. Coral's loose curls appear in silhouette. *Gillian's* loose curls . . . or so she'd thought. Funny, Coral always had her hair in a bandanna; Lenna never noticed.

Sarah sits up, gaping at her in horror. *"Coral?"* she cries. "Honey, why?"

"Where's Jacob?" Lenna says at the same time. "What have you done with him?"

Coral ignores this question, looking at Sarah. "You really have no idea why I'm here?"

Sarah shifts to sitting. "I-I'm sorry, but no . . ."

"How about you, Lenna?"

Lenna shakes her head, too terrified to speak.

"Come on. You're smarter than that." Coral puts her hands on her hips. "She told you about me. I know she did. Some friend *you* are. Then again, you pushed her into a canyon, so . . ."

"Gillian?" Rhiannon whispers.

Coral points at her. "Good job!"

Lenna looks over. Rhiannon had put the pieces together, then. Or had she always known? She was *acting* surprised, but were she and Coral in on this together?

But in a snap, she sees how terrified Rhiannon looks. And confused. She looks at Coral again. "Did you *know* Gillian?"

Coral crosses her arms. "Yes and no."

Lenna blinks hard. Then, suddenly, something comes to her. *She told you about me.* Gillian didn't, in so many words . . . but maybe she did.

"Oh my God," she whispers.

"What?" Rhiannon whispers. "What is it?"

Lenna's voice is shaky. "Gillian . . . she was dancing around this secret the night before she fell. About Sarah's baby, about how it was triggering . . . but she didn't tell me the whole story."

Coral tips her head up, staring at the cave's ceiling. "Like you would have believed her even if she did?"

"I . . . I don't know," Lenna says.

"Please. You thought she made shit up. You thought she just wanted attention. You'd written her off."

"Wait a minute, Lenna," Sarah gasps. "On Gillian's Instagram, she talked about telling you this huge secret."

"She didn't actually tell me, though. She was drunk, and rambling, and not really making any sense, and then she just left."

"You should have asked her about it." Coral rolls her eyes. "You should have run after her and actually cared. But you just thought she was weird. And awkward. And *dramatic.* Isn't that right, *Rhiannon*?"

"I don't get it," Rhiannon cries, looking back and forth between all of them. "Who are you to *her*?"

Coral glances at Sarah, maybe waiting for her to guess. Sarah looks like she's figuring it out, too, but she shakes her head. Coral then looks at Lenna, who breathes in cautiously and turns to the others in the dim, gauzy light.

"I think . . . I think Coral is Gillian's daughter."

DM Message Board for @GillianAnxietyBabe

July 23

@lonely_girlRZ4540: Hi. My name is Coral. I'm not
supposed to have your name until I turn eighteen, but
I think I know who you are. Sorry, I'm super nervous, I
don't know how to go about this.

July 24

@lonely_girlRZ4540: Hi again. Did I come on too
strong? Like, I've read all of your posts, I struggle with
the same things you do. I really would love to connect
with you. I feel like I've known you all my life. In a way,
I sort of have. I'd love to know your story. I'm here,
patiently waiting.

July 24

@lonely_girlRZ4540: Just in case you're confused:
Jefferson Memorial Hospital, August 18, 2005. I was
there, too.

37

LENNA

Lenna stares at the woman looming over her. She takes in Coral, realizing that without her bandanna, she has Gillian's wavy hair. Her same square shoulders and petite, slender build.

But she can't fully process this—not yet. "Where's Jacob?" she asks Coral. When Lenna tries to stand, Coral lunges toward her, gun raised.

"Sit *down,*" Coral growls.

Lenna lets out a whimper. Every cell in her body wants to run to her baby. The helplessness she feels is debilitating. She can barely breathe.

"I don't understand," Sarah whispers. "You're really Gillian's . . . daughter?"

"I always knew I was adopted," Coral says. "My parents told me when I was a little kid, maybe four or five. I had a good childhood, don't get me wrong. My parents were great—loving, gave me everything anyone could want. But they told me nothing about my birth mother. Which, like, I *get.* But I knew I could search for my mom when I turned eighteen, and I had a feeling they had the paperwork somewhere. So I snooped. I was fifteen. That's when I found her name. Gillian Winters. She was seventeen when she had me. I don't know the exact circumstances, but she was from this real churchy part of the state, so I can't imagine her parents were pleased."

Sarah breathes out. Rhiannon makes a little whimper. "My mom was eighteen when she had me. Young mothers—it's hard."

"Cry me a river," Coral says, bored. "Anyway. I looked Gillian up online. She only had an Instagram account, and though it was private, I could see her profile picture. I just knew she was my mom. It's hard to say how—our hair is the same, but it was more than that. A *feeling.* I requested permission to view the account, not that I said who I was right away. She granted me permission, thank God. I was able to read her posts—and her comments. So many people loved her. She bolstered a lot of people. I read the posts about social anxiety . . . about a roommate who was mean to her, S; and a best friend who took her for granted, L; and a total bitch named R. I didn't even know who you all were at first—that came later. It was heartbreaking, reading about how difficult it was for her to navigate the world. Funny enough, I had the same problems. The same anxieties.

"I wanted to reach out to her, but I was afraid to send her a message. It took me months to work up the courage, but when I did, I got no reply. I was crushed. I sent another, and then one more basically spelling it out. *Still* no reply. Know why? Because she'd already fallen into a fucking *canyon.* I found out on her Instagram account, actually—her readers were talking about it. *Mourning* her. They said her death wasn't an accident or suicide, and I didn't think so, either. She was striving for things. She wouldn't throw it all away. So I went back through her page, especially her recent posts. I kept reading about L and R and S. I needed to know who you were. I was able to break into her GillianAnxietyBabe Instagram account—she didn't even have two-factor authentication. *Then* I was able to get into her email . . . which told me a lot. I got Sadie's name and, Lenna, you were all over her messages. Rhiannon was a little harder to track down, but I worked backward through the list of magazine employees. Et voilà," she adds, stretching out her arms triumphantly. "She tried so hard, but you pushed her away again and again. It also hinted that maybe she tried desperate measures to make sure you stayed friends—especially you, Lenna. She cared about you so much. All she wanted was for you to be happy. But you didn't care."

"I did care!" Lenna cries. "But I was confused. She went into my phone. Sent texts as me. She lied to make me get my friend in trouble."

"She only did it because she cared about you."

Lenna blinks. There's probably no negotiating. Better just to agree with Coral. But also, Coral is sort of right, in a way. She's thought plenty about Gillian and her motivations, her misguided protectiveness. "You're right. I failed to see that. I failed to see *her,* I think. I should have asked about her past more. I should have given her more grace." Her voice cracks. "I'm sorry, Coral. You don't know how sorry I've felt since she died. It *ruined* me, basically."

Coral sniffs. "Poor you. Got married. Had a child. From my perspective, your life doesn't seem so bad."

"But I still think about it all the time." Lenna swallows hard. "Can I please have my baby? Please, Coral."

"Not yet," Coral says.

"Let her see her baby," Sarah croaks. "And, Coral, you should have reached out to me. You could have stayed with me. We could have talked about all of this."

"*Could* we have, now?" Coral snickers. "And would you have told me that you were the one who killed her?"

Sarah's mouth hangs open. Coral's smile is knowing. Lenna tries to understand how she *could* know the truth. Maybe it isn't so hard to figure out. Lenna glances at Sarah, thinking of the night before, their confessions in the darkness. Coral easily could have been hanging around, listening.

"I listened in on your little conversation yesterday," Coral explains, as if reading Lenna's mind. "But even before that, I had my suspicions," she continues. "I was the anonymous tipster who pressured the police to question you in the first place."

"Oh." Sarah sounds sick. "Oh God."

"I wasn't the only one who thought it. All of her followers were saying the same thing. But I couldn't believe they let you go. Some alibi! It still didn't seem right. I tried to report Lenna, too, but at that point, the cops had already deemed the fall an accident. They didn't want to open the case back up. So I decided to bring you here. I wanted *answers.* I knew one of you was at fault, I just didn't know who. But now I have my answer. I have a recording of everything you two said, by the way." She points at Sarah and Lenna. "Just in case you try and wriggle out of it."

Coral smiles. "I wonder what everyone here would think. Marjorie wouldn't be very pleased."

"So Marjorie isn't in on this?" Rhiannon asks.

"Nah. All she wants is money."

"*You* paid my fees," Rhiannon says miserably. "How?"

"I have a trust fund from my parents." Coral smiles. "Put it to good use."

"And then you made me recruit Sarah and Lenna?"

Lenna twists around to stare at Rhiannon. "You were made to *recruit* us?"

"Now, now, Rhiannon didn't know," Coral scolds. "She had no other choice—she needed the money, and she has no rights to her baby outside these walls."

Rhiannon turns guiltily to Lenna. "Teddy's my mother's. That's where I went, suddenly, when I left LA. My mom . . . she didn't try and kill me when I was a kid. She's a shitty person, but she didn't do that. I didn't know how to tell you."

Lenna looks away. "Sarah and I found a photo in your room of you and this woman—we were trying to figure out where you'd gone. We thought it might be her in the picture, but we weren't sure. There was a message on the back." She glances at Coral. She can only guess Coral was the one who wrote that creepy note about being the only one who knew whose baby Teddy really was.

"But, Rhiannon," Sarah protests. "You could have fixed things— custody of Teddy, all of that. There are ways. You didn't have to come here. Or bring us here."

"I didn't force her," Coral reminds them. "Rhiannon wanted to come."

"It's true," Rhiannon admits. "It's always been sort of a dream."

"You thought you'd escape your past, right?" Coral goads. "You thought you'd become brand-new people. Shiny happy."

But then Lenna has a thought. She looks at Rhiannon. "If Coral gave you my name to recruit, why didn't that set off alarms? Why didn't you see it might be . . . a setup?"

"She didn't give me your name, exactly," Rhiannon sounds miserable. "She just said to look for a friend. I came up with you all by myself. I'm so sorry. I'm an idiot."

"I did give her Sarah's, though," Coral adds. "But that was different—Rhiannon and Sarah had never met. And I conveniently left the Gillian connection out of it. That's Rhiannon's fault not to look up Sarah's background. Guess she was too desperate to follow my instructions and didn't care."

"I . . ." Rhiannon trails off, sounding distraught. "I didn't have the money to stay. I had nowhere else to go."

But Lenna still doesn't understand. If Coral wanted to punish her, why not just do it in California? She thinks of all the walks she took with the baby on her own, the desolate neighborhood. Then her heart twists. "Please tell me where Jacob is?" she begs.

"He was already hurt." Coral's voice cuts deep. "You've exposed him to the sun all day. Subjected him to the dust storms. Kept him up at strange hours, and, if I recall, placed him in the arms of a complete stranger the very first day you arrived. It's not like you're the world's best mother."

"Coral, listen," Rhiannon interrupts. "We want to help. Whatever you need. Just, *please,* you don't have to do this."

Coral scoffs. "My mom needed help, too, but you overlooked it. A social outcast who wasn't your vibe. None of you actually *paid attention.*"

"But I did pay attention," Lenna begs. "And if I could change what happened, if I could take it back . . ." Tears roll down her cheeks. "You have to believe me."

"I mean, sure, of course you regret it *now,*" Coral says dejectedly. "You need to understand: We're all at fault. We all lied. We all did things that are terrible. *All of us.* I'm the bad guy right now, fine, but so are all of you." She straightens. "Anyway. Gang's all here. I'm kind of loving this."

She steps toward them. A shiver goes down Lenna's spine. Her heart starts to race. In all of her fears of her past coming to a head, she'd never thought it would be quite this harrowing. But now it's time to face what she's done. Time to learn what Coral has been plotting all these years.

"People know we're out here," Sarah warns in a shaky voice. "And they must know *you're* gone, too. They're going to figure out what's going on."

Coral waves her hand. "Marjorie thinks I'm in my room. I have a feeling, in all the chaos, she's not too concerned about looking for her little scullery maid."

Lenna swallows hard. The dog lets out another growl. "Cosmo," she says, touching him gently.

But Cosmo doesn't let up. Coral reaches behind her for an object, and Lenna flinches at a glint of metal. It's an iron golf club. She *thwacks* it against the rock. The dog yelps. "Okay. Back to back. Do it now."

Sarah whimpers. "Wh-what are you going to do?"

"No more questions."

She knocks the club against the rock again. Sarah shifts toward Rhiannon. Rhiannon sniffles as she pivots. Lenna presses her back against her friend. She can smell the dried sweat on Rhiannon's body. The fear. She can feel the bones of her spine.

Coral checks that their hands are secure. Then she begins to wrap heavy twine around their waists to keep them all together. After she's finished, she stands over them, hands on her hips, the rope trailing from her hands.

The dog snarls as Coral shifts from woman to woman. At first, Lenna thinks his anger is directed at Coral, but then she notices his body is positioned toward something outside the cave. When Lenna breathes in, she smells something . . . *strange.* It's not something she's smelled before, but there's something familiar about it. Something hormonal. *Musk.*

She cocks her head, listening. There's that familiar shuffling of sharp, sturdy hooves. *Javelinas.* They're out there. Moving in a herd. *Close.*

The dog beside her stiffens, tipping his nose to the air. He snarls toward the mouth of the cave. Lenna knows what Cosmo smells. Suddenly, there's a shadow of . . . *something.* And suddenly . . . *there.* That low-profile beast. The edge of a snout.

The dog is really barking, straining under Lenna's knee, where she's trying to pin him so he won't make trouble. Coral stares at it murderously. "This thing has to fucking *stop.*"

Another snout. A cluster of bodies. Eyes shining into the darkness, *seeing* them. Coral pivots, and just like that, Cosmo leaps out from under Lenna's knee and toward the animals, his teeth bared. Coral twists to grab him, and when her back is turned, Lenna stretches her leg toward the golf club that Coral abandoned in order to tie them up. It takes every effort of strength, but her foot makes contact. She hears the club clatter across the rocks, out of Coral's immediate reach.

A howl rises up. When Lenna turns again, fear strikes her—she worries the pigs have gotten the dog. But it's Coral who tips forward at the mouth of the cave. A javelina chomps into the flesh of her calf.

"What the fuck!" Coral beats at the snorting animal. It rears back, squealing, tusks raised. Lenna winces. Then she hears something off in the distance. A tiny wail. Her heart cracks in two.

"Jacob?" she splutters, looking toward the cave's opening. She turns to Coral, still on the ground. "Wh-where is he?" Adrenaline surges through her. It sounds like he's just outside. On a rock? In that swirling dust? "Please let me see him. He's not safe."

Coral is still on the ground, clutching her calf. From the distant wails and squeals, Lenna guesses that the javelinas have moved on. She hopes the dog is okay. Coral is panting, and there's a layer of sweat on her forehead. She's clearly in pain and trying not to show it. Blood seeps through her khaki cargo pants, black and thick, dripping onto the rock.

"Please, Coral," Lenna whispers. "Let me have Jacob."

Coral groans. "Fine."

She staggers to her feet and disappears from the mouth of the cave. Lenna only feels bewilderment. That was too easy. But also, where was Jacob all this time?

A few minutes later, Coral is limping back, carrying Jacob in her arms. A primal sound escapes from Lenna's lips. Her baby. She doesn't want to think about where he was, but he's with her now.

She reaches her arms out, her wrists still tied, her elbows pressed together in a makeshift platform. Once she has Jacob, she eases him toward her chest, wriggling around so that he can get in her bra. It takes a minute, with her wrists together, but she gets a nipple free. She tries to let him nurse, but he pulls away quickly, too agitated.

"Come on," Lenna whispers to him. "You're dehydrated." She looks up at Coral. "Thank you."

"Yeah, well." Coral twists her mouth. "You can go together."

Jerkily, she turns to a faded army-issue knapsack at the mouth of the cave. From it, she extracts a variety of materials Lenna can't quite make out. One of the objects is in the shape of a firework.

Lenna lets out a gasp. It's not a firework but a stick of dynamite.

"Please," Rhiannon whispers, her voice trembling. *"Please."*

Lenna switches Jacob to the other breast, which is leaking. It astounds her that her breasts can provide milk at a time like this.

Coral looks over her shoulder, wincing as her injured leg twists. "It's kind of a funny expression. Blowing something up. We toss it around all the time. My phone is *blowing up.* Her career is *blowing up.* We talk about it like it's something getting bigger and bigger— I've always wondered how that got misappropriated. Because in essence, blowing something up is *eliminating* it. Making it cease to exist. Turning it into nothing." She gets wistful. "It's hard not to appreciate the beauty of this peak right in the middle of the land. But there's also something so . . . *godlike* . . . about altering rock. People are going to look at this peak years from now and wonder why it's shaped the way it is. And that's going to be because of me. Of us. You know what Marjorie says about this land: It's *magical.* It changes people. It reveals the truth."

"Coral, please," Sarah says. "You want to know more about your mom? I'll tell you anything you want to know. I knew her well."

Coral's eyes blaze. "Yeah, and then you *killed* her. All of you did."

"We're sorry," Lenna blurts. "You're right, all of us did, but we are so, *so* sorry. Please understand that. Please don't do this."

Coral doesn't answer. She places the wrapped dynamite at the mouth of the cave. She pulls out more sticks and places one each behind Lenna, Sarah, and Rhiannon. Wires link each stick. The women wrench against the twine Coral has used to tie them, but there's no way they can break free.

"I'm the one who did it, really," Sarah suddenly cries out. "I'm the one who pushed her. Just take me."

Coral's expression remains unchanged. "The blast is going to make beautiful colors in the sky."

And then she lights the match.

Lenna screams. Her heart bangs against her chest. Next to her, the others are struggling, yanking their ankles, screaming at Coral to change her mind. Then, at one point, Rhiannon awkwardly grabs Lenna's hand.

"Lenna," she wails. "This is my fault. I should have been open with you. I should have told you the truth. And I should have never brought you here. I should have seen the writing on the wall."

"It's okay," Lenna says, her body swimming with guilt. "I'm sorry, too. I'm just as at fault as you are."

Lenna watches as the spark travels down the fuse. Her baby's skin is warm against hers. He's going to perish before even living. Suddenly, she realizes she has another option. A *terrible* option, but maybe it's the only one.

"Coral, wait," she cries. "Take Jacob with you. Please."

Coral pivots, blood still trickling from her wound. She narrows her gaze like she doesn't understand what Lenna has asked.

"I'm serious. Get in touch with my husband. He'll take care of him. I just want him to live. *Please.*"

"Lenna!" Rhiannon screams. "What are you *doing*? She won't do what you ask!"

Maybe that's true, but Jacob has a better chance surviving outside the cave than inside. It's the only thing Lenna can think to do.

The flame travels down the fuse. It's getting closer and closer to the explosives. Coral shifts, considering, and then holds out her arms. "Have it your way."

Lenna stares into her baby's eyes for a moment, the sobs racking her body. Jacob looks back at her, his eyes blank and tired. She can barely breathe. Barely *think*. "I love you so, so much."

She hands him over, which causes him to burst into tears. Lenna sits back on her haunches. Her mind is numb. The spark moves hungrily. It won't be long now. She closes her eyes, trying to find strength within herself. A minute, maybe. Sarah's chains rattle. Fifty-nine seconds.

And then a shot rings through the air.

Lenna's eyes snap open just as Coral shrieks and slumps awkwardly to the ground outside the cave, Jacob still in her arms. "Jacob!" Lenna screams, rising up awkwardly on her knees. The way Coral crumples, she has broken the baby's fall, but now Jacob is lying awkwardly on his side. He starts wailing even harder.

And Coral . . . she's writhing in pain. More blood spills across the rock.

"What the hell?" Rhiannon screams.

"Someone fucking shot me!" Coral screams.

A figure steps over the body. She's in silhouette for a moment, but as she turns her head, Lenna recognizes her short stature and glasses.

"Matilda?" Coral shrieks.

The young girl stares at the shotgun in her hands like it's a rattlesnake. She sets the gun down on the rocks as though she's afraid it might go off again. Then she scoops up Jacob.

"What are you doing?" Coral screams.

"I didn't . . . ?" Matilda looks completely confused. Then she looks more steadily at Coral. "I *knew* something was off. I asked you, again and again, and you wouldn't tell me."

"You wouldn't get it," Coral argues.

"Matilda, run!" Lenna cries. "It's going to explode!"

"No, get us out of here!" Rhiannon screams. *"There's still time!"*

Matilda looks at Coral for a beat. "They don't deserve to live," Coral growls. "And, anyway, you won't be able to untie them. You have an illness, don't you? Even if you're better, you shouldn't push yourself. Your mom's always saying that."

Matilda eyes the women in the cave, then looks at Coral again. "I'm not sure I am sick," she says in a small voice. "I'm not sure I ever was."

She walks over to her friend, looming over her body. Then she squats down. For a moment, it seems like she might sit right next to Coral to become part of the explosion, too. But then her hand reaches for something at her hip. She extracts a Swiss Army knife from her pocket. Her gaze rests, for a beat, on her friend's face. Lenna swallows hard. Matilda looks like she might be sick.

Then she stands. Scampers into the cave, the knife blade raised.

"We're tied around the waist!" Lenna instructs. "Get that first!"

Matilda rushes to them, sawing at the twine that connects the three of them together. It snaps quickly, and Lenna lurches forward.

"We have zip ties," she says. "On our ankles."

"Lenna," Sarah's voice trembles. "She won't be able to get all of us. She should go. The baby . . ."

"I can do it," Matilda insists. Awkwardly, while still holding the baby, she starts on Rhiannon, who is closest to the mouth of the cave. "I have to try. This is my fault," she adds sadly. "I should have seen this coming."

"This isn't your fault!" Lenna cries. "How could you have known she'd do something like this?"

"I'm her friend. I'm supposed to look out for her."

"And as *your* friend, I'm telling you that you need to leave!" Coral screams.

There's a *click*, and Rhiannon is free. She scampers over to the sparking fuse, though when she tries to blow on it, it's useless.

Matilda snips Lenna next. Her hands tremble. When Lenna's ankles and wrists are freed, she darts from the cave on wobbly legs. Sparks from the fuse lick her ankles. She yelps in pain. She grabs the baby from Matilda and steps over Coral, who lies in a heap on the ground, felled by the gunshot. Lenna makes the mistake of looking at the depth of her injury—it seems the bullet has sliced the bottom part of her leg cleanly off. She is hemorrhaging blood. Her face has grown pale.

Lenna hesitates, then stops above Coral and extends her hand. "Come on. I'll help you. There's still time." She isn't sure why she does this. Maybe because everyone is capable of mistakes. Maybe because she understands Coral's misguided rage, just a little. Mostly because she can't have another thing to feel guilty about.

But Coral's eyes are dim. She already looks like she's somewhere else. She shakes her head, bottom lip protruding, a single tear pouring onto her cheek.

Sarah is screaming inside the cave. "It's going to go off! Matilda, you have to get out of here! You, too, Lenna!"

And then Lenna's limbs move without her consent. She stumbles over Coral and down the rocks. When she glances over her shoulder, she doesn't see Sarah *or* Matilda, and her heart twists. But she keeps running. It's the only way to save herself, her baby.

The cave is close to the basin of the ravine, and she shoots across it, out the other side, and across the desert sand. She feels the explosion before she sees it—the vibration, the heat. She whips around just in time to see pieces of rock shooting into the sky. She screams, hitting the ground, covering Jacob with her body, covering her head with her arms. Something knocks against her—at first, she worries it's rock, but then she realizes it's bone. A dusty shape huddles at her feet, covering her head. And then a second. Matilda. Sarah, Rhiannon, too. But no Coral.

The boom blows out her eardrums. She covers her baby's ears and grits her teeth. But shortly after, there's only silence. Slowly, Lenna lifts herself from the ground. The air is full of putrid-smelling smoke that's so thick, she can barely see.

"It's okay," she whispers to Jacob, who stares at her with wide eyes. "It's okay."

A few feet away, Rhiannon lies in a heap. She looks stunned. "Are you okay?" Lenna screams.

Rhiannon makes a small sound. Lenna hears another whimper just as Matilda and Sarah struggle to stand. They're covered in dust. Even their eyelashes. Matilda is holding her ears.

"Here," Lenna says, reaching out her arm. She pulls the girl to her feet. The gun is once again in Matilda's hand. She stares at Lenna shakily, like she's about to shatter.

"Where are you?" voices scream. "Hello?"

And then, Marjorie appears through the smoke, followed by Amy, Ann, Melissa, and Gia, who is holding Teddy's hand. When they see Lenna and the others standing on the rocks, they cry out and sprint for them.

Rhiannon lets out a scream as her son runs for her. Amy wraps her arms tightly around her daughter, staring in horror at the gun Matilda is holding.

"Wh-where the hell did you get that?" she asks, grabbing it from her.

"It's mine," Gia volunteers. She shrugs. "I wasn't about to be out here in the middle of nowhere without a weapon. I guess she found it . . ."

Matilda, Lenna realizes, is sobbing—hard. Her cries are so

forceful, it's difficult for her to speak. "I just—when I saw Coral was gone, *and* Rhiannon, I knew I had to come out here. I knew something was really wrong."

"We were worried *sick,*" Amy whispers.

"I know." Matilda's face collapses. "I'm so sorry."

"Baby." Amy strokes her arm. "It's okay. You didn't do anything wrong. You were protecting your friends."

But then Matilda looks up and shakes her head. "Mom, *no.*" She points at the gun Amy is now holding. "I didn't pull the trigger. I swear."

"Of course you did," Amy says. "You probably just don't remember. You're in shock."

Matilda is firm. "I *didn't.* I don't even know *how.*"

Amy glances at Gia, and Gia raises her palms. "*I* certainly didn't teach her how to fire a gun. I've never even fired that thing myself."

"You saved us," Lenna tells Matilda. "It's okay."

Matilda starts to shake. "She's in shock," Marjorie says firmly, stepping toward her.

Amy catches her arm. "*I've* got it from here, thanks."

"Actually?" Matilda's teeth chatter as she looks back and forth between her mother and Marjorie. "I'd rather not be around *either* of you."

Her tone isn't lost on Lenna. She wonders what went down at the house, after that call where Lenna made her accusations. She'd mentioned that post Carina wrote. Maybe some of it was true.

So it's Rhiannon who limps over to Matilda. "Sit down. Just rest. And here." She gives her the sweatshirt tied around her waist. "I'm sorry if it smells. You're a hero. You saved us."

"But . . . I didn't." Matilda stares at her hands, then the gun. She says it again and again: *I didn't, I didn't, I didn't.*

Some of the other women look at Lenna and Rhiannon, still deeply confused about what even happened. Lenna is too overwhelmed to explain. There will be time. Instead, she turns toward the hole that's now in the rock face. Splinters mar the smooth surface. Mist hangs in the air like a ghost. The cave is obliterated. There isn't a trace of what was inside—not Coral's pack, not the chains she used to keep them there, nothing.

The women turn to the cave, somehow knowing without knowing. They stand solemnly for a beat, hands over mouths. The wind blows gently—hauntingly. By her side again, Rhiannon takes Lenna's hand. Sarah joins her on the other side, wraps her arm around Lenna's waist, and squeezes, too. They are all dusty. Wounded. Broken. But as Rhiannon and Sarah squeeze, and as Lenna presses her cheek into the top of Jacob's head, she feels something commingling with her trauma and fear and grief—for Coral, for Gillian, for the mess left behind.

Hope.

EPILOGUE

LENNA

They meet at the same café Rhiannon chose for her recruiting mission. There is a certain symmetry to it, but it's also the first café that comes to Lenna's mind when Rhiannon suggests they finally hang out again.

Lenna climbs out of the car and rolls back her shoulders. It still feels a little strange not having the baby strapped to her 24/7. Her gait is still a little off, too, from the injuries she sustained while in the cave. But most of all, her stomach teems with nerves. She feels like she might be sick.

And yet she steadies herself. Shoots off a text. I'm going in.

A response comes back. You've got this.

She breathes out, then pushes through the door. It's such déjà vu seeing Rhiannon at the same table as last time—though now, she and Teddy wait together, and Lenna comes without Jacob. It's better she's come alone, though—there's some truth to what Rhiannon said about babies sensing tension, and Jacob really does do best when things around him are calm. She feels a pinch of dread—she hadn't wagered on Teddy coming, though at least the little boy is wearing headphones and intently staring at an iPad. He'll be distracted, hopefully.

"Hey, Len," Rhiannon says, spreading out her arms, just as before.

"Hey," Lenna says back, stepping into the hug, but only for a moment. When they move apart, Rhiannon smiles warmly. Lenna thinks she smiles, too. But her heart is banging.

"Sit," Rhiannon says.

Lenna gives a little wave to Teddy, but he is lost in his screen.

"How's it going?" Lenna points at Teddy. She's glad to see that Teddy is still in Rhiannon's custody, though she heard Rhiannon had to explain to the state of Oregon what had happened. It's been touch-and-go what the state wants to do about the adoption process.

Rhiannon looks down at the table. "My lawyer is great. We should have stuff sorted soon. There's a lot of paperwork to file. A lot of things to prove."

"And *your* mom? Did you ever—"

Rhiannon shook her head. "Never found her. Not even after all of us in the news." Then she lifts her gaze to Lenna. "I feel awful about what I told you about her. It was so . . . misleading. Awful. I'm a piece of shit."

Don't, Lenna thinks. Feelings well up in her throat. So many feelings.

Since leaving Halcyon, Lenna has stayed in the suburbs outside the city, trying to only see what is in front of her. After everything went down, the members of Halcyon made a pact not to tell the authorities about the reasons Coral had come after Lenna, Sarah, and Rhiannon, instead reporting the young woman as tragically unstable, and the violence she inflicted on the women as a product of a troubled, delusional mind. It protected all three of them that way, and it also protected the community from even more bad press. After all, Marjorie had let this happen under her nose.

Not to mention everything *else* that would come out—including the gossip about Marjorie's sons, but also Carina's post about the place, as much of it was true. Everyone had noticed that Naomi and Melissa hated each other but were also codependent, and then something came out that even the residents didn't know—they'd both gone in for IVF at the same time, and they'd put their eggs into a shared pool. Melissa's children might actually be Naomi's, except Melissa was the one who successfully carried to term. Once the babies were born, Melissa was treating them like they really *were* hers. Which, maybe they were after all. The twins were identical. There was no way to know.

And Matilda had been questioning her medical history for a while, but it took reading Carina's post to push her over the edge. As it turned out, the girl had had lots of mysterious symptoms before coming to Halcyon, but no doctor could make heads or tails of what might be causing any of it—or provide any diagnosis. Was coming here a miracle . . . or did her mother just *want* it to be a miracle? Matilda finally confronted Amy, and Amy confessed, sort of, that perhaps she had no *real* illness—but still, the world was toxic and scary, with danger at every turn, and she was only doing what she thought was best.

Whispers surfaced about Ann, too. Apparently, she was a ketamine dealer, having swiped it from her veterinary practice, where she specialized in the care of large animals. It was unclear how Marjorie scooped her up or prevented her from going to jail, but this was why Ann felt indebted to her—and had given Marjorie her life savings.

Well, all of them had done that, Lenna supposed—and they'd never get that money back. When they forced Marjorie to pay them their share from the Halcyon bank account, Marjorie revealed that the account was nearly empty. As it turned out, Marjorie had spent all of it not on property upkeep or even the IVF fund, but on paying off her own past debts, which she'd amassed before and after starting the community, and which were astronomical. Gia had an inkling this was going on; it was why Marjorie put up with Gia's snide attitude and general lack of participation.

The day after the explosion, Marjorie opened the gates and let everyone who wanted to leave go. She tried a last-ditch effort of saying that she had a new philosophy for the place, that she was going to slash the fees, that she would work on *herself*, but Lenna had no interest in staying. Still dazed and exhausted, Lenna immediately flew back home. She hadn't even downloaded what had happened with Rhiannon or Sarah, not really. She just wanted to get the hell out of there. Daniel picked her up. He'd heard nothing about the explosion—no one pressed charges, Coral was the only one who'd perished, and Lenna's injuries were fairly minor. It was just a blip in the desert—and maybe Lenna could have kept it that way. All of it. A proud part of her would rather he knew nothing of the ordeal she'd gone through.

But something had changed in her. This was no way to start a marriage or parenthood. She needed to tell Daniel. *Everything.* She needed to tell him the hold Rhiannon had on her, the lies Gillian told her, but also that she'd bought into those lies, that these two women had pulled at her arms like she was a rag doll, manipulating her one way and then another. But she wasn't a victim. She had reported Rhiannon out of spite, and she'd cost Rhiannon her job. She had believed Gillian's lies, even though she probably knew, deep down, that some of them might not have been completely true. It felt so petty, in hindsight. She dreaded admitting how she'd behaved. She also had to wonder how things would have turned out if Rhiannon hadn't been fired.

Daniel needed to know who she was as well as the headspace she'd been in when they'd gotten together—a headspace, if she was perfectly honest, that had extended through their marriage. *All* of it was built on a shaky foundation he wasn't completely aware of, and that wasn't fair. The funny part, though? Just being at Halcyon, just going through the danger she'd gone through, Lenna realized how much she wanted to be with Daniel after all. She didn't realize how much she loved him, despite the fact that she'd clung to him at first more out of necessity and desperation than love. The love had developed slowly, almost without her knowing.

This was how she ended her confession, this realization of how important he was to her. Lenna worried what Daniel would make of her secrets. There was a very good chance he'd want a divorce. One thing helped, anyway—at least she knew, for certain, she wasn't a murderer. Daniel couldn't take Jacob away from her. It was something she still was scared to truly believe—she'd been carrying around the secret for so long that it kind of felt . . . *part* of her. She realized, too, that unlike how she'd run to Gillian after Rhiannon left, and then how she'd run to Daniel after Gillian died, she would have no one to run to if Daniel chose to end things. She'd never stood on her own, but suddenly, she was pretty sure she could.

It empowered her, knowing this. Her mother would be proud, too. Independence, finally. It gave her the courage to tell Daniel everything she needed to say. She didn't want him to leave her, but even if he walked away, she knew she could go on.

Now, she clears her throat and dares to look at Rhiannon across the table. Her old friend looks so repentant. She has no idea about the grenade in Lenna's hands. Lenna presses her fingernails into her palm five times, but when she looks around the café, for the life of her, she doesn't see anything yellow. But that's okay, surprisingly. Since Halcyon, despite the trauma she went through, she finds she needs the coping mechanisms a little less. She presses through regardless. This will suck, but she can keep going.

"I don't think we can do this, Rhiannon," she says quietly.

Rhiannon blinks. "Sorry?"

"I figured I should tell you in person. But I just . . . I don't think we're good for each other. As friends. I don't like the decisions I make around you. This isn't easy for me to say, but . . ."

Rhiannon shakes her head. "Lenna. I feel so terrible about dragging you to Halcyon. You *know* that."

"Yes, but even before you knew there was some master plan involving Sarah and me, you were still bringing me there under false pretenses. There were reasons you hadn't entirely shared with me." Lenna is so nervous, she's gripping her kneecaps hard. *Push through.* "And that thing you told me about your mom—"

"I told you, I'm so sorry about that. I feel awful."

"I know, and I understand it. But I mean, that you'd tell *that* kind of lie, and not just the first day of our friendship, but after we'd developed a rapport . . ." She feels tears on her cheeks. For some reason, this lie hurts the most. That Rhiannon manipulated her feelings so brutally—almost indifferently. "I feel like I know nothing about who you really are."

"But you do," Rhiannon begs. "I swear."

Lenna worried about this happening. Rhiannon pushing back. Rhiannon trying to get Lenna to change her mind. People talk about the art of breaking up with a significant other; there are plenty of articles to refer to, tactful scripts of how to do it. But breaking up with a friend? Those scripts don't readily exist.

Lenna certainly knows that firsthand. If there had been a script, maybe she would have done a better job ending her friendship with Gillian before that moment on the cliff. Maybe Sarah would have, too, instead of both of them resorting to panic and frustration and threats and death. And Lenna sees the other side of things, too—from Rhiannon's perspective, and from Gillian's. To them, these are friendships desperately worth fighting for.

She closes her eyes. *Gillian.* In the aftermath of things, Sarah showed her Gillian's private Instagram posts, which she'd combed through during the investigation. Finally Lenna could read through Gillian's Instagram posts herself. It was fascinating to see how *justified* Gillian thought she was in her behavior, how she only saw herself as a true and caring friend—and also how much her readers were on her side. But maybe she had reason to have such a skewed view of the world, now that they knew about Coral.

Or, well, what they *presumed* they knew about Coral. Sure, Gillian had told Lenna, in so many words, that being pregnant with Coral had been a terrible ordeal. But it wasn't as if Lenna knew what exactly happened. She'd tried to inquire into Gillian's family, who she was finally able to track down. They lived in central California, and they declined to answer her emails. But then a cousin, Heather, reached out randomly, saying she'd heard Lenna had been a friend. Heather was the chatty type, one of those people endlessly interested in family history and 23andMe connections, and her cousin Gillian's saga was the biggest story of her uninteresting life.

"All of us used to hang out when we were kids," Heather said on a phone call. "But even then, Gillian was kind of . . . dorky, I guess? Laughed too late at stuff, and her jokes weren't funny, didn't quite catch references about things, all around a little bit of a doofus. And there were some days she just didn't want to hang out at all. And if we were going to meet people she didn't know—forget about it. She went home."

"Social anxiety," Lenna said sadly. "Did her parents acknowledge she was going through that?"

Heather paused. "Her parents . . . they weren't the type who believed in any sort of mental troubles, you know? They'd just try and pray it out."

"Ah," Lenna said, thinking about what Coral said. *She was from this real churchy part of the state.*

Heather continued. "This one summer, she bragged about having this serious boyfriend. She showed us a picture, but we didn't really believe her. I mean, she kind of lied about a lot of stuff, you know. Embellished the truth, made things seem better than they were. Like, maybe he was just a good friend? Or she got a mixed message? Anyway, I only saw her once that summer—she got this awful flu. Or, well, her parents *said* she had a flu—it was only later that I wondered if it was something else. I only found out much, much later what actually happened, and that was only from a girl whose mother worked as an OB/GYN and . . . heard things."

"That's when she was pregnant," Lenna guessed.

"Obviously her parents didn't want anyone to know. They must have told her not to tell anyone, either, because I talked to her that following year—even saw her!—and she didn't say a thing about it. Acted like everything was fine—sort of. She was a lot quieter."

"Did she say what happened to the boyfriend?"

"I don't think she ever mentioned him again. And then I lost touch with her after she moved to LA. She never spoke to her parents after that, though."

"Because of how they covered up what happened?"

"Well, no—actually, I think they were the ones to cut her off, not the other way around."

It was heartbreaking. If only Gillian had told her. Had she been able to talk to anyone about her pregnancy? Had anyone *cared*? But it was a huge missing piece to the puzzle. Maybe Gillian wasn't interested in relationships because someone had scarred her in her teens. And maybe Gillian was so clingy with friendships because she had little practice with them—since she'd been awkward even when she was young. There was also the trauma of teenage pregnancy, the childbirth, the way she'd had to lie . . . it seemed she'd grown up to believe that lying was easier. Things could be swept under the rug. And so she kept lying.

It was no excuse for Gillian faking texts from Lenna's phone. It was no excuse for Gillian teasing about tampering with Sarah's meds—or maybe doing it. But could they really despise Gillian, if she'd had no guidance? She was doing what she thought she needed to do to hold on to precious relationships. They were so hard to come by, in her world.

It was what Rhiannon was doing now. But it all felt too tangled, too messy.

"I loved being friends with you," Lenna says to Rhiannon now. "And I'm so happy for you and Teddy, and I really think it'll all work out. But . . . I need to go my own way." She shoots her an apologetic smile. "I'm sorry."

Rhiannon's gaze falls to the table. "I guess part of me saw this coming."

"Maybe you can go back to Halcyon, after the adoption comes through?"

The community is still going. Naomi and Melissa stayed on the property. So did Amy, though not Matilda—she left to live with an aunt. Ann was awaiting trial on drug charges. And Gia—it turned out she never actually rejected her fortune, just needed a break from that life. She joked about buying an island, maybe starting a community there. But Lenna had a sneaking suspicion no Halcyon guest would be invited.

Those who remained demanded that Marjorie leave, and Marjorie did; Lenna has no idea where she went. From what Lenna's heard, Halcyon is a little shaky without her—they hadn't realized, apparently, how handy Marjorie was. They're limping along for now. There's still a magic to the desert, a value in that kind of community. For some, anyway.

Rhiannon shakes her head. "I can't go back." She looks up, tears in her eyes, too. "It'll remind me too much of how I thought we could be there together. And change and grow."

"That's the thing, though. Were we ever really going to change? Our friendship, or even just *us*?" Lenna puts the strap of her bag over her shoulder. "We were all looking for this big transformation at that place, but I'm not sure it comes by simply living in the desert and, like, eating organic food. We were all still . . . us." Lenna goes on. "It's like this conversation I had with Gia, before we both left. I never really figured out what Gia's deal was, except that I don't think she was very good at interacting with people. Maybe that's *all* it was. But she said that everyone she met at Halcyon, every single person, was damaged. And also, that every single person she met wasn't *really* getting better. Oh sure, Matilda might feel healthier, so maybe she's the exception, but for most people, they needed to look at who they *were* before they came, in order to heal. And no one was actually doing that."

Rhiannon presses the heels of her hands to her face, letting out a long, defeated sigh. "So I guess Gia's not a murderer, then? Like that post said?"

"I don't think so. Carina wasn't right about everyone, I guess."

"I got a look at Gia's closet once. She had *tons* of clothes. All beautiful. I get the feeling that she didn't wear a lot of stuff twice. Even in that place."

Lenna laughs. "But what about the one-bag-of-garbage-a-day policy?"

"Oh right." Rhiannon groans. "That was impossible. Ann would literally watch me like a hawk if I so much as tried to throw away an orange peel."

Lenna feels a twinge. She's going to miss Rhiannon. Rhiannon seems to read her thoughts, because she looks up as a tear rolls down her cheek. But she doesn't say anything. Her chin wobbles.

Someone comes through the front door, distracting them. It's a young woman, not that much older than Coral. She wears a gray hoodie pulled over her head, and she's studying something on her phone, a half smile on her face. Lenna watches as she wanders to the back and ties on an apron.

This could have been Coral's path. Lenna had actually spoken to Coral's parents after the explosion, as they'd called to apologize for their daughter's actions, especially when they found out Coral held Lenna's baby hostage. They were good people, Coral's parents. They really did give her everything they could. Maybe *too* much of everything, without many rules. Still, they couldn't fathom that their daughter had plotted such a bizarre sequence of events. They didn't even know she'd found out her biological mother's name—she wasn't supposed to know it until later. As for her escape to Halcyon, she'd always wanted to travel. She graduated high school a year early; they thought she was just taking a "gap year" before college. "We thought she was farming, finding herself, making crafts," said Coral's mother, Jana, a small, fine-featured woman with diamond studs in her ears. "Could we have brought this on? Simply by not sharing with her the details about her birth mother? We didn't think she was old enough yet. We didn't think she was ready to know." As for how Coral paid for her and Rhiannon's Halcyon fees, Jana admitted they let her have a teenager-friendly credit card with a high line of credit, and they'd been lax that summer about monitoring her charges. "I wanted her to be independent," Jana said. "She was old enough." *And yet she wasn't old enough to know her birth mother's name?* Lenna wondered. But maybe she wasn't one to judge. Motherhood and all its decisions were so complicated.

Now, Lenna stands, shaking herself from her thoughts. "I

should go," she says. As an afterthought, she places her hand on top of Teddy's little head. The boy glances up at her placidly, and their eyes meet for a moment. *Take care of your mommy,* Lenna tries to telegraph to him. "Bye, Rhiannon."

Rhiannon looks at her emptily. "Bye," she whispers.

Lenna turns and takes a few steps toward the door, and then she is outside. She walks to the end of the block before the expected call comes. Lenna had said it would take about ten minutes or so; it surprises her how on the mark she was.

When Lenna answers, the normal recorded message that a prisoner from Chino State Correctional Facility is looking to contact her, and does she accept the call, blares forth. Hastily, Lenna presses a number on the keypad, and Sarah's voice floods in.

"So?" she asks. "Did it go okay?"

"Yeah," Lenna breathes out. "I think so."

But then she bursts into tears.

"Oh, Len." Sarah sighs. "It's hard."

What's harder is that Sarah is locked away and can't be here with her. After they left Halcyon, despite the pact the women made to keep Coral's motives quiet, Sarah hadn't been able to live with herself. Finally, she said she had to confess. She'd pushed Gillian, after all. A death that affected so many people.

And so, Sarah called a lawyer. They came up with a plea deal, and she was serving eleven months in a women's correctional facility in Chino. Though her attorney said it was likely she'd get out sooner, Sarah could have her baby in prison. And she wouldn't be able to see the child until she got out—Sarah's family agreed to take the baby for a few months. Lenna can't imagine. She remembers those first months with Jacob. They were brutally hard, but she wouldn't trade them for anything.

"It's not like she's the only one who did things wrong," Lenna blubbers. "I was wrong, too."

"You both lied to each other. Sometimes, friendships have too much mess to fix. You know that. And it's okay."

"I know," Lenna says miserably.

She thinks of the mindset she'd been in when meeting Rhiannon in this café for the first time. How she promised herself not to utter a word about Gillian, how she vowed to stand firm and indifferent, like their friendship didn't matter. Maybe on her side of the table, Rhiannon was reminding herself not to talk about the lies she'd told about her mother, or the fact that someone—Coral's ambiguous voice—was more or less *forcing* Rhiannon to bring Lenna to the commune. What does it mean, to leave all these pieces out of a friendship, to have so many cracks? And Lenna feels guilty, too, for not instantly calling the police when Rhiannon was missing. Is it the same guilt Matilda felt when she came upon Coral in the desert and raised her gun?

It's hard to know the boundaries and responsibilities in friendship. That last night, Gillian had told her something important, but Lenna hadn't wanted to see it. She hadn't wanted to make the emotional commitment; she was in her own emotional swarm. Now, she wishes she had. Now, feeling so much older and wiser, she thinks she *would*.

All these missed chances, all these mistakes. It's amazing people invest in friendship at all.

"So is your day going better than mine?" she asks Sarah, kind of as a joke.

"Hardly." Sarah laughs. "But I'm trying to get through it. I'm reading up on alternative careers for when I get out. I'm really thinking social work. And I am selling the house—that'll help."

"That's good," Lenna says. "And I like the idea of you in social work. You have the heart for it." Because of her conviction, Sarah said she doubted she'd be able to be a physician again. But she'd always gravitated toward psychology. And after coming up against someone like Gillian, maybe the right way to give back was to help more people suffering through the same things she suffered with.

"Listen, I only have another minute, but I wanted to bring up something that's been on my mind." Sarah clears her throat. In the background, someone shouts, and there's a clattering noise. Lenna has visited the prison; she pictures the harsh overhead lighting. "About that day."

"Okay . . ." Lenna slows her walk.

"You know how Matilda kept saying she didn't fire the gun? There's part of me that kind of . . . believes her."

"Really?" Now Lenna stops completely. "What do you mean?"

"I think . . ." Sarah pauses. "I think I saw someone out there. In the desert. Someone else."

"What? Who?" A warm, oozing feeling flows through Lenna's veins as she understands. "Oh come on, Sarah," she says gently. "You can't actually mean . . ."

But it's not the first time she's considered it. Despite her best efforts, Sarah's theories about Gillian being alive have wormed their way into her brain and stayed there. For so long, you can believe one thing without ever considering an alternative. It's astonishing how easily, though, your mind can be changed, if you're open to it.

Lenna thinks of how quiet it was when she woke up on that bench next to the canyon trail more than two years before. She heard the rain pelting the wrought iron and sidewalk. She heard her own cries, too, moans so disassociated from her she didn't even realize she was making them at first. Only, that was the thing— *had* she been making them? What if they were coming from someone else? And how had she gotten on that bench, anyway? Sarah swore she wasn't there when she left. Had Lenna crawled up there on her own? Had someone *else* put her there?

Someone who'd fallen but hadn't perished. Someone who'd been pushed, but who'd only slid halfway down.

Someone who could still climb up and save herself.

No, she scolds herself now. That's *impossible.* And yet . . .

She thinks, too, of that *crack* of gunfire, Coral falling forward like a stone. And the horror on Matilda's face as she stared down at the rifle in her hands, swearing she hadn't pulled the trigger. She'd also overheard a cop muse, later, that the bullet's exit wound from Coral's body didn't quite match up to the angle from where Matilda theoretically took her shot. Could it be explained away? Maybe. Lenna knew nothing about forensics. And as far as she knew, no one was looking into another shooter on the property. *Should* they have?

Only, would Gillian kill her own child? Perhaps if it meant saving the people she'd once thought were her closest friends?

A chill goes through Lenna. She glances over her shoulder now, half expecting to see Gillian on the street. She thinks of the words Gillian wrote in her posts. How if Lenna and Rhiannon had just given her a chance, she would have made a great friend. It might have been possible. Imagine if they had just given her a chance. What would *that* life have looked like?

The street is empty. "I don't know," she tells Sarah. "I think we should let it go."

"Yeah," Sarah says, suddenly dismissive. "Maybe you're right."

The automated voice tells them that their call is coming to an end. Lenna promises Sarah she'll visit soon and bring Sarah some snacks she likes from the outside. "Go kiss that baby for me," Sarah orders. "I bet he's getting so big."

A warm feeling of well-being surges through Lenna's bones. It's mixed with sadness, of course, as she hangs up, but all at once kissing Jacob is exactly what she wants to do. And someone else, too. She reaches for her phone and opens the text. I did it, she types. Come pick me up.

Lenna waits on the corner, jiggling up and down in the

midwinter California chill, until she sees Daniel's sporty BMW round the corner. She breaks into a smile.

Daniel pulls to the curb, and Lenna runs around to get into the passenger's door, first peeking into the back and waving at Jacob sitting backward-facing in his car seat. Daniel has put him in a knitted hat shaped like a pumpkin.

"Do you think it'll feel scratchy?" he'd asked, still so jittery when it came to the baby. "I don't want him to get a rash." Jacob has fallen asleep, so clearly the hat isn't bothering him *that* much. He still cries, of course. Though maybe a tiny bit less. Maybe Halcyon did do something.

She opens the door and peers in at her husband, who is looking at her with sympathy and worry but also pride. They'd talked through how hard the conversation with Rhiannon would be. Rhiannon was Lenna's first love. Her *fiercest* love. It's hard to let go of that. But now, Lenna gets that rush of surprise and also gratitude at his presence. Her second love, maybe. Or perhaps third—after the baby. Regardless. Love. She's getting there.

"You came," she breathes.

Daniel reaches out to grab her hands. "Babe. I've got your back."

ACKNOWLEDGMENTS

First and foremost, a huge thank-you to Maya Ziv, who has believed in this idea from the very start—and believed in me *in general* for a very long time now. It sounds cliché, but a good editor is so hard to find, and I'm glad I've found someone so kind, insightful, and smart.

Thanks to other members of the Dutton team, Isabel DaSilva, Juli Menz, and Sarah Brody, for the book's amazing cover design. Thank you also to Richard Abate, Tom Lassally, and Hanna Carande at 3 Arts for all your hard work and dedication.

Also, this book is in loving memory of my father-in-law, Mike Gremba, whom I've relied on for many years for insider knowledge about private investigation, police procedure, a detective's thought process, how actual crime scene investigations work, how first responders behave, what happens when a gun is fired, how a body decomposes, and more—in other words, all of the interesting stuff an author researches when writing a thriller novel. I will miss you so much—not only for your wisdom but for your gift of storytelling, your thoughtfulness, your dogged handiness, your watchful protectiveness, and how you brought joy to everyone's life. The world isn't the same without you in it.

ABOUT THE AUTHOR

SARA SHEPARD is the #1 *New York Times* bestselling author of the Pretty Little Liars series, the Lying Game series, *The Heiresses, The Elizas,* the Perfectionists series, *Reputation,* and *Safe in My Arms.*